Droris
Thatia
Lamalt's Sea
Palace
Starspell
Avrearyn
Ceveasea
Vidaica
Dekresian
Zourin
I0838191

THE CURSED WATERS DUET

C.A. VARIAN

Main Dust Jacket Design Leigh Graphic Designs

End Page Design D'Arte Oriel

Edge Design Artwork by Leigh Graphic Design

Edge Design Embedding on Global Distribution Copies by Painted Wings Publishing

Hardcase Design by G-CAT Designs

Main Jacket Reverse Art Design by Just Venture Arts (JV Arts)

Alternate Jacket Front and Back Design by Swampy Sloth Studios

Paperback Cover Art Alijah Arts

Paperback Cover Text and Design D'Arte Oriel

Paperback End Page Art Leigh Graphic Designs

Full Artist & Designer Credits in Back of Book

1st Edition 2025

Global Distribution Paperback ISBN 978-1-961238-72-5

Global Distribution Hardback ISBN 978-1-961238-64-0

SeSe Printing Special Edition Hardback ISBN 978-1-961238-76-3

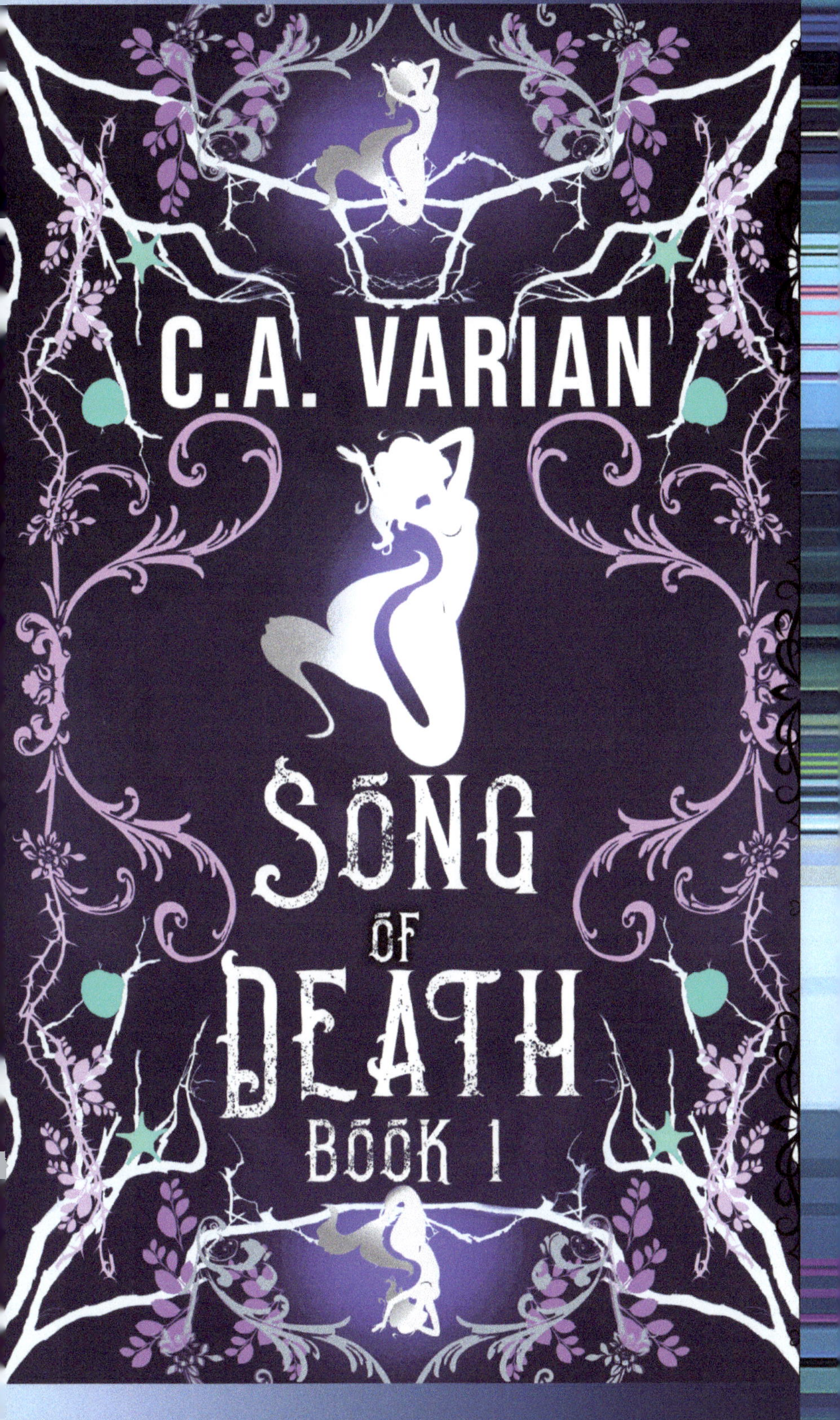

C.A. VARIAN
SONG OF DEATH
BOOK 1

Book Cover by Leigh Graphic Designs

Page Edge Design by Painted Wings Publishing

Chapter Header design by Leigh Graphic Designs

Hardcase Design by Athena Crest Arts

2nd edition 2025

This novel contains mature content and themes that may be distressing or triggering for some readers, including but not limited to:

Graphic violence and physical torture
Captivity and imprisonment
Abuse of power by a deity
Depictions of trauma and PTSD
Mentions of suicidal thoughts and emotional despair
Sexual content (consensual)
Body horror and transformation
Murder and drowning
Human trafficking and slavery (fantastical context)
Mentions of childhood trauma and parental neglect
Loss of autonomy and consent under magical coercion
Death and graphic injury
Reader discretion is advised.

Chapter One

THE DARK BARGAIN

"Help!"

The word tore from my throat, raw with desperation.

"Someone! Please! Save her!"

Daneliya's small form vanished beneath the raging waves, swallowed whole by the merciless current. My little sister, only seven years old, was slipping away, and I was too far. I had only looked away for a moment, just long enough for her to drift beyond my reach.

Panic surged through me as I sprinted into the water, the tide slamming into my legs and nearly knocking me off balance. Salt stung my eyes and lips, but I barely registered the burn. My fingers brushed hers... so close... before another wave rose like a wall and crashed between us, tearing her from me again.

"No! Daneliya!"

She was gone.

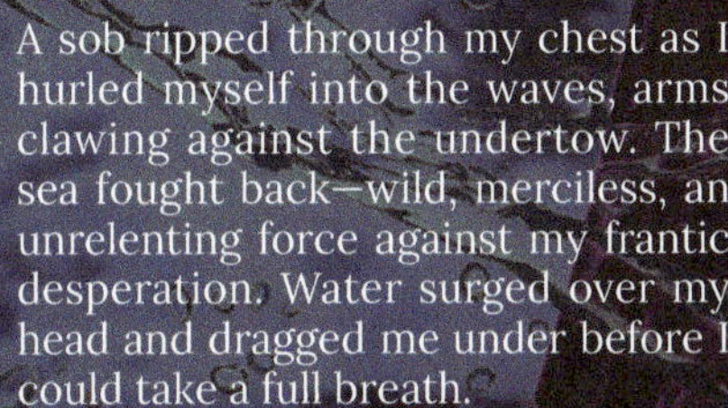

A sob ripped through my chest as I hurled myself into the waves, arms clawing against the undertow. The sea fought back—wild, merciless, an unrelenting force against my frantic desperation. Water surged over my head and dragged me under before I could take a full breath.

Thick darkness closed in, smothering me.

The sea roared in my ears, filling every space, pressing in from all sides. Pressure mounted like invisible hands shoving me deeper. My chest burned. My lungs screamed. Still, I kept going. I couldn't stop. I wouldn't.

"Someone! Please!"

No answer. No help. No hope.

And Daneliya did not surface.

The abyss yawned around me, vast and empty. My hands sliced blindly through the water, searching, begging. At last, they found something solid—her arm.

Terror crashed over me again. She was limp, weightless. I seized her and dragged her close, clutching her lifeless body to my chest as I kicked toward the surface. My limbs ached. Every motion felt leaden, but I refused to let go.

I won't lose you.

Breaking through the waves, I gasped a lungful of air, choking on it as I fought toward the shore. Her weight, so small yet impossibly heavy, pressed fear deeper into my bones.

"Please, no..."

My feet found sand. I staggered onto the beach, collapsed to my knees, and pulled her into my lap. Her skin was icy beneath my trembling fingers. Her lips, once full of laughter, were blue.

"Daneliya!" I sobbed, pressing my hands against her chest. "Come back to me. Please..."

Nothing.

Lightning split the sky, illuminating the shoreline in a blinding flash. Thunder rolled above, a low and distant drumbeat that echoed the chaos inside me. The storm was coming, but all I could feel was the unbearable stillness in my sister's body.

She was gone.

A broken sound tore from my throat, hoarse and desperate, but the wind devoured it. I clutched her tighter, rocking her gently, my fingers tangled in her drenched hair.

This was my fault.

I had only looked away for a second. One breath. One moment. And now my sister, my last remaining family, was lost.

The wind shifted.

At first, it was only a whisper in the trees. Then the humid air thickened, pressing against my skin like unseen hands, smothering me. Droplets of moisture hovered in the air, unnaturally suspended, as if even the storm had paused to watch.

Behind me, the ocean whispered.

The same waves that had taken her could take me too, I thought. I had no reason to resist. Nothing to return to. No one left to hold on to.

Letting the thoughts fester, my gaze drifted toward the sea. All I had to do was let go.

Just as I was about to stand, something touched me.

Cold as the grave, it brushed against my shoulder.

I froze, breath catching. The sensation sank deeper than flesh, slipping beneath my skin like frost under the surface of a pond. Something unseen had reached into me, but when I scanned the space around me, nothing was there.

As I tried to convince myself that I'd imagined it, the wind died, and the trees stilled.

The air, dense with the scent of salt and coming rain, grew heavier, pressing down on my lungs. My skin prickled with a feeling I couldn't name, and my pulse faltered.

Slowly, I turned, but one stood behind me. We were alone.

The beach stretched empty beneath the bruised sky, but the presence remained, invisible yet overwhelming. Waves lapped at the shore in eerie silence, as if the ocean itself held its breath.

Reaching for Daneliya, I cradled her small frame protectively against my chest. Although I knew she was gone, I needed to take her somewhere safe. I couldn't leave her exposed to the fury of the coming storm.

Then the touch returned, stronger this time. *Unmistakable.*

A sound rippled through the air. It was not thunder or the wind. It was something older. A resonance that vibrated in my bones like the hum of the world itself.

Heart thundering, I twisted sharply, my eyes wide, expecting to see nothing, but this time, a figure stood beside me.

Perfectly motionless and cloaked in black with its hood drawn low, the figure's face was lost in shadow. It did not move, but the space around it bent and darkened, as if the air itself recoiled from its presence, as though it refused to touch it. Power radiated from it in slow, unseen waves, coiling through the thick air and pinning me in place.

I couldn't see its eyes, but I felt their weight—ancient and unfeeling, like a god's gaze.

The air reeked of rain. Of salt. Of something older than time. Although I didn't know who, or what, it was, fear clawed at my throat. I swallowed it down, knowing I needed help, no matter how frightened I was.

"Help her," I whispered, the words breaking as they left me.

Still, the figure remained silent. I stared up at it, trembling, my hands clenched so tightly that my nails drew blood from my palms.

It didn't speak, but the sea surged, and lightning cracked overhead, splitting the sky.

The storm had heard me.

Without speaking, the cloaked figure lowered itself beside Daneliya's body with a fluid, silent motion. One pale hand emerged from the folds of its robe and came to rest on my sister's chest. She didn't stir. Her small form remained limp, cold, and breathless beneath the stranger's touch.

My breath faltered, catching on the edge of hope and fear. I pressed my palms together in a trembling prayer, unsure if they could help me, but knowing I had nothing left to lose. The storm around us seemed to pause, as though nature itself waited to see what would come next.

"Can you help her?" I whispered. My voice cracked, barely carrying over the whisper of waves. "Please... I'll do anything."

The words slipped out before I could second-guess them, scraped raw from the hollow space inside me where grief had begun to take root. Was I speaking to a god? A phantom? A figment of my unraveling mind?

Then the figure responded, and her voice was unmistakably real. Soft. Feminine. But devoid of warmth. Each word carried cold precision.

"Would you trade yourself?"

I flinched. The sound wasn't cruel, but it pierced through my skin. She still didn't look at me, yet her presence coiled through the air with quiet dominance, curling around my ribs.

The meaning was clear, though I hesitated to repeat it aloud.

"Trade myself how?" I asked, though in my heart, I already knew the answer.

"Her soul for yours."

No hesitation colored her voice. No cruelty either. Only certainty. The weight of those words pressed down on my shoulders like the tide itself. My chest tightened until I could hardly draw breath. Even so, the answer had formed long before the question had been spoken.

"Yes."

The word emerged soft, but sure. I would give anything. My life. My soul. Whatever was left of me. Daneliya was only a child. Too small to die on this shore. Too innocent to vanish beneath the waves like our parents.

The figure reached for me.

Her hand felt cold as stone, inhuman in its stillness. Fingers closed around my wrist, and I gasped. Her grip held the strength of iron, her nails slicing into my skin. Sharp pain lanced through me as blood welled beneath her touch and spilled in slow rivulets down my arm.

"Stop! You're hurting me!" I cried, trying to pull away, but it was no use. The stranger didn't respond. She simply held me, drawing my blood like it was the price of the deal I had agreed to.

When she finally let go, I staggered back, my wrist throbbing. I clutched it to my chest, the heat of pain mingling with the cold air. Blood still dripped, dark and vivid against the sand.

Ignoring me completely, she turned back to Daneliya and pressed those same bloodstained fingers to my sister's heart. Her lips moved, though the words were barely audible—whispers carried on a wind that had gone too still. I didn't recognize the language, but I felt its power. Older than prayer. Older than the sea.

Time fractured.

The storm waited.

And as I watched in awe, Daneliya gasped.

The sound was sudden and violent. Her back arched as air tore into her lungs, limbs twitching with the desperate instinct to survive. She coughed, sputtered, then whimpered—drawing another breath. Color rushed into her cheeks, her tiny lips softening from blue to life.

My vision blurred as tears spilled down my cheeks. A choked cry escaped me as I reached for her, pulling her into my arms. For a long moment, I held her like the sea might try to take her again.

Without a glance, the cloaked figure stood. Her silhouette remained still. *Unreadable.*

"You must return to these waters before the sun descends," she said, her voice calm but final. "If you do not, you will not live to see the morning."

I turned to face her, too many questions crashing through me all at once, but she was gone.

No footprints marked the sand. No sign she had ever stood there at all. Only the fading storm and the blood on my arm bore witness to what had happened.

As I scanned the beach for our savior, the clouds split, and light spilled through the heavens. Golden sunlight warmed my face, and it should have felt like salvation. Instead, it felt like the edge of something vast and terrible.

A miracle had happened. Or a curse. I didn't yet know which.

"Sissy?" Daneliya's voice was faint, hoarse from her ordeal.

My heart broke anew. Pressing a kiss to her forehead, I pulled her closer, burying my face in her damp hair. She was warm, *breathing*.

Tears streamed down my cheeks and soaked into her dress as I gathered her in my arms and stood. My body shook with the weight of everything I didn't understand. Turning away from the sea, I took a single step.

Behind us, the waves whispered against the shore. They no longer crashed. They crooned. The sound was not of wind or tide, but something deeper. Something watching. *Listening.*

The ocean sang a new song. One of death and rebirth.

"It's okay," I whispered, my voice cracking under the weight of the lie. "Everything's going to be okay."

The storm had gone. The birds had begun to sing again.

But deep in my marrow, I knew, nothing would ever be the same.

CHAPTER TWO

WEIGHT OF THE DEEP

Three Years Later

Pain flared across my back, sharp and unrelenting, and I hissed through clenched teeth. The sting of raw, torn flesh throbbed with every breath, each inhale shallow, like drawing air through broken glass. Sweat pooled along my spine, sliding into the wounds like acid.

"Just a little longer." Ocevia's voice was soft but steady as she worked. She blew gently over my back, trying to cool the fire in my skin before sealing the tin of ointment with a quiet snap. "They should scab over soon. If you would stop defying her, she would stop having you whipped."

Rolling my eyes, though she couldn't see me, I exhaled through clenched teeth. We both knew that wasn't true. It didn't matter how obedient I was. Miris would always find a reason to punish me.

"Even if I stayed out of trouble, she would still find a reason to beat me."

"You're probably right." Ocevia rinsed her hands in the salty water that pooled along the rocky floor. Outside, the violent waves battered the entrance of our cove. It was a dangerous place for humans, but for us, bound to the sea, it was a sanctuary.

"Are you going to be ready to go back out tonight?"

Turning toward the markings I had carved into the cave wall, I let my fingers brush over the rough indentations. One hundred and forty-three souls. That was all I had claimed. A pitiful number. A drop in the endless ocean of what Miris demanded from me. Five thousand souls—stolen from the living and delivered to the abyss—and only then would she free me.

If she even kept her word.

Each mark was a wound carved not into the stone but into my soul, a tally of screams and sinking ships, of faces I never let myself remember.

The weight of that reality settled over me like a crushing tide. My chest tightened. How many more years would I have to endure? How much more blood would stain my hands before I could step onto land again? Would Daneliya even remember me when that day finally came?

Would I even remember myself?

I forced the lump in my throat down and looked back at Ocevia. "I don't think I have a choice. My back can't take any more lashings just yet."

She pursed her lips, brushing strands of her long golden hair over one shoulder. Ocevia was my age, though she hardly looked it. None of us did. Mermaids were crafted to be ethereal, their beauty unnatural, haunting, irresistible. It was what made us so effective at what we did: luring men to their doom.

"You really don't. You'll never be free if you keep putting more marks on your back than on that wall." She nodded toward my tally of stolen souls.

With a grunt, I sat up, biting back a sharp breath as the movement pulled at my torn skin. She was right. I had taken more lashes than souls these past three years, more pain than progress.

"Yeah... that's going to hurt you for a while." Ocevia grimaced as I adjusted my posture, her sharp turquoise eyes filled with sympathy.

"I'm aware. I'm the one who always takes the whip, after all." Studying her for a moment, I tilted my head. "Have you ever even been punished by Miris?"

She hesitated, just for a second, but, it was long enough for me to notice. Her gaze flickered to the horizon, where foreboding storm clouds churned over the endless sea. The scent of brine filled the cave, thick and heavy, mingling with the rhythmic crash of waves against jagged rock.

"I have not." Her voice was distant, *unreadable*. Then, with a small shake of her head, the cloudy look in her eyes cleared. She exhaled, as if shaking off something invisible. "It's a stormy one today. Bad for the sailors, good for us."

Sighing, I pulled my top back over my breasts, wincing as the coarse fibers brushed against my tender skin. It was little more than a strip of woven seaweed, barely enough to cover me. Modesty had long since lost its place in my life. I had been shaped into something designed to entice men to their doom with little more than a glance and a song.

"I don't consider it good for me either." The words escaped in a low mutter. "I never wanted to be a killer."

Ocevia's turquoise eyes softened, their glow catching the dim light of the cove. "The water takes lives. We're just bystanders."

A bitter huff slipped from me as I tucked a damp strand of onyx hair behind my ear. Even the smallest things felt foreign now—the silken smoothness of my locks, the violet sheen they had taken on since my transformation. I used to have deep brown hair, warm and familiar. Now, it shimmered like an oil slick, a cruel reminder that nothing about me remained the same.

Sometimes I wondered if that girl had ever existed at all. Or if Miris had drowned her too, reshaping what remained into something beautiful, hollow, and cruel.

My gaze dropped to a shallow pool on the cave's rocky floor. My reflection stared back at me, unrecognizable. The same cursed turquoise eyes all mermaids bore, so unnatural, so otherworldly, bored into me like a taunt. There was nothing human left in them.

Slowly, I pushed myself to my feet, careful not to jostle my aching back, and joined Ocevia at the mouth of the cave. The sea raged beyond, waves crashing against jagged cliffs with a hungry fervor. We could shift into human form and walk as they did, but we were forbidden from stepping onto any land humans claimed as their own. The caves, the lonely islands, and the dark depths of the goddess's palace were the only sanctuaries we were allowed.

"That's just wishful thinking and you know it," I said, my voice barely audible over the surf. "Most of those ships would make it safely across if it weren't for us. She has turned us into monsters. The water is the weapon, but we're the ones who wield it to claim the victims."

Ocevia sniffed and turned away, wiping her cheek. "We don't have a choice, Azure. You try to deny our fate, but all it does is get you whipped. It's not getting you any closer to seeing your sister again. Surely you must know this."

The thought of Daneliya growing up without me sent my heart plummeting into my stomach. My voice softened. "I know." Reaching out, I placed my hand on her icy elbow. "Look, I'm sorry. I just hate this."

Wrapping me in an embrace, Ocevia silently cried on my shoulder. "I do too. We are all in this together. None of us want to live like this."

A snort escaped before I could stop it. "I can think of a few who might. The Seawraiths."

Oona and Lucia, two mermaids I despised, had fulfilled their life debts long ago but remained in this cursed form, forsaking their human lives. They enjoyed being monsters who played as though they were gods with innocent mortal lives. They were evil and vicious to their very cores.

Ocevia nodded against my shoulder. The blond beauty was not a monster. If anything, she was the kindest among the forsaken merfolk. She'd been paying off her life debt since she was a young girl. If she remembered her life prior to her transformation, she didn't talk about it, but it had not hardened her. She was not defiant like me. She followed the rules, and her back was as unblemished as her record. I didn't know what she'd received in exchange for her extensive life debt, but the fact that she owed fifty thousand souls to Miris was enough to tell me it was something big. She'd never offered an explanation, and I wasn't even sure if she had any memory of the exchange.

"Come on. Let's get something to eat."

I changed the subject, hoping to distract her from the heaviness of my words, and led the way to the crates that lined the far wall. Grabbing a few pieces of the dried fish that made up most of our meals, I handed her one before taking a bite of my own.

Honestly, I was tired of fish. I hadn't enjoyed eating them before being dragged into the sea, and that hadn't changed. Sometimes, I managed to find fruit or vegetables on one of the small islands that speckled the sea, but it wasn't often enough for my liking.

Handing Ocevia a handful of the small fish, we sat on the stone platform that served as a bed.

"I could really go for something other than dried fish right now." Ocevia held her nose as she took a bite.

I snickered. "Me too. I don't remember my mother's cooking, but my father made a tasty stuffed goose. I could go for either at this moment."

"That sounds delicious. I don't actually remember my mother's cooking either, but I can imagine she was great at it." Her voice became softer, more melancholy. "When I gain my freedom, you must take me to meet your family."

My heart thudded. "All that's left is my little sister. I hope she found a home with someone who cares for her. With only one hundred and forty-three souls after three years, my sister will be grown and married by the time I'm free. With my luck, she will have moved away, and I'll never be able to find her."

"I'm sorry, Azure. I didn't mean to bring that up. I didn't realize about your parents."

I squeezed Ocevia's hand. "No. It's okay. It's my fault for never telling you about them. I've moved past that loss."

"I understand. It's hard to bring up things that cause us pain, especially when we are supposed to be hardened out here."

My friend could not be more correct. Hardening our hearts was the only way to survive this captivity. If I didn't, watching the life drain from the drowning victims, after witnessing my own sister suffer the same fate, would be enough to break me.

I met Ocevia's eyes. "And what about your family? Will I ever be able to meet them?"

No matter how much I tried to open that door, she never let it stay open for long.

Ocevia sighed and fidgeted with the shell necklace that never left her neck. She clutched it now, as if it could anchor her to something she no longer dared name. I had always thought it beautiful, but now it shimmered strangely in the dim cave light, like a memory trying to stay alive.

"Maybe someday."

Ocevia's noncommittal response held no hope. I didn't know for sure, but something told me I would never be able to meet her family.

And that, perhaps, was the cruelest fate of all.

THE DAMNED AND THE DROWNING

By the time Ocevia and I dared leave the cave, the storm was raging. The howling winds sent waves crashing violently against the jagged shore, each impact a deafening roar. The storm would aid us, hiding our movements, tearing apart weaker ships, but it would also limit the number of vessels brave enough to cross the sea tonight. Fewer ships meant fewer souls.

I wasn't sure if that was a blessing or a curse. Every life I sent into the abyss chipped away at my debt, bringing me closer to freedom, but at what cost?

Daneliya would be long gone by the time I ended five thousand innocent lives. That much was certain. The dream of returning to her, of finding her waiting in our old cottage, was nothing more than a cruel fantasy. The girl I once knew would be grown by then, a stranger living a life I no longer belonged to.

So why did I still fight? Why did I still cling to the hope of a reunion that would never come?

A gust of wind sprayed salt across my face, snapping me from the spiral of my thoughts.

"Usual spot?" Ocevia's voice cut through the storm, steady despite the fury around us. She shifted, her human legs dissolving into an iridescent turquoise tail as she slid to the edge of the rock, waiting for my answer.

Our usual spot was near the southern shipping channel, close to the Kingdom of Thatia, my homeland. Though the sea stretched vast and lawless, most ships followed predictable routes, sticking to the deeper waters that offered safer passage between kingdoms. The channel was a vital artery connecting Thatia to Avrearyn, Zourin, and Vidaica. It carried merchants laden with goods, noble ships bound for diplomacy, and pirate vessels that prowled the waters for prey.

We had been taught to target the pirates first. They were already killers, already doomed by the nature of their existence, but the distinction was meaningless. Miris demanded a soul, and the sea did not care whose lungs filled with water.

"Our usual spot works for me."

I settled beside Ocevia, my skin prickling as the cold wind lashed against my bare arms. With a deep breath, I let my legs dissolve, the transformation as effortless as a sigh. My iridescent purple tail, unnatural in its beauty, shimmered beneath the storm's fractured light. Without hesitation, I slid from the rock, plunging into the waiting darkness below.

The ocean swallowed me whole.

My stomach always twisted when we set out for the hunt. It was a quiet war within me, one I had been fighting since the moment I was dragged beneath these waves. But there was no escape. The only way to shed this cursed form was to fulfill my debt. Five thousand souls. That was the price of my freedom.

It was either that or death.

And if there was another way, I had yet to find it.

Every time I swam toward a ship, my stomach turned to ice. I remembered the first sailor I lured, how his wide, disbelieving eyes locked onto mine before the water closed over his head. I could still hear his scream beneath the waves, muffled and brief.

With my heart a leaden weight in my chest, I swam forward, Ocevia at my side. The storm raged above, violent enough that we had to remain below the surface to avoid choking on the endless spray of saltwater. Even beneath the waves, the currents pulled at us, turbulent and restless. The water was frigid, but I barely felt it. I had long since grown accustomed to the cold. My body no longer withered in its embrace. My skin didn't shrivel. My hair no longer clung to my face like it once had. Even my voice had changed—clearer, sharper, hauntingly melodic.

Everything was different now.

Everything had been altered to make taking lives easier.

But no matter how well I had been shaped into a predator, my conscience refused to be dulled. The weight of every stolen breath, every final cry swallowed by the sea, pressed down on me, heavier with each passing year.

And on this night, I would add more names to the list of the damned.

We reached our hunting grounds an hour later, emerging from the churning sea to scan the storm-darkened horizon. The sky was a mass of roiling black clouds, swallowing what little moonlight dared to peek through. Rain fell in a relentless sheet, its cold bite doing nothing to phase me. I had long since learned that the sea's cruelty did not end with its waters.

No ships in sight.

Still, we waited. Lightning forked across the sky, a jagged wound tearing through the heavens. A heartbeat later, the deafening crack of thunder followed, sending a shudder through the air. Instinct drove me below the surface, away from the open sky where death could strike in a flash.

I resurfaced, shaking the water from my face. "Anyone foolish enough to be out on the water tonight deserves what's coming."

And yet, here we were. Just as reckless. Just as desperate.

My fingers curled into fists beneath the waves.

Ocevia treaded water beside me, using her tail and hands to keep herself steady against the restless tide. "I admit that tonight doesn't seem like it will be very productive. The storm is too severe. However, let's wait a little longer. A ship might still arrive."

I wasn't keen on staying in the open much longer, but I nodded anyway. We needed souls. As it always did, my conscience protested, but I forced it down. If I let myself falter, I would never be free.

Were the other mermaids out hunting, or were we the only ones stupid enough to try?

The question had barely settled when the water around us began to bubble.

It was our only warning.

The surface broke violently as Oona and Lucia emerged, their eerie grins flashing in the darkness. My muscles tensed. The storm seemed to hush for a moment, as if the world itself was holding its breath in anticipation of blood.

My lips curled before I even registered what I was saying. "This is our spot. Find somewhere else to hunt."

A foolish thing to say, but I never hesitated to mouth off to them, no matter how dangerous they were.

Oona's predatory smile widened. Her midnight-black hair spread around her like an ink spill, her turquoise eyes glittering with cruel amusement. "You and your weak little friend do not own this water. We hunt where we choose. Go ahead. Try to take souls from us. It won't end well for you."

A surge of anger pulsed through me, tightening every muscle in my body. I parted my lips, ready to spit a venomous reply, but a flicker of movement in the distance caught my attention.

A *ship.*

Even in this storm, even amid fury and darkness, the ship gleamed like an offering. My breath caught. That a vessel had made it this far into the storm was a miracle, or a curse.

It appeared from the direction of Vidaica, its sails billowing violently in the storm winds. The vessel rocked precariously against the raging sea, struggling to maintain its course. Even through the thick sheets of rain, I could see the desperate figures aboard, scrambling to keep control of their doomed vessel.

Silence fell between us, all other tensions forgotten.

Grabbing Ocevia's hand, I pulled her toward the ship, ignoring the presence of our rivals behind us. They were nothing. The only thing that mattered now was reaching the target first.

We swam through the storm-churned water, pushing forward until we reached a jagged outcropping of rocks that lined the channel. It was the perfect vantage point.

Hovering in place, my tail swayed in the current to keep myself above water. With Ocevia by my side, I opened my mouth and sang.

My voice cut through the storm, smooth and haunting, carried by the wind and the waves. Ocevia joined in, her voice seamlessly weaving with mine, an intricate harmony as beautiful as it was deadly. It wrapped around the ship, an unseen net tightening around the minds of the sailors.

The song wasn't just sound, it was power. It coiled in my chest, curling behind my ribs like smoke and starlight, rising on the breath Miris had stolen from me. Every note pulled tighter, reaching across the waves like a net of silk and sorrow.

Across the channel, I caught sight of Oona and Lucia, their forms barely visible through the rain. Their lips moved, but the storm swallowed their song, drowning it beneath the tempest's roar.

Good.

I sang louder, pouring every ounce of power into the melody, my voice rising above the chaos.

I glimpsed their faces through the rain, wide-eyed and frozen, their fates sealed by a song they didn't even hear. The water surged beneath me, alive with hunger.

Lightning split the sky as the wind howled, tearing through the storm with relentless fury.

The ship veered toward us, drawn by an unseen force toward its doom.

Chapter Four

THE PRICE OF SALVATION

The ship veered in our direction, and a shiver of anticipation, laced with self-loathing, raced through me. It was time to carry out my cursed duty.

Tonight, I would kill, and I would hate myself for it.

Moving swiftly, Ocevia and I slipped behind a jagged rock outcropping near the edge of the channel, keeping ourselves hidden as we continued our haunting song. The vessel drifted toward us, no more than a ghost ship now, sailing helplessly across the thrashing waves, bound for ruin on the jagged rocks ahead.

The sound of splintering wood struck like a lash, sharp and final. I squeezed my eyes shut, willing myself to believe it wasn't me who had taken those lives. That it was the sea. That it was the storm. But I couldn't lie to myself.

Screams followed, raw, panicked, and unmistakably human. They pierced the night, loud even over the wind and thunder, echoing in a chorus of agony that jolted me to my core. The same cries clawed through my dreams each night, dragging me from sleep with cold sweat on my skin.

From the sound of it, at least fifty men had been aboard. Half a hundred souls, now trapped in a death they hadn't chosen. Ocevia and I would share the offering, just as we always did. But I already knew the others across the channel would come to challenge us. Oona would never let us keep the credit for the wreck, not with our song dragging it under before hers could reach them.

"I'm going to head for the stern, see how many are already in the water," Ocevia said, her voice low and steady. She slipped away before I could respond, her tail vanishing into the darkness.

I didn't follow. I didn't need to see more.

The screams began to fade, one by one, as the sea claimed its due. I sat motionless in the shadows, waiting for the last cries to fall silent. Each death twisted something inside me, turning another screw deep into my ribs. I forced myself to breathe through the nausea, but bile still rose in my throat.

The fire in my chest refused to burn out.

Above me, lightning cracked the sky open. White veins arced across the clouds, jagged and furious, illuminating the wreckage in brief, violent flashes. I tilted my face upward, daring the gods to strike me down.

They didn't.

They never did.

A sudden splash jolted me. Water slapped against the stone, and I flinched, instinctively retreating a few feet from the wreckage. Blinking through the darkness, I searched.

A man.

Alive.

Adrenaline surged through me, and for the first time in three years, my pulse lifted with something dangerously close to hope. A survivor clung to the rocks, his coughs ragged, fingers clawing against the jagged surface.

Saving him would mean death. It would mean betrayal, but something deep inside me refused to look away.

Maybe sparing one life could balance the scale.

It wouldn't. I knew it wouldn't. Nothing ever would.

And yet, the thought took root. A foolish, reckless wish in a life where hope had no place.

The man coughed again, his clothes soaked through. His hair clung to his forehead in soaked tangles. Still, he didn't let go. He fought. He clung to life like his soul depended on it.

A fighter. A *survivor*.

Every instinct in me screamed to turn away. Let him drown. Let the sea take him.

But I couldn't. Not this time.

I had watched others die. I had stood motionless as men begged for help. I had told myself it wasn't my fault, that it was the curse, but this wasn't the same.

The ocean clawed at him, hungry, and I wanted to resist it. I needed to resist it.

Even as my heart pounded, even as every memory of pain urged me to stay hidden, I found myself watching the curve of his jaw, the sharp line of his cheekbone. He was young. Strong. Breathing through sheer force of will.

And something in me broke.

If you save him, you'll never be human again. You'll never see Daneliya.

The thought sliced through me like a blade.

But what kind of life was I pre-serving by killing strangers? I was no closer to redemption than I had been the day I was cursed. Five thousand souls? I could mur-der until my fingers bled, and it still wouldn't be enough. Daneliya would be dust by the time I ever saw her again.

Saving this man, this one soul, was something I could do.

My tail flicked once, cutting through the current. I surged forward, my hands clenched at my sides. I tried to hold on to reason, to duty, but the tide had already turned.

I moved without permission, without thought. His breathing was growing more labored, his grip on life loosening with each crashing wave. Just a few more seconds and the sea would win.

But not tonight.

Not him.

He had fought too hard. I wouldn't let it end like this.

With a final surge, I cut through the waves and reached for him, toward a decision I could never take back. The first true choice I had made in years.

And it was *mine*.

As I darted toward the barely conscious man, I caught sight of Oona in my periphery. She moved through the water like a predator, eyes locked onto her prey. I knew exactly what she intended. She would rip the life from him without hesitation, claim his soul, and savor the cruelty of it.

Not this time.

Even if it cost me my own life, I would not let her take his. In that moment, I made a vow to myself—a silent, defiant promise.

He will *not* die tonight.

I had no plan. Only desperation. I wrapped my arms around his limp body and held him close.

The instant his skin touched mine, something strange surged through me. Warmth bloomed beneath my ribs, deep and consuming, like fire lit beneath the waves. It wasn't mermaid magic. It was something else. Something I hadn't felt in a very long time. Something that still belonged to me.

I didn't have time to question it.

I pried him from the rocks, but he resisted instinctively, still clinging to the jagged stone. His eyes fluttered open, glassy, dazed, and filled with disbelief. He looked at me like I was a dream, or a hallucination sent by the sea to torment him before death.

"It's okay," I whispered, tightening my grip. "I'm going to get you out of here."

He didn't speak. He just stared for a moment, then gave a weak nod. Slowly, as if surrendering to fate, he wrapped his arms around my neck and let me pull him away from the wreckage.

I swam with his full weight pressing against me, slowing my movements. He was heavy, and unconsciousness had stripped him of any ability to help. But my mermaid form was built for endurance, and adrenaline burned through my limbs, giving me the strength I needed.

Still, fear gnawed at me. His body was far too cold. What if I had risked everything, only for him to die of hypothermia in my arms?

No. I wouldn't let that happen.

I pushed harder. The storm continued its relentless assault. The violent seas made swimming a challenge, even though I could carry his weight. Usually, when the waters were so turbulent, I would have swum far below the surface and out of the current, but I couldn't do that with him in my arms. He would drown. I just hoped the men still screaming in the water would serve as enough of a distraction for Oona and Lucia to leave us alone. I had only one soul. The sea held dozens. They didn't need him, but I did.

So, I kept to the surface, my movements slow and controlled. I fought the sea, refusing to be pulled under.

Oona and Lucia might still be nearby. That thought chilled me more than the storm. I hoped the chaos of the wreck would keep them distracted. Dozens of men still thrashed in the water. Surely, they would choose easier prey over me.

Taking him to the cove where Ocevia and I sheltered would be too dangerous, too exposed. The mainland wasn't an option either. If the humans saw me, it would all be over.

There was only one place left.

I turned toward the open sea, swimming for one of the uninhabited islands that dotted the horizon. Barren and remote, they offered no comfort, but they might offer safety.

If I was caught, Miris would do worse than punish me. She would torture me, and she would take him, too.

I could already see it—his body shackled beneath her throne, his soul devoured by the abyss that had nearly claimed mine.

The thought lit something inside me. I swam faster, harder.

I had never wanted to be a killer. But tonight, I was choosing something else.

The dark silhouette of an island loomed in the distance, jagged and unfamiliar. Overwhelming relief surged through me. I pushed forward, my limbs screaming, my breath growing heavier with each stroke.

When my tail finally touched the sandy bottom, my muscles gave out. I nearly collapsed under his weight but forced myself to hold on. Carrying him while swimming was one thing, but all my muscles were strained from the long journey, and I could barely support his weight above water.

I dragged his limp body onto the shore, the waves still licking at his legs with greedy persistence. He remained motionless in my arms. His skin was pale, but I wasn't ready to accept the worst.

"You're going to be okay," I whispered, the words more a plea than a promise. I inhaled deeply, clinging to the fading trace of his scent through the salt and rain. It grounded me, something human and real.

With one last effort, I pulled him farther up the beach, beyond the reach of the sea. My body trembled from the strain. Every inch sent fire through my muscles, but I didn't stop until he was safe.

Only then did I allow the shift.

With the little energy I had left, my tail dissolved into legs, the magic flickering through my veins in a rush of aching cold. I gasped, falling to my knees beside him. My damp hair clung to my bare skin as I leaned over his still form.

He lay unmoving, barely breathing, his chest rising so faintly I had to watch for it.

For one brief moment, I saw someone else.

Daneliya.

Her blue lips. Her lifeless body. The way her chest had refused to rise no matter how I begged.

A broken sob tore free from my throat as I doubled over, shaking. The relentless flood of memories crashed through me like another suffocating wave. I had failed her. I had failed Daneliya.

But I would not fail him. I couldn't.

Still, the thought pierced me—sharp, cruel, impossible to ignore. *What if I had been too late again? What if everything I had done, every rule I had broken, every risk I had taken... still ended in death?*

The past and present blurred, collapsing into a single unbearable moment. Her face. His silence. That helpless weight in my arms... again.

Nausea surged up my throat. I turned away and vomited into the sand, my body wracked with violent shudders. When it was over, I dropped to my knees again, hands buried in the earth, sobbing as quietly as I could. But I couldn't stop. I couldn't hold it in anymore.

The dam had broken.

Grief. Rage. Guilt.

They spilled from me like a tide I could no longer contain, dragging everything with them. My body trembled with exhaustion, my heart splintering under the weight of too many regrets. I had buried it all for so long—every death, every punishment, every song—and now it clawed its way to the surface, demanding to be felt.

I knew I couldn't afford to break. Not now. Not here.

But I did.

Because he was alive. Because I had risked everything for him. And because some part of me, deep down, feared it would never be enough.

Chapter Five

STRANDED IN SECRETS

Walking along the moonlit bank, I searched for kindling and dried logs, suppressing a shiver as a cool breeze skimmed over my wet skin. The islands were warm during the day, but night had stripped away their heat, leaving the air sharp and biting. My body was still damp, completely bare, and the chill dug deep, making me tremble. Fear only worsened the cold, the unshakable feeling that we were unsafe.

As cold as I was, I knew he would fare far worse. Without the magic of the curse to shield him, the chill could sink deep, steal his breath, stop his heart. Fire came first. By morning, I would search the caves inland, hoping to find a breast band and bottoms left behind by another mermaid, but right now, survival was all that mattered. I was used to being exposed. Our kind wore little beyond what the sea permitted. But this was different. There was no ritual to it. No seduction. Just me, bare and trembling, tending to a dying man, trying to remember what it felt like to be human.

My gaze flickered to his unmoving form, still trembling in his unconsciousness. I forced myself to work faster. I hadn't risked everything just for him to die now.

After the curse claimed me, fire was one of the first things I taught myself—how to coax it to life with shaking hands and cold skin, how to wield it like a secret. Now, my fingers moved out of memory, not thought, arranging driftwood in a careful nest. The flames came slowly, then all at once, licking at the wood with quiet hunger. It wasn't much, just enough to keep the cold from crawling into our bones, but not enough to betray our presence to the sea.

Yet, I couldn't shake the gnawing worry about Oona and Lucia.

If they found us, there would be no mercy. Miris would see to that personally. I could only hope I had put enough distance between us that the vast sea would work in my favor. The world beneath the waves was endless, full of places to hide, but I had defied my fate tonight. That kind of sin was not easily forgiven.

Once the fire was stable, I turned my attention to him. His weapons, a sword and dagger, were still strapped to his belt, their edges gleaming in the firelight. Carefully, I unbuckled them and set them aside before moving to his boots.

The real challenge, though, was his clothing. His drenched tunic and trousers clung to his body like a second skin, making it a slow, frustrating process to peel them away. The sea breeze and insects would make him miserable without clothes, so I handled the fabric carefully, ensuring it wouldn't tear. His undergarments remained in place. I wasn't that bold, but the rest I spread over a large rock near the fire, hoping the heat would dry them faster.

When I turned back, my gaze lingered.

I was just checking his coloring, I told myself... Making sure he was warm enough.

It was a flimsy excuse, even to me.

My eyes traced the defined lines of his chest. The firelight danced over the hard planes of his stomach, over the slow-drying rivulets of water that slid down his skin and disappeared beneath the waistband of his undergarments.

I swallowed, forcing my eyes upward.

A tattoo covered one of his pectorals, an image of a circular chain, its links severed at one point, the broken ends flaring outward. It should have been a mark of freedom, but at that moment, it felt like a mockery.

I wore no such emblem, but every inch of me was bound.

Sitting at his feet, I rubbed from his calves down to his toes, willing warmth into him as I studied him. He was tall, his muscles firm and toned. His physique suggested skill with the sword I had found strapped to him.

I had never been this close to a man before, not like this.

Aside from the desperate sailors who leapt from their ships in last-ditch attempts to escape, I had never touched one, felt their warmth, or watched them sleep.

And this one, this unconscious man, was more handsome than most.

Embarrassed by my wandering thoughts, I forced my gaze back to his face.

But when my eyes met his, the world narrowed to that single point of connection.

He was awake.

I froze, my pulse hammering.

Curiosity flickered in his expression as he stared at me, his gaze unfocused but undeniably aware. I wondered what thoughts must have been racing through his mind. It couldn't be every day that a man woke up drenched, in nothing but his undergarments, on an uninhabited island with a naked stranger sitting at his feet.

His stare flickered downward, dipping to my bare chest before quickly darting back to my face.

His eyes widened.

Not just from confusion, but from realization.

I swallowed hard, forcing myself to speak. "I was trying to warm you back up." My voice was softer than I intended, making me sound unsure. "Your clothes were all wet. I didn't want you to die from hypothermia."

He turned his face toward the fire, his expression unreadable, but he didn't pull his foot from my hands. Taking that as permission, I resumed massaging his icy skin, hoping to stimulate his blood flow. The silence between us stretched, the only sound the crackling fire and the crash of waves against the shore.

The quiet gnawed at my nerves.

After what felt like an eternity, I cleared my throat, drawing his attention back from the dancing flames. His gaze locked with mine, and I felt myself drowning in the deep blue of his eyes. The color pulled at me, endless and fathomless, like the ocean's call.

My breath caught, and I had to steady myself before I spoke. "What's your name? I'm Azure."

He lifted himself onto his elbows, his movements slow and stiff, as he ran his fingers through his damp hair. "Elios... My name is Elios." His gaze flickered across the darkened shoreline, his brow furrowed as he tried to make sense of his surroundings. "Where are we? How did I get here?"

A sharp pang of uncertainty twisted in my stomach. How could I tell him the truth? That it was all my fault?

"Your ship crashed," I admitted, heat rushing to my cheeks. "And I... uh... saved you. I carried you here."

His head tilted slightly, skepticism darkening his expression. "How? I'm probably twice your weight, and the waves were brutal. Where's the rest of the crew?"

My breath caught in my throat. I opened my mouth, but no words came. There was no easy way to explain the things he wanted to know, not without revealing the very nature of what I was.

But I couldn't hide the truth forever. He would have to see it eventually.

My chest tightened beneath the weight of his gaze. I lowered my eyes to the sand at my feet, unable to meet those piercing blue eyes as I admitted what I could. "The rest of your crew has probably already drowned."

They *have* drowned. I had felt their souls shatter into the abyss, their light fading into the endless depths of the sea. It was a sensation I could never escape, no matter how much I wished to forget.

A tremor wracked my hands, and I clenched them into fists to hide the shaking. Without another word, I turned and walked toward the water, my body heavy with the weight of my secret. The tide licked at my legs as I sank onto the damp sand, the foamy surf washing over my skin. Taking a deep breath, I allowed the shift to take hold, my human legs dissolving into the shimmering violet of my tail.

I didn't look at him initially, afraid of what I might find on his face. But I felt his eyes on me, the way his breath faltered, the sharp edge of silence settling between us. Slowly, I chanced a glance.

He was watching me, unmoving. His stare dragged over the length of my tail, blinking rapidly as his mind struggled to process what he was seeing. Then, slowly, his hand lifted to cover his mouth.

I wasn't human, and now he knew it.

"This is how I managed to carry you to this island," I said at last, my voice quiet against the crashing waves. "As for where we are... the best answer is far from the shipping channel and even farther from the shores of Thatia. Bringing you here was the best option."

I hesitated, my gaze drifting toward the endless sea. The sea was dark, its depths unknowable. Were there eyes in the water now, watching and waiting?

"I'm not allowed to approach human lands," I admitted. "I brought you here because I thought you would be safe, but I didn't have much time to think. You needed to get out of the water before you froze to death."

Silence stretched between us, taut and uncertain. My heart pounded as I forced myself to shift back, my tail dissolving into legs once more before I returned to my seat near his feet. I searched his face for any sign of anger, disgust, or fear, but his expression had softened, his features no longer etched with suspicion.

"What did my ship crash into?" he asked at last. "I thought the channel was clear."

I exhaled slowly. "There's a rock outcropping on the side of the channel. The ship veered off course and crashed into it. I saw you swimming away, trying to save yourself."

It was a half-truth. A fragment of the real story.

I thought about telling him more. About the song that lured his ship into the shallows. About the voices that led his crew to their deaths. About *my part in their deaths.*

But I swallowed the words before they could form. He wouldn't trust me if he knew the truth. If he knew I had played a role in his crew's demise, in destroying countless lives...

There was a chance he would find out eventually, but not now. Not yet.

Our fragile alliance would shatter if I revealed too much, and I needed him to trust me if I was going to get him out of this alive.

Elios nodded, but his eyes remained full of questions. Questions I could answer but wouldn't.

"So, what now?"

That was the one inquiry I had no response to. There had been no time to form a plan before, or after, I'd saved him from the rocks. Survival had been my only concern. Keeping ahead of my enemies. Keeping him alive. That was all that had mattered.

"My only plan for now is to keep you alive," I admitted, staring into the flames. "That's been my plan since I pulled you from the rocks."

He let out a quiet breath, shaking his head. "Aside from having no way back to shore, I guess I'm okay. *Alive*. So, thank you."

A Life Worth Saving

A cool breeze swept over the island, ruffling my damp hair. He rubbed his arms against the wind, his body still shaking from the remnants of the cold. I rose and added more wood to the fire, debating whether to tell him more. He deserved some answers. Even if I couldn't tell him the truth about everything.

"I guess there's something you must know about mermaids," I said, my voice hesitant.

His brows furrowed. "Okay."

Swallowing my hesitation, I forced myself to continue. "We're all slaves to the Sea Goddess, Miris. We were taken from our human lives to fulfill a debt after striking a bargain with her." Glancing away, I blew out a breath. "She grants what you beg for and takes what you never thought to lose. That's the price," I said. "She's a goddess of wishes, twisted ones."

His expression fell, but his eyes softened. Pity flickered in his gaze. I turned back to the fire, pretending not to notice. I wasn't asking for sympathy. I didn't deserve it.

"Why were you taken?" he asked, his voice quieter. "What was your debt for?"

I clenched my fingers around a stick, prodding at the burning logs. The embers danced into the night, glowing orange against the darkness. My chest tightened. I wasn't comfortable being vulnerable, especially not with him. Admitting my truth left me feeling raw, exposed in a way that my nudity never could.

Taking a deep breath, I exhaled slowly. "Three years ago, my little sister..." My voice trembled, and I squeezed my eyes shut, steadying myself. Even after all this time, speaking of that day felt like reliving it. The terror. The helplessness. The unbearable grief. "My little sister, Daneliya, drowned. We were on the beach, and I looked away. Just for a second.

Just a second. But..." My throat closed, and I trailed off, suppressing the tears that burned behind my eyes.

Shame coiled through me like a serpent, constricting tighter with every passing second. The image of her lifeless body flashed behind my closed lids—her small, still frame, her lips tinged blue. It was all my fault. Her death. My enslavement. The never-ending curse that bound me to the sea. I had done this. I had failed her.

"She was only seven years old."

Elios moved closer, his warmth seeping into my chilled skin. A calloused hand covered mine—grounding, steady. I flinched at the warmth of it, not because it startled me, but because it soothed something in me that had gone untouched for too long.

Tears slipped down my cheeks before I could stop them. I had spent so many years drowning in silence, in guilt, in self-loathing. But here, with his hand over mine, it all felt too raw. Too *real*.

"I'm so sorry you lost your sister," he murmured. His voice was deep, steady. *Gentle*. "That's such a tragedy. I can't imagine what that was like for you."

Sniffling, I wiped my damp cheeks with the back of my hand. I hesitated, not because I didn't trust him, but because saying it aloud made it feel like it was happening all over again. Like I was standing on that beach, soaked and screaming, *all over again*.

"She didn't remain dead."

Elios' fingers tensed slightly against mine but didn't pull away. Instead, he listened.

"Miris appeared on the beach as I cried over Daneliya's lifeless body... as I screamed for help." The words lodged in my throat like broken glass, but I forced myself to keep going. "She offered to save my sister if I traded my life for hers. I didn't know what that meant, but I agreed anyway."

A part of me had known it was foolish. That nothing came without a price. But I was desperate. I was helpless.

My voice wavered as the memory surfaced with razor-sharp clarity. "I couldn't let her die. Miris brought my sister back to life, but I was turned into a monster in exchange. I could either accept my life like this or die and never have even the *slightest* chance of seeing Daneliya again."

Elios' fingers tightened around mine, his grip firm, reassuring.

"You're not a monster, Azure."

His words were so genuine, so immediate, that I flinched.

He didn't know the things I had done or the lives I had taken. If he had, he would never have touched me so gently.

I still remembered the look on the first sailor's face as he slipped beneath the waves, lured by a melody he didn't understand. If that wasn't monstrous, I didn't know what was.

Fresh tears burned down my cheeks as I turned my face away. "I wasn't, not until I made the deal with Miris. Our curse... mermaids are forced to repay our debts with souls. We have to kill if we ever hope to be free." My voice dropped to a whisper, the weight of my confession suffocating. "If I'd known before... if I had known that I would have to claim five thousand lives to retrieve my own, I would've died that first night. I would've never stepped foot into the sea. Living like this? Being this? It isn't worth it."

Elios pulled his hand from mine, rubbing his forehead. The absence of his
touch felt like another wound to my
already battered heart.

"You have to kill five thousand people?" he repeated. His tone wasn't
angry, but the words still cut like a
blade.

I swallowed hard. "Most mermaids
don't kill with their own hands," I
admitted. "We create situations that
result in casualties instead."

I don't even know how many names I'd forgotten. They blurred together in my mind—faces I would never recall, screams I could never unhear. And still, I was expected to collect more.

Shame coiled around my ribs like a vice. I couldn't bear to see the disgust I already felt for myself mirrored in his expression. Rising swiftly,

I walked toward the shoreline, letting the cold breeze sting my damp skin. The storm had passed, leaving the water eerily calm. *Too calm.*

The stillness made me anxious. If we had been followed, it would be easy to spot us now.

I hoped we had traveled far enough. I hoped Oona had lost my trail. But hope was fragile, and I had learned long ago not to trust it.

"What happened to your back?"

Elios' voice was closer than before.

I stiffened, my stomach twisting as I realized he had moved to stand behind me. The heat of his gaze burned against my skin, and I knew—*knew*—he had seen the scars.

His gaze was a physical thing, like the sting of salt in a wound. I hated the way those scars made me feel exposed, weak, *human.* The fragile nature of human life wasn't what I missed most.

Turning slowly, I crossed my arms over my chest as if that could some-how shield me from his scrutiny. "That's what happens when you disobey Miris."

His expression darkened.

"Just because I'm cursed doesn't mean I want to kill," I continued, my voice quieter now. "Disobedience doesn't go unpunished."

Elios reached for me.

I should have stepped back. I should have put more distance between us. But I didn't.

His fingers found mine again, sending me a strange, unexpected warmth.

When our eyes locked, something passed between us, something un-spoken, something I couldn't name.

His deep blue gaze darkened, not with fear, not with pity, but with un-derstanding.

"Will you be whipped for saving me?"

His question knocked the wind from me. His voice was strained, as if the thought of it unsettled him as much as it did me.

I licked my lips, trying to rid myself of the dryness in my mouth, but it didn't help. The truth was bitter and suffocating, and I knew I couldn't soften it.

"Saving a sacrifice has never happened. Not to my knowledge," I admitted. "But Miris is cruel. She'll torture me, then either add to my debt or kill me. Probably the former. I'm worth too much to her to kill."

I had seen what she did to those who displeased her, how she stretched their pain across years, how she turned their screams into songs that echoed through her halls like dirges.

A humorless smirk twisted my lips. How ironic. I had prayed for death so many times, and yet Miris would never grant me that mercy.

"Killing me would give me what I want," I added, bitterness poisoning my tone. "So I doubt she'd ever give me that satisfaction."

Elios' jaw tightened, something unreadable flashing across his face. "And what about me?"

That was the part that terrified me the most.

His soul was far more valuable than mine.

Unlike me, he had a future, a life stolen from him, but still waiting. He was the reason I had risked everything. He was the reason I had broken every rule and defied every order.

Taking a slow breath, I forced myself to answer. "That's why I chose an island so far from the wreckage. You were supposed to die tonight, Elios."

His entire body tensed.

"Miris is greedy," I continued. "To her, your soul is already hers to claim. She'll have her henchmen hunting for you. We need to move farther away soon, but honestly... I don't know where we can go to escape them."

I turned toward the water again, scanning the horizon and searching for unseen threats.

"Mermaids aren't allowed to go into human lands," I murmured, half to myself, half to him. "But Miris would let her people do so if it meant retrieving the stolen sacrifice. I don't know where you or I would be safe."

Dragging a hand down his face, Elios let out a slow, frustrated breath. "So, our only option is to run? To keep running?"

I nodded, my stomach twisting with the weight of it all. "Until I figure something else out... Yes."

The words felt like a death sentence, because deep down, I knew the truth.There was nowhere to run.

Not from Miris. And certainly not from the sea.

I inhaled deeply, my gaze lingering on the midnight-colored water before returning to Elios. Though still pale from the cold, his face was striking in the firelight—sharp angles softened by exhaustion, blue eyes reflecting the flickering embers like shattered glass.

Without thinking, I squeezed his clammy hand, feeling the roughness of his calloused palm against mine. He was so human. So *alive*.

"Come back to the fire," I murmured. "You're freezing."

To my relief, he didn't resist as I gently tugged him toward the flames, his fingers tightening around mine in silent gratitude.

We sat beside each other, the warmth of the fire licking at our damp skin.

"So," he said after a beat, his voice quieter now, steadier, "when do we leave?"

His grip didn't loosen. If anything, it tightened, as though the touch reassured him as much as it reassured me.

With my eyes fixed on the driftwood as it turned to ash, I shrugged a single shoulder. "We'll hide in the cave once the sun rises. Then, we can look for food and—" I gestured at my bare skin with a wry smirk. "—something I can use as clothes. My people store things in caverns when they rest, so I hope there's a stash somewhere."

Elios' gaze flickered over me, his expression unreadable.

Clearing my throat, I continued, "I've never traveled beyond this point, so I don't know what other islands or caves exist farther out. Hopefully, we can find somewhere safe to hide for a few days. For now, you should try to get some rest."

"You should as well."

I shook my head. "I'd feel better keeping watch."

Elios studied me for several moments before his lips quirked into a small, unexpected smile. It was the first time I had seen such an easy, effortless expression on his face, and it sent a sharp, unfamiliar ache through my chest.

"I'd feel better knowing you won't pass out from exhaustion while we travel tomorrow," he said, cocking his head slightly. "I can't exactly swim to another island by myself."

My eyebrows shot up. Although his words were dire, his tone was teasing.

I scanned the beach, letting his lightheartedness wash over me, even as the tension in my body refused to ease. We could avoid detection if we put out the fire and moved further inland, but the thought of Elios braving the elements without warmth didn't sit right with me. We had no idea how large the island was or what creatures lurked within its shadows.

"It would be too uncomfortable for you," I admitted, weighing the risks. "Between the breeze and the bugs, you wouldn't last the night. We'd have to put out the fire and venture into the caves to let our guard down, but predators could be inside. My kind isn't the only threat."

Elios glanced toward the darkened direction of the caves. Instead of fear, his shoulders squared with quiet determination.

"If we have to, we can share body heat," he said matter-of-factly.

I froze.

Touch had always meant something dangerous. Something weaponized. But when he said it, it felt like safety. Like a *choice*.

He must have noticed, because he quickly added, "You're not the only one who can protect us." He reached for his weapons, his fingers brushing the hilt of his sword. "If we have to fight, I can help."

His confidence was almost amusing. He had no idea what kind of creatures existed beyond his mortal realm. But something about how he said it, so unwavering, made my lips twitch despite myself.

Biting my lower lip, I tucked a strand of violet-tinged black hair behind my ear as I considered his words.

He was right about one thing. Exhaustion was already settling into my limbs, making them feel like dead weight. And if we needed to move quickly tomorrow, I'd be a liability if I didn't rest.

"Alright," I conceded, sighing. "If you're sure."

"I am."

I watched him for a second longer, searching for hesitation in his expression, but there was none.

"Okay," I relented. "Let's grab your things and put out the fire. Then we can try to find a place to sleep."

Standing before I finished speaking, Elios extended his hand to help me up. His grip was firm. *Steady.*

I hesitated for only a breath before taking it.

Before kicking sand into the fire, he fashioned a makeshift torch. A flurry of embers scattered into the air, burning briefly before fading into the night. The flames died, leaving nothing but the ghost of smoke curling into the sky.

I gathered his still-damp clothing while he retrieved his boots and weapons.

Then he smiled at me again, that same soft, easy smile made my pulse stutter in a way I did not appreciate.

We simply stood there for a moment, the silence between us strangely comfortable.

After a slow heartbeat, he tilted his head. "Are we ready?"

I blinked, realizing I had been staring. *Again.*

"Oh. Yes. Sorry."

Shaking my head, I reached for his hand and led him away from the dying embers, across the moonlit beach, toward the unknown. I didn't know where we were going, or how long we had left, but for once, I wasn't walking into the dark alone.

Chapter Seven

The Hidden Refuge

The trek across the wild island was far easier with Elios' torch, its glow stretching long, restless shadows over the uneven terrain. My cursed eyes, sharper than any human's, picked out three caves in the distance, their yawning mouths blending into the darkened cliffs. Though their sizes varied, there was no clear sign of habitation, but that didn't mean they were unoccupied.

The cave on the right and the one in the center shared a split entrance, a jagged fissure that splintered into two smaller tunnels. I chose the nearest one first, peering inside cautiously. Disappointment curled through me. The shallow cavern barely extended beyond the entrance, offering no real protection. We'd never be able to hide there.

The scent of salt and memory clung to the stones, and I couldn't help but wonder who had used this place last. Had she survived? Had she escaped Miris' grip, or vanished into it?

With a quiet sigh, I stepped back, allowing Elios to search through the scattered remnants left behind by one of my kind. He collected the dried fish, scraps of fabric, and what might have once been a blanket—little comfort but better than nothing. When he finished, I grasped his wrist and guided him toward the second tunnel within the split entrance, heart pounding with the fragile hope that this one would be different.

It was larger, more spacious than the first, but still too exposed. The cavern stretched wide, its open space leaving us vulnerable to discovery. If the weather turned, we could shelter there, but it was no stronghold. If another mermaid, or worse, set foot on this island, we'd be defenseless.

Frustration gnawed at me as we abandoned the second cave. We still had no proper refuge, but we weren't empty-handed. I dressed in the spare fabric Elios had found before we ventured toward the third and final cave, our last chance for safety. Unlike the others, this entrance was blocked by a massive boulder, leaving only a narrow gap, just large enough for someone to crawl through. A rush of cautious optimism fluttered in my chest.

If it's deep enough, this could be the safest option.

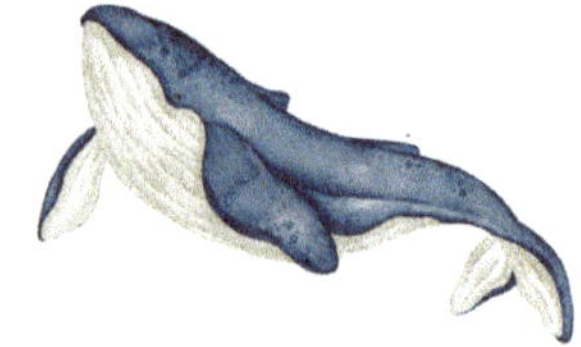

There was only one way to find out.

I handed the torch to Elios and inhaled deeply before wriggling through the gap. Darkness swallowed me whole, thick, and impenetrable. The air inside was cool, carrying the scent of damp earth. I reached my hand back through the opening. "Give me the torch."

Elios passed it to me, and I lifted it high, letting its warm glow chase away the suffocating blackness. The space stretched farther than I had hoped, the cavernous chamber unfurling before me. My heart stuttered.

Could this be more than a temporary hideout?

It was foolish to consider staying here long-term. But if we had time to rest, plan, and figure out our next move, maybe survival wouldn't seem so impossible.

Shaking the thought away, I turned to the entrance and began shifting some of the looser stones, widening the gap just enough for Elios to squeeze through. It was still tight, his body far larger than mine, but he made it inside with a grunt and some awkward contorting.

The cavern was bigger than I had dared hope. The ceiling loomed high, like the vaulted roof of a forgotten temple. A small opening near the top allowed for ventilation, perfect if we needed to light a fire without drawing too much attention.

Slowly, I moved along the perimeter, taking in the details. Elios followed close behind, his warm hand resting lightly against my bare shoulder as a guide. I tensed at the contact but didn't pull away. His presence was steadying. *Grounding.* The torchlight flickered over the jagged walls, the shadows it created twisting and dancing in unnatural shapes.

He touched my shoulder like it was nothing, like this wasn't a haunted corridor leading to who-knows-what. I envied that steadiness, even as I leaned into it.

Let nothing be waiting for us in the dark.

To my relief, the space appeared abandoned. A few desiccated droppings and ancient bones littered the ground, remnants of creatures long gone, but there were no fresh signs of life.

As we ventured deeper, something shifted in the torch's glow. I narrowed my eyes. In the farthest corner, shadows warped around a strange indentation in the rock. I moved closer, my pulse quickening.

What I had first assumed was a solid wall had a gap, a sliver of darkness that stretched beyond my line of sight.

"It looks like an opening to another chamber," Elios murmured, stepping close. His chest hovered inches from my back, his warmth a stark contrast against the cool cave air. A shiver coursed down my spine, not from fear, but from something far more dangerous.

Don't be foolish.

I tilted the torch forward, letting its light spill into the narrow passage. The corridor curved sharply, disappearing into the unknown.

Elios exhaled, his breath brushing against the shell of my ear. "I don't know where this leads, but it could be a good home for animals." His voice dropped slightly. "Or for us."

Setting down our supplies, he unsheathed his dagger, the blade glinting in the torchlight.

"I'll check it out," he said, taking the torch from my hands. "Stay here until I give the all-clear."

I clenched my fists as he disappeared into the shadows, fighting the instinct to follow.

Please, let this place be safe.

I didn't like the idea of him searching the unknown space alone, but I let him go first since he was the only one with a weapon. As soon as he disappeared into the narrow gap, I scooped up the supplies he'd left behind and followed him into the darkened corridor.

Our footsteps were nearly silent as we crept forward, the sound of our breaths the only thing to reach my ears. Without warning, Elios halted before me, causing me to collide with his muscled back. I barely suppressed a gasp as the sudden contact sent a shiver down my spine.

In the faint flicker of the torch's light, I saw him place a finger to his lips, and I stiffened at the nonverbal command. I hadn't sensed any threat but held my breath and trusted his instincts.

After a few seconds, a faint, rhythmic tapping reached my ears, reverberating through the stone walls.

"Do you hear that?" Elios whispered, his lips so close that they brushed against the shell of my ear. His warm breath skittered across my face, making it difficult to focus. I nodded, too tense to respond aloud. "I think it's dripping water."

The momentary fear melted away, replaced by excitement. We resumed our slow journey deeper into the cave, drawn forward by the promise of fresh water.

The corridor opened into a secondary chamber, and Elios had been right. The dripping sound grew louder, echoing throughout the enclosed space. At first glance, I couldn't determine where it was coming from. No moonlight filtered in, leaving the chamber an abyss of blackness beyond the torch's reach. The flame flickered, weaker from burning so long, barely illuminating a foot before us.

We circled the room at a painfully slow pace, hoping the small steps would prevent us from rushing upon an animal—or worse, slipping on unseen damp ground. My fingers tightened around the bundle of supplies as we moved. The monotony of the stone wall finally broke as it curved back, and the floor dipped to reveal a pool of water, fed by several small streams trickling down the rock face from the ceiling.

"This place is amazing," Elios murmured, crouching as he submerged his hand in the water. "It's warm. Do you think this is a hot spring?"

"It's possible. The sea is full of volcanic activity. It could be why these islands exist."

Elios straightened and strode toward the far side of the chamber. "It should be safe to start a fire here. There's plenty of space, and the ceiling is high."

"I was wondering the same thing. My only concern is ventilation, but we can try a small one first." I shifted my weight as I scanned the cavern, my vision adjusting to the darkness. "This cave is more secure than I expected. Even if someone were searching for us, they'd likely only check the more obvious openings. If we reseal the entrance, they wouldn't see this back chamber. We might be able to stay here longer if we don't spot any activity nearby."

A slow smile spread across Elios' face. "With all the trees around, there must be resources. Well, if the water dripping down the wall is drinkable. If not, we might need to find a way to collect rainwater."

His optimism was infectious. Unlike me, he didn't dwell on misfortune. He adapted, moving forward with a quiet resilience that made warmth spread through my chest.

I wish I could be like that. To meet danger with determination instead of dread.

"Should we gather wood, then?" I asked, trying to match his resolve.

Elios' grin widened as he took my hand, his calloused fingers rough against my skin. "Let's do it."

The night air was crisp as we stepped out into the open. I wasn't sure how much time had passed, but the sky was still cloaked in darkness. The torch's light barely stretched beyond a few feet, but the moon offered enough glow to illuminate our path to the forest. As soon as we stepped beyond the tree line, the thick canopy swallowed the silver light, plunging us into near-blackness.

The island was larger than I had expected, most of it densely wooded. Kindling was abundant, so we gathered as many sticks and dried twigs as possible before retreating to the safety of the cave.

When we returned to the rear chamber, Elios wasted no time building the fire. I hadn't even set my wood down before he coaxed the first spark to life. I watched, impressed, and intrigued, as the flames grew under his careful touch. He continued to surprise me. For a merchant sailor, his survival skills were remarkably honed.

I had forgotten what it was like to work beside someone who didn't expect obedience or sacrifice in return. His quiet efficiency, his calm, it steadied something in me I hadn't realized was still shaking.

I found myself wondering was that really what he was? Perhaps he hadn't been working aboard that ship at all. Some men purchased passage on merchant vessels to travel to distant lands. That explanation seemed to fit him better.

But I didn't have the nerve to ask. *Not yet.* There was so much I didn't know about him, but I wanted to.

As the fire crackled, filling the cavern with much-needed warmth, Elios moved to inspect the water trailing down the wall into the pool. He dipped his fingers and touched them to his tongue, nodding in approval. "It's fresh. Not saltwater."

I let out a slow breath. I could hardly believe our luck. Out of all the islands scattered across the Lamalis Sea, we had managed to escape to one with a hot spring. It was an incredible advantage, and a reason to stay as long as it remained safe.

FORBIDDEN DESIRE

Sitting beside the fire, I tried to absorb the warmth, but it did little to chase away the chill beneath my skin. The cavern flickered with shifting light, the flames throwing long, twisting shadows against the stone. Elios and I shared some of the dried fish we had found while searching the other caverns. I hated the staple food of my kind. I had despised it even before my transformation, but I forced it down anyway, chewing mechanically as I focused on anything but the taste. We were lucky to have food at all.

After eating, we washed in the warm spring water, the heat easing the tension that had settled into my muscles. Elios, once clean, pulled his barely dried trousers back on, his broad shoulders and toned chest gleaming in the firelight before he settled beside me again. He was still damp, his skin chilled from the water, but he was human—far more susceptible to the cold than I was.

When he tried to hand me the blanket we'd scavenged, I shoved it back at him. "You need it more than I do," I murmured, my voice softer than intended.

He chuckled, his gaze gleaming. "Then let's share."

I hesitated, my pulse quickening at the suggestion. It was logical, I supposed, but the thought of lying beside him, pressed close for warmth, sent an unfamiliar heat curling in my belly. I wasn't sure what unsettled me more—how my body reacted to the idea, or that I didn't entirely want to resist it.

In the end, we found a quiet compromise side by side, close enough to share the fire's warmth, but not quite touching. He curled beneath the blanket while I stayed above it, the flickering flames painting restless patterns across the sharp lines of his face. Sleep claimed him quickly, his breath falling into a steady rhythm that betrayed just how deeply fatigue had taken hold.

I, however, did not sleep.

Instead, I watched over him, tending to the fire as the hours bled into one another.

The fire used to mean danger, used to mean drawing men close before they sank beneath the waves. But now it felt like something else. Something alive. Something shared.

I had never wanted a man before. A lover had never interested me. Desire was an unknown hunger, a distant concept that had never stirred within me even when I had still been human. But Elios was different. His scent alone made my pulse quicken, the warmth of his body luring me in ways I didn't understand. I wanted to press closer, to bury my face in the hollow of his throat and breathe him in.

But I didn't.

I clenched my hands into fists against the impulse, forcing myself to remain still. *You are cursed. He is human. There is no future here.*

Whatever this was, this pull between us, it was nothing more than longing for something I could never have. A foolish, fleeting dream. I had saved him. That was all. And once I ensured he was safe, we would go our separate ways. I could not afford to forget that.

Letting out a slow breath, I turned my gaze back to the fire, allowing the rhythmic crackling to soothe my frayed nerves.

I had only ever seen men in terror—clawing at the sea, gasping for breath, their eyes wide with fear. Watching him sleep, unafraid, was a kind of cruelty I didn't know how to bear.

We had decided to remain on the island for now, until we could determine our next move, but the longer I sat in the silence, the stronger the urge to flee became. A deep, instinctual need to keep moving pressed against my ribs like an iron weight. Staying in one place too long made us vulnerable. The longer we lingered, the more time Miris had to send her hunters after us.

And she *would* send them.

The first scouts would be fast and merciless—one or two mermaids tasked with tracking us down before the goddess unleashed her full wrath. If we were careful, if we saw them before they saw us, we could eliminate them before they reported back. That might buy us time and prolong our survival.

But we had no real way to defend ourselves on the island, not against Miris and those she trained to carry out her punishments.

Elios had his sword and dagger, but I had nothing. *You should have taken something from the ship,* I scolded myself. I hadn't been thinking about fighting then, only escape. But now, it was all I could think about.

The fire crackled, spitting embers into the darkness as I stared into the flames, my mind whirling with possibilities.

If I had a weapon, I would use it, because if Miris sent her hunters, I would not hesitate.

Not this time.

I would kill before I allowed them to take him from me.

We were too deep inside the cave to see the sunrise, but I knew it had come when Elios' bright blue eyes fluttered open. His gaze, still heavy with sleep, softened when it landed on me. He stretched, rubbing at the remnants of slumber, his rich brown hair tousled from the night. Seeing him like that—unguarded, still caught in the haze of waking—sent a strange warmth through my chest, something dangerously close to fondness.

Stop it.

I steeled myself against the feeling, schooling my expression into neutrality, but then he grinned, and the kind of smile melted through all the walls I tried to build.

"Good morning," he said as he sat up. "How did you sleep?"

I glanced toward the fire, its embers still glowing from the fresh wood I had added before he woke. "Not much, honestly. I kept the fire going and had a lot on my mind."

His smile faltered, making me regret my words immediately. I didn't want to add to his burdens, not when he had already lost everything.

"You need your rest, too." His voice was gentle but firm. "I'll do fire duty tonight."

I waved him off, forcing a small, dismissive smile. "It's okay, really. I'm used to working at night and resting during the day." *Used to luring men to their deaths. Used to stealing souls while the rest of the world slept.*

A pit formed in my stomach, but I pushed past it. I had made my choice. I had saved Elios, and for that, I would fight.

"I can take a nap later," I added.

He nodded, slipping his feet into his boots. "That's a good idea. What were you thinking about?"

I turned to him, feigning confusion. "What do you mean?"

"You said you had a lot on your mind last night." His gaze was inquisitive, patient. "I was just curious what you were thinking about."

My throat tightened and I turned back to the fire, pretending to be more interested in the flickering flames than how his piercing stare unsettled me.

"If we're going to stay here longer, we need to make more weapons," I said instead. "Mermaids sleep most of the day since our nights are so long. Well... unless Miris is making them search for us. We should spend the late afternoons and nights hidden away, just in case. If the Sea Goddess has already sent scouts to look for us, we must be prepared. I'm not sure how long we can stay here. We're still close to her underwater caves and the main shipping channels."

Elios' brow furrowed as he considered my words, his fingers absently brushing over the stubble on his jaw. I found myself staring at the shadow of it, the way it framed his sharp features, the way it made him look older, rougher, dangerously alluring. Realizing where my mind had wandered, I tore my gaze back to the fire.

"We could probably sharpen rocks as blades and fit them with wood to make knives or spears." He pulled his dagger free from its sheath and offered it to me. "*Here.* You can use this for now."

I hesitated momentarily before accepting the weapon, pressing the cool leather grip to my chest.

I'd never been trusted with a blade. I was the blade—sharpened by Miris, wielded without mercy. But this... this felt different.

In the dim light of the cave, I couldn't make out the details of the blade, but the weight of it in my hand was reassuring. I might not have much experience wielding weapons, but I felt better having one.

"Thank you," I murmured.

He nodded, flashing another of those easy, disarming smiles before he finished lacing his boots.

I pushed to my feet, shaking off my exhaustion. "Should we go outside and get our day started? I'd feel better if we collected supplies quickly and returned to the cave immediately. Especially today. They will almost certainly be searching for us."

Standing, Elios reached for my hand as he grabbed the torch. The unexpected touch sent a quiet thrill through me. I instinctively leaned into him, my body betraying me before my mind could protest. I was more tired than I had realized. The weight of a sleepless night clung to my limbs, making my movements sluggish.

You're useless like this.

I would need to sleep soon if I wanted to be of any help to him.

His hand remained firm around mine as he led us toward the exit. I knew I had better night vision than he did, but I didn't say anything. I liked the excuse to keep holding onto him.

As soon as we stepped into the daylight, he tapped out the torch, preserving it for later. The sun had already begun her slow ascent into the sky, bathing the island in soft gold. The storms from the night before had passed, leaving behind a crisp breeze that rolled in off the sea. It carried the scent of salt and damp earth, the remnants of rain still clinging to the leaves of the dense forest.

Now fully dressed in his dry clothes, Elios looked perfectly at ease as he stretched beneath the morning light. I, on the other hand, felt far too exposed. My breast wrap and loincloth covered little, and the thought of how stark the difference between us must have seemed sent a ripple of unease through me. But my lack of coverage wasn't the worst of it. What I regretted most as we picked our way across the rocky terrain and into the forest was the lack of shoes.

Every step over the jagged stones and uneven ground sent small jolts of discomfort up my legs, but I clenched my jaw and bore it. Complaining wouldn't do any good. I would find a solution.

Elios glanced at me, catching how I winced when my foot scraped against a sharp rock. He frowned, then, without a word, reached down and pulled a strip of fabric from his shirt.

"What are you—?"

"Give me your foot," he said, kneeling before me.

I stiffened. "I don't need—"

"Azure." His voice was quiet but firm. "Let me help."

Something in the way he said it made my argument die on my tongue. Swallowing my pride, I hesitantly lifted my foot. He wrapped the cloth around it with deft, careful hands, tying it securely before moving on to the other.

His fingers brushed the arch of my foot, light and careful, and my breath stilled. *It was nothing. A kindness. But still... no one had touched me like this before.*

The warmth of his touch lingered long after he pulled away.

"Better?" he asked.

I flexed my feet, testing the makeshift wrappings. They weren't shoes, but they were enough to dull the worst of the sharp edges beneath me.

"Yes," I admitted, unable to stop the smile that tugged up the side of my lips.

Seeming satisfied, he grinned and turned, leading the way toward the trees. I followed, my heart a tangled, aching thing in my chest.

I had fought so hard to keep my distance from him, to remind myself that we were nothing more than two lost souls crossing paths for a fleeting moment, but every time he touched me and looked at me with that quiet, unwavering kindness, I felt myself slipping. *Falling.*

And that was far more dangerous than any blade.

Desire was one thing. Trust was another. And trust could get us both killed.

Chapter Nine

BETWEEN THE TIDES OF DESIRE AND DOOM

The forest was lush, brimming with life and color. A wild tangle of oak, palm, and unfamiliar fruit trees stretched high above, their sprawling canopy filtering sunlight into golden beams that scattered across the mossy floor. Vibrant mushrooms sprouted from decaying logs, their strange, twisting shapes lending the land an almost otherworldly feel. Thick vines coiled around the trees like lovers in an embrace, their tendrils winding between splashes of bright flowers that reached desperately for the sun, determined to outgrow the shadows.

Above the rustling leaves, birdsong rang out in a jubilant melody, a chorus of life that clashed against the distant crash of waves. The scent of damp earth and salt mixed with the faint sweetness of over-ripe fruit, a fragrance so achingly familiar it made my chest tighten.

I closed my eyes, drawing in a slow breath. This is what home used to feel like.

For a fleeting moment, I allowed myself to pretend—to believe I was back on the shores of Thatia, running barefoot through the fields with Daneliya at my side, her laughter ringing like wind chimes in the breeze. But the illusion was fragile, breaking apart the moment Elios spoke.

"Here."

My eyes snapped open to find him standing before me, smiling as he held out an egg-shaped piece of green and orange fruit.

"Are you hungry?"

Warmth bloomed in my chest before I could stop it. A genuine, un-tainted happiness, something I hadn't felt in so long it almost frightened me. Without thinking, I threw my arms around him, hugging him tightly.

He stiffened in surprise, but before I could fully process what I had done, I quickly pulled away, my cheeks flaming. "You found a mango!" Clutching the fruit, I stared at it in awe. "Thank you! They're my favorite!"

I wasn't someone who reached for others. Touch had always meant danger, or debt, or seduction. But with him, it had simply meant warmth.

His grin widened, amusement flickering in his sea-blue eyes. He didn't seem to mind the sudden embrace, which only made my embarrassment burn hotter.

To distract myself, I bit into the firm skin of the mango, peeling it back with my teeth. The tangy sweetness exploded across my tongue, a blissful contrast to the salt and fish that had been my main diet for years. Juice trickled down my chin, sliding down my throat and pooling between my breasts, but I didn't care. I would gladly drown in the nectar if it meant savoring something this delicious.

It had been so long since I'd tasted anything that wasn't stolen or salt-soaked. The sweetness felt undeserved.

I ate anyway.

Elios chuckled, shaking his head. "Hand me the dagger, and I'll cut that for you."

I stilled, realizing how ridiculous I must have looked, devouring the fruit like some starved animal. Dragging my forearm across my chin, I only managed to smear the sticky mess further.

With a huff, I handed him the dagger and watched as he effortlessly sliced through the mango's thick skin, peeling it back to reveal the glistening flesh beneath. I tried to wait patiently as he cut off a sizable chunk and handed it to me, but the second it touched my tongue, I nearly moaned.

We shared two more mangoes before continuing our search for supplies. Weapons were our top priority, but anything else that could be useful—food, materials, tools—was equally important.

After scavenging the forest, we moved to the beach, combing the shoreline for whatever the sea had abandoned there. The waves had been generous in their offerings. Among the scattered debris, we found several glass bottles, a large piece of leather, and a torn sail that could be repurposed.

I used to scour shipwrecks for gold or proof of conquest, relics to bring to Miris. Now I searched for wood and water like a mortal clinging to survival. In a way, I was just that.

When we returned to the cave, our arms were full of treasures. It took several trips through the small opening to bring everything inside, but it was worth it. We had gathered enough food and firewood to last us for days. With any luck, Miris' scouts would have searched this island and moved on before we needed to leave the safety of our sanctuary again.

At least... that was my hope.

We got to work once the last of our supplies were placed beside the hot spring. Elios crouched near the fire, his dagger flashing in the dim light as he whittled a long branch into a spear. I sat nearby, stripping a section of leather into something resembling proper clothing.

Our movements were synchronized, and our teamwork was seamless. It was strange how natural it felt, like we had been doing this for years instead of mere hours. I glanced at Elios as he worked, his brow furrowed in concentration.

What are you doing to me?

I hadn't thought much about the kind of man I was saving when I pulled him from the wreckage. At the time, he had been nothing more than a nameless survivor, a desperate soul clinging to life. I hadn't known his face, his voice, his smile, but I knew them now, and that made everything more complicated.

"What are you thinking about?"

His voice pulled me from my spiraling thoughts, and I looked up to find him watching me.

"Not much," I lied. "Just trying to turn this section of leather into something that actually covers me."

His gaze flickered downward, just for a heartbeat, before quickly return-ing to my face, a mischievous smirk tugging at the corners of his lips.

My cheeks burned.

Oh. He liked what I was wearing just fine.

I cleared my throat, determined to ignore how my pulse fluttered be-neath my skin.

"Do you need some help?" he asked, his expression turning genuine.

My heart stumbled at the offer. His voice was steady, his intentions sin-cere, but the thought of his hands on my skin, of him helping dress me, was enough to make my stomach twist into knots.

Shaking my head, I focused on my task. "Since I have no thread, it won't take long. I'm just going to cut this and close it with knots." I nodded to-ward his project, eager to change the subject. "How are the weapons coming along?"

He looked regretful as he held up the spear. It was roughly made, and the wood still bore the scars of his carving.

"It's getting there," he said. "The branches are sturdy, so that's a plus, but it'll take time to sharpen the stones without the proper tools."

I examined his work, nodding in approval. "It's better than nothing."

"I agree."

Reaching for the dagger, I shifted closer to work side by side. I had never been this close to someone without danger hanging in the air. With him, the danger came from wanting something I couldn't name.

The fire crackled beside us, the air between us thick with unspoken words and unacknowledged tension.

He was human. I was a cursed thing.

And yet, in the dim glow of our temporary sanctuary, with only the sound of our breathing, water dripping, and the steady scrape of stone against wood, I found myself thinking...

Maybe I don't want to let him go.

I should have been thinking of Daneliya, of my promise to find her again, but instead, I was memorizing the way his fingers curved around the wood, the way his voice softened when he spoke to me.

I studied how Elios' expression darkened. His thoughts were lost somewhere I couldn't follow. His silence, his hesitation, made my chest tighten.

Without another word, I turned my back to him and untied the flimsy breast band I had been wearing. The leather cover I had made was crude, just a wrap with haphazardly cut armholes, but it would do. I tied the ends into a knot below my breasts, the snug fit offering a bit more support than before. My chest was small enough that the covering sufficed. Had I been built differently, the garment would have been useless.

The bottom piece was no better, just a slightly larger loincloth, knotted at my hip, with another strip layered over it to mimic a skirt. Functional, if nothing else.

At least now, I don't look like a half-dressed sea sprite.

When I turned around, Elios still sat by the fire, knocking two stones together. Still, I caught how his eyes flickered toward me from the corner of his vision before darting away.

"Okay," I said, brushing my hands over the leather to settle it into place. "Now I can help you with the weapons."

He seemed lost in thought when I spoke, as if my voice had startled him out of whatever reverie he had slipped into. He blinked hard, shaking his head slightly, and cleared his throat.

"That, um..." He swallowed. "That would be great."

The cave's dim firelight couldn't quite mask the heat blooming across his cheeks, and the realization also sent a rush of warmth through me.

Is he blushing?

I looked away quickly, focusing on the fire as I forced my nerves to settle.

Stop being ridiculous.

Trying to ignore the sudden awareness curling low in my belly, I moved to sit beside him again and held out my hand. "Tell me how to help."

For a moment, he simply stared at my outstretched palm as though deciding something before finally placing a long piece of wood and a rough stone into it.

"Sand this down," he said, "and we can use it to make another spear."

I nodded, turning the materials over in my hands before setting to work, but I felt his gaze linger on me for another beat before returning to his task. We worked in silence, our hands busy, our thoughts louder than the fire, but neither of us dared to speak the truth simmering just beneath the surface.

Chapter Ten

Where Fire Meets Water

The cave grew hotter as the hours stretched on. Between the fire crackling near us and the lingering warmth of the day outside, the air had turned thick, almost stifling, but we needed the light, so we endured it.

Elios eventually removed his tunic, and I nearly lost my grip on the wooden shaft I was working on.

He had been handsome before, but now, with his tunic discarded and his skin damp from sweating, it was impossible not to look. The sharp cut of his muscles, the sheen of sweat glistening along his chest and arms, made my chest tight. I forced my attention back to the task at hand, willing my gaze to stay put. But my resolve wavered with every slow roll of his shoulders, every subtle movement that sent another bead of water sliding over his skin.

I swallowed hard and returned my attention to the weapon I was crafting.

After a brief break to share some fruit, we created smaller fires around the chamber, hoping to ease the oppressive heat. Banking the main blaze brought instant relief, though it meant we had to tend to the scattered flames more often. Still, it was a fair trade to be able to breathe again.

For the next few hours, we worked in comfortable silence, occasionally breaking it with light conversation. We discussed the best ways to craft weapons with what we had, making mental lists of what to search for during our next scavenging trip. I wanted to ask him more—where he was from, why he had been on that merchant vessel, who he had left behind—but I couldn't find the courage to pry.

I told myself it was because I didn't want to risk getting too attached. Knowing him too well would only make things harder when the time came to say goodbye.

But deep down, I knew that was a lie.

Hours passed, and exhaustion pressed down on me, my lack of sleep gnawing at my focus. As I worked, my skin prickled with unease, my mind conjuring images of Miris' scouts scouring the sea for us. *Are they close? Have they already passed over this island?*

I tried not to let my fear show. If Elios had noticed, he didn't mention it.

But as I stared at the fire, my thoughts circling endlessly, my body gave in. The fire hissed as I leaned back against the stone wall. My limbs ached, my soul frayed, and for one foolish breath, I pretended this was peace.

Without my permission, my eyelids grew heavier, and darkness pulled me under.

I jolted awake at the sound of Elios' voice.

"Do you know how to use a spear? Any weapons?"

I blinked, my mind scrambling to catch up. I hadn't even realized I had drifted off. Judging by his expression, neither had he.

I shook my head, more to wake myself up than to answer his question. "I was cursed at eighteen." The words came out quieter than I intended. Thinking about Daneliya and the life I had lost was a knife in my gut, but I pushed the memories back, forcing them into the depths of my mind. "Up until then, I never needed a weapon. And once I became this…" I gestured vaguely to myself, my voice edged with bitter disgust. "I definitely didn't need them."

Elios studied me in silence, his expression unreadable. Then, without a word, he stood and handed me one of the newly crafted spears, offering a small, sympathetic smile.

Although I appreciated his attempt to shift the subject, the self-loathing still coiled in my chest, refusing to loosen its grip.

I eyed the weapon warily before standing and taking it. It was heavier than I'd expected but surprisingly well-balanced, especially considering how roughly it had been made.

"How do you catch fish if not with a spear?" Elios asked, watching as I tested the spear's weight. "Do you use nets?"

Shrugging my shoulders, I switched the handle from hand to hand. "I found a net that washed up on shore a while back. It's stored in the cave I use most of the time. It works well enough, but I can catch them with my hands... if I have to."

His eyebrows lifted, a smirk playing on his lips. "When it's safe to go out again, I need to see that. I don't think I've ever seen someone catch a live fish with their bare hands."

A flicker of something strange and unfamiliar unfurled inside me. *Excitement?* It had been so long since I had felt anything close to that, since I had wanted to do something just to impress someone. I had never cared to show off before, but now? For him?

I *wanted* to.

Before I could dwell on the feeling, Elios gave me only a moment's notice before swinging his spear at me.

Instinct took over, shoving every thought from my mind as I blocked the strike. The scattered fires cast shifting shadows across the walls, making it harder to track his movements, but I adjusted quickly.

The dance began.

The wood vibrated in my hands with each impact. My wrists ached. My breaths came fast, not from fear, but from effort. This was not seduction. This was survival.

Sparks flared between us as our weapons clashed, the sharp crack of wood-on-wood echoing through the cave. He was strong, stronger than I had expected, but I was fast. Faster than I ever was as a human.

My heart pounded, blood rushing hot through my veins as we circled each other. When he feigned left, I lunged forward, twisting the spear just in time to catch his counterstrike. The firelight flickered across his face, illuminating the sharp edges of his jaw and the glint of his smirk.

My breath stilled.

And in that single heartbeat of hesitation, he struck.

The force of his next attack knocked the spear clean from my hands. Before I could react, he was on me, twisting my wrist and pinning me in place with an ease that made my pulse stutter.

His face was inches from mine, his grip firm but careful.

Swallowing hard, I tried to ignore the way his breath fanned against my lips, the heat of his body so close to mine.

Elios grinned. "You're fast, Little Tempest."

I swallowed past the dryness in my throat, not missing the nickname. "You're stronger."

Lips twisting into a smirk, he leaned in, his voice dropping to a whisper. "You let me win."

I shivered, because he was right.

His weight pressed against me—not crushing, but unyielding, and I hated how much I liked it. How easily I could have leaned up and kissed him, just to see what it would change, but I didn't dare. It was one boundary I knew I couldn't cross.

Once our impromptu sparring session ended, Elios began showing me the basics. He adjusted my stance, corrected how I held the spear, taught me how to block an attack, and even guided my hands as I learned to wield his sword. When he handed me his dagger, demonstrating how to grip and throw it properly, I absorbed every instruction like a sponge.

He patiently but unrelentingly tailored each lesson to the meager skills I had displayed, and it was startling how much I learned in such a short time. Every correction was accompanied by a wry smirk, and every successful maneuver met with an approving nod. He often reminded me, half-joking, half-serious, that when all else failed, I needed to just jab the pointy end into my enemy. *Simple enough.*

His dry humor was as appreciated as his teachings, easing some of the tension wounding into my bones. Practicing helped me gain something I had not possessed in a long time... confidence. It was just a drop in an otherwise empty bucket, but it was more than nothing. I wasn't ready to face an enemy, not yet. But the burn in my muscles, the way sweat slicked my skin, the rhythm of movement, helped to release some of the suffocating anxiety that had been pressing down on me since the moment I'd stolen him from the sea.

I had always been the weapon—my voice, my beauty, my curse—and the moment I stopped being useful, I would be discarded like the rest.

By the time we ventured outside again, the moon hung high in the sky, this time with a purpose beyond training. We wanted more wood and stones—enough to obscure the small opening leading into our cave.

We hadn't planned to leave so soon after our last trip, but as we rested by the fire, the idea came to us simultaneously: we needed more security. The entrance had to be hidden. In theory, the branches and stones would serve as an alarm system. If someone tried to move them, the noise would wake us, giving us enough warning to prepare.

That sliver of assurance made me feel better about sleeping at the same time as Elios. It was foolish to take shifts when we both needed our strength. Still, the thought of being vulnerable, of closing my eyes and allowing myself to trust someone else to keep watch, was a foreign and terrifying concept. It was worth the trouble if the makeshift barricade could offer us even a small measure of peace.

The boulders at the entrance were too large for a single person to move, and once we arranged the branches and stones, the cave appeared abandoned and impassable. We would have to clear the entrance whenever we left and rebuild it upon returning. Still, the added security was well worth the effort.

Each stone I laid over the entrance felt like a word I couldn't speak. We *were not prey. We were not done. We were not hers.*

Once we finished, we made other improvements to our temporary home. A large piece of sail, repurposed with a few sturdy branches, became a crude privacy screen in the back corner of the front chamber for when we needed to relieve ourselves. It wasn't much, but it was something. We gathered thick foliage to line the bedding area, layering it beneath the leather to soften the hard stone floor. If we were to remain on this island for a while, we needed to make the space as livable as possible.

By the time we returned to the heart of the cavern, a larger fire burning steady beside the smaller ones we had lit for additional light, exhaustion dragged at my limbs. My muscles ached, my body sore from hours of exertion. Even though I knew how filthy I had become, the grime didn't bother me. I had endured far worse discomforts before.

Sitting beside Elios, the heat of the fire warming my skin, I let out a slow breath and allowed myself to relax just a little.

We shared a simple supper of dried fish and fruit, the meal sparse but satisfying. The hunger in my stomach was nothing compared to the hunger that had gnawed at my soul for years. I had expected nothing but suffering when I stole Elios from the depths.

I should have let him drown. Should have saved myself instead.

But now, sitting beside him, feeling his presence like an anchor in a world where I had always been adrift, I knew the truth.

I would do it all over again.

ELIOS

A Kiss Stolen from Fate

"Do you want to bathe first, or should I?" Elios asked, rinsing the sticky nectar from his dagger. We had just finished eating another mango, which was a tasty improvement on my usual fish.

I shrugged, trying to appear nonchalant, though the mere thought of submerging myself in the water with him sent a flicker of heat curling through my core.

"You've already seen me naked." The moment the words left my mouth, my face burned with embarrassment. I hadn't meant to say it so boldly. The memory of his body, slick and half-bared beneath his drenched undergarments, flashed through my mind before I could banish it. I might have only seen *most* of him, but little had been left to the imagination. I cleared my throat and added, "So, it doesn't matter. I don't care if we clean up at the same time. The pool is big enough. Whatever you're most comfortable with."

A slow silence stretched between us.

I could feel his gaze on me, assessing, *considering*. The attraction that simmered between us was undeniable, an unspoken thing that neither of us had dared to name. I had no real experience with men, but that didn't matter. How Elios made me *feel*, how my body responded in ways I didn't fully understand, was proof enough.

When I had pulled him from the sea, something had snapped into place. A *bond*. An invisible tether between us, one that I suspected would never break, no matter how much time passed. *Did he feel it, too?* It felt like fate had led me to him that night. To save him. Maybe even to *love him*.

I glanced up just in time to catch him staring, his piercing blue eyes flicking over my face, searching for something. He didn't speak, but his expression told me he was debating whether I was serious.

I *was*.

Neither of us moved toward the water right away.

Maybe I *was* being reckless, but my future was a short road ending in nothing but death. There was no path forward, no bright horizon waiting for me on the other side. If Miris didn't find me tomorrow, she would find me the next day, or the one after that. My life was a borrowed thing, stolen from the goddess herself, and I knew how these stories ended.

So, why deny myself the few pleasures I could still take?

"What?" I asked softly, stepping toward the water as my fingers loosened the knot on my top.

Elios didn't answer, but I could *feel* the shift in the air, thick and crackling, stretching between us like the final moments before a storm broke.

For three years, my existence had been nothing but misery, a ceaseless tide of hunger, cold, and death. I had nothing to look forward to but more of the same. If these were my final days, I refused to let them pass without feeling something good, something warm, something *real*.

I had no idea if someone was waiting for him back home, some woman who had claimed his heart. But there had been no ring on his finger, no whispered name on his lips as he had nearly drowned. That was enough comfort for me.

I untied the last knot with steady fingers, letting my loincloth fall in a soft heap at my feet.

I didn't look back as I stepped into the water.

Let him follow or let him stay, I thought, I wouldn't regret it either way.

When I glanced at Elios, he was still standing in the same spot, his boots discarded beside the fire. His expression was relaxed, though curiosity shone in his bright blue eyes. His lips parted slightly as if he meant to speak, but instead, he shifted his weight, lingering at the water's edge.

"Are you sure you don't mind?" His fingers raked through his damp hair, the muscles in his forearm flexing with the motion. Then, almost hesitantly, he took a small step back. "I don't mind going back to the fire and waiting."

His nervousness delighted me. For someone who had spent so long feeling powerless, I reveled in how I had the upper hand in this moment, in *this* kind of battle. It gave me a confidence I hadn't known I possessed.

I let my movements slow, drawing out each one deliberately, acutely aware of the way his gaze followed the path of my hands as I wet my hair, arching my back just enough that my breasts crested the surface. Heat pooled low in my stomach, an unfamiliar but intoxicating sensation.

I shouldn't have been doing this. I hardly knew him, but *what did it matter*? These weren't normal circumstances. Death loomed on the horizon, and caution had no place in a life so thoroughly damned. There was *nothing* to lose.

A thrill surged through me as I dragged my fingers down my throat, over my collarbone, trailing the curve of my breasts beneath the guise of washing them. The touch sent a jolt of pleasure through my limbs, drawing a soft gasp I couldn't suppress, but I didn't stop. Not as long as he watched me like that, like I was something rare, something he couldn't look away from.

Elios hovered near the water's edge, his mouth slightly open, his body taut as though warring with himself. *Come to me*, I silently willed, my pulse hammering. He had yet to move and yield to the tension thickening between us. He was waiting for a sign. *As if my words hadn't been enough.*

I chuckled softly before rising from the pool, water cascading down my body as I balanced on the tips of my toes. I let him *see* me, let him take in every inch before I shifted my legs into iridescent purple scales beneath the surface.

"I meant what I said, Elios. I don't mind."

His Adam's apple bobbed, and for a moment, I thought he might change his mind. But then, with slow, deliberate movements, he untied the waist of his trousers and let them fall, kicking them aside.

The faint glow of the dying fires spilled over his body, revealing just enough—the carved lines of muscle beneath sun-bronzed skin, the broad strength of his shoulders, and the scars etched into his forearms like echoes of old battles. He was beautiful, and the sight of him had my lips parting, my tongue sweeping over them in a weak attempt to moisten my suddenly dry mouth.

The urge to look *below* was unbearable, but I didn't dare.

Elios stepped into the pool, sinking in one fluid motion beneath the water. I exhaled, forcing myself to look away. *Gods, what was I doing?*

I reached for the small handful of juniper berries resting on the pool ledge, grateful for the distraction. This was the best we had without soap, and it would at least mask the scent of salt and sweat. I started to set them beside where he was submerged, my tail flicking idly in the warmth, but the water rippled just as I was about to turn away.

Elios surfaced *right in front of me.*

A sharp tightness coiled in my chest, every muscle locking as his face hovered mere inches from mine. Water clung to his skin, droplets tracing down the sharp angles of his jaw and his full lips. His dark lashes dripped, framing eyes so impossibly blue that I found myself drowning in them.

Neither of us spoke.

The air between us was thick, charged with something unspoken, something that made my heart beat so wildly I thought he could surely hear it. His gaze flicked to my lips, and my breath shuddered out.

He's going to kiss me. Please, kiss me.

The corner of his mouth lifted in a half-smile as if he had sensed my anticipation. He leaned forward, his lips close enough that I could feel the warmth of his breath, and my pulse became erratic, my body thrumming.

But he *didn't* kiss me.

Instead, he reached past me, grabbing the berries from where I had placed them.

I stood frozen, my lips still parted, my entire body still *waiting.*

As though he hadn't just sent my heart tumbling into the ground, he crushed the berries in his palm, the fragrant scent rising between us, and turned away.

Disappointment crashed over me like a cold wave, and I clenched my jaw to keep my frustration at bay as I swam to the other side of the pool. *What was I expecting? That we'd simply forget that we were running for our lives? That he would give in to this unbearable tension between us?*

Maybe he hadn't realized I had wanted him to kiss me, or maybe he had. Maybe he was simply choosing not to.

It was bad timing, after all. The *worst* timing. We were hiding in a cave, fugitives of a goddess, no more than strangers.

But gods help me, I still wanted him to.

I wanted him, regardless of our circumstances.

Maybe I had misread the way he looked at me, how his gaze lingered just a breath too long, or how his lips parted when I stepped from the water. Maybe he had a woman waiting for him back home, someone he was loyal to and loved. *Maybe I had imagined the entire connection between us.*

The thought twisted inside me, sharp as a blade.

Swallowing against the bitter taste of disappointment, I reached for the crushed berries and worked them into my hair, scrubbing vigorously as if I could wash away my foolishness. I hated how easily I'd fallen into something so reckless, so *desperate*. Nothing in my life had ever prepared me for romance, and it wasn't as if I *deserved* it anyway.

And yet, there was a hollow pit inside me, a deep ache that I didn't know how to fill.

I exhaled a shaky breath and let my tail shift back into legs beneath the water, stretching them out against the smooth stone floor of the pool. The shift was effortless now, as natural as breathing. My limbs ached from all the walking earlier, but the warmth of the spring soothed the tension in my muscles.

When I finally turned around, still lost in misery, I found Elios standing barely a foot away. He was so close that I could feel the heat of his body, the slow, steady rise and fall of his breath.

My pulse stumbled, then quickened.

His gaze locked onto mine, steady and unreadable, though something burned behind those blue depths, something I didn't quite understand.

"Are you angry with me?" His voice was low, tinged with something dangerously close to concern.

I swallowed hard, willing my voice to remain steady. "No."

He didn't look convinced.

"Tell me about your family, Elios," I said instead, forcing the conversation in another direction. "Do you have siblings? A wife? Children?"

The corner of his mouth lifted slightly, but his gaze didn't waver. "A wife? No. No wife. Or children. I travel too much to create attachments."

My chest loosened, and a shallow breath slipped free. There was no other woman. No one was waiting for him back home.

But before the relief could settle too deeply, his words echoed in my mind. *I travel too much to create attachments.*

The ache in my chest tightened. *And yet, here I was, already attached.*

"I do have a sister, though," he continued. "Her name is Angelia."

I nodded, grateful for the distraction. "Why do you travel so much?"

His expression darkened as though the answer carried more weight than he would admit.

"I travel because it's better than being back home. Seeking adventure is a better use of my time at this stage in my life." A chuckle escaped him, though there was something forced about it. "Though I guess I've found quite the adventure with you."

A small laugh slipped past my lips, but before I could respond, he moved closer, tracking my movements as I washed my arms.

A moment later, I climbed out of the pool and slid on my clothes, knowing it was barely enough to cover me. Behind me, the water splashed as Elios stepped out of the pool as well. I felt the shift in the air before he even spoke.

"Why were you angry?" His voice was softer now, lower. "Did I do something wrong?"

I opened my mouth to deny it, but he closed the space between us in a single step, his hand lifting to tilt my chin up, forcing me to meet his gaze.

"And don't tell me you weren't mad. I could tell."

A quiet jolt ran through me at the touch, his fingers warm against my cool skin, calloused yet gentle. *Gods, how did he unravel me so easily?*

I shrugged, unable to speak, too embarrassed to admit the truth, that I had been expecting him to kiss me and *aching for it.*

I *wanted* whatever he was willing to give me.

That I had accepted death the moment I had stolen him from the sea, and that if I was going to die, I didn't want to leave this world untouched, *unloved*.

I wanted to know what it was like to *belong* to someone, even for a fleeting moment.

As if he could hear my thoughts, Elios leaned in, slow, deliberate, like a man drawn to something he didn't dare rush.

His lips brushed mine, featherlight at first, a question hidden in the contact.

The answer came in the way my body shivered. In the way my heart stuttered and then soared.

And then he kissed me like he meant it.

No hesitation. No holding back. Just the heat of his mouth on mine, unrelenting, reverent, like he had been waiting to do this for far too long.

The butterflies in my belly didn't just stir, they ignited. My lashes fluttered closed as I kissed him back, sinking into the warmth of him, the taste of him, the spark we'd been circling for days.

Fire bloomed behind my ribs, hot and breathless and real.

When we finally pulled apart, the silence between us wasn't awkward or uncertain.

It was full.

And in that fullness, I let myself hope for something more than survival. For something like this.

Chapter Twelve

A Fate That Cannot Be

Our fingers were laced together, his warm hand resting against my thigh, the weight of it searing through me. We hadn't moved beyond kisses, but the hollowness between my legs was undeniable. If he wanted to take me, I would let him.

I swallowed against the aching need in my chest, desperate to focus on anything else.

"Where were you headed?" My voice was quiet in the hush of the cave, just loud enough to break the silence that had settled over us.

Elios let out a sleepy hum, pressing a lingering kiss to my temple. "Hmm?"

I tilted my head slightly, reveling in the feel of his lips against my skin. "You were on a merchant ship. I assume you paid for passage. I was just curious where you were going?"

His face brushed against mine as he shifted, his thumb tracing slow, lazy circles over the back of my hand. Such a simple touch, yet it sparked through me, tightening something low in my chest and setting every nerve alight. "I was going wherever the wind took me," he admitted. "As long as the ship wasn't returning to Zourin, I didn't care."

I frowned slightly, my curiosity deepening. "What do you do in unknown places? How do you support yourself?"

I knew I was prying, but I couldn't stop myself. I wanted to know more about him. About his life before the sea had stolen him from it.

He didn't seem to mind my endless questions, his thumb continuing to stroke mine as he answered. I watched how his tanned skin contrasted against mine, tracing the path of his fingertips as they ghosted over my wrist. I imagined what that same hand would look like against my stomach, between my thighs, gripping me in the throes of pleasure. Heat curled low in my belly at the thought, at the possibility.

And then, as swiftly as desire had taken hold, guilt returned.

The suffocating weight of all the lives I had taken pressed down on me, a constant reminder that I didn't deserve this moment, this warmth, *him*.

I swallowed hard. "I'm sorry."

The words came out in little more than a whisper, as if I didn't want him to hear them. But, of course, he did.

Elios kissed my cheek, his arm tightening around me, his warmth grounding me even as my mind threatened to unravel. "For what?" His voice was calm, steady. "If you hadn't crashed the ship, another would have." His fingers tightened around my hip like he needed me to hear him, needed me to believe him. "I know the guilt must eat away at you, but you didn't have a choice. Not with the way those scars look."

A bitter taste rose in my throat. The kind of bitterness that came from years of regret, of self-loathing. I tried to swallow it down, but it lingered.

"I did have a choice," I murmured. "I still do. I could die, and my life debt would die with me."

Elios tensed. His grip on me tightened as he twisted, pulling me to face him. His expression darkened, his brows furrowing in a way I had never seen before.

"Please don't talk like that, Azure." His voice was rough, his fingers firm against my skin. "The Sea Goddess will continue her monstrous games, with or without you. Your dying doesn't change anything except taking you away from me."

The words startled something inside me, something brittle and starved. No one had ever spoken to me like that before. Like I was more than the curse wrapped around my soul. Like I was worth saving.

His care for me filled my chest like the sweetest wine, warming me from the inside out. But no matter how much I wanted to believe him, to let myself hope, I knew he was wrong. My life was worth nothing—less than nothing. With every mark I etched into the cave wall, with every life lost to my cursed song, I became more and more confident of that.

The world would be better if I were put down, like any other dangerous beast, but I couldn't bring myself to say it. Not when it would only deepen the anguish in his gaze.

Elios swallowed hard, his voice low but steady. "Instead of thinking about removing yourself from the equation, why not find a way to remove her? That's the only way to truly save lives. Surely, there must be a way to defeat her."

Elios swallowed hard, his voice low but steady. "Instead of thinking about removing yourself from the equation, why not find a way to remove her? That's the only way to truly save lives. Surely, there must be a way to defeat her."

"I just don't know... She's a goddess," I said, shaking my head. "She seems untouchable. If there's a power that can destroy her, I don't have it. I don't think anyone does. And even if there was..." I trailed off, voice hollow. "Whoever kills her has to take her place. That's the price of slaying a god, and that's not a position I would ever want."

His jaw tightened. "But you don't know for sure, do you? You don't know that no one can stop her."

A sharp, cynical laugh escaped me. "And what if there is a way?" I met his gaze, my expression unreadable. "Would you take it? Would you be willing to risk it?"

Elios didn't hesitate. "If it meant saving you? Yes."

Something shifted inside me, tight and breathless, locking everything in place.

No one had ever fought for me before. No one had ever looked at me like this, with unshaken resolve, with a conviction that sent shivers through my blood.

Turning away, I stared into the fire. Its low glow mirrored the unrest coiling beneath my ribs.

He was wrong.

There was *no* way to kill Miris.

Because if there had been, I would've done it long ago.

Elios pressed his forehead to mine, his grip firm but careful, grounding me. The firelight shimmered across his skin, painting molten gold over the sharp lines of his face.

"I don't want you to take her place either," he murmured, voice a steady anchor in the chaos. "But don't give up on her destruction just yet. You're stronger than you think, and I'll help you however I can."

The words should have stirred hope. Should have offered some fragile glimpse of a future beyond servitude and death.

But they didn't.

Because I wasn't strong.

I was a coward—a woman who killed because she wasn't brave enough to die.

The moment his forehead lifted from mine, the spell between us broke. Whatever closeness had formed dissolved into the cool cave air. We rose together, reaching for our scattered clothes. The tension between us shifted, no longer intimate, just quietly uncertain.

My body still ached for him, still burned with the echo of his touch. But I wasn't ready. Not when the war inside me made everything feel too sharp, too exposed.

To my relief, Elios didn't push. He moved at my pace, as if sensing how close I stood to the edge. And maybe he did. Maybe he knew.

Because the truth was, I didn't know if it was love, or if it was just the storm pressing us together.

Would we cling to each other like this if we weren't fugitives? If death wasn't hunting us? If I hadn't dragged him from the wreckage of his life?

I tried to tell myself that what I felt for him was survival. That needing someone, needing *him*, was the only thing keeping my head above water.

But I knew it wasn't true.

Because no matter how much I tried to guard my heart, I was already his.

And clinging to that lie, that it was just necessity, I let it lull me as we stirred the fire and prepared for sleep.

Elios lay beside me, pulling the worn blanket over us. When I turned toward him, I didn't hesitate. Our bodies tangled beneath the weight of silence, his arm slipping around my waist, his breath warm against my temple.

I should have pushed him away. Should have protected whatever pieces of myself remained untouched, but instead, I leaned in, pressing closer.

As sleep crept in, heavy and irresistible, Elios' voice echoed through my mind. He wanted me to fight. To see myself as something worth saving.

But nothing had changed.

My life wasn't greater than, wasn't even equal to, the five thousand souls I had been ordered to steal.

For now, I had a reason to keep breathing: *him*. Keeping him safe. Making sure he survived. That was enough.

But beyond that?

I had already accepted the truth of my fate.

I would resist the curse for as long as I could. But when every option ran dry, when the path narrowed to its inevitable end, I knew how my story would close.

Only death could free me from this nightmare.

Chapter Thirteen

THE DREAM THAT WARNS

Elios' arm tightened around me, his grip gentle yet possessive as if he could sense the dark thoughts winding through my mind. Shifting slightly, he brushed the hair from my face, his fingers lingering before he pressed a soft, lingering kiss to my cheek.

His lips burned against my skin, not in heat, but in tenderness, making a lump form in my throat.

"What are you thinking about?" he asked, his voice edged with quiet concern. He propped himself up on an elbow, his hand tracing along my side in lazy, soothing circles.

I closed my eyes for a breath, savoring the touch before answering. "Everything and nothing," I admitted. "Today was too easy. Tomorrow isn't promised." I rolled onto my back, meeting his gaze, letting the flickering firelight reveal the raw fear I couldn't bring myself to mask. "What if they're watching? What if they're just waiting for us to show ourselves?"

Elios' hand trailed from my hip to my stomach, his fingers tracing slow, idle patterns against my bare skin. Each delicate stroke made it harder to focus and think beyond the heat of his touch and the way my body ached for more.

"We can't fight a battle that doesn't exist," he murmured. "If they're watching us, then it's too late to run anyway. We deal with problems as they come."

I barely heard him over the rapid pounding of my heart. His fingers continued their perusal, teasing circles just above my navel, and I want-ed—*gods*, I wanted—for him to slide his hand lower, to claim the space between my thighs with the same certainty he wielded his sword.

"All we can do is survive, Azure," he continued. "Worrying serves no purpose."

Though my thoughts were elsewhere, I nodded, my pulse thrumming wildly beneath his touch. Reaching up, I cupped the back of his head and pulled him into a kiss. His lips were warm, firm yet impossibly soft, and as our mouths moved together, I let myself sink into the moment, into him.

Perhaps he was right. Perhaps worrying was as fruitless as the tides raging against the cliffs. But the fear never left me, lingering beneath my skin like an old wound that refused to heal.

"So, we just prepare?" I whispered against his lips. "Make weapons and train?"

He hummed in agreement and kissed me again. My fingers tangled in his hair, reveling in the silky texture as I arched into his embrace. Firelight danced across the sharp planes of his face, cloaking him in shadow and flame. For a moment, he looked otherworldly, like a god sent to tempt me into sin.

Arm tightening around my waist, he dragged me against the heat of his body, and when his teeth scraped my lower lip, a moan escaped before I could stop it.

I should have resisted. Should have let logic guide me instead of the unbearable hunger twisting low in my belly. But when the hard length of him pressed against my hip, answering the pulse of need between my thighs, I found myself on the precipice of something dangerous, something inevitable.

And I *wanted to fall.*

A sound from the front chamber of the cave shattered the moment.

We tore apart, breathing hard, frozen as we listened. My heartbeat thundered in my ears, loud enough that I swore it would give us away.

A long silence stretched between the walls of the cave.

Then came a sound—*a scrape*. A slow, deliberate dragging, followed by the dull clatter of something hitting the ground.

My pulse spiked.

Before I registered our next steps, Elios was already moving, shoving the blanket aside as he reached for his sword. I snatched the dagger beside me, the cold steel reassuring against my palm. The air had turned thick, suffocating in the darkness.

Another thud.

Elios crept toward the entrance without making much noise, his body coiled with tension. I followed in his shadow, my grip tightening around the dagger's hilt.

We had no idea what, or who, had found us.

The silence stretched, the only sound being the whisper of our breaths as we neared the narrow passage leading to the main chamber. The air smelled of damp stone and cooling embers, but there was something else, something off beneath that.

Another stone tumbled from the barricade we had built.

Sucking in a sharp breath, I gripped the waistband of Elios' trousers, grounding myself in the warmth of his presence. Without a word, he reached back and squeezed my hand before continuing forward.

The cave suddenly felt too small, the air too thin.

Through the small gaps in the barricade, moonlight streamed into the front chamber, illuminating the disturbance. My heart clenched as I spotted another rock shift and roll to the ground. Whoever, or whatever, was outside was trying to get in.

Elios' body vibrated with tension, his breath slow and measured. We stood still, watching, waiting. If it was an animal, it might lose interest and leave.

Or it might not.

A deep, guttural growl rumbled through the air, primal, agitated, making the hairs on the back of my neck stand on end.

Heavy footsteps followed, retreating. Fading into the distance.

Elios exhaled, leaning so close that his lips nearly brushed my ear. "Just an animal," he whispered. "And it seems to have given up." He punctuated his words with a playful nip at my earlobe as if trying to ease the lingering tension.

I let out a shaky breath. "Any idea what kind?"

Wrapping an arm around my waist, he guided me back toward the warmth of our chamber. "I'm not sure what creatures are native to this island. Maybe we'll find signs of it in the morning." He settled before the fire, pulling me onto his lap as if he could shield me from whatever still lurked beyond the cave's entrance. "It's too dark to see anything now anyway."

I nodded, letting the tension drain from my limbs.

The late-night intruder had doused the fire between us like a cold wave against burning embers, leaving nothing but smoldering heat beneath the ashes. The hunger was still there, but it would have to wait.

Tonight, there would be no surrender.

Instead, we curled together beneath the blanket, his arms a fortress around me, my body fitting against his as if we had always belonged.

The barricade had done its job, keeping the island's creatures at bay, but I prayed it would be as effective against the monsters that hunted us.

My worries warred against the weight of exhaustion. Still, eventually, the warmth of Elios' embrace dulled the sharp edges of my thoughts, lulling me into uneasy sleep. His steady breaths against my hair, the rhythmic rise and fall of his chest beneath my cheek, these small comforts tethered me to the present, a fragile shield against the nightmares that lurked at the edges of my mind.

But the darkness always found me.

Waves crashed against the shore, their ceaseless rhythm washing away the sand beneath Daneliya's feet. Her tiny body stood motionless, stiff, and gray, her skin taking on the pallor of death as the sea threatened to claim her once more.

My breath came in ragged sobs, but the sound was swallowed by the void pressing in around us. The landscape was barren, endless, a world reduced to nothing but black water and shifting sand. There was no sun. No wind. No voices. Just me and my lifeless sister.

I dropped to my knees beside her, the force of my grief stealing the air from my lungs. My hands trembled as I cupped her cold cheeks, stroking the softness of her skin with desperate reverence. Come back to me. Please, come back.

There was no warmth in her body, no hint of life behind her closed eyes.

I tried to scream for help, but no sound escaped my lips.

No one would come.

It was too late.

A jolt of terror shot through me.

The irises that had once been a warm, lively brown were now pure black. Obsidian pools devoid of light, devoid of life. Her lips parted, tinged blue with death, but her expression was not hers.

It was something else.

Something wrong.

My stomach twisted violently, nausea clawing its way up my throat as those soulless eyes locked onto mine. A cold dread spread through my limbs, turning my blood to ice. I wanted to move. I needed to move. Every instinct screamed at me to run, to shove her away and flee, but my arms refused to let go.

A strangled cry wrenched from my throat as I clutched her to my chest, my fingers tangling in the damp strands of her hair. I rocked her,

whispering frantic, useless apologies, my tears carving hot trails down my face. I had failed her. I had failed the only person who had ever truly mattered.

Then, impossibly, her eyes snapped open.

A sickening silence stretched between us, thick and suffocating.

Then she spoke.

A voice not her own.

A voice that slithered from her lips like a hissing tide, warping the air around us.

"She's coming. She'll find you. You will never be safe."

A scream tore from my throat, but the void devoured it whole.

And in the darkness, something laughed.

Chapter Fourteen

TIDES OF VENGEANCE

By the time the fifth day arrived, necessity finally overpowered my fear.

We were out of dried fish. The island provided enough fruit to sustain us, but it wasn't enough, not for long. If we stayed here and survived, I had to do what I had been avoiding.

I had to return to the water.

The realization twisted in my gut as I lay beside Elios, his arm draped heavily over my waist, his warmth an anchor against the creeping unease in my chest. I didn't want to leave his embrace or slip out from under the security he provided, but we needed food.

We needed me to be what I had spent the last three years despising.

With careful movements, I slipped from beneath his arm, rising from our shared bed of ferns and leather. He stirred slightly, his brow furrowing in sleep, but he didn't wake. I exhaled, relieved. He would have insisted on coming with me, and though I craved his presence, the sea was my battlefield.

The chill of the early morning air prickled my skin as I left the cave and stepped onto the deserted beach.

Overhead, dark clouds loomed at the horizon, heavy and foreboding, promising an oncoming storm. As I strode toward the tide, the winds rolling off the water carried a sharp bite, tousling my hair. The ocean was restless, *uneasy*. I could feel it in the way the waves crashed against the shore, in the salty spray that clung to my skin like an omen.

I hesitated. *Maybe I should have woken him.*

The realization struck me like a wave to the chest, but it was too late to turn back.

Fingers tightening around the crude spear I had fashioned days ago, I adjusted Elios' dagger at my waist, securing it against the makeshift leather belt I had crafted. The weight of it was reassuring, but it did little to ease the tension coiling in my stomach.

Overhead, a flock of white birds fled inland, away from the storm and the churning depths. I tracked them with wary eyes, my gut twisting as they vanished beyond the treetops—a silent warning.

I exhaled a sharp breath, shaking off the unease before stepping into the frigid embrace of the tide.

My body reacted instinctively as soon as the water closed around my legs. With a single thought, my human form melted away, iridescent scales shimmering beneath the surface as I shifted.

For the first time in over a week, I was home.

And yet, it didn't feel like home at all.

I hovered in the shallows, scanning my surroundings for any sign of movement. The sea was deceptively empty before me, but I knew better than to trust its stillness. Even if no ships sailed close and I saw no mermaids lurking beneath the waves, the water was never truly empty.

Something was always watching.

Something always waited.

But hunger demanded action.

Drawing a deep breath, I gripped my spear and dove, cutting through the waves like a blade.

The deeper I swam, the more the storm's chaos faded. The surface turbulence gave way to eerie stillness, the world below untouched by the brewing tempest above.

The ocean floor stretched endlessly beneath me, teeming with life—vibrant coral, darting fish, creatures that pulsed with soft bio-luminescence in the darkened depths.

It should have been breathtaking.

Once, long ago, I marveled at the wonders hidden below the tide. I ran my fingers along the swaying fronds of seaweed, traced the spirals of delicate shells, and laughed as Daneliya gasped in delight at the creatures that flitted past.

But I no longer saw the beauty here.

Now, the sea was nothing more than a prison. A graveyard.

I didn't deserve to admire it, not when it had become my hunting ground, my cage, my punishment.

Jaw tightening, I steeled myself against the rush of self-loathing and angled my spear toward the shadows moving along the seabed.

I wasn't here to mourn.

I was here to kill.

And if I was lucky, if the gods still had even a shred of mercy left for me, I would return to shore before the storm hit.

I forced myself to ignore the beauty around me—the kaleidoscope of color, the way the water danced through swaying fronds, the iridescent shimmer of passing fish—it was all meaningless.

With slow, deliberate movements, I glided closer to the underwater foliage, careful not to startle the prey concealed within. The plants undulated in the shifting current, a safe haven for fish seeking shelter from predators, but they would not find safety from me.

I tightened my grip on the spear, muscles coiling with anticipation, and then I struck.

The stone tip pierced flesh in a single, brutal thrust. The fish barely had time to react before the spear pinned two of them in place, their bodies jerking violently in protest. Their struggles ended quickly as I twisted the weapon, ensuring they felt no more pain.

A rare sense of satisfaction bloomed in my chest, dulling the ever-present ache of guilt. At least this death meant something. This was not a senseless sacrifice, not another meaningless life stolen by my cursed hands. This would sustain us.

I slipped the fish into the pouch fastened at my waist, already imagining the pleased look on Elios' face when I returned with fresh meat for dinner. I could picture how his eyes would light up, and his lips would curl in that crooked smile that made my stomach flutter.

For once, I was bringing him something other than ruin.

But the moment of triumph was short-lived.

A shadow moved above me, massive and slow, blotting out the fractured sunlight that filtered through the surface.

A sharp chill crawled down my spine.

I went still, my breath locking in my throat.

Something watched me.

The water around me turned heavy, thick with the weight of unseen danger. I swallowed hard, forcing back the rising panic, and in one fluid motion, propelled myself upward.

The instant I broke through the surface, there was chaos.

The wind howled through the sky, carrying the scent of impending violence. Cold and relentless rain lashed at my face, turning the world into a blur of shifting grays and churning waves. I blinked rapidly, struggling to find my bearings as the storm loomed closer, swallowing the distant horizon in its black maw.

But the storm was not the worst thing waiting for me.

Through the dense curtain of rain, I saw them.

Elios stood on the shore, sword drawn, his stance rigid and unyielding as he faced two figures.

Oona and Lucia.

A violent tremor tore through me, dread sinking its claws deep into my chest. I had seen the cruel smirks on their lips too many times before and had watched them hunt and destroy with cold precision.

Elios was in their sight.

My pulse thundered, louder than the crashing waves, louder than the growl of distant thunder rolling in from the sea.

I have to reach him.

Every instinct screamed for me to rush forward, to stand between him and the nightmare looming before him. But what could I do? I was no warrior. My body was built for endurance, for speed, for seduction, but not battle.

The only advantage I had was the element of surprise. If I lunged too soon, I would lose it.

I forced myself to remain submerged, barely keeping my head above the surface, eyes fixed on the confrontation unfolding on the beach.

Oona stood with her hands outstretched, her expression of pure, wicked amusement. She was toying with him, savoring the power she held. If she decided to act, she could kill him in seconds. She could twist the air from his lungs with a flick of her fingers.

Ever the loyal shadow, Lucia stood at her side, dagger glinting in her grasp, poised and ready to strike the moment Oona gave the command.

And Elios stood defiant before them.

"I've already told you," he said, voice strong and steady, unshaken by the monsters before him. "I don't know who she is. I'm here alone."

My chest clenched so hard it hurt.

He was lying for me. He was risking everything to protect me.

A bitter taste rose in my throat. He shouldn't have to protect me. That was my job.

Oona sneered, scanning the island with a predator's patience. "Lies," she spat, the single word laced with venom.

I held my breath, praying she wouldn't sense me lurking beneath the waves. Praying she wouldn't decide to test her patience on Elios' flesh.

If she so much as blinked in his direction the wrong way, I would kill her. I would kill them both.

But my heart slammed against my ribs with the knowledge that I wasn't strong enough.

Oona was more than just a mermaid.

She had served Miris longer than I had been cursed, spending decades twisting her gifts into something monstrous. The power at her disposal was beyond my understanding, beyond my reach. Strength, endurance, impeccable sight—those were the only gifts my curse had granted me.

And my song.

The haunting, sultry melody that could lure a man to his doom.

But Oona was more than just a hunter, she was something darker. There was an unnatural edge to her, a shadow lurking beneath her skin, something ancient and cruel that went beyond her love of the kill.

Something wrong.

My fingers tightened around the dagger at my waist, my pulse pounding.

I had no magic. No divine gifts. No weapons but the crude blade in my grip.

But if she took one step toward him, I would carve her open myself.

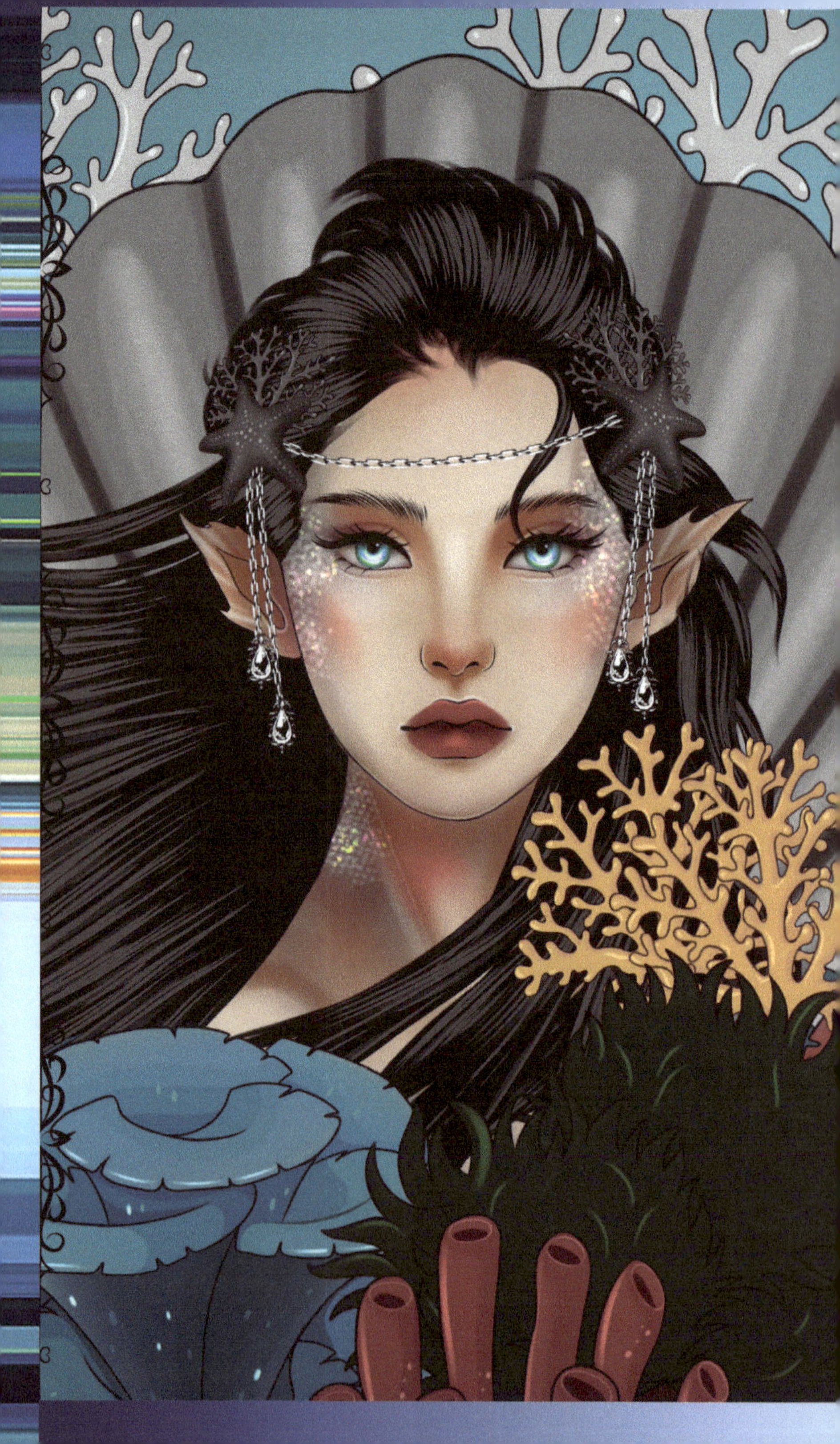

Chapter Fifteen

A Monster Awakens

While Elios held their attention, I slipped onto the bank, my body shifting seamlessly as I dragged myself onto the sand. The rain battered my skin in cold, stinging sheets, but I ignored it, moving silently toward the cover of the trees. My heart pounded as I melted into the shadows hidden beneath the thick canopy.

I wished I could signal to him, wished there was some way to let him know I was here, that I hadn't left him to face them alone. But there was no way to do that without revealing myself, and I needed the advantage of surprise. I forced myself to remain still, to breathe through the chaos in my mind.

Think, Azure.

But no matter how I tried to focus, the storm inside me refused to settle. It was just like the night I had pulled him from the sea—acting on instinct, on raw desperation, rather than any real plan.

Over the last several days, Elios and I had hidden weapons throughout the island, precautionary measures for a moment just like this. There weren't many, but I knew where they were. My hands moved swiftly, brushing through damp foliage as I found what I sought—a crude dagger, its stone blade sharpened to a jagged point.

I still had Elios' dagger tucked against my belt and my spear slung across my back, but I wasn't ready to use them. Not yet. I needed to be careful and wait for the right moment.

Something I prayed I would recognize when it came.

My grip tightened around the handle.

Oona's voice rose through the veil of rain, sharp with anger. Another threat. Another demand. My blood boiled, the heat of it burning through the cold.

I didn't wait.

The blade flew from my hand.

A scream ripped through the storm, high and piercing.

Oona collapsed, clutching at her right shoulder, where my dagger was now buried deep, just below the shoulder blade, a wound meant to weaken, not to kill. *Not yet.*

She twisted, her gaze wild, scanning the trees. Searching.

But I was already gone, swallowed by the dense undergrowth.

Elios didn't hesitate. With a powerful thrust, he lunged at Lucia, his sword knocking her dagger clean from her grasp. The weapon clattered to the mud, but she was too fast. She darted forward and snatched it up before he could reach it.

"You're going to regret that, human," Lucia snarled, her lips pulling back in a feral grin.

She pivoted and yanked the blade from Oona's shoulder without hesitation. Oona let out a sharp hiss of pain, her blood mingling with the rain as it ran down her back. But even as she staggered, her dark eyes burned with unrelenting fury.

She wouldn't stay weak for long.

Oona was powerful, stronger than most of Miris' servants, and even wounded, she was still dangerous. If I hesitated and wasted even a second, she would regain her focus and bring her powers crashing down on us.

And then it would be over.

Elios and Lucia circled each other, their weapons raised, their bodies taut with lethal intent.

He's a skilled fighter, but she's a monster.

I had to act.

I had never prepared for a battle like this before. I had never been a warrior, but I was willing to die to save him.

Oona was too powerful. Lucia was too ruthless. They wouldn't stop until they had me.

And Elios—Elios was just an obstacle in their way.

To them, he was already dead.

The clash of metal rang through the storm, a violent song of survival. I turned just in time to see Lucia leap at him, her legs wrapping around his torso as they crashed onto the mud-soaked ground. Their blades were lost, forgotten in the fray.

She was smaller than him, but she was vicious and unrelenting.

Elios fought back, his arms straining against her grip, but she was stronger than she looked. Her fingers clawed at him like a wild animal, her lips curling into something savage.

My chest constricted. *He doesn't have the upper hand.*

And Oona was regaining hers.

I reached for my other dagger. My heartbeat pounded against my ribs, erratic and wild, as adrenaline surged through my veins. I needed to act. *Now.*

My trembling fingers wrapped around the hilt of Elios' dagger, my grip slick with rain. With a sharp inhale, I took aim and hurled the blade.

The weapon cut through the air like an arrow, but missed.

Oona ducked at the last second, the dagger sailing just over her head before disappearing into the mud. Her head snapped up, and for a single breath, I thought she had spotted me. Instead, a slow, venomous smirk curled at the edges of her lips. Without hesitation, she drew her knife and turned toward the trees, her narrowed eyes scanning the dense foliage.

I clenched my jaw, forcing my ragged breathing to steady as spots flickered at the edges of my vision. I couldn't afford to panic now.

Behind her, Elios wrestled beneath Lucia, straining toward the weapons scattered across the ground. Her tangled blond hair was slick with rain, plastered across her face as she bared her teeth in frustration.

Then, with a victorious snarl, Lucia's fingers closed around the bloodied dagger she had ripped from Oona's shoulder.

Before Elios could react, she placed it against his throat.

My breath caught, my grip tightening around my primitive spear until the wood groaned beneath my fingers.

"I know you're there, Azure," Oona taunted, her voice laced with cruel amusement. Her head tilted slightly as she smirked in my direction, though I remained concealed in the shadows of the trees.

Behind her, the fight came to an abrupt halt. Elios had gone still beneath Lucia, though his chest still rose and fell in quick, shallow breaths. He was waiting. Watching.

Waiting for me.

Lucia's lips curled into a wicked sneer as she pressed the dagger harder against his throat, her nails digging into the rain-slicked skin of his jaw.

"Come on out, or we'll kill your lover boy," Oona drawled, glancing over her shoulder at Elios. The words were laced with boredom, like his life meant nothing. Because to them, it didn't.

My stomach twisted, bile rising in my throat.

"Not that we won't kill him anyway," she added with a lazy chuckle. "He's already a dead man."

Lucia spat on the ground beside Elios' head. He bucked beneath her, his muscles coiling as he tried to throw her off, but she was too strong. A creature made for violence. The blade remained against his throat, poised for the final cut.

No.

I fought back the urge to scream, to rush at them in blind fury. I had no options. No time.

Only one choice.

Taking a shaky breath, I stepped out from my hiding place.

"If I surrender, you have to let him go."

Oona barely spared me a glance. Unimpressed, she twirled her dagger between her fingers as if I had been an inevitability rather than a threat.

"I don't know, Azure," she mused, flicking a bit of dirt from her nails with the blade's tip. "Our Goddess would be quite angry if we set him free. His soul belongs to her."

My blood ran hot with fury.

"He belongs to no one," I spat, fists trembling at my sides. "He's a free man—an innocent." My pulse roared in my ears, drowning out the storm, the ocean, everything except the hatred boiling inside me. "And she is *not* my Goddess."

Oona clicked her tongue. "Kill—"

The word barely left her lips before the sea erupted behind her.

A monstrous shape burst from the water, dark as the abyss.

Tentacles, massive and writhing, lashed out and wrapped around her before she could react. She let out a strangled shriek, her body jerking violently as she was ripped off the ground.

I stumbled back in shock.

No.

This wasn't real. It couldn't be real.

Oona's eyes went wide, the whites flashing in terror as she twisted in the beast's hold, but the grip was unrelenting. The last thing I saw before she was dragged beneath the surface was the sheer, unbridled panic on her face.

And then she was gone.

The sea swallowed her whole.

For a long, frozen moment, no one spoke. The rain hammered against my skin, my breaths coming in short, frantic bursts as I stared at the churning water. My mind refused to process what I had just seen, to accept the truth of what had taken her.

No. It *wasn't possible.*

The Kraken was just a myth. A *legend.*

Lucia's scream shattered the silence. "Oona!"

She scrambled off Elios and bolted for the shore, shifting midair before she hit the water. Her form disappeared beneath the waves, going after the monstrous creature she was no match for.

And then there was nothing.

No sign of the beast. No ripple of movement. No trace of the two mermaids who had been there just moments ago.

Just silence.

My lungs ached as I tried to force air back into them, my mind still spinning. It wasn't real. I must have imagined it. The Kraken didn't exist. It couldn't.

But the ocean said otherwise.

A pair of strong, familiar arms wrapped around me from behind, anchoring me back to reality. Elios pulled me against his chest, his warmth sinking into me as his lips pressed frantic kisses along my temple, cheek, and jaw.

"Are you okay?" he murmured, his voice rough, breathless. His hands traced over my arms, checking for wounds. "You were amazing."

I barely heard him. My gaze remained locked on the horizon, on the dark, empty sea where the monster had vanished.

"What was that?" I whispered, though I already knew the answer.

Following my stare, Elios exhaled and pulled me closer. "I've heard stories of such a monster before. Sailors love to tell tales of the Kraken, but I never believed they were true." His fingers curled against the small of my back as if grounding me in the present. "Until now."

I closed my eyes, letting his warmth chase away the bone-deep chill that had settled inside me. The Kraken was real. It had taken Oona as if she had been nothing more than an insect caught in its grasp. And if it was real, what else lurked beneath the waves?

Elios exhaled softly against my ear. "Come," he murmured. "Let's go sit by the fire and warm up. You're shivering."

I wasn't cold. The tremors racking my body had nothing to do with the rain.

But I let him guide me back toward the cave, my feet moving without thought, my mind still stuck in the moment Oona had been ripped from the shore.

Because I couldn't shake the feeling that this was only the beginning.

And that whatever had come for her, whatever had risen from the depths, would come for me next.

Surrender to the Storm

The fire had burned low by the time we returned to the back chamber of the cave, its glow a dim echo of the chaos that had preceded it.

"Let's get you cleaned up," I said softly, eyeing the streaks of blood and dirt still drying on his skin. The sight of him—smeared with battle, still breathing, still here—made my throat tighten. "The hot spring will feel good."

Undoubtedly exhausted, Elios didn't argue. He just stood, wincing slightly as the movement tugged at his shoulder, and offered me his hand. Fingers twined, we crossed the stone floor to the small, steaming pool nestled at the far edge of the cave. The heat wafted up in curling tendrils, scented faintly with minerals and earth.

He stripped off his soiled tunic and stepped into the water, submerging with a soft hiss. I followed, easing in beside him, the warmth enveloping me like a second skin.

For a moment, we said nothing. Just breathed.

"I didn't expect to survive that," he said finally, voice quiet in the steam. "When I saw them, I thought that was it."

I moved closer, cupping water in my hand and letting it pour gently over his shoulder. Dirt and blood trailed away into the spring.

"You didn't give up," I murmured. "Even when they surrounded you."

A tremor moved through me at the memory of Oona's eyes, of Lucia's grin. "I thought they were going to kill you," I admitted, my voice barely above a whisper. "And I didn't know if I could survive that... not that they would have left me alive to try."

He turned toward me, eyes dark with understanding. "But we survived," he said. "And we'll keep surviving. You and me—*together*."

Doing my best to push the negative thoughts away, I reached for the cloth set beside the spring, soaking it and gently wringing it out. Without a word, I ran it across his chest, wiping away the remnants of dried blood and dirt. The touch was slow, intentional. Each pass of the cloth was a quiet thank-you—for surviving, for staying.

He let me tend to him, his eyes never leaving mine. When I leaned in to press a kiss to his shoulder, he drew in a breath and let it go slowly, like the last remnants of fear were slipping away with the water. Not because I had healed him—but because I was here, and we were still standing.

"You're shaking," he murmured, cupping my elbow. The touch forced me to pause, if only for a moment.

"I think I'm only just realizing how close it was," I whispered. "How close I came to losing you."

A silence settled between us—not heavy, but humming with everything unspoken. Then he reached for me. I let out a small, surprised breath as he gathered me into his arms, but I didn't resist. I folded into him, the warmth of his body steadying the last of my trembling.

The heat of his skin pressed into mine as he carried me across the stone floor, banishing the chill the spring had left behind. When we reached the makeshift bed of palm fronds and leather, he knelt and laid me gently among them, his gaze lingering over me like a caress.

He didn't speak—not at first. Instead, he reached for a few fresh sticks and coaxed the fire back to life. The fire stirred to life, casting a warm, amber glow across the stone walls and softening every sharp corner of the cave. Its light played across Elios's skin in shifting patterns, illuminating him with a quiet brilliance that felt impossibly tender. The heat radiated outward, chasing the damp from our skin and anchoring us in the fragile peace we'd fought to earn. As the flames took hold, he sat before them and pulled me gently into his lap. I melted against his chest, the warmth of him easing a tension I hadn't realized I was still carrying.

Outside, waves crashed faintly against the rocks beyond the cave mouth, a constant rhythm beneath the crackling of the fire. The air smelled of salt and smoke, and of him—earth and wind and something deeper, something uniquely Elios, like warmth woven through danger.

"Who were they?" he asked, voice quiet near my ear. "Did you know those mermaids?"

I nodded, grimacing. "Unfortunately. The one you fought was Lucia. She's feral, prefers to kill with her hands rather than her voice. The one I hit with the dagger was Oona. Her magic is... *terrifying*. She could've killed you with a single thought if she'd wanted to." I swallowed hard. "Miris must have ordered them to bring us back alive. Otherwise, they wouldn't have hesitated."

The words left a bitter taste in my mouth. Just imagining what would've happened if the Kraken hadn't intervened made my stomach twist. Whatever future awaited us in Miris' grip would've been cruel—slow, sadistic, and final.

The creature from the sea had bought us time. Not freedom. Not safety. But time enough to breathe. To be here. To hold each other before the next shadow crept in.

Elios tucked a loose strand of hair behind my ear. "I don't think Oona will be coming back from that. Lucia... I'm not sure."

His fingers skimmed along my spine, slow and steady, and I closed my eyes against the sensation. I didn't want to think about the future. About danger. About escape. Not yet.

"I was so scared something would happen to you," I murmured. "I'm sorry I didn't wake you before I went fishing. I wanted to let you sleep. It was stupid."

He turned me toward him, his lips brushing mine in a kiss that stole my breath. Even after everything we'd been through, even after fighting for his life, he was still so gentle with me.

"You have nothing to apologize for," he said softly. "You couldn't have known they were watching."

He was right, but I wouldn't make the same mistake again. Not when everything I cared about was wrapped up in this man.

It was us now. Us against everything.

I kissed him again, deeper this time, my fingers sliding into the softness of his hair. I needed the feel of him. Needed the distraction, the grounding. I could have lost him today, and that reality made every breath, every heartbeat, feel borrowed.

We weren't promised tomorrow. Only this. This one moment, and each other.

As his mouth found my neck, I tilted my head back with a soft gasp, letting the heat in my belly curl deeper. I would no longer waste time pretending I didn't want him. That we didn't want each other.

Desire surged between us, and I gave myself to it.

He groaned softly when I shifted in his lap, turning to straddle him. There wasn't much separating our bodies. Only the thinnest scraps of cloth. My thighs cradled his hips as I settled against him, and the contact made my lungs struggle to expand.

I relished how scandalous it felt—the closeness, the warmth, the press of him beneath me. His hands found my hips, guiding me gently as I began to move, rocking against him.

It was my first time being so close, but with Elios, it didn't feel frightening. He looked up at me like I was something rare, something precious—like in that moment, I was the only truth that mattered.

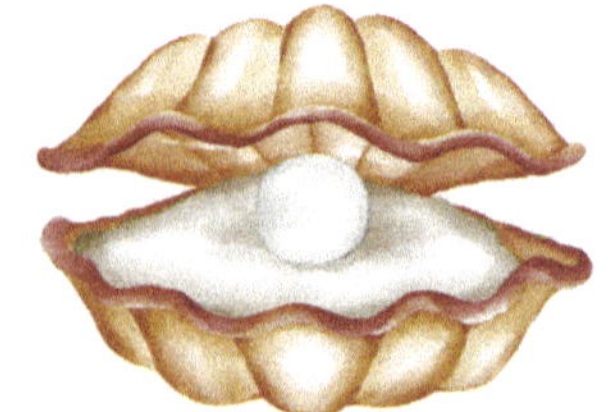

It felt inevitable.

With his lips on mine, his hands slid down my back to my waist, then lower, gripping and kneading, drawing my body more tightly against his. The friction set me ablaze. I moaned, let-

ting my head fall back, and he met
each motion with a slow grind of his own, pulling a deeper sound from
my throat.

"Wait," he whispered, voice husky. "We don't have to go further, not if
you're not ready."

His restraint only made me want him more. The way he held back, the
way he waited for me—it wasn't distance. It was reverence.

I leaned in, pressing my lips to his neck. I nipped gently at the skin just
above his collarbone and whispered against his pulse, "I don't want to
stop."

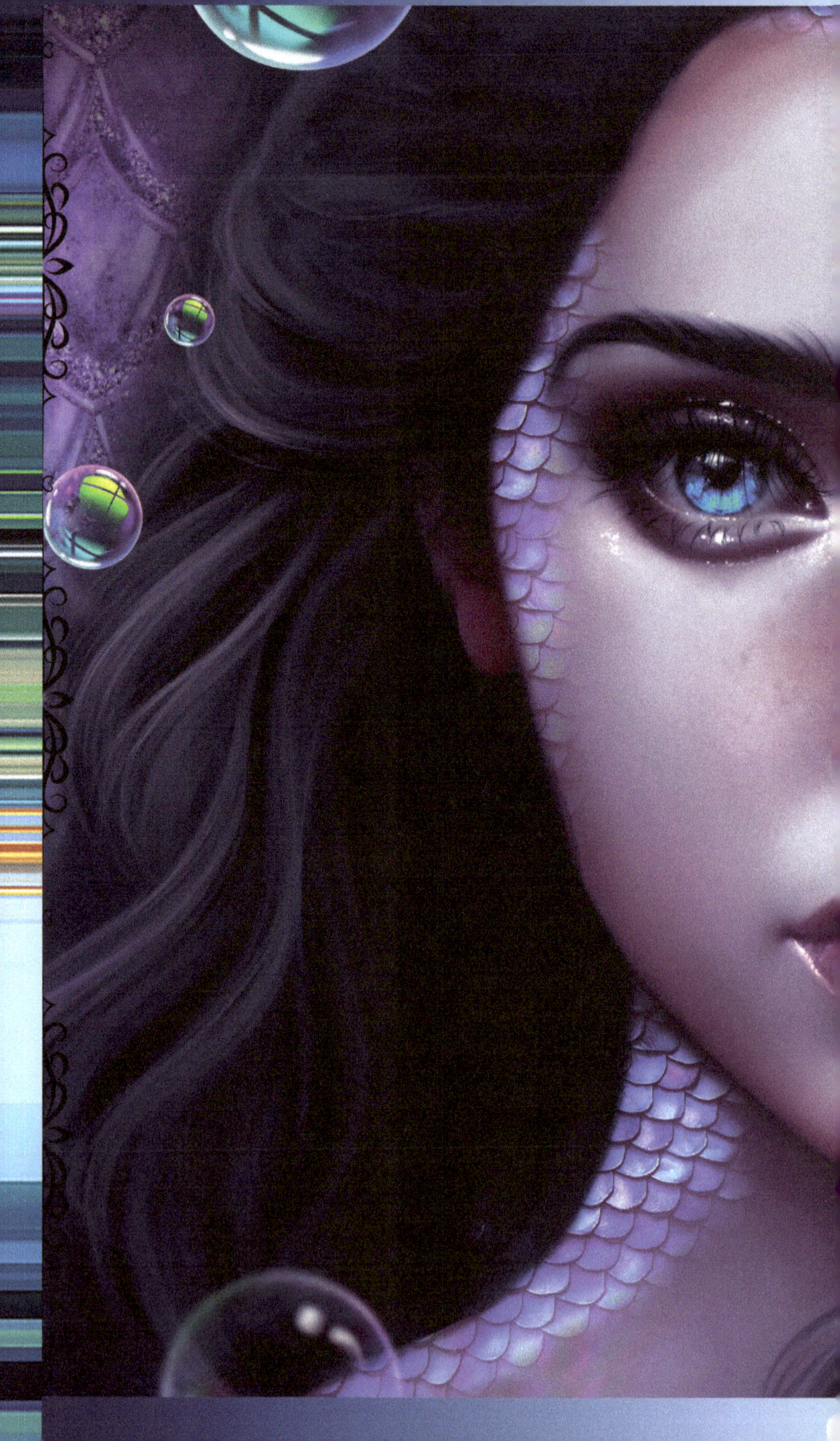

Chapter Seventeen

No More Waiting

He had changed everything. Not with grand gestures or elaborate declarations, but with quiet understanding, unwavering patience, and the way his eyes always found the parts of me I tried hardest to keep hidden. In ways I couldn't have foreseen, I was beginning to believe he had saved me.

Now, with his mouth trailing a burning path down my torso, the truth of that settled deep and low, blooming through every inch of my skin like wildfire. His lips left behind heat and adoration with every kiss, each one more deliberate than the last, edging steadily toward where I ached for him most.

A shaky breath left me as his tongue moved lower, a slow drag down the center of my abdomen. Every flick of it sent new sparks skittering across my skin, each one a tease that made my thighs tense, my hips lift of their own accord—not boldly, but pleadingly. I wasn't demanding. I was offering. Asking. Silently begging for mercy.

I hadn't been taught how to want. Not like this. But my body knew. With aching clarity and primal certainty, it understood what it meant to burn, to crave, to be undone by the promise of someone else's touch.

Whispers had echoed behind coral walls—mermaids trading secrets in hushed tones about shadowed coves and stolen pleasures. I'd watched human lovers on moonlit shores, their bodies tangled in devotion. Those glimpses painted a picture in my mind, piecing together fragments of what this might feel like. But nothing, not their stories or my stolen glances, had prepared me for *him*.

His breath skimmed lower, drawing a whimper from deep in my throat. The anticipation coiled tighter with each slow kiss he placed beneath my navel. My fingers slid into his hair again, not to guide but to anchor, because I didn't know how to stay tethered without him.

When he looked up at me, something in his eyes made the world tilt. There was no teasing there. No hunger without meaning. Only a quiet devotion that shattered me more than any kiss.

He hooked one of my legs over his shoulder, the motion confident but unhurried, like he wanted to savor the way I trembled beneath him. His hands trailed along my thighs, thumbs brushing the inside edges, coaxing them farther apart until there was nowhere left to hide.

"I need to taste you," he murmured, voice roughened by restraint. "Let me?"

"Yes," I whispered, breath catching. "Please."

When his mouth touched me, it carried no urgency—only intent, and a kind of tender curiosity that made my breath catch. A slow, exploratory stroke of his tongue sent a jolt through my spine, my back arching from the bed. I gasped his name, the sound escaping my lips like it had been waiting for this moment to be set free.

He groaned in response and did it again, deeper this time, his hands holding me open as though I were a gift. Each flick of his tongue pulled me further from reason, until the cave, the fire, the world all faded to the place where only we existed.

My breath came in broken gasps, each one chasing the next. I couldn't hold still beneath him, my hips rising in plea, in offering. He read each movement like a language he was born knowing—answering with another slow, devastating stroke.

When he groaned against me, the sound vibrated through my center. My fingers tangled tighter in his hair. I didn't know how to stay still. Didn't want to.

Then his fingers joined his mouth.

I cried out, sharp and breathless, as one slid inside, followed by another—slow, sure, grounding. The stretch of it pulled me wide open, winding the tension in me so taut it nearly snapped, but he was gentle.

My name slipped from his lips in a low rasp between strokes. I gasped his in return.

"Elios."

He looked up at me, eyes dark and unguarded. "I've got you," he whispered.

And then I shattered.

Pleasure tore through me like lightning through open water. My body seized, bowed, then broke apart with a cry that filled the chamber. He held me through every wave, mouth and fingers working me through the storm. Even when I had nothing left but gasps and shudders, he stayed with me.

Only when I whimpered from the sensitivity did he pull away, pressing a kiss to my thigh. One, then another. Then he rose slowly up the length of my body.

He kissed my hip, my stomach, my ribs, the underside of my breast. He kissed me like he needed to relearn me inch by inch. And when he reached my lips again, he hovered there.

Unable to stop myself. I pulled him down to me and kissed him.

The world was still unraveling beneath us, but in that kiss, everything came back together.

When our lips parted, I didn't open my eyes right away. I just stayed there, wrapped in him, letting the rhythm of our breathing slowly align. The world was soft now. Gentle in a way it hadn't been for a long time.

His forehead rested against mine, the weight of his body a comfort, not a burden. I could feel his heart still thundering beneath his skin, feel the tension coiled in him that he hadn't let spill.

He was waiting. Holding back. For me.

I opened my eyes and found him already watching me, his gaze searching. Not demanding. Just... present.

"I want you," I said, my voice low, certain. "All the way."

His breath seized, and for a moment, he didn't move—like he was giving me time to change my mind, even now.

Realizing he needed encouragement, I slid my hand between us and wrapped my fingers around him, feeling the heat of him against my palm. The soft hiss of breath he let out nearly undid me.

"I want this," I whispered. "I want you."

He groaned and pressed his forehead to mine again, trembling. "If I move now, I won't be able to stop."

"You don't have to."

His lips curled against my jaw. "Then let me take my time with you."

As if he were still waiting for some final confirmation, he kissed me slow, lingering against my lips, but I didn't hesitate. I kissed him back with all the tenderness and certainty I carried in my chest.

"Come here," I whispered, curling my arms around his neck.

Deliberately, he shifted his weight and pressed himself against me, skin to skin. My legs opened around him without thought, drawing him closer, anchoring him to me. The head of him brushed against my entrance, and I gasped, not from fear, but from the rush of anticipation.

Elios stilled, his eyes searching mine. "Tell me if it's too much."

"It won't be." I cupped his face, thumb brushing along the line of his cheekbone. "I want this with you."

He nodded once, his throat working as he swallowed. Then, with exquisite care, he began to ease into me.

The stretch stole the breath from my lungs. My fingers clutched his shoulders, holding on, not from pain but from the sheer intensity of the feeling. Every inch of him slid into me with exquisite slowness, each new depth pushing a wave of sensation through my spine. It was as if my body had been waiting for him without knowing it, made to welcome him, to hold him. Heat bloomed low and heavy, and I couldn't tell where my breath ended and his began.

He didn't move right away. He stayed there, completely still, as though honoring the threshold we had just crossed. As though the moment itself deserved silence. My body adjusted to the fullness of him, and something unspoken passed between us—an agreement, a promise, a belonging.

"You're perfect," he whispered. "You feel like home."

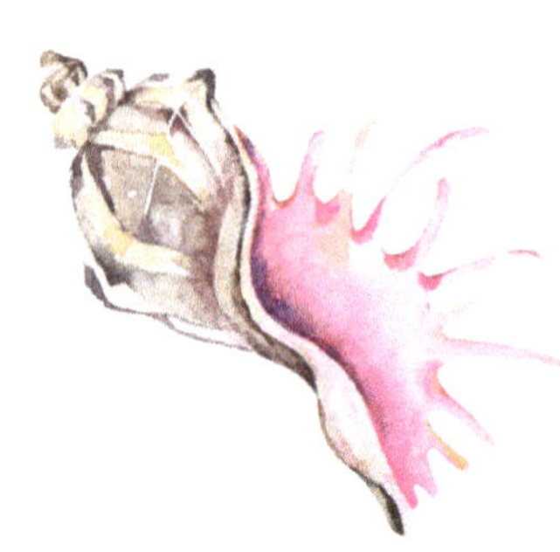

I couldn't answer. Not with words. Instead, I cupped his face and drew him down to me, our lips meeting in a kiss that held more than desire. It was a confession, a letting go, a claiming. I poured everything I felt into it—want, trust, awe—hoping it would reach the pieces of him I couldn't touch any other way.

When he began to move, he moved slowly at first, his hips rolling in a rhythm that reminded me of the tide. Every stroke was measured, intimate. His hands braced beside my shoulders, grounding me while his body eased into mine. I moaned softly, overwhelmed by the sensation of being filled and surrounded, the friction sparking heat low and deep.

He paused, resting his forehead against mine, anchoring us both. My hands roamed across his back, feeling the tension in every line of him, the effort he made to keep his pace controlled, intentional.

I wanted to tell him what it meant—that it wasn't just the pleasure, but the closeness, the way he made me feel more like myself. More whole. But the words were buried beneath the pulse of sensation and the rise of breath between us.

His hips moved again, slow and deep, and I met him willingly, offering everything.

Our bodies learned each other in that rhythm. The fire beside us crackled gently, waves lapping in the distance, as if the entire world had quieted to let us exist in this single, sacred moment.

We clung to each other, and with every movement, I felt us both unraveling—together, slowly, beautifully.

"I love you," I whispered, the words falling from my lips on a trembling breath.

He stilled, just for a moment, and looked into me. "And I love you."

Then he kissed me, and I surrendered to him, giving him everything I could until he chased me over the edge again.

Afterward, we lay tangled together in the fading warmth of the fire, breath mingling, limbs entwined. He stayed inside me, unmoving, as though neither of us could bear to break the connection just yet. I stroked his back slowly, memorizing the curve of every muscle.

"Are you alright?" he asked, his lips pressing gently against my temple.

I nodded, eyes closed, utterly spent. "I've never felt safer."

Outside, the sea murmured to the shore, soft and steady. Inside, the silence stretched comfortably around us, wrapping us in something deeper than words.

He shifted finally, easing us gently apart, and lay beside me, one arm wrapping around my waist to draw me close. My head rested against his chest, listening to the slow, grounding beat of his heart.

We didn't speak. We didn't need to.

In the quiet, we simply held each other. And for the first time in my life, I knew what it meant to belong.

Chapter Eighteen

BLOOD IN THE TIDE

Images flickered across my mind—fast, unstable, shifting like reflections on water before a storm.

Miris sat before a fire, the flames painting her sharp, regal features in flickering orange. Shadows clung to her like a second skin. Her fingers tore through a stack of parchment, flipping page after page with quick, agitated snaps. With a hiss of frustration, she tossed the documents into the flames. They curled, blackened, and vanished into smoke.

The acrid scent of burning parchment filled the air, thick and clinging. It coated my throat, made my eyes sting.

Flash.

Ocevia crouched inside a narrow undersea cavern, pressed into the jagged crevice of a rock wall. Her arms clutched her chest, eyes wide, scanning the abyss beyond. The water around her shifted, dense and heavy, cloaking the unknown in a silence that felt far too deep.

Flash.

The vision shattered—splintered into pieces too sharp to hold. Images blurred together in a rush of motion and noise. Faces, places, voices. None I could focus on. All I could do was feel them pressing in, drowning me in chaos, a hundred moments collapsing into one.

I tried to hold on. Tried to make sense of it.

But the dream slipped further out of reach.

Then, everything stilled.

I stood on the beach where everything had gone wrong.

The air held that familiar weight, thick with salt and memory. The sky arched pale and cloudless overhead, but the sea churned at the edges, waiting.

And there she was.

Daneliya danced barefoot across the wet sand, her laughter rising like birdsong, delicate and free. The tide kissed her ankles, retreating with each step she took.

My chest ached at the sight of her.

She spun, arms lifted, carefree. Then her smile faltered. Just slightly. Enough.

And she began to fade.

"No," I whispered, stepping forward. Reaching.

I knew what came next.

The current would take her. The waves would rise. Arms of water would wrap around her, greedy and cold. She would thrash. She would cry out. And I—

I would stand there. Watching. Powerless.

Her small body would vanish beneath the surface. Her lips would turn blue. Her eyes would go still.

The sea would take everything.

I lunged to move, but my legs locked in place, trapped by something invisible and unyielding. I strained, screamed, sobbed, but nothing worked.

I watched her go.

The moment fractured me... again. Grief cracked through my ribs like lightning.

The world collapsed inward, curling in on itself until only darkness remained.

Only silence.

Only loss.

"Wait."

The sound of stone hitting stone jolted me awake.

I gasped, lurching upright, heart slamming against my ribs. My cheeks were wet, the remnants of whatever dream I'd escaped still clinging to my skin like mist. Each breath came shallow, *jagged*. Grief pressed tight against my lungs, sharp and physical.

Elios hadn't stirred. His arm remained draped across my waist, warm and unmoving. His breathing was steady, untroubled by the noise that had pulled me from sleep.

Had I imagined it?

I froze, every muscle tightening. The silence around us felt too complete—heavy, unnatural. I strained to listen, eyes wide in the darkness, dread curling low in my gut.

There it was again.

A dull thud. Followed by the unmistakable scrape of rock against rock.

The hairs on the back of my neck lifted. That wasn't part of any dream.

Then came another crash, louder this time. *Closer.*

I clutched Elios' arm and shook him hard. "Elios," I hissed.

He stirred with a soft, sleepy groan, rubbing his eyes. The moment his gaze met mine, his expression sharpened. He read the tension in my body without a word.

A groan followed from the front chamber—low, *human.*

Elios was on his feet instantly, sword in hand, already moving toward the entrance. I scrambled after him, snatching up his dagger, my pulse racing.

The thin screen that separated our sleeping space from the front chamber fluttered faintly. Whether it was stirred by wind or something else, I couldn't tell. Shadows twisted in the dim firelight, stretching long across the uneven stone.

Elios halted at the divider, lifting a finger to his lips in silent warning. Narrowing his eyes, he leaned forward to peer around the corner, every muscle held in quiet tension.

I knew he was silently telling me to stay back, but I couldn't, drawn by the pull of dread and the need to see for myself.

The front chamber was dark, lit only by a sliver of moonlight seeping through the barricade. Just enough to see the figure lying crumpled on the stone floor.

Blood glistened beneath the body.

Another groan rose from the figure, weak and broken.

"Azure?"

The voice barely carried, slurred with pain, but unmistakable.

"Azure... are you still there?"

Something cracked open in my chest.

I dropped the dagger without thinking. Before I even registered the movement, I was on my knees beside her.

Ocevia.

Laying naked on the stone floor, my friend trembled, her body curled in tight like a wounded animal. Each breath came shallow and uneven, rasping through clenched teeth.

I hovered above her, hands outstretched but useless. I needed to help—*had* to help—but I was frozen, terrified to make it worse.

Where is she hurt? Where is the blood coming from?

My eyes dropped lower.

A deep gash split the skin across her thigh, the edges ragged and red. Blood poured from it in thick, steady pulses, warm and slick beneath my fingers when I reached to stem the flow. Bruises marred her arms and ribs, already darkening to a deep, sickened purple.

Her body jerked suddenly, spasming as she tried to rise, but the effort broke her. With a strained grunt, she collapsed again, limbs folding inward, her strength gone.

"Stay still," I whispered, the words catching in my throat.

A strangled sound escaped her, barely more than a breath.

Silence pressed in.

Her body slackened against the stone, breaths shallow, uneven. Each one thinner than the last, faltering like a flame caught in the wind.

Panic rose like a tide inside me, and that's when I realized we had to stop the bleeding.

"Elios," I said, turning to look over my shoulder. "Come help her. Let's get her back to the fire."

He hesitated, but only for a moment. His hand tightened on the hilt of his sword, his eyes scanning the shadows behind her. We had been hunted that morning. The instinct to be cautious was still fresh.

But this was Ocevia.

Whatever had happened, it wasn't a trick.

With a sharp breath, he crossed the chamber and knelt beside her. When he lifted her into his arms, blood smeared across his chest where her skin met his. She let out a soft sound—half whimper, half breath—but didn't resist. Her limbs hung limp.

We moved quickly, stepping over the scattered coals and toward the fire. Elios laid her down carefully. I grabbed one of the blankets and tucked it around her while he crouched beside her, checking her pulse, her breathing.

The fire crackled beside us, steady and quiet.

But something in her stillness made my chest tighten.

She was here. She was alive.

But whatever had found her out there in the dark... it had nearly finished the job.

CHAPTER NINETEEN

SURVIVING THE NIGHT

Minutes dragged by, thick with silence. I rinsed my bloodstained hands in the pool, the water swirling red before clearing once more. The metallic scent clung to my skin, to the air, as I added more wood to the fire, stoking the flames until they burned brighter, chasing away the damp chill of the cave.

Trading places with Elios, I pressed down on the wound, keeping the pressure steady as he lifted her unconscious form and moved her closer to the fire's warmth. The fire was our only source of light so deep in the cave, and it wasn't enough.

I wanted to shake her awake, to demand answers—*who did this to you?*—but she was too weak, too lost to the pain to respond. Clenching my jaw, I forced myself to be patient.

She would tell me when she could. If she survived the night.

Thankfully, after a few more agonizing minutes, the wound finally clotted. A human would not have survived such a fatal blow to an artery, but mermaids healed faster. I watched the sluggish rise and fall of her chest, willing her to breathe stronger, *deeper*. She would be weak for a while, but at least she was no longer at risk of bleeding out.

With her as stable as she could be, Elios and I retreated to the pool to wash off the blood. My hands were still shaking, and my mind was still spinning, but my friend was alive. We all were, at least for the moment.

The warm water lapped around me as I sank deeper, letting the gentle heat soothe the tension coiled in my muscles. I pressed my cheek against Elios' chest, listening to the steady rhythm of his heartbeat. It grounded me, calmed the whirlwind of thoughts fighting for dominance in my mind.

His arms tightened around my waist, holding me close. "Do you trust her?" His voice was quiet, the worry clear in his tone.

"With my life," I murmured without hesitation. "She's my best friend."

Exhaling softly, he leaned back against the rocky side of the pool, pulling me with him.

"Was she able to tell you what happened?" he asked after a moment. "I mean, before I picked her up?"

I shook my head, frowning. "No. She mostly just said my name." The memory of her broken, desperate voice sent a shiver down my spine. A terrible thought struck me, and I pulled away from Elios' embrace, whipping around to face him. My breath caught. "You don't think Oona or Lucia attacked her, do you? Or that creature?" My stomach clenched. "Oh gods, Oona couldn't have survived that. *Right*?"

Elios caught my wrist, tugging me back against him, his hand moving in slow, soothing strokes down my back. "I don't think there's any way Oona survived that creature," he said. "As for Lucia... I don't know."

His hand paused for a fraction of a second before continuing. "But if she was injured then, why did it take her so long to find us? I mean, I guess the wound could've slowed her down, but it's been more than half a day since Oona was attacked. The timing is strange."

He was right.

I swallowed hard, considering it.

It had been hours since the other mermaids vanished beneath the waves. If Ocevia had been injured then, she would have surfaced much sooner, or not at all. So *where had she been? What had kept her away for so long?*

Mermaids weren't invincible, but it was too much of a coincidence for her to be wounded now, right after the attack on our island.

I chewed my lip, heart hammering as unease settled deep in my bones. *We will have answers soon,* I told myself. *As soon as she wakes up.*

I could only hope—*pray*—that neither Oona nor Lucia had survived the Kraken's attack.

Because if they had...

They would come back.

And they would not fail a second time.

Sleep did not come easily.

Even wrapped in Elios' arms, his warmth a balm against the chill in my soul, my thoughts refused to quiet. My stomach twisted, anxiety creeping through my veins like a slow-moving poison.

If Miris' people survived the Kraken, they would regroup. They would return. And next time, they wouldn't let us escape.

I squeezed my eyes shut, trying to force the fear away, but it coiled tighter.

Eventually, I gave up on sleep entirely.

Slipping from Elios' grasp, I moved silently across the cave, my eyes adjusting to the dim glow of the fire. I lowered myself beside Ocevia, watching the steady rise and fall of her chest. Her face was slack with exhaustion, her breaths too shallow for my liking.

What happened to you?

I wished she could answer me.

I wished she would open her eyes and tell me I had nothing to worry about.

But she remained unconscious, making my mind spiral with worst-case scenarios.

My gaze flickered to the cave's entrance. We couldn't stay here. Not for much longer. The moment Ocevia was strong enough to travel, we had to leave. We weren't safe here. Not anymore.

We never were.

With Ocevia and Elios depending on me, I would not wait for Miris to send more of her hunters. I would not sit idly by and allow another attack to come. We had to disappear.

Even if it meant risking the human lands.

The idea sent a wave of unease through me. My kind was forbidden from setting foot in their world. If we were caught, there would be consequences, but that no longer mattered.

All I cared about was keeping Ocevia safe. Keeping Elios safe.

I stared into the flickering fire for hours, lost in the dance of the flames, the shifting embers mesmerizing enough to pull me into a fitful, dreamless slumber.

Each time I woke, my heart pounded, expecting to see Lucia's sneering face hovering over me, waiting for the kill. But every time I opened my eyes, the dim interior of the cave was the only thing that greeted me.

Still, the unease never left me.

The silence stretched, broken only by the distant crash of the tide beyond the cave walls. But then, at some point during the long night, a soft groan broke the silence.

I jolted upright, pulse spiking as I turned to Ocevia's form.

She shifted slightly, rolling onto her back, the movement triggering another pained noise, but she didn't wake. A jolt of fear surged through me, tightening my chest. I scrambled to her side, reaching for the water we had set aside, but her eyes remained closed, her body limp with exhaustion.

Not *yet*.

I exhaled hard and set the water back on the ground. The fire had burned low, its embers casting a soft, uneven glow across Ocevia's face. She looked too still. Too quiet.

She would wake up soon. She had to.

For now, all I could do was wait.

I pressed my hands flat against my thighs, willing them to stop shaking. Every muscle in my body ached, but still I turned toward the cave's entrance, listening. Every shift of stone, every rustle of wind in the branches made me flinch.

Elios had reinforced the barricade after Ocevia stabilized, layering more stones and branches to better conceal the entrance. It was more secure now, but security didn't mean safety. We'd already been found twice in one day. If someone else came looking, we might not survive again.

The thought left my skin crawling. I wanted to run, to disappear into the trees or the sea, anywhere but here, but we couldn't leave. Not yet.

Not without her.

So, I curled near the fire, my body heavy, my thoughts louder than the wind outside. Hope wore thin. All I could do was wait... for her breath to steady, for morning to come, for anything that might feel like safety again.

I woke to the scent of boiling water and the quiet murmur of Elios tending to Ocevia's wound.

Blinking away the remnants of sleep, I pushed upright and found him crouched beside her, a strip of cloth in hand as he carefully cleaned the gash along her thigh. Above the fire, a leather pouch of hot water hung from a tripod, steam curling into the air in soft, ghostly ribbons.

My gaze dropped to Ocevia's leg.

The wound had begun to scab.

Relief broke over me like breath after a long dive. Healing had begun.

Elios glanced up as I stood and offered a small, tired smile. "Good morning."

I knelt beside him, leaning in for a better look. The scab was larger than I expected, covering the wound entirely. No signs of infection. No swelling. It was a good sign.

"How's she doing?" I asked, brushing hair from her forehead.

He leaned closer, his breath warm against my ear. "It looks good, but she still hasn't woken. It's healing faster than I expected."

"One of the few perks of being a mermaid," I murmured, trying to ease the knot tightening in my chest. "Fast healing."

He arched a brow at that, tucking the detail away without comment. Then he finished wrapping the wound and folded the blanket more securely around her sleeping form.

Once we were both sure she was stable, we stood and made our way toward the pool so he could wash the blood from his hands.

"What's the plan now?" he asked, dipping his hands into the water and cupping it to his face.

I watched as the droplets traced slow lines over the curves of his chest, following the contours of muscle and scar. My thoughts scattered. I swallowed hard.

By the time I lifted my gaze, his smirk told me I'd been caught.

Heat rushed to my face.

Folding my arms, I looked away, trying to recover some dignity. "Plan for what?"

His grin deepened, mischief lighting his eyes. "Plan for what we do next. It's not safe to stay here now that we've been found."

He wasn't wrong.

But we were cornered. I exhaled slowly, rubbing my temples as I tried to focus.

"We can't leave until Ocevia can shift and swim," I said. "I can't carry both of you. But you're right. I don't feel safe here anymore."

Elios turned toward the cave entrance, his expression sharpening. "We can make a raft," he said after a moment. "There's plenty of wood outside. We could use vines and strips of the sail to bind it. If we fashion paddles, neither of you would need to shift or swim."

I blinked at him, surprised by the clarity of the idea.

That could actually work.

If no one was watching the cave, we wouldn't leave a scent trail in the water. Normally, a mermaid's scent could be picked up and carried on the current if our pursuers were close enough to track it.

But if we never entered the sea...

The idea clicked into place, sharp and clean.

I nodded, explaining the tracking risk to Elios. He listened closely, his attention fixed on me.

"So, if we stay out of the ocean entirely," he said slowly, "we might actually be able to disappear."

"Yes," I said, my pulse quickening with something I hadn't felt in far too long—*hope*. "It's a risk, but it's a better one than waiting here to be hunted."

His head tilted slightly as he studied me. "Shall we go collect wood, then?"

I glanced over my shoulder at Ocevia, watching the rise and fall of her breath. She was still resting.

Turning back to Elios, I reached for his hand.

"Let's do it."

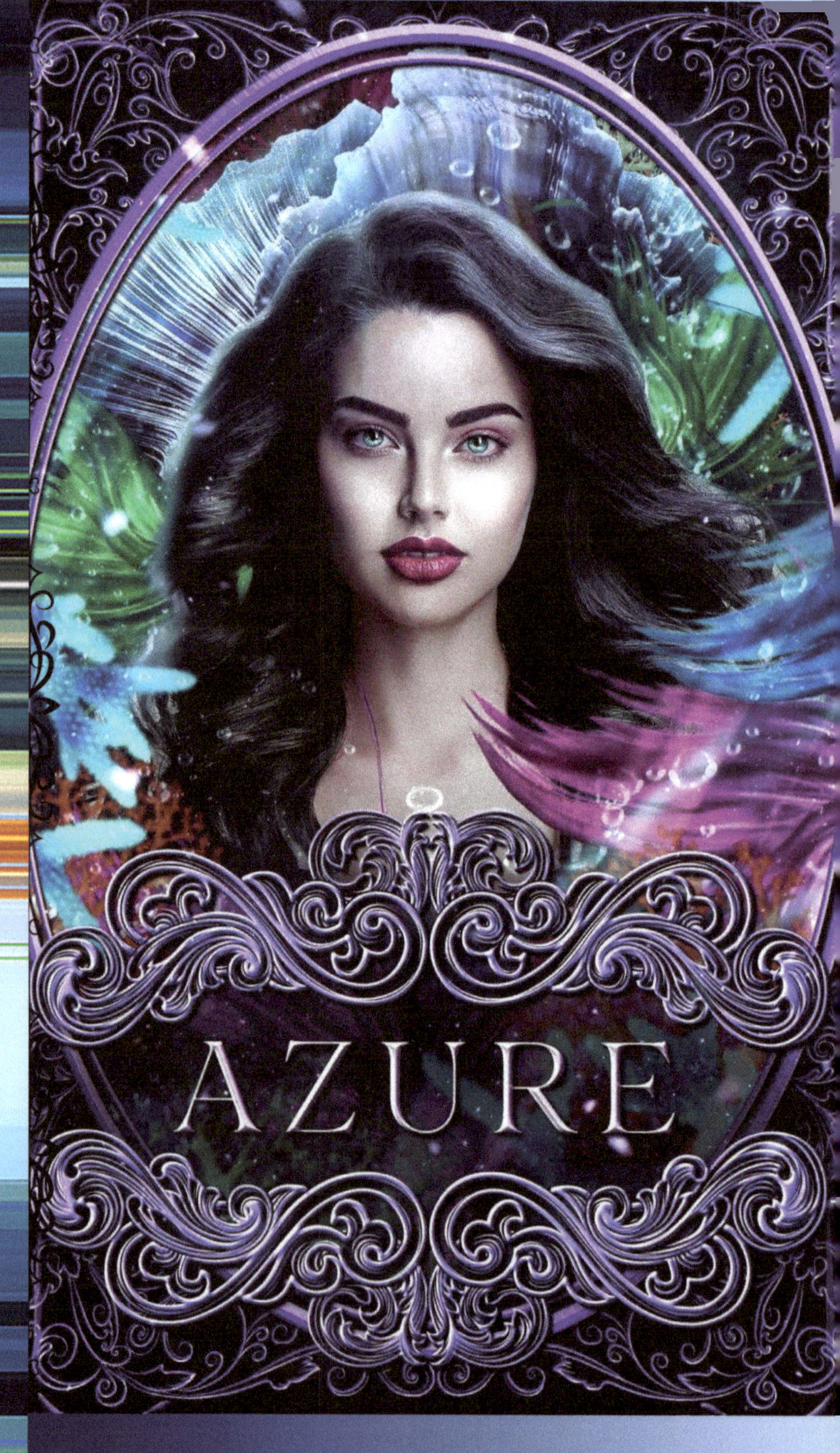
AZURE

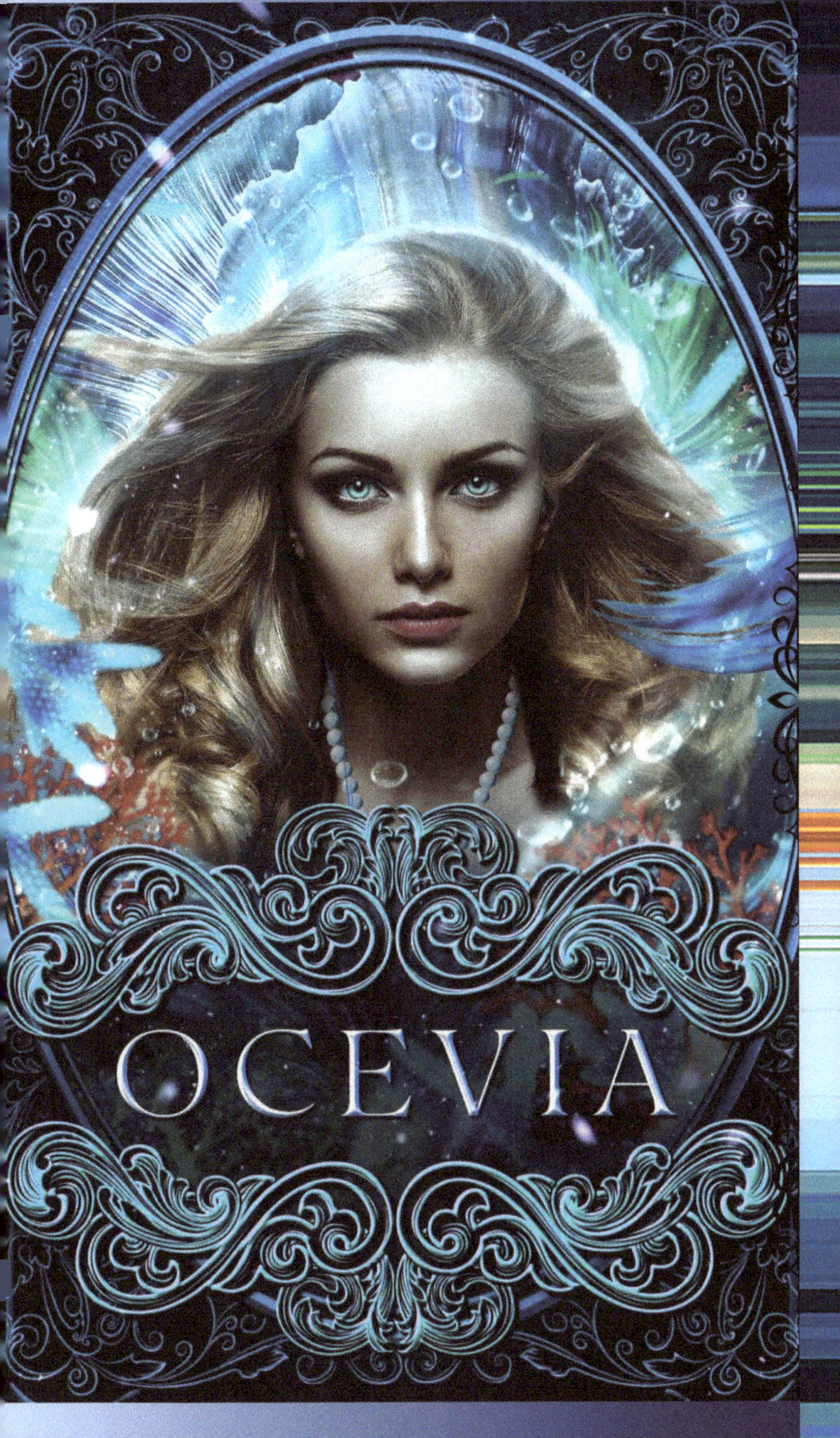

OCEVIA

A PERILOUS PLAN

My heart stuttered when we returned to the back chamber for a late lunch.

Ocevia's eyes were open.

Bloodshot, *dazed*, but open.

Relief and worry collided, crashing through me so hard I nearly lost my footing. I dropped to my knees beside her, the air stalling in my lungs like it didn't know whether to stay or flee.

"What happened?" Her voice was hoarse, raw with sleep as she tried to sit up. I lifted a cup of water to her lips and helped her drink, but she coughed on the first sip, wincing as it rushed down too fast.

"Easy," I said, steadying her with one hand. "You need to take it slow."

She nodded and tried again, this time managing without sputtering.

"I was going to ask you the same thing," I told her, still trying to reconcile the image of her pale, battered body with the person I knew. "You showed up with a deep gash in your leg, collapsed in the cave, and you've been unconscious ever since."

Her fingers brushed the bandage, and a soft wince escaped her lips. When she pressed too hard, I caught her wrist and pushed her hand away, gentle but firm. "How did you get that injury?"

She blinked slowly, rubbed at her face. Her movements were sluggish, her thoughts clearly struggling to reassemble themselves.

"I... don't remember much after seeing the Seawraiths," she murmured.

A cold shiver prickled down my spine. It was what I'd feared—what I hadn't wanted to hear.

I poured more water, slower this time, and offered it again, careful not to let her gulp.

"I overheard them talking about finding you, so I followed them," she said, her voice thin. She twisted the shell necklace at her throat, the familiar gesture a small comfort. Her gaze drifted to the stone wall, unfocused. "I was under the sea when something pulled Oona under. Then... something dragged me down too. I didn't see it. There was too much chaos. Someone's dagger got me in the leg."

My throat tightened, my grip on the cup steady only through force of will.

Wiping the water from her chin with my fingers, I tried to keep my voice calm, even as a hundred awful possibilities unfolded behind my eyes. "Did they survive the attack? From the creature?"

She gave a little shrug and reached again for the cup. After she drank, she leaned back, bracing herself on her elbows. The exhaustion in her face hadn't faded. If anything, it had sunk deeper.

Elios took the cup from me, refilling it without needing to be asked. Quiet, steady—always steady.

Ocevia's gaze slid toward him. Sharp again. Curious. *Measuring.* Her eyebrow arched, and I could already hear the comment forming.

"And who is he?"

I cast her a sideways look. "This is Elios. I pulled him off a rock outcropping after the shipwreck and brought him here."

She didn't say anything right away, just let her eyes trail over him from head to toe with that slow, surgical precision that could make grown warriors squirm.

Elios didn't even blink. Instead, he raised one brow in return, as unbothered as a man could be.

A sly smile curved across Ocevia's lips as she looked between us. She didn't need to say what she was thinking.

"I see," she murmured.

With a huff, I stood, folding my arms. I could lie to others. I could hide from myself. But never from her. Ocevia had always seen through my defenses like they were nothing but mist.

Instead of offering an explanation she wouldn't believe, I turned away and sifted through the pile of fruit, pretending to look for something useful. I handed Elios a mango. He took it without a word. I watched him a second too long, pretending it was about the fruit and not the way quiet moments like this felt more dangerous than any blade.

Once I had wrestled my expression into something blank and unbothered, I returned to Ocevia's side and crouched beside her. She looked pale, the shadows under her eyes deeper than usual, her body still stiff with pain. Quietly, I pressed a chunk of mango into her palm.

She didn't hesitate. Just accepted it and bit down, like her body remembered hunger even if her mind hadn't caught up yet. It wasn't a stuffed goose or roasted duck, but it was sweet and fresh and not dried fish. A small mercy, at least.

Hours ago, we'd found her bleeding and half-conscious at the cave's entrance, her body limp and covered in salt. Now she was awake, chewing slowly, alive. It shouldn't have felt like a miracle, but it did.

She needed this. Food. Rest. Something to root her to this world again, because whether she liked it or not, we needed her to stay.

"We don't have the luxury of time," I thought, the words beating in my head like a second pulse. If she couldn't walk soon, she wouldn't survive the next run.

"Elios and I made a raft this morning," I said, watching her closely as she chewed. "We can't stay here now that the others have found us. We need to leave as soon as you're strong enough."

"Good plan," she replied, her words soft and muffled around the fruit.

Mango juice slid down her chin, catching the firelight as it trailed toward her collarbone. She looked almost absurdly young for a moment—mouth sticky, cheeks full, like the girl she might've been in another life.

I bit the inside of my cheek to keep from smiling.

She swallowed and tilted her head at me, sharp and curious again. "Any idea where you're headed?"

I glanced toward Elios. He gave the smallest shrug, a gesture that somehow said both *I trust you* and *don't look at me.* I exhaled through my nose and faced her again.

"We were thinking we would all travel to Starspell and then inland," I said, not sure how much of the plan I believed in, but it was something.

Ocevia waved a hand, brushing off the details like they bored her. "I'll be fine."

But she moved too quickly, pushing herself upright with more will than strength.

Pain punched the breath out of her lungs, and a hiss escaped her lips as she dropped back down, one hand clamping around her thigh.

Frustration burned in her eyes, bright and raw. She hated this—being slowed, being fragile.

"On second thought... guess I'm stuck with you two for a while."

Elios chuckled, the sound low and honest and stupidly warm. I turned to glare at him, but it only made him grin wider.

He held up both sticky hands in mock surrender, fingers glinting with mango juice. "What?"

"Don't encourage her," I muttered, though we both knew he would.

Ocevia batted her lashes in a parody of sweetness, perfectly matching his tone with a look so over-the-top I almost snorted.

I groaned and tipped my head back toward the ceiling, dragging a hand over my face.

Traveling with these two? I was never going to get a moment's peace.

The sun dipped lower, casting the jungle in molten gold. Light threaded through the canopy in ribbons, flickering across our skin like half-formed spells. The shadows had started to stretch long and thin across the forest floor, a silent warning of what came next.

We moved quickly, gathering what we could before the dark claimed us.

No one said it aloud, but neither of us wanted to be out here when the light died.

Mermaids hunted at night. Their numbers multiplied in the dark, drawn to moonlight like blood in water. We had seen it for ourselves. Oona and Lucia didn't care if the sun still hung in the sky. The old rules meant nothing anymore.

Every step felt like it might be our last.

The underbrush was dense and bristling with thorns. Each footfall cracked twigs or stirred leaves, every sound sharp as a blade. I flinched at the smallest rustle, my pulse ticking fast and nervous behind my ribs. We kept to the trees, staying away from the shore. Whatever cover the jungle could give us, we'd take it.

I kept looking behind us, unable to help myself.

I didn't expect safety. I only hoped to avoid surprise.

Staying out of the water might help us go unnoticed, but if it came to a fight, we were outmatched. Aside from Elios' dagger and sword, our blades were chipped stone and scavenged wood. No armor. No magic. No allies.

Only each other.

And still—it didn't feel like enough.

"I was thinking," Elios said quietly beside me, dropping a handful of small berries into my satchel. His voice was calm, but there was a careful weight behind it. "If we can make it to the kingdom of Avrearyn, we could travel inland—by horseback, or on foot if we must—to Ceveasea. There's someone there I trust. Someone who owes me."

I paused, a piece of fruit half-forgotten in my hand.

Inland.

Farther from Miris' reach, but farther from the ocean, too.

My chest constricted, a sudden squeeze that made it hard to draw a full breath.

"How far would the trek overland be?" I asked, pushing the words out past the tightness in my throat.

Elios lifted his head, eyes scanning the horizon like he could map the route from here. "We can dock in the port city of Starspell. From there, the mountain pass should take less than a week."

He looked at me then—really looked—and something in his expression shifted, softening as if he could already feel the storm rising inside me.

"You're worried about being too far from the sea," he said.

I gave a faint nod, then shrugged, as if pretending not to care might make it true.

"I've never told you this before," I murmured, voice rough with something I didn't want to name. "But mermaids have to submerge in water every twenty-four hours. If we don't…" I hesitated, swallowing the knot in my throat. "Miris told us we'll rot from the waist down."

His entire posture changed.

The wood in his arms slipped from his grip and hit the ground with a hollow thud.

In two steps, he closed the distance between us. His arms wrapped around my waist, anchoring me with a gentleness I didn't expect. His hold was strong. Steady.

"I won't let that happen," he said, voice low and certain, like a vow spoken to gods he didn't believe in. "There are creeks, rivers, hot springs... we'll find something. And if we don't, I'll pour water over you myself, drop by drop if I have to."

My breath caught, not from fear, but from the unbearable tenderness of it.

How did he always know how to break through the fear like that? To find the seams and stitch me back together before I even realized I'd come undone?

Without giving myself time to question it, I leaned up and kissed him.

It was grounding. *Real.* His warmth seeped into my skin, his breath mixing with mine in that hush between heartbeats. I pressed closer, steadying myself with the shape of him, the solid, unyielding quiet that lived in his bones.

The last twelve hours had been a storm.

But this—*this moment*—was the eye.

The ache low in my body, a leftover ember from the night before, sparked anew as his grip tightened around my waist. He didn't press forward. He never did. But the look in his eyes... *gods,* the way he looked at me...

"How do you make something like that sound so sexy?" I whispered against his mouth.

Elios smirked, then brushed his lips over mine again—slow, coaxing, addictive. His tongue slid against mine in a rhythm that made me dizzy. Dazed. Drunk on nothing but him.

When he finally pulled back, it wasn't abrupt. It was a soft press of lips that felt less like an end and more like a promise.

He stooped to gather the wood again, his eyes never leaving mine.

"We should head back. It'll be dark soon."

I exhaled slowly, realizing only then how tightly I'd been holding everything in. The fear. The longing. *The need.*

The thought of the cave's cool stone walls and the suffocating close-ness of that space tightened something in my chest. I didn't want to return—not yet. Not after standing here in the golden peace beneath the canopy, with sun on my skin and space to breathe.

But we couldn't stay.

The cave was imperfect. Cramped. Fragile. But it was shelter, and we had nothing else.

Still, my feet didn't move.

I stood there for one last moment, staring into the trees as the breeze carried the scent of salt and soil. It smelled like memory. Like the edge of a life I used to have.

The stillness wouldn't last. It never did.

I felt the shift coming—the invisible pull of the tide, and in that quiet before the dark, I made the choice.

We would leave before dawn.

We'd take the raft to Starspell, then head inland. We'd walk the mountain pass. Watch the tides. Guard our sleep. Count the hours. Count our breaths. Never stop looking over our shoulders.

If we were careful, if the sea didn't swallow us, if fate was feeling merc iful...

Maybe, just maybe, we would find a place where we didn't have to flinch at every shadow.

A place we could finally call safe.

A place we could call home.

Chapter Twenty-One

A Journey into the Unknown

The air in the cave that night was heavy with silence, as if the walls themselves were holding their breath. It wrapped around me like seawater, pressing against my chest, settling into my bones. I lay awake beneath the jagged ceiling, unmoving, watching the shadows dance across stone as the fire dwindled to coals. Each flicker cast uneasy shapes into the corners—elongated, uncertain, too much like the thoughts circling inside me.

Sleep tugged at the edges of my awareness but never quite took hold. My mind churned restlessly, too full of what-ifs, too wary of what waited beyond dawn. The cave had become a fragile refuge, but we were about to leave it behind, stepping into water where the rules shifted and nothing could be trusted. The sea belonged to Miris, and her reach was long.

And if she wanted to find us, she would.

No matter how far we rowed or how well we hid.

Ocevia's breath was uneven in the dark. She hadn't stirred in hours, but I could still hear the faint rasp of discomfort in her lungs, the soft tension threaded through each exhale. Her wound had scabbed over, but her body hadn't yet forgiven the trauma. And Elios—he slept deeper than either of us, but even sleep didn't disguise what he was.

Human. Mortal. *Breakable.*

He didn't carry the curse that slowed death, the magic that stitched wounds closed or numbed agony to a dull roar. One blade in the wrong place could end him. And I couldn't stop it.

That thought stayed with me, sharp and unyielding.

We had no allies. No guarantees. Only a raft built from salvaged wood, a plan carved out of desperation, and the brittle hope that we might reach land before the sea took us.

I must have drifted for a moment—some shallow, restless version of sleep—but it didn't soothe me. When I opened my eyes again, the fire had burned low, and the pale blush of dawn had begun to bleed across the cave floor.

It was time.

I moved quietly, limbs stiff from tension, packing the last of our supplies. The woven cord I'd salvaged held the fabric sail in place, though it sagged slightly at the edges. It wasn't beautiful. It wasn't strong. But it might carry us forward a little faster than paddling alone, and that was enough.

Every choice now had to serve one purpose: survival.

I crossed the cave in silence and knelt beside them, my voice low as I woke them. "Elios. Ocevia."

They stirred slowly, caught in that groggy space between rest and reality. Neither of them had spent the night staring at stone and imagining how quickly things could go wrong. I didn't resent them for that. If anything, I envied them.

By the time they sat up fully, rubbing sleep from their eyes and adjusting their packs, I had already prepared everything we could carry. Our food. Our water. A few weapons. The sail. The raft.

It wasn't much.

But it was everything we had.

The morning air was still and thick, clinging to the walls of the cave like breath held too long. Light seeped in from the narrow opening above, faint and gray, not yet strong enough to chase the chill from the stones.

"How are you feeling, Ocevia? Are you in any pain?" I asked, folding the last of our leather blankets and glancing toward her where she sat near the fire.

She didn't look up as she wrestled with the salvaged shoes, her movements careful and stiff. "Like I was thrown off a cliff and then eaten by a shark," she muttered, tightening a strap with unnecessary force.

Despite everything, a small smile pulled at the corners of my mouth. The sarcasm was a good sign, if not a comforting one. Her color was still off. The sharpness in her eyes dulled. And though she moved with that familiar stubbornness, her body lagged behind her will.

"We'll need proper shoes before we hike into the mountains," she added, her tone clipped as she adjusted the bandage beneath the leather.

Behind us, Elios moved through the chamber with quiet purpose. He passed close, and without a word, pressed a kiss to the side of my head before shouldering his pack. The gesture warmed something in me, even as the weight of everything we were about to do pressed harder against my chest.

"I have credits in Avrearyn and Ceveasea," he said, taking a few more steps toward the exit. "You can get whatever you want."

At that, Ocevia's head snapped up. Her eyes lit with mischief, a grin already forming.

I didn't even look at her. "No," I said flatly. "We are not going on a shopping spree with Elios' coins."

She snorted in response, unbothered and entirely too pleased with herself. The sound cut through the tension like a blade through kelp, but I didn't lean into it. Not now. I followed Elios into the next chamber instead, letting motion take over where words failed.

Playfulness was a kind of armor, but even armor cracked under fear.

"I think this is the last of it," I murmured, adjusting the straps of my pack and reaching for one of the lashing ropes. "I'll help you bring the raft to the beach."

Elios nodded, tugging at his pack until the straps lay flat against his shoulders. "Let's wait until we're ready to bring Ocevia down. I don't want to risk it floating off without us. But we can move it closer."

We bent together, lifting the bulk of the raft between us. The bindings creaked as the structure shifted, rope groaning against wood. It wasn't graceful, but it held.

I had already cleared the brush and debris in the night, unable to sleep and too restless to do nothing. The work made our exit swift and clean. No noise. No delay.

The raft waited at the edge of the water—two uneven halves lashed together and praying to float. Elios checked the knots again while I inspected the makeshift sail, running my hands along the seams, testing the tension. The sea would test it harder than I ever could.

And still, for a long moment, I stood there, my hand resting on the wooden edge as I looked back.

The cave had given us more than shelter. It had cradled our exhaustion. Held our secrets. Let us laugh, even love, for a little while without the sea dragging us under, but that chapter had closed. Comfort was dangerous now, so we couldn't stay. Not with Miris' reach creeping ever closer.

I exhaled, slow and quiet, then turned back to the task.

Getting Ocevia to the raft was the hardest part. She insisted on walking, naturally, her pride louder than her pain, but every step was a betrayal. Her leg trembled beneath her weight. Her jaw was set too tight.

Before she could argue further, Elios stepped forward and swept her off her feet.

She shrieked in protest, half outrage, half disbelief. Her fists thudded against his back, though there was no real force behind them. "I can walk, you brute!"

"You're limping like a drowning cat," he replied evenly, utterly unfazed.

I bit the inside of my cheek, smothering a laugh as she scowled, pouting all the way to the shore.

The raft rocked slightly as we loaded our supplies, every creak a reminder that it wasn't built for this. But it would have to do. With a final push, we left the sand behind and drifted into open water.

I didn't feel lighter. Not yet.

But the horizon stretched wide before us—unclaimed, uncertain, and terrifying in its promise.

And it was forward.

And that, at least, was something.

The raft drifted out into the open water with a groan of wood and tension, every shift of weight a test of its fragile construction. The sky above was streaked with pale blue and soft gold, the horizon stretching endlessly before us—wild, quiet, and terrifying in its promise.

The cave, with its fire-warmed stone and close safety, was already fading behind us, shrinking into the morning mist like something imagined.

We pushed forward anyway.

The weight in my chest didn't lessen with distance. If anything, it grew heavier with each slow pull of the paddle. The sea stretched in every direction—broad and unmoving, deceptively calm. Its stillness was a trap. It watched in silence, as it always did, biding its time.

Ocevia sat against the raft's edge, cloth pulled over her face to shield her from the growing heat. She was quiet now, conserving her strength, but I could tell the movement of the waves still jarred her wound. Her jaw was clenched, her hands tucked beneath her knees. I was grateful when she dozed off.

The morning passed uneventfully, though nothing about it felt easy. The further we floated, the harsher the sun bore down, seeping into my skin and turning each breath thick with salt and sweat. I cursed myself for not fashioning a canopy with the extra cloth. I'd been so focused on water, weapons, and food, that shade had seemed like a luxury we couldn't afford.

Now, the luxury I craved was the ability to breathe without heat sinking into my spine.

The wind, once a faint gift, gave up entirely by midday. The sail sagged, motionless. The sea became a sheet of glass beneath us, too still. Too silent. The kind of quiet that hummed beneath your skin and made you feel watched.

We didn't speak. Didn't dare.

We paddled instead, trading shifts in silence, each stroke a slow repetition of ache and discipline. The raft creaked beneath us, the sound loud in the absence of wind. Every movement, every breath, felt like a ripple we couldn't afford.

We were too exposed. No rocks to hide behind. No currents to carry us. Only the slow, grinding effort of survival.

Ocevia, mercifully, slept.

The rise and fall of her breathing beneath the cloth offered a strange comfort—proof that for now, she was healing. That we hadn't dragged her across the sea for nothing.

The hours blurred, marked only by the pulse of sun and the growing burn in my shoulders.

Then, just as I began to question whether I could keep going, the sail stirred.

A tremor of air kissed the cloth, barely more than a breath. Then another—*stronger*. The fabric lifted like it remembered how to fly, and in the next moment, it snapped fully open, catching the wind with a sound like hope.

Relief flooded me so suddenly it made my hands tremble.

I let the paddle rest in my lap and rolled my shoulders, shaking out the ache, though the tension wouldn't fully leave me. My gaze slid

toward Ocevia, still resting. Then to Elios, his back strong and sure as he watched the horizon.

"We should wet our tails before the sun sets," I said quietly.

"How long will it take us to reach land?" Ocevia's voice was groggy as she pushed the cloth aside, blinking against the brightness. Her movements were slow, but she slipped into the water with ease, her legs melting back into their true form beneath the surface.

Elios set his paddle down and leaned forward, squinting into the distance. "If this wind holds, we might reach the coast by tomorrow."

Tomorrow.

My fingers tightened around the edge of the raft, knuckles gone white.

Tomorrow felt like a promise the sea wasn't ready to make.

We had no cover. No weapons that could match the magic Miris had at her command. If she sent someone after us now, out here, with no place to run...

We wouldn't stand a chance.

Still, I forced myself to focus on what we *could* control.

"Have you ever been to Starspell?" I asked, eyes scanning the horizon, hoping to see land where there was only water.

Elios bit into a strip of dried fish before answering. "I've been to every kingdom surrounding the Lamalis Sea, some beyond. I haven't visited Starspell in about five months, but I have contacts and resources there."

That word, *resources*, settled like a balm against the rawness in my chest. It wasn't a solution, not yet, but it was a thread. And threads could be followed.

Could be built into something more.

I looked at him. Really looked. Salt crusted his jaw. His lips were dry. His eyes squinted slightly against the glare of the sea, but even now, something about him remained unshaken. He looked like someone who kept promises.

"I'll take you to a tavern near the docks," he added. "We'll rent a few rooms for the night before heading inland."

The idea of a bed—of four walls, food, warmth—tugged at something buried deep in me. I hadn't realized how much I longed for those things until he said them aloud.

I nodded slowly, letting myself feel it for just a breath.

It wasn't forever.

But it was a place to begin.

Chapter Twenty-Two

The Tempest Between Worlds

The sea was too quiet.

Darkness had fallen reluctantly, as though the sun itself had been hesitant to leave us. Now, only a scattering of stars blinked overhead, veiled behind gauzy, drifting clouds. They moved without conviction, like thoughts lost in the fog of exhaustion. The raft rocked gently, its creaks dulled by the stillness around us. Even the sail hung limp in the dead air, a tired banner surrendered to a sky that no longer cared. The repurposed ropes, once straining with tension, sagged silently, too waterlogged to moan against their knots.

We drifted through silence so profound it seemed unnatural, a void that swallowed even the faintest noise. This wasn't the sea I knew.

This was something else.

Something that felt like waiting.

I sat curled against the edge of the raft, arms wrapped around my knees, listening—for wind, for the distant cry of a gull, for anything that might remind me the world was still moving. But no sound came. The ocean stretched around us, black as ink, its surface disturbingly smooth, like obsidian glass. Not a ripple stirred. Not a breeze touched our skin.

It felt like we'd drifted into the space between heartbeats, where nothing dared to move for fear of what might wake.

Ocevia lay bundled at the rear of the raft, her injured leg folded beneath her. Even in sleep, her features were strained, lips parted in uneasy breaths, brow drawn tight with whatever pain or memory lingered just beneath the surface. Her skin glowed faintly in the moonlight, pale and ethereal, like a candle's last gleam before it gutters.

Behind me, Elios checked the sail again. His movements were slow, methodical. I could hear the whisper of rope in his hands, the quiet strain of fabric adjusting. He didn't speak. Didn't complain. Just moved with the kind of steady, silent presence I'd come to rely on.

I didn't look back.

My eyes stayed fixed on the horizon, on the perfect line where the ocean swallowed the stars. I was waiting... for something to stir. Something to break the stillness. My skin prickled with the feeling that we were not alone. That the sea was watching us.

Waiting, too.

Elios crouched beside me without a word. The warmth of him at my side eased something tight in my chest. When his hand brushed lightly against my leg, it was instinct, not comfort, but I welcomed it just the same.

"Still nothing?" he asked.

I shook my head, my voice low. "It's not right. The sea isn't supposed to be this still."

His gaze followed mine out toward the horizon. "Storm coming, maybe."

"Maybe."

I didn't lean into him. I didn't answer again. But I stayed close.

The hours dragged in a stillness too thick to name. The air hung heavy, swollen with an invisible pressure, as if the sky itself was bracing for a scream that hadn't come yet. Every breath felt like it carried weight. The quiet stretched so far, so deep, it felt like it came from beneath the water, like the sea had pulled everything down into its depths and left us here alone in the silence.

I had never feared the ocean. Not even when it cursed me. But tonight, the water felt sentient—*aware*, listening, waiting for the moment to strike.

When Elios slipped his arm around my shoulders, I didn't flinch. I leaned into the solid comfort of him, closed my eyes, and listened, not to the water, but to the silence that said the water was listening back.

Then came the breath.

A whisper of air across the water, so faint it could've been imagined. Then another, sharper. The heat broke like a fever. The sail rustled. Then snapped. Once. Then again.

I sat bolt upright.

The wind came all at once, sharp and slicing, cutting through the stagnant air like a blade. Elios was already moving, already at the mast, tightening ropes, hands moving fast and certain. "Hold on," he called. His voice was calm, but I could hear the urgency beneath it. "The wind's coming in hard."

I didn't hesitate. I scrambled toward Ocevia, shaking her shoulder. "Wake up. Something's wrong."

She groaned, slow and thick with sleep, but her eyes snapped open at the sight of the rippling water. The sea, once flat and still, had begun to churn. A low growl rolled across the surface—thunder, distant at first, then closing in fast.

Above us, the clouds coalesced into a single, dark mass, swallowing the stars whole. Lightning split the sky, illuminating the ocean in stark flashes of bone-white. And in one of those flashes, I saw it.

A wave. Rising in the distance. Tall. *Too tall.*

My blood turned to ice.

"Grab the rope!" Elios shouted. The raft jolted as the first swell struck. Water crashed over the bow, soaking us in a breath. My hands found the rope and clung tight, the fibers slick and trembling in my grip.

Then the second wave came. Harsher. Meaner. It tore across the raft, snatching one of our supply bundles and dragging it into the dark. It disappeared without a sound.

Ocevia screamed. The raft pitched violently. Elios caught her, pulling her against him with one arm while bracing the mast with the other.

Then the rain came.

Not a drizzle. Not a storm.

A wall of water fell from the sky in one massive sheet, so cold it shocked my breath from my lungs. The sea rose up to meet it, both elements conspiring to drown us. I couldn't see *anything*. Not the sail. Not the stars. Only the blur of rain and shadow, only the lightning and the roar.

"Azure—hold on!" Elios shouted again. His voice came from somewhere to my left, barely audible above the wind.

The raft tipped hard. I nearly lost my grip.

"I can't—I can't keep it straight—" His voice vanished into thunder.

Ahead of us, a monstrous wave loomed. A wall of water, taller than the mast. My scream tore through the storm.

"Brace!"

We hit it.

The raft launched into the air, lifted by the force of the swell, then crashed down into the trough with a violence that stole the breath from my lungs. The world went white. My vision blurred. My ears rang with the scream of the wind.

Somewhere in the chaos, I heard Elios, closer now, desperate.

"Don't let go. No matter what happens—don't let go."

So I didn't.

Even when my arms shook. Even when the sea howled like a wounded god. Even when it felt like the storm would never end.

I held on.

When the storm passed, it left a silence behind, not the heavy stillness from before, but a hollow, haunted quiet. The kind that settles over something broken.

The raft floated in limping rhythm, pushed along by the weakened pull of the current. The torn sail hung uselessly, dragging at its corner. Everything was soaked—our clothes, our packs, our skin. My arms throbbed, and my palms were raw and bloodied from the rope. The inside of my cheek stung, and the sharp tang of copper lingered in my mouth.

Elios slumped at the rear of the raft, his fingers still curled around the mast, like part of him hadn't realized it was over. When I knelt beside Ocevia, she stirred faintly, her lips cracked, her breath shallow.

"We made it," I whispered.

She nodded, too exhausted to speak.

The sky above us had shifted to gray, clouds thinning into long ribbons streaked across the pale horizon. The light of morning crept slowly behind them, hesitant and thin.

Elios joined me at her side. His touch on my back was soft, reassuring.

"We lost the sail," he said, his voice hoarse. "And half the food."

I nodded, swallowing hard. "But we're alive."

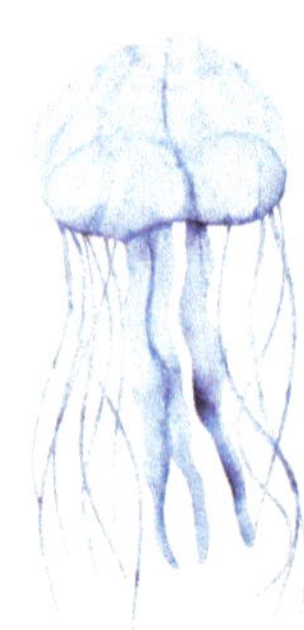

It didn't sound like enough, but I meant it. We were still breathing, and that counted for something. The sea, for now, had let us go.

The raft rocked gently beneath us, as if nothing had happened. As if the storm had never come.

But we remembered. We always would.

For a long while, no one spoke. The silence was no longer a threat, but something we could rest inside.

Elios reached for my hand, and I took it. Held it tight.

Above us, a single streak of sunlight broke through the clouds.

Far ahead, a dark shape rose against the horizon.

Land.

"We're almost there, ladies," Elios said, his voice breaking through the haze of half-sleep that had settled over me.

Ocevia sat upright, her eyes wide with wonder as she stared at the approaching shoreline.

"I haven't been to the human lands since childhood," she murmured, her voice hushed, reverent. "I don't even remember what it was like."

The words struck deep.

She had spent her whole life beneath the sea, cursed into servitude. And though my own fate had been cruel, I still remembered. I had memories of warm bread, firelight, a mother's song. She had nothing but water and silence.

Before we reached shore, we wet our tails once more, careful not to capsize the raft. The water was a comfort this time, not a threat. Familiar. Reassuring.

As I shifted back into my human form, I caught Elios watching me. His smirk was subtle, but unmistakable.

Ocevia's laugh shattered the quiet. "Just for the record," she said, eyes glinting, "I am not sharing a room with you two lovebirds."

I groaned, dragging my hands over my face.

Of course she noticed.

With a dramatic sigh, I shook my head and looked away. Although my face burned with embarrassment, Ocevia's expression told me she enjoyed being able to tease us, and I was happy she was in good spirits. Even if it was at my expense.

I shifted again, legs returning with a familiar ache.

We reached for the paddles, pushing forward one last time.

It wasn't long before Starspell rose ahead of us, framed by the velvet sky and jagged mountain peaks. Lanterns glowed along the harbor, their light dancing across the water in golden waves. It didn't look like safety. Not really.

But it didn't look like Miris.

And that, for now, was enough.

"My friend's tavern is close," Elios said, nodding toward the clustered buildings near the dock. "We'll go there first. He can get us new clothes. A real meal. Something hot."

He glanced at us both, his gaze lingering just a moment too long on our tattered clothes.

"Real food," he added, smiling. "Not just dried fish and fruit."

A laugh broke loose from my chest, bright and sudden. For a heartbeat, I forgot the ache in my muscles, the rawness in my throat.

I had spent years surviving on punishment and fear, forgetting that food could be joy. That fire could mean warmth, not pain.

But here, in this place where the sea couldn't follow, we would choose.

THE HARBOR'S REFUGE

As Elios promised, the tavern was close to the harbor, mercifully so. After days adrift and hours under the burning sun, our limbs ached and our clothes clung damp to our skin. We moored the raft with quiet relief, exchanging no words as we gathered our few belongings. None of us said it aloud, but we all hoped to never see that raft again.

The buildings along the harbor's edge stood close together, their stone facades bleached by salt and sun. The tavern stood out, not for its size, but for its charm. It was intimate and cheerful from the out- side, its sandstone bricks softened by age, the marble detailing along its archways still catching the lamplight with a quiet elegance. The windows were weather-worn, clouded with sea spray and sand, but the sounds inside told a different story. Laughter, clinking glasses, the muffled melody of music and merriment drifted through the cracks like a promise.

Anticipation sparked through me, jittery and quick, as I stepped ahead and swung open the tavern door. The iron was cool beneath my fingers. I held it open for Elios, who followed with Ocevia in his arms. She didn't resist, but her glare was sharp enough to cut through solid bone. If looks could kill, Elios might've dropped her on the steps.

Warmth hit me first, the heat of firelight, of too many bodies pressed close in revelry. Then the scent came, thick and intoxicating: roasting meat, spiced wine, fresh bread still steaming from the oven. After weeks of dried fish and foraged fruit, it was dizzying.

The tavern was alive with movement. Servers weaved between crowd- ed tables. Patrons shouted over each other with laughter thick in their throats. Music swirled from a corner stage—a fiddle, a horn, and a drum joining in a song I didn't recognize but instantly wanted to dance to.

We wove through the crowd, Elios guiding us through the noise. My excitement grew with each step, drawn forward by the promise of food, warmth, and temporary safety. At the far end of the bar, an elderly man with an eye patch broke from his conversation, his smile spreading the moment he spotted Elios.

The man strode forward and clapped Elios so hard on the back he nearly lost his grip on Ocevia. She grumbled as he lowered her to the floor, her legs still unsteady from the journey. For a moment, she leaned against me, then straightened with quiet determination, her balance improving as pride took over where strength hadn't fully returned.

Elios offered the man a smile that was all warmth and memory. "Vasso, it's good to see you, old friend. Business looks like it's going well."

Vasso's grin widened. He threw an arm around Elios' shoulders, sweeping his other hand toward the crowded tavern. "It's been a good season," he said with satisfaction, then turned a more curious eye on him. "What brings you back to Starspell?"

I shifted beside them, tension bristling at the back of my neck. We hadn't planned a cover story, but Elios didn't hesitate.

"We're just passing through," he said, glancing toward me with a brief, reassuring smile. "We probably won't stay more than the night."

Something unspoken passed between them. Vasso's gaze sharpened, but he nodded slowly. "Off the record, it is then. One room or two?"

"Two, but near each other if possible. We also need supplies—clothes for my companions and something to eat. Unfortunately, we've had to travel with little more than the clothes on our backs."

I crossed my arms over my chest, instinctively trying to hide the truth of our journey beneath threadbare leathers. The tavern's soft candlelight offered little in the way of shadow, just enough to be seen, never enough to disappear. My clothes were little more than undergarments, and I felt every inch of exposed skin under the weight of unseen stares.

"Are my credits still adequate?" Elios asked, though he already seemed to know the answer.

Vasso clapped him on the shoulder again. "Your credits are more than enough. Let me grab those keys for you, and I'll bring food and drink to your rooms. Chryssa will dig up something to wear until the stores open in the morning."

As Vasso disappeared behind the bar, Elios reached for my hand and laced his fingers with mine. His thumb brushed slow circles over my palm. It should have calmed me. It didn't. The tavern's laughter seemed distant now, drowned by the roar in my chest. I felt raw. Underdressed. Not quite human.

No one stared, but I knew we didn't belong.

Vasso returned and pressed two keys into Elios' hand. Without a word, he led us toward a narrow stairwell tucked into the back of the tavern. The light dimmed as we climbed, and the noise below faded behind us like a distant tide.

Ocevia climbed on her own, determined as ever, though she leaned slightly on the railing. Her limp was still pronounced, but her chin was lifted in defiance.

I followed behind, conscious of every creak in the wooden steps, every whispered voice that carried through the walls. Shirtless, wounded, underdressed—what must we have looked like to the others?

I didn't want to know.

A few sconces along the stairs and hallway lit our path. Still, the dim illumination made it challenging to see our surroundings clearly. However, Elios was familiar with the place and had no trouble finding our rooms.

Unlocking the last door on the right, he motioned to Ocevia. "Make yourself comfortable. One of us will come to knock when Vasso sends up food and clothing. Get some rest. There are usually towels in the bathing room and a bathtub for your tail."

Ocevia needed no further convincing. When she heard about the bathtub, she darted into the candlelit guest room and slammed the door behind her. I snickered as I waited for Elios to point out our own room.

My stomach fluttered at the thought of spending the night with him in an actual room, on a proper bed.

The human lands were forbidden to me, but it no longer mattered after breaking so many rules since rescuing Elios. Screw it, I decided to just enjoy myself. I hadn't spent a night in a human dwelling or felt the comfort of a mattress and blankets in over three years, and I intended to relish every second of it. With my new romance blossoming, there was much more to look forward to than just the comfort of a bed. I could finally feel Elios' skin against mine again, and my body heated at the thought.

The room that Elios and I would share was the last one on the left, directly across from Ocevia's. I wondered if he always chose the farthest room from the tavern and why Vasso seemed so familiar with his need for "off-the-record" transactions. I didn't know much about Elios other than that he was a traveler who stayed away from his family. There was so much more I wanted to know about him, but for now, I pushed those questions aside.

Elios unlocked the door and let me into our small but cozy room. A large wooden bed frame occupied most of the space, complemented by a small table, two chairs, and an armoire in the main bedroom. A door led into a bathing room equipped with a sink, toilet, and soaking tub. Moonlight streamed in through a window overlooking the sea. Elios lit some candles around the room, creating a romantic atmosphere. Although the room had a faint smell of dust, I opened the window to let in the cool sea breeze and refresh the scent. I took a deep breath and felt mixed emotions as I took in the familiar fragrance.

As Elios continued tidying up, I gazed at the starry sky reflected on the water's calm surface. "I've never seen the sea like this," I said.

Elios paused and wrapped his arms around my waist, looking over my shoulder at the view. "Like what?" He planted a kiss on my neck, sending shivers down my spine.

"Sparkling. It's beautiful."

A knock at the door broke the quiet between us. The barmaid entered swiftly, balancing a tray of food and wine. She didn't speak, just offered a polite nod before placing it on the table and slipping back out into the hall, the door clicking softly shut behind her.

The moment she left, the scent hit me—rich, savory, *mouthwatering.* My stomach let out a sharp growl in response, loud enough to make me wince. After weeks of dried fish and foraged fruit, the aroma of fresh stew and warm bread was almost overwhelming.

"Are you hungry?" Elios asked, already reaching for the wine as he uncorked the bottle and poured two glasses.

I nodded, perhaps too quickly.

"I'll go get Ocevia. I'm sure she's ready for dinner too." Elios moved to set the table, his movements relaxed, unbothered—such a sharp contrast to the chaos we'd just escaped that it made my chest ache.

I slipped into the hallway, the tray's warmth still lingering in the room behind me and crossed to Ocevia's door. After a brief knock and no reply, I eased it open.

Relief softened my shoulders at the sight before me—Ocevia, very much alive and seemingly at peace, was singing to herself in the tub. Her tail draped lazily over the porcelain edge, flicking water onto the tiled floor with every idle splash.

"Food is ready," I said, stepping into the bathing room, my voice raised just enough to carry over her tune.

She paused to rinse her hair with a nearby glass. "I'm in the bathtub."

I laughed, unable to help it, and handed her a towel as I gestured toward the floor. "You're lucky it was just me and not one of the staff checking on you."

She waved a dripping hand in dismissal. "They shouldn't enter my room without permission."

I raised an eyebrow and pointed toward the hallway. "It was unlocked."

Her smirk faltered into a wince. "I haven't been in the human lands since childhood. I couldn't figure out how to lock it. I don't know how to use half the stuff in here. It took me forever just to figure out how to turn the water on."

The words hit like cold water. Guilt followed quickly behind.

"I'm sorry, Ocevia," I said quietly, sitting on the edge of the counter. "I should've shown you around. I didn't think."

She didn't seem fazed. With a playful smirk, she reached for the plug and tugged it free, the water gurgling down the drain as she began shifting her tail back into legs. "Don't worry about it. I'm the one who ran off at the promise of a tub. If you and your muscled brute give me food and clothes, I'm sure I can figure out how to use the bed on my own. I don't plan to do much other than sleep after eating."

I shook my head with a smile and made for the door as she wrapped herself in a towel.

"I'll bring you a plate of food and wine while you dry off," I said, pausing at the threshold. "I expect they'll bring up clothing soon. I'll be right back."

When I walked into the hallway, Elios was already in the open doorway of our room, holding a bowl of steaming stew, a piece of bread, and a glass of wine.

"Chryssa should be here with clothes soon. It'll be enough to get us through the night, at least. How is she?"

The scent of the rich stew wafted toward me, coaxing another growl from my stomach. I hadn't realized just how hungry I was until that moment. "She's doing well, but I feel bad for not realizing she wouldn't know how to work anything. It's been too long since she's been in a human structure. She figured out how to run a bath independently, though, so she's quite content."

I crossed the hall again, easing open Ocevia's door with the tray in hand. What I found made me freeze and snort softly under my breath.

She was stark naked, kneeling by the hearth with her damp hair curling over her shoulders, furiously attempting to light the fireplace.

With a sharp kick, I closed the door behind me before anyone else could witness the scene. "Ocevia," I sighed, setting the tray on the side table, "the food's here. And maybe don't flash the hallway next time."

"I'm trying to figure out this fire stick," she muttered, not at all bothered. "It's not like we had one of these in the caves."

I crouched beside her, grabbing the fire starter from the mantle and demonstrating. She watched intently as the sparks caught. One of the first things she had ever taught me was how to make fire from stone and tinder—out in the wild. But this? This modern contraption might as well have been sorcery.

It struck me again how little she remembered of this world, how unprepared she was for it. The human realm moved fast. Too fast. And she'd been left behind for far too long.

Elios knocked lightly, cracking the door just enough to reach through with a bundle of clothing in his hand. I accepted it and passed it to Ocevia, then helped her figure out the strange fastenings and the way the nightdress slipped over the shoulders. She grumbled under her breath, tugging at the unfamiliar fabric.

Before I left, I gave her a quick rundown of the basics—how to use the toilet and how to lock the door.

She raised an eyebrow. "The bed won't attack me, right?"

I laughed. "Not unless you deserve it."

Dinner was already cooling when I returned to our room, but I couldn't bring myself to care. Elios stood as I entered and pulled out my chair. The simple act made my heart squeeze. I sat, flushing despite myself, and offered him a tired smile.

"Is she all settled now?" he asked, waiting for me before starting his own meal.

I nodded and reached for the wine. The first sip was sweet, but the bitterness that followed made me grimace. Still, I took another.

"I don't think she likes human clothing much," I said between sips, "but she's enjoying the food. I'm certain she will jump on the bed, even though I told her not to."

Elios chuckled, topping off his glass. "After all her time away, she deserves to jump on the bed."

I nodded, chewing a piece of bread as I glanced toward the door. My laughter faded as the worry returned—the memory of Ocevia's limp, her brief flashes of exhaustion. She was healing.

But healing didn't mean whole.

Chapter Twenty-Four
A Mermaid's Desire

After being tempted by the rich aroma of the stew for what felt like hours, I finally gave in and devoured every bite. Even at room temperature, it was easily the best thing I'd tasted in three days. I didn't just eat—I inhaled, scraping the bowl clean before I realized Elios was watching me.

Not in admiration. Definitely not for the sake of romance.

More like I reminded him of a starving animal.

Internally, I cringed. But that didn't stop me from licking the last bit of butter off my fingers.

Trying to salvage whatever dignity I had left, I set the bowl down and reached for my wine, finishing the rest in a few hasty gulps. The taste was bitter, but I welcomed the distraction.

"Would you like more stew? I can have some brought up," Elios offered. His face was composed, but I could see the restrained amusement in his eyes.

I hiccupped, realizing the wine had hit harder than expected. My head felt oddly light, like my thoughts were floating just above me, and I supposed that was the point of drinking it. A giggle bubbled up before I could stop it. I pressed my hand to my mouth, and Elios grinned.

"I've had enough food but would like more wine."

He arched an eyebrow, clearly debating the wisdom of giving me more. But he poured anyway, just a small amount, I didn't argue. A half-filled glass was probably wise. The last thing I needed was to pass out in the bath.

"Are you ready to get cleaned up? It's been a long couple of days. I'm sure you're as tired as I am," he said.

I glanced at the bathing room, which now looked like it was a hundred miles away. My tail needed the water. My body craved weightlessness. But everything spun just slightly, and the idea of standing on my own two feet seemed questionable at best.

Still, I nodded and tried to rise. The floor tilted under me. Elios chuckled and offered his arm. Gratefully, I took it.

In the bathing room, I sat on a low stool while he filled the tub, steam curling into the air. I couldn't take my eyes off him. The steady movement of his arms, the way the candlelight flickered over his skin. It sparked something hot and deep in my chest.

I peeled off the rough-spun clothes Chryssa had given me, my hands moving slowly, reverently. It had been so long since I'd worn anything real. But before I could think about dressing, I needed to wash away the layers of salt, sweat, and memory still clinging to my skin.

With Elios' help, I slid into the water and shifted into my mermaid form. The tub was barely big enough to hold me. After all our time sharing the hot spring pool, it felt strange to be in the water alone.

He offered to leave, to give me privacy, but I shook my head. We hadn't spent more than a few breaths apart since he'd pulled me from the sea. I didn't want that to change now.

He sat beside me again, dipping a wooden cup into the water and pouring it gently over my tail. My eyes slipped shut, letting the warmth soak into my bones.

Every sensation felt more intense than it should have. The rhythm of water on skin. The lavender soap in my hair. The scent of Elios beside me. The way his fingers worked shampoo into my scalp like he was learning me by touch alone.

Desire stirred low and slow, building with every pass of his hands.

It had been days since our first intimate encounter, and I craved that feeling again. The hunger lingered beneath my skin like a slow-burning ember. Every time Elios touched me, even something as simple as rinsing my hair or caressing my arm, I imagined more. I wanted more. I ached for it.

But I waited.

I held myself back, deciding to save that fire for when we were in bed. There, I could let go completely.

When it was his turn to bathe, I stayed beside him. The wine's haze had faded, leaving a soft warmth in its place. A kind of gentle surrender.

I watched him without shame as he washed, 1watched the way water rolled over his shoulders and chest, how the candlelight danced across his skin in shifting golds and shadows. Every muscle moved with quiet purpose, honed and familiar, and my gaze lingered too long.

He noticed.

Of course he noticed.

Every time our eyes met, he smiled. Not the sly kind of smile, but something slower. Smoldering. Mischievous. And when he reached between his legs to wash, he didn't rush. He gave himself an extra stroke, deliberately slow, meant for me.

"Do you like what you see, Azure?"

My face flushed, heat rising like a tide. I didn't look away. I didn't even try.

"Why don't you get out of that tub?" I murmured, voice thick with anticipation. "I'll show you exactly which parts I like."

Even I was surprised by how boldly the words came out. Judging by the spark in Elios' eyes, he was too.

But surprise turned quickly to heat.

He rinsed the soap away in record time, stepped from the tub, and dried off in a few swift, eager motions. Before I could blink, he was on me—towel tossed aside, arms wrapping around me like he meant to hold me there forever.

"I hope you weren't planning on getting much sleep tonight, Little Tempest."

His voice was rough silk, brushing over my skin like a promise. I bit his bottom lip, teasing.

"Who needs sleep?"

There were no more words after that. Just mouths finding mouths, skin finding skin. We came together with a need that bordered on desperate, a frantic tangle of limbs and breath and heat. The world outside the room vanished. There was no sea, no curse, no looming threats. Just this—this moment. This *man*.

Elios touched me like I was sacred. His hands mapped every curve, every line of me like a territory he never wanted to forget. I returned the favor, memorizing the way he gasped when I kissed the hollow of his throat, the way he trembled when I traced the line of his ribs.

His lips were fire. His body, a storm. And I surrendered to it, to *him*.

There was no fear. No hesitation. Only the rhythm of our bodies moving together, finding solace in one another, chasing pleasure that felt like salvation.

Wrapped in his arms, I felt the world shrink to nothing but the heat between us and the heartbeat beneath my ear.

He had saved me. Not just from drowning, but from silence. From isolation. From a life that had been about survival and little else.

And as I held him, trembling with the aftershock of everything he made me feel, I knew I would never stop being grateful—for him, for this, for the chance to choose something more than pain.

Waves slammed against the shore, their roar echoing in my ears as the briny scent of the sea filled my lungs. I spun in place, breath quick and sharp, heart thundering against my ribs. Panic surged through me—wild and unreasoning.

But there was no threat.

No monsters. No shadows. Nothing but an open stretch of sand beneath a bruised sky.

Still, the fear coiled tight around my lungs like a fist.

I knew this place. Knew the way the tide curved along the rocks, the way the dunes dipped and rose like sleeping giants. This was the beach I had played on as a child, barefoot and sun-drenched, before everything fell apart.

But something was wrong.

The sky churned with storm clouds, dark and low, trailing threads of lightning too far to hear. And yet, it wasn't the weather that raised goosebumps on my arms, it was the feeling that I had been here before.

Then I heard it.

A giggle—light, unbothered, spilling across the wind.

I turned sharply.

Daneliya.

My little sister splashed through the shallows, her hair clinging to her cheeks, her laughter bright and innocent. She spun in place, arms out, as if the world had never hurt her. As if it never could.

A smile tugged at the corners of my lips, but it died just as quickly. Something twisted in my chest. A wrongness that echoed too loudly.

This wasn't just a dream.

It was a memory replaying itself in real time, and I already knew how it would end.

"Daneliya, no!"

I ran, legs pounding the wet sand, arms reaching, but I was too slow. The tide surged in a sudden swell, sweeping beneath her feet and dragging her under with a merciless pull.

"No!"

I dove into the surf, the cold hitting me like stone. My eyes burned as I forced them open beneath the surface, blinking against the sting, searching desperately for a glimpse of her—blond hair, pale arms, anything.

But the water gave nothing back.

Only silence.

Only loss.

Daneliya was gone.

A sharp knock shattered the remnants of sleep, dragging me back into the waking world with a jolt. I groaned, curling into the blankets as my empty stomach twisted painfully. My head pounded in rhythm with the relentless banging on the door.

Muted daylight filtered through the curtains, soft but unforgiving. I blinked against it, my eyes aching. Beside me, Elios stirred with a groan of his own, running a hand through his tousled hair as he sat up. He moved slowly, like every muscle was still half asleep, then reached for his trousers and pulled them on without a word.

I struggled with the ties of my borrowed tunic, cursing the wine, and myself, for overindulging. My fingers fumbled, still clumsy from sleep, still shaken by the dream.

Then the door creaked open.

Ocevia stood in the hallway, wild-haired and barefoot, her tunic barely holding itself together. The collar had slipped low, exposing far too much of her chest.

I was across the room in seconds.

"Ocevia," I hissed, grabbing her arm and tugging her inside. I fumbled with the fabric, working quickly to cover her. "You can't stand in the hallway half-dressed."

She blinked at me, utterly unfazed. "I usually wear a lot less than this, Azure. You're being ridiculous."

I sighed sharply, pressing both hands to her shoulders. "Mermaids wear less, but humans don't. Remember, you're pretending to be human right now."

She didn't argue, which was as close to agreement as I could hope for.

Her gaze shifted to Elios, then back to me. "So, what's the plan for today?"

Her tone was casual, but her eyes swept the room with curiosity, with excitement.

Elios sat on the edge of the bed, adjusting his boots without looking up. "Let's head down to the tavern for breakfast first."

Then his gaze lifted to meet mine.

And just like that, the warmth returned, spreading through me at the memory of his hands, his mouth, the way he had looked at me in the dark.

"Or I can have it brought up if you'd prefer."

I opened my mouth to reply, but Ocevia had already turned for the door, her steps light and unapologetic as ever.

I rolled my eyes and followed, my stomach growling louder now, a reminder that desire wasn't the only hunger I had left to answer.

Chapter Twenty-Five

FORCED TO RUN

The tavern bustled even in the early morning, filled with cheerful patrons savoring their food between sips of cider and conversation. The warmth of the hearth, the clatter of dishes, and the hum of voices created a rhythm that made it almost easy to forget what waited for us beyond these walls. We settled at a quiet table tucked into a corner, grateful for the illusion of peace, and ordered plates of eggs and fried potatoes. It wasn't the healthiest meal, but after surviving on dried fish for years, it tasted like salvation.

"This is so good," Ocevia groaned. She sank her fork into the eggs like she might never stop. I watched her with quiet amusement, barely containing my laughter. She'd been taken from the human world far too young to remember what real food even tasted like, and now she ate with the abandon of someone reclaiming something they'd never realized they'd missed. Every exaggerated moan of delight made it clear she intended to make up for lost time.

"What?"

Before I could do more than stifle a laugh behind my cup, a woman approached—middle-aged, sharp-eyed, and self-assured. Chryssa, the tavern owner's wife. She dropped several bags at our table with a soft grunt, the weight of them thudding against the wood. Clothes, provisions, basic supplies. The things we'd need for the road ahead, though none of it made the journey feel any more real.

We barely had time to look inside before Vasso appeared, his usually easy demeanor replaced with something tight and unreadable. His expression alone made my stomach clench.

Without a word, he reached out and grabbed Elios by the wrist, tugging him toward a narrow, dimly lit hallway at the back of the tavern. No questions. No explanations. Just tension, immediate and unspoken. Ocevia and I rose without hesitation and followed, our footsteps quiet on the stone floor.

The change in Vasso was jarring. His movements were brisk, his shoulders tense, his eyes flicking toward the door like he half-expected someone to burst through it.

"I don't mean to rush you off, Elios," he said, voice low and clipped, "but some individuals were asking questions in town last night about a woman with her description." He nodded toward me.

A chill swept over my skin, ice threading through my veins.

"They came into the tavern after you three went to bed," Vasso continued. "I didn't recognize them under their cloaks, but I ran them off. Still, I doubt they've left the city."

Elios exhaled sharply, rubbing his brow with the heel of his hand. He wasn't surprised.

But I was.

Miris' people had found us. Too fast. Too close. The walls of the hallway felt like they were closing in. The air thinned, each breath harder than the last.

"Send word to our contacts," Elios said, his voice tight. "We'll set out for Ceveasea today."

Vasso nodded, the tension in his face unrelenting. "I can spare a few men from *The Circle*. I don't want you traveling with these lasses without some extra swords."

The Circle?

My pulse stuttered. The name settled in my mind like a weight I didn't yet understand. *What was that? Why did Elios seem to expect it?* My skin prickled with unease.

Elios didn't answer. He simply turned and led us quickly back to our room, urgency now pulsing in his every movement.

"Take a moment to wet your tails while you can," he said. His tone was all business, calm but stern. "I'll get our packs together."

Then his eyes found mine, holding there.

"You know what Vasso said. They're already here. If we don't leave now, we may never get the chance."

I swallowed hard, my throat tight with fear and frustration. "Elios…" I hesitated, then asked, "What is The Circle?"

His jaw tightened as he reached for my hands. He glanced around before answering, as if the shadows might be listening.

"I promise to tell you everything once we're safe. But for now, we need to get moving. I imagine Vasso is preparing the horses and men right now. The sooner we leave, the better. The longer we wait, the more danger we'll all face."

It wasn't the answer I wanted, but it was the one we had.

I nodded, heart pounding as I turned toward the bed. I pulled fresh clothes from one of the supply bags, fingers trembling slightly as I gripped the fabric. I didn't speak. Neither did Ocevia. She grabbed her things and slipped out ahead of me, both of us silently preparing for a journey we could no longer delay.

By the time we returned downstairs, the alley behind the tavern had come to life with purpose. Vasso stood near four saddled horses, flanked by three armed men whose cloaks stirred faintly in the breeze. One stepped forward, his red hair catching the early light like fire. "Dimitris," he said, offering a firm nod. The others, Markos and Aris, gave silent greetings, eyes sharp, expressions unreadable.

Ocevia shifted beside me, clearly uneasy. Her gaze fixed on the horses with open suspicion.

"I don't know how to ride a horse, Azure. That thing may kill me," she muttered.

I fought back a laugh, my shoulders shaking slightly. "I haven't ridden a horse since I was younger, and I have barely any experience either, but I'm sure you won't be alone. You'll ride with one of those fine men."

She studied the group like a shopper picking fruit, then pointed at Markos with all the decisiveness of someone making a life-altering choice. "I want that one, I think."

I nearly choked on a laugh. "I'm not sure if you get to choose, but I'll see what I can do."

As Elios helped me onto his horse, I leaned close and whispered, "I think she wants to ride with Markos."

Elios chuckled, a glint of mischief in his eyes, and winked at me. Then he turned to the man still standing quietly beside his mount. "Hey, Markos," Elios called.

The man flinched slightly at the sound of his name, clearly not used to being singled out, but jogged over without question. Elios tilted his head toward Ocevia, who still lingered near the tavern's shadow. "Can you look after Ocevia for us?"

Markos gave a silent nod and made his way toward her, expression unreadable.

Elios steadied me as I adjusted into the saddle of our horse, Night Step, then swung up behind me as though he'd done it a million times. His presence at my back was warm, steadying, *familiar*. Across the alley, Ocevia followed Markos to his own horse with a mix of bashfulness and curiosity. The poor man didn't know what he was getting into with her, but I hoped he would be kind. She deserved that much. For all my inexperience, I still understood more about men than she did.

Vasso and Chryssa stood at the edge of the alley, waving us off as our group set into motion. The clop of hooves echoed between the narrow buildings, a steady rhythm that felt strangely final.

Leaving was bittersweet.

I longed for a life lived freely, with safety and possibility. Still, I couldn't help feeling the pull of Starspell. There was so much here I would never get to experience. I'd barely begun to reacquaint myself with the human world, and already I was being forced to leave it behind.

But we didn't have a choice.

I clung to that truth as Night Step carried me farther from the Lamalis Sea, farther from the ocean's call, and deeper into territory where my kind wasn't meant to go.

Elios' arm was warm around my waist as he held me close, steadying me with each gentle sway of the saddle. The horses trotted along the cobblestone path, hooves echoing in quiet rhythm through the empty streets. The strength of his body behind me brought a kind of safety I wasn't used to. It settled over me slowly, like warmth seeping into frozen skin. So, even as thoughts of our uncertain future churned through my mind, I leaned into that strength and let myself breathe.

The city faded around us. With no pedestrians or vendors behind the businesses we passed, slipping away in relative secrecy proved surprisingly easy. A few early risers moved through their morning routines—a woman sweeping dust from her doorstep, a man loading crates of vegetables into a cart—but none spared us more than a passing glance.

Still, Elios kept my hood drawn low. Markos did the same for Ocevia. The protection was necessary, not just from eyes, but from recognition.

We weren't the only ones concealing our identities. Before leaving, the men had donned identical cloaks, their faces hidden beneath deep hoods. Their movements were practiced, silent, coordinated. Whoever they were, they were used to moving unnoticed. And though the cloaks were too warm for the climbing sun, I knew I'd be grateful for them once night fell and the cold crept in.

The cobbled road gave way to dirt as we left Starspell behind, the path narrowing as the terrain sloped upward into the mountain pass. The moment the last rooftop vanished behind the trees, a weight lifted from my shoulders. Not entirely, but enough to draw a breath without feeling like I was being hunted.

"How long until we reach Ceveasea?" I asked, leaning into Elios' chest and tilting my head to glance up at him.

He rewarded me with a soft kiss on the temple, a touch that sent a ripple of heat across my skin. His hand slipped from my waist to my hip, resting there as his voice rumbled low beside my ear.

"It should only take a few days, depending on the length of our stops and the weather." He began tracing slow, idle circles on the fabric of my trousers, the pressure of his fingers burning through the layers. "There are some camps and large cave systems in the mountains. There'll be ample places to rest along the way. Still, we need to take water into consideration for you and Ocevia. Also, I don't want to be stuck in the pass overnight without cover."

The reminder of our curse, the need to submerge in water every twenty-four hours, soured the air in my lungs. My stomach twisted. A part of me had always wondered if it was true, if Miris had told us the truth about what would happen if we went too long without soaking. But I wasn't brave, or foolish, enough to test it.

I nodded, eyes fluttering shut as a cool breeze swept through the trees. It slipped beneath my hood, catching on the sweat along my spine, and I shivered.

Hoofbeats grew louder as Markos pulled up beside us, his horse matching our pace. "Any ideas where you want to stop tonight, Brother?" he asked.

His arm was curled around Ocevia's waist, and the look on her face, pure delight, made me smile despite everything. I hoped she wouldn't rush into something she wasn't ready for. But I didn't have the heart to caution her. I hadn't exactly taken things slow with Elios.

We had both gone so long without real touch, without connection. We had grown up in isolation, denied affection and freedom. Could anyone really blame us for grasping whatever warmth we could find?

Not that I cared if they did.

Elios glanced up at the sky, squinting against the light, then turned back to Markos. "We need a place we can defend, somewhere with a water source, before sundown. You know the creatures that roam these lands at night. I don't want to be vulnerable once we lose the protection of daylight."

Markos nodded, the lines of his face tightening. Whatever Elios meant, it wasn't just folklore. His voice held too much weight. My stomach turned at the thought of what might be waiting in the dark—real monsters, not just the ones Miris created.

Markos scanned the narrow path ahead before speaking again. "There's a camp about five hours from here. Maybe less if we pick up the pace."

"Let's try to get there before sundown," Elios replied without hesitation.

Markos nodded again and lifted his reins, urging his horse ahead. Aris and Dimitris followed silently behind him, falling into formation without needing to be told.

Elios adjusted his grip on me, his arms tightening around my waist as he nudged Night Step into a faster rhythm. The world blurred around us as trees, rock, and rising mountain air gave way to motion and breath. I let myself be held, nestled between his thighs, my body pressed flush to his.

We galloped into the pass, the city behind us, the unknown ahead.

And though my heart beat with fear, it also beat with something else.

Hope.

DIMITRIS

SANCTUARY IN THE CLIFFS

Exhausted and sore from riding, we reached the camp just as the sun touched the horizon, staining the sky in streaks of fire and gold. The mountain loomed above us, its cliffs softening into dusk, sheltering a lively camp that pulsed with the warmth of firelight and voices.

I had expected an empty clearing, maybe a cold firepit and a few makeshift shelters at most. Instead, dozens of people moved through the space, forming what looked like a small, self-sustained community tucked safely away from the outside world. Children played barefoot in the dust. Adults gathered around a massive bonfire, their laughter rising beneath the crackle of flames. An entire animal carcass turned slowly on a spit, the savory scent curling through the air and making my mouth water.

It smelled better than anything we'd eaten in weeks, aside from last night's stew.

Markos moved ahead of the group and dismounted, handing the reins to Dimitris before approaching a man standing near the edge of the firelight. The native was tall, his frame solid, the muscles beneath his skin carved by labor and time. A heavy spear rested easily in one hand, and thick braids hung down his back like ropes of dark thread.

"This is the Arcane River Tribe," Elios whispered behind me. "Markos is getting permission from a tribal elder for us to stay the night. We'll be safe here. A river flows through the cave system, for you and Ocevia to… soak."

He hesitated on the word. The pause, the way he glanced sideways, made me wonder what else he wasn't saying.

I turned to look at him. "A river inside the caves?"

I felt him nod, his chin brushing my temple. "A warm one. It's fed by a hot spring."

The memory hit instantly—our island cave, the steam, the peace. The nights we shared there, feeding the bond that burned between us. I closed my eyes and let myself sink into the thought for just a moment, pretending the mountains might offer something similar.

When I opened them again, Markos was returning with the tribal elder beside him. My heart skipped. I didn't know what we'd do if they refused us shelter. The idea of continuing into the pass after dark sent a cold shiver down my spine. Elios' warnings echoed again—of what hunted these mountains once the sun slipped below the trees.

"We can stay," Markos announced, nodding toward the large man at his side. "This is a tribal elder, the Great Protector."

The man said nothing. He gave a single nod, then turned and walked away, heading back toward the fire.

Markos pointed toward the far end of the cliffside. "The Great Protector said we can use the caves over there. There are rooms inside, and the river runs through them. Drinking water. Bathing water. He exchanged gold for the night."

Elios nodded once, and the rest of our party began to dismount. Markos moved to Ocevia's side without needing to be asked, his hand already reaching for hers. She accepted it with an easy smile, one that made something unspoken pass between them, quiet but sure, like the beginning of a promise neither of them had voiced yet.

As we moved toward the assigned caves, a few tribe members watched us pass, their expressions curious but not unkind. Most carried on with their tasks, offering little more than a glance. Whether they were used to travelers or simply respectful of space, I couldn't be sure. Still, I felt the brush of their eyes—fleeting, but present.

"Elios," I murmured, leaning closer as he reached up to brush a loose strand of hair from my face.

"Hmm?"

"You mentioned creatures that make traveling at night too dangerous. I was wondering... what kinds of creatures?"

His arms tightened around me. The reaction was immediate, and more telling than any words.

"There are creatures that hunt in these mountains," he said, his voice low. "They drain the blood from their victims and leave the corpses for lesser predators to consume. They're the ones we avoid at night."

Ice crawled across my skin. Every shadow sharpened. Every whisper of wind felt more pointed. I gripped the saddle horn tighter.

"That sounds like a nightmare."

He held me even closer, so firm I could feel the tension locked in his shoulders. "They are, but we'll do our best to avoid them. Don't worry. As long as we set up camp before sunset, we'll be safe. The Arcane people have lived in this pass for generations. If anyone knows how to protect themselves from the beasts, they do."

As we approached our temporary lodgings, we passed an enormous cave secured with a sturdy wooden gate. From the gaps in the slats, I could just make out the broad silhouettes of horses shifting inside, their flanks gleaming in the low firelight. It was no surprise the tribe kept their animals well-guarded. If creatures stalked the pass after dark, the stables would be a target.

Markos led us to the gate, where a member of the tribe stepped forward to collect the reins. He took the horses without a word, guiding each one away and toward the troughs.

With Elios' help, I slid from Night Step's saddle, wincing as my boots met the ground. My legs ached, stiff from the hours of riding, and I paused to stretch them. Every movement sent a dull throb through my hips and knees. After years in the sea, I'd forgotten how unforgiving long rides could be.

We waited as the stable hand led the last of the horses through the gate. Ocevia approached as soon as Markos set her on the ground. Her face was flushed, but her smile stretched wide across her cheeks.

"Markos said there's a heated river inside!" she said, practically bouncing where she stood.

The excitement in her voice was contagious. I couldn't help the smile that curved my lips. "Are you having fun? You seem to be."

She smacked my arm lightly, the blush in her cheeks deepening. "Yes, I am, actually. Markos smells so good and has been such a gentleman. Plus, he's really handsome."

I reached for her hand, intertwining my fingers with hers as the men led the way toward the caves. "I'm glad you've enjoyed his company, especially since you were with him all day on a horse. Do you still want to ride with him tomorrow?"

She practically skipped ahead, golden hair swaying as she moved. "Of course I'm going to ride with him again. I'm going to make him my husband."

Choking on a laugh, I squeezed her hand again, resisting the urge to roll my eyes.

I didn't want to see her heart broken, but who she chose to love wasn't mine to govern. Ocevia had already been denied so much, and I refused to be one more voice telling her what she couldn't have. She deserved softness. She deserved choice. And if Markos accepted her truth the way Elios accepted mine, then maybe, *just maybe*, there was hope for both of us.

As we neared the cave entrance, I slowed and tugged gently on her hand, speaking low.

"You don't have to tell him about us if you're not ready," I murmured. "You can wait until he falls asleep to soak properly. Don't feel pressured."

The caves we were assigned were far more expansive than I had anticipated. From the outside, they appeared unremarkable, just another jagged opening carved into the cliffside. But once we stepped inside, the space opened into a wide, domed chamber glowing with firelight.

At the center, a large fire pit crackled with an already blazing flame, its smoke curling through a hole in the ceiling. The walls were rough and natural, but someone had taken the time to smooth the floors and hang leather screens over each of the doorways that led deeper into the cave.

Sleeping quarters, I realized. There had to be at least four... maybe more.

A faint sulfuric scent lingered in the air, sharp but not unpleasant. I followed it toward the back of the cave and stopped at the sight of a wide pool nestled against the stone wall. Steam rose from the surface, curling like mist into the cooler air above. A narrow stream fed the pool, trickling from a crevice at the far end, its path glistening as it snaked through the rock. Behind it was a path that appeared to link the caves in both directions.

Behind me, Ocevia and Markos slipped into one of the private rooms together, disappearing behind the screen. Elios rested a hand at the small of my back and gently guided me to the next doorway over. I stepped inside, my boots muffled by thick rugs layered across the floor.

The room wasn't large, but it was warm and comfortable. A fur-covered platform lined the far wall, fashioned into a bed. There was no mattress, but after years of sleeping on cold stone, the sight of soft fur and a raised surface felt luxurious. I dropped my bag beside it and ran my fingers across the thick pelts, letting the texture slide through my hand like water.

Elios lingered in the doorway for a moment before retreating toward the main chamber, his footsteps fading into the quiet. With a sigh, I sank onto the furs, letting my weight settle into the soft layers, muscles still sore from the long ride. Stretching my legs out slowly, I wiggled my toes to coax the blood back into them.

For the first time in hours, I let myself breathe deeply.

It smelled like earth and smoke and something faintly floral—maybe a dried herb tucked into one of the storage baskets in the corner. My body ached in places I hadn't realized could ache, but the quiet peace of the room sank into my bones like warmth.

Still, my thoughts drifted.

Ocevia was with Markos. After only one day. I couldn't judge her, not when I'd done the same with Elios, but I worried all the same. She barely knew him. We barely knew any of them.

Yet, somehow, I trusted them.

I had to.

For a while, I lounged on the fur-covered bed, fingers lazily combing through the silky pelts beneath me. Each stroke was a small luxury, a quiet rebellion against the years I'd spent sleeping on bare stone with nothing but cold air and harder truths to keep me company.

Firelight flickered through the leather screen at the doorway, its glow shifting gently along the cave walls. From the main chamber, I could hear Elios speaking softly to one of the others, the occasional clink of gear being unpacked. The sounds reached me faintly, softened by the space between us.

Even so, I listened for Ocevia.

My thoughts wandered to her, curled up behind a screen not far from mine. I knew I shouldn't worry. She wasn't fragile. She was clever and fierce in her own right. But my heart still clenched at the idea of her trusting someone so quickly. I knew the vulnerability that came with hope. The risk of it. The danger.

It felt hypocritical—this concern—when I had thrown myself headfirst into Elios' arms with little more than instinct and trust to guide me. But still, it lingered.

I hoped Markos would treat her gently. That if he learned the truth of her, it wouldn't change the way he looked at her. I hoped she wouldn't face rejection, not after all she had endured.

She deserved someone who saw her fully and chose her anyway.

Just as Elios had done for me.

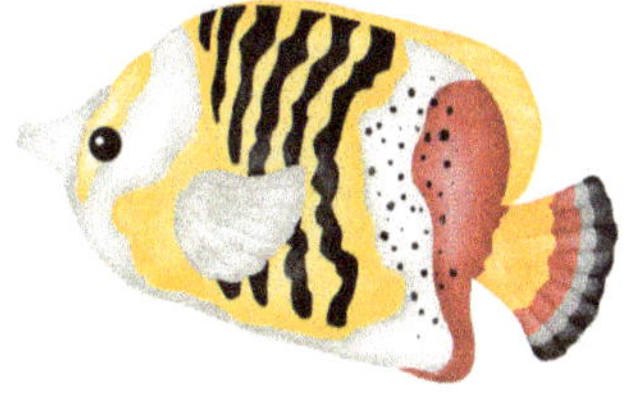

That thought stirred something warm in my chest, and I let it settle there as I stretched out along the bed. The fire's heat reached me even here, distant but steady. The scent of smoke and hot spring water clung to the air, earthy and grounding.

Through the screen, I caught a glimpse of Elios returning. I didn't rise. I didn't need to. I felt safe.

And for the first time in a long while, I allowed myself to rest in that feeling.

BY FIRE AND FLESH

When Elios returned, he opened his mouth to speak, but whatever words he'd planned died instantly. His gaze landed on me, stretched across the fur-covered bed, and something inside him shifted. His eyes darkened, a wicked grin curling slow and dangerous across his face, like he'd found prey instead of a lover.

The change in his expression sent a ripple through me, not fear, but something deeper—*hotter*. Anticipation burned low in my belly.

His beard had grown since the day I pulled him from the sea, the rough edge of it lending his face a rugged, almost wild appeal. He looked like something dangerous. Something meant to be devoured.

He crossed the room in two strides, his hands sliding up my legs, pausing just long enough to squeeze my backside before continuing their ascent. Then he shifted, positioning himself between my thighs and leaning down until his mouth found mine.

The kiss was fire, hungry and deep. His tongue explored mine, stoking the heat already building beneath my skin. His arousal pressed against me, a silent, fevered promise of everything he wanted to give me. The heat of him, the tension in his body, said everything his lips hadn't yet.

We broke apart, breathless.

"Sorry," Elios gasped, bracing himself with one arm while the other guided me gently onto my back. "I came to tell you that everyone else went to get food from the main campfire."

My fingers slipped beneath the hem of his tunic, tracing the waistband of his trousers. "And Ocevia?"

"I couldn't tear her away from Markos if I tried. They left together."

A flicker of worry clouded the haze of desire. I bit my lip. "I hope she doesn't get hurt."

He kissed my forehead, the corner of his mouth lifting in a small smile. "Markos is a good man. We've known each other since we were kids."

"Okay, I trust your judgment since I don't know him." I glanced up at him beneath my lashes, my fingers slipping a little lower. "But I have one more question."

Elios raised a brow, lips curving into a knowing smile. "Yes?"

"You said everyone else went back to the main fire. That means we won't be disturbed, right?"

His grin widened into something deliciously wicked. "Of course," he murmured, pressing a kiss to my neck that sent warmth cascading down my spine. His hand slipped beneath my tunic, fingers finding the sensitive peaks of my breasts and teasing them in slow, circling strokes that left me breathless. His hips pressed against mine, his cock already hard for me.

"Do you like that, Azure?" he whispered, voice rough with want. "How much my body craves you."

His lips brushed the shell of my ear. A soft nip followed, gentle but possessive, and a whimper escaped me. I tugged him closer, breath catching as my body arched to meet his. Every inch of him was pressed to me, solid and hot and impossibly close. Our breaths mingled—uneven, hungry—as if we couldn't get close enough.

A moan tore from my throat, half surrender and half plea. Elios answered with a low groan of his own, the sound rumbling through his chest. He pulled back, just far enough to slide his hand from beneath my tunic and rise onto his knees.

He made quick work of the laces, untying them and casting the tunic aside. I reached for the ties of his trousers, but he swatted my hand away with a playful smirk.

"Not yet. Be patient."

Groaning in frustration, I let myself fall back as he lowered over me again. His mouth closed around my nipple, warm and wet, while his palm kneaded the other. My back arched instinctively, seeking more friction where I needed it. I was already aching for him—every nerve alight, every muscle drawn tight with need.

Already impatient, I reached for him again, and this time, he twisted away just enough to laugh softly against my skin.

"You're so demanding tonight, Little Tempest."

"And you're infuriating," I shot back, my breath shaky.

His hand drifted down my body, tracing the curve of my waist, my belly, then lower still. When he pressed between my thighs, I cried out, hips jerking toward him, desperate for more than teasing.

"I'm not trying to tease you, love," he murmured, nuzzling my throat. "I just want to give you the kind of pleasure you'll remember tomorrow."

He was teasing, no matter what he claimed, and I was past the point of self-restraint. I writhed beneath him, biting back a plea as he kissed a slow path down my stomach. His smirk was infuriating. *Addictive.*

He ground against me, the thick press of him still trapped behind the cloth of his trousers, and my gasp turned sharp. The friction was maddening.

"If you want to make me feel good tonight," I panted, "take off your trousers and give me what I want. Save the teasing for another night. I'm ready *now.*"

That did it.

Whatever control he'd been clinging to vanished. His mouth crashed into mine, desperate and hungry, while his hips ground against me in a rhythm that made my whole body quake.

I reached for him again, and he didn't resist. Instead, he helped me. We tore at each other's clothes like we were drowning.

The moment the last barrier dropped, he slammed into me, and the scream that left my throat echoed through the cave. They might have heard me at the fire, but I didn't care.

Passion surged between us, hard and fast and desperate. We moved together like we'd been chasing this moment forever, our bodies falling into a rhythm that felt instinctive, inevitable, chasing release with an urgency that blurred everything else.

When I came, it was slow at first, a trembling, unraveling of tension, followed by a release so fierce it left me dazed. We collapsed together, tangled in limbs and breath, the heat of us lingering like lightning after a storm.

My stomach interrupted the quiet, growling like a beast untamed, and I couldn't help but laugh.

Elios chuckled and leaned in to kiss me again, slower this time—soft and lingering—before rising from the bed. He extended a hand to me, still catching his breath.

"Let's get you something to eat."

It was a suggestion I couldn't argue with. I sat up slowly, the cool air brushing against my flushed skin. Around us, discarded clothing lay scattered across the stone floor, tangled like the aftermath of a tsunami.

I dug through the pile and pulled on what I could find, cleaning up and dressing quickly. The tunic clung to my damp skin, and I fought with the ties as I tried to fasten it properly.

"Do you think I'll be able to bathe and soak my tail tonight?" I asked as I adjusted the hem. "I feel disgusting after hours of travel."

And after everything else, but I left that part unsaid.

I glanced at Elios as he pulled on the same trousers I'd just so desperately ripped off. His chiseled form was a distraction, every line of muscle still glowing faintly in the firelight. He looked sinfully good, and I cursed my tunic's complicated ties for slowing me down.

"You'll be able to bathe later," he said, tugging the laces of his trousers into place. "I'll talk to the guys and make sure they all give Ocevia and you the privacy you need... unless Ocevia decides to tell Markos."

The thought made me cringe.

She might. She could. And if she did, it was her right. But part of me still felt protective, maybe overly so. Ocevia had lived her entire life wrapped in the sea and its secrets. She'd never been taught how to navigate human intimacy or judgment. Her understanding of love was still half-shaped by tides and silence.

"I guess she'll have to if she intends to pursue him," I murmured. "I just hope he handles it as well as you did. I know it's still soon, but we're in a dire situation. It feels like death is looming over us at every turn. I don't blame her for wanting a companion."

Elios stepped behind me and wrapped his arms gently around my waist as I finished dressing. His embrace was steady, grounding.

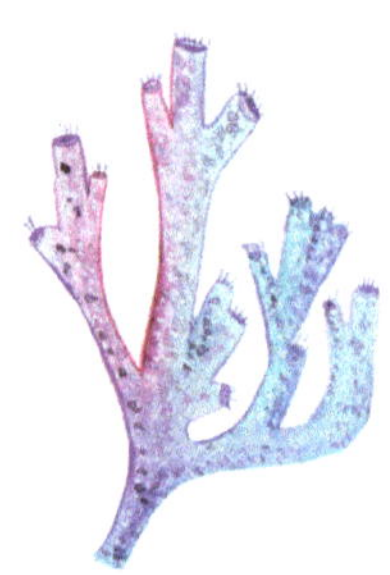

"Don't worry so much," he whispered near my ear. "I promise Markos is one of the good ones. Some of us have heard stories about mermaids in the Lamalis Sea. I didn't believe them before, but... it's hard to deny when you come face-to-face with a woman with a tail. He'll handle it well, even if I have to talk to him first."

I nodded, still uncertain. There was no way to predict how someone would react to the truth, but Markos had volunteered to protect us. He'd left the safety of his world to escort two strangers without knowing why. That had to mean something.

I clung to that thought as we dressed, gathered our things, and stepped out into the night. The beat of the drums had quieted, replaced by the lower hum of voices and the scent of meat curling in the air.

The campfire flickered ahead of us, the light growing steadier with each step. The roasted animal was being carved, its savory scent thick in the air, while wide bone plates passed from hand to hand. The fire's warmth hit us first, a welcome contrast to the cool mountain wind, and laughter drifted among the crowd, easy and unrehearsed.

We found a spot near a large gathering of Arcane tribespeople and eased into the warmth of the group. Dimitris' booming voice rang out before we could sit, his red hair wild and cheeks flushed with drink.

"You guys have to try this drink brewed by the Arcane people!" he shouted, throwing his arms around us in an unexpected group hug. "It's stronger than any whiskey I've ever had!"

His voice was loud enough to reach the other side of the fire, and I giggled, patting him on the back. The scent of fermented fruit and smoke clung to his clothes. He was definitely enjoying himself.

Accepting the bone mug Dimitris offered, Elios gave his friend a squeeze on the shoulder. "You need to slow down, Brother, or you'll retch right off your horse come morning."

Dimitris raised a finger like he was about to argue, then dropped it with a nod. "You're probably right, Boss. I think I need to eat some of that bear."

"Bear?"

The word caught in my throat. The idea of eating bear turned my stomach for half a second, until the scent hit me again. Rich, smoky, and delicious. Hunger quickly won out over hesitation.

Elios and I joined the line for food, trailing behind the still-swaying Dimitris. The Arcane people were generous, either that or Markos had paid with more gold than I realized. Our plates were heaping with roasted meat and dense, dark bread. My stomach rumbled as we made our way back toward the fire.

To my surprise, Ocevia was already seated with Markos, tucked against his side on a wide log surrounded by Aris and several Arcane men and women. Her eyes were bright, her cheeks flushed from laughter. Markos had his arm loosely around her waist as Aris told what must have been a particularly wild story, judging by the roaring laughter from the group.

No one else seemed as deep in their cups as Dimitris, but the energy around the fire buzzed with warmth and ease. It was clear we'd missed quite a gathering while we'd been... otherwise engaged.

And honestly? I didn't regret it.

Elios slid in beside Markos and pulled me onto his lap, wrapping one arm around my waist while reaching with the other to steal a piece of meat from our plate. The warmth of his chest pressed into my back, solid and reassuring.

Markos handed me a bone mug filled with something cloudy and strong. I took a sip, and immediately coughed as it burned down my throat. After the wine from the night before, I wasn't eager to repeat the headache. Instead, I passed the drink to Elios with a smirk, grateful when a tribal woman offered me a mug of water in its place.

I took a few sips, then passed it to Dimitris, who looked like he needed it far more than I did.

We spent the rest of the evening at the fire, full and content, listening to the Arcane tribespeople tell stories that blended myth and memory. Aris, ever the performer, spun tales of sea monsters, pirates, and narrow escapes with flair, his hair catching the firelight like threads of spun gold.

Ocevia looked radiant, laughter dancing from her lips as she leaned into Markos with unexpected tenderness. Although their posture was casual and not overly affectionate, they still moved like two people who had quietly decided something important. It wasn't just companionship—it was connection. Watching them, I found myself quietly hoping the choice would hold.

As the night wore on, my thoughts wandered to the impossible. What if we could stay? What if Ocevia and I could live here—on land, as women, not weapons? What if the sea didn't come calling again?

It was foolish. *Naïve.*

But I couldn't stop myself from dreaming.

Later, after we soaked privately and bathed in the warm river, my exhaustion returned with a vengeance. I barely made it to the furs before I was drifting. No dreams came that night. No memories. No fear.

Just silence.

And sleep.

ARIS

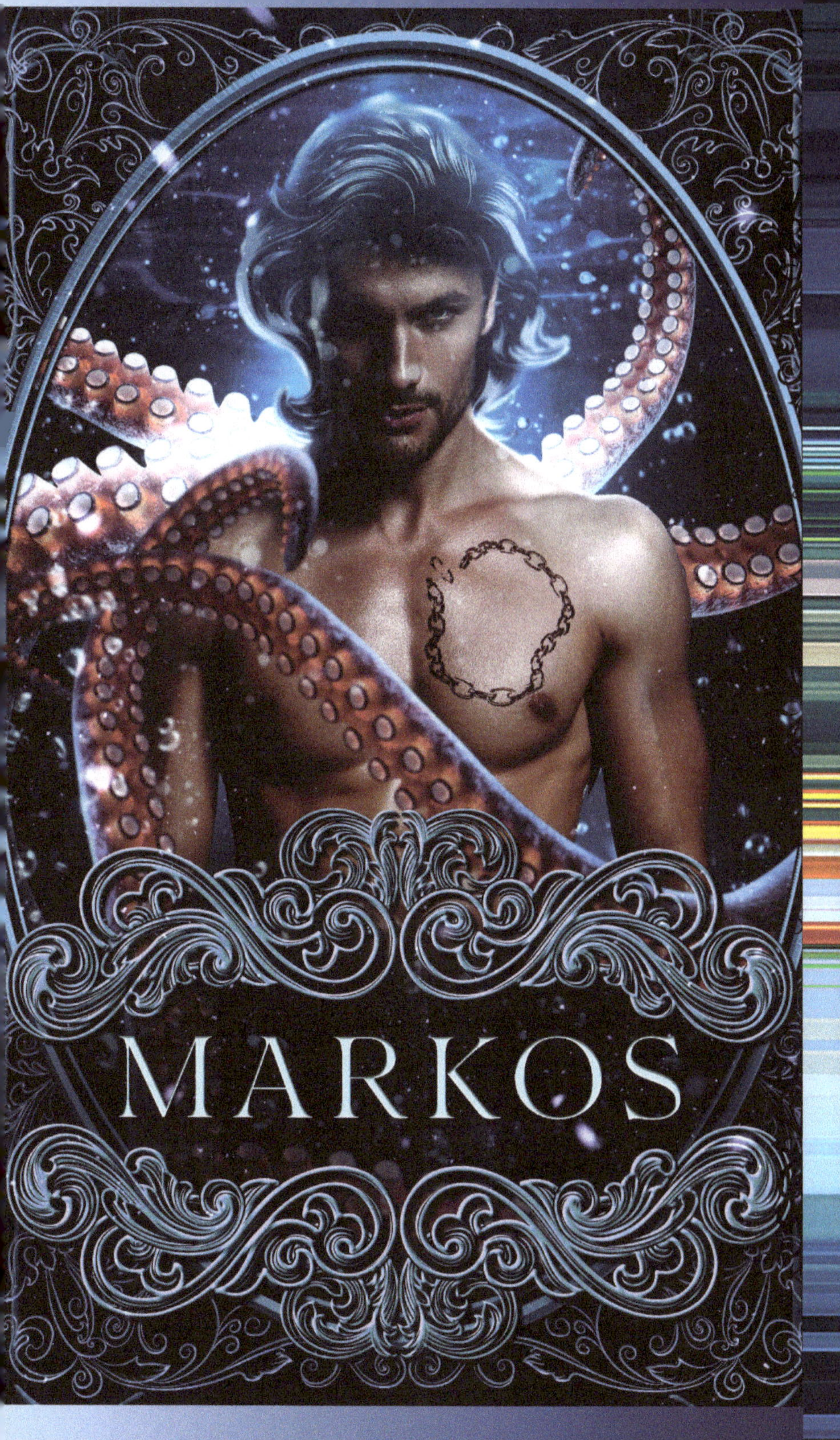

MARKOS

WHEN THE STORM BREAKS

The first light greeted us with more storm than sunrise. Sheets of rain pounded the cliffs, fierce winds bending the trees as if trying to uproot the mountain itself. Travel was out of the question. Our plans dissolved in the downpour, buried beneath the weight of wind and water.

Markos believed the Arcane camp would remain safe for another day, but the fear of Miris' people catching up to us never left my chest. It pulsed beneath every breath.

Still, the storm was too much. Even if it broke by afternoon, leaving would be reckless. We couldn't risk getting caught between camps as night fell, not with the blood-drinking beasts Elios had warned us about. Better to be still than exposed.

The main bonfire had been moved into a large central chamber, its glow now flickering deep within the cliff-side tunnels. Aris called through the leather sheet that hung across our room, letting us know breakfast was being served beside the fire.

But there was no rush.

The storm outside howled, but inside, we were warm. *Sheltered.* Elios echoed his thanks through the curtain, then nestled against me, burying his face in the crook of my neck. I leaned into him, drawing the fur blankets higher as I pressed back into his chest. He radiated heat and safety, rare comforts in our world, and the steady rhythm of his breath lulled me toward sleep again.

Being held like this was a gift. One I didn't take for granted.

I'd barely known him a month. And yet, he'd become something solid in a world that had given me nothing but shifting tides and shattered trust. His touch, his voice, his presence felt like an anchor. I couldn't imagine a future without him in it.

For a while, we didn't speak. We didn't need to. The quiet said enough.

Eventually, the smell of food found us, rich with smoke and salt and something sweet drifting in on the draft from the tunnel. It pulled us from the warmth of our bed, reluctant but hungry.

When we finally stepped into the central fire chamber, warmth met us first, followed by voices and stories already halfway told.

I settled between Elios' legs as we found a space near the relocated fire. His arms wrapped securely around my waist, drawing me back against his chest. The heat from the flames was immediate, chasing away the damp cold that clung to my skin.

The cave was crowded but calm, the entrance screen propped to the side where it had fallen again and again under the force of the wind. Inside, though, the space felt protected. Steady. The tribe had gathered early, their voices overlapping in easy conversation. Laughter rose in soft bursts. The fire snapped and flared, its light dancing against the stone walls.

We nibbled on dried bear meat, the richness of it lingering on my tongue. I wasn't hungry, not really, but the act of eating, of participating in something ordinary, was grounding.

As I looked around the firelit chamber, I took in the unfamiliar faces of those who had accepted us so easily. Strangers, all of them, and yet I felt no fear. No suspicion. Only a quiet sense of belonging I hadn't expected.

Then I saw Ocevia.

She sat between Markos' legs, her posture mirroring mine. Their fingers were laced together, resting between them like a quiet declaration.

Markos leaned forward to whisper something in her ear, and she smiled, genuine and radiant. Her cheeks were flushed, not with embarrassment, but with something warmer. *Softer.*

They looked comfortable together.

And yet, beneath the comfort, my worry stirred.

She was still learning what love meant, what freedom meant. So was I. And neither of us had been taught how to guard our hearts.

If Miris caught us, even if the men escaped, I knew what the loss would do to me.

I only hoped Ocevia wouldn't have to feel that kind of devastation. I hoped she would never know what it felt like to lose the one person who made you feel safe.

I forced myself to look away.

She was happy.

That mattered more than anything else.

Dimitris arrived well after the rest of us, dragging his feet as he slumped beside Aris with the weight of the previous night still hanging off his shoulders. He didn't say a word, just reached for a canteen and drank as though the water could undo his choices.

His eyes were bloodshot, rimmed in fatigue, and his ginger hair stuck up in every direction, matted and tangled from restless sleep. A woman handed him a strip of dried meat with a sympathetic smile and urged him to eat. He took it but didn't bite, staring at it like it was a test he hadn't studied for.

Even holding down water seemed difficult.

Watching him struggle, I felt oddly thankful for the storm. It had held us hostage, *yes*, but it had also given him the one thing he needed most.

Stillness.

Time passed strangely in the cave. Minutes, maybe hours. I lost track somewhere between the shifting firelight and the way the voices hummed around us, soft and constant like the sound of waves against stone. No clocks. No obligations. Just stories and food and weather.

Here, the world moved differently.

The Arcane people didn't live by rigid rules or schedules. They measured time by tradition, by hunger, by the sky. They told stories not to fill silence, but to pass memory from one voice to another. They lived like a family, even if they weren't one by blood.

And somehow, in their quiet, ritual rhythm, I felt welcome.

Not like a guest. Not like a secret.

Simply welcome.

We sat for what felt like hours, legs aching from the stone floor, bellies warmed by roasted root vegetables and bits of leftover meat. I listened to tales passed around the fire, my eyes half-lidded as I leaned into Elios, full in a way that had nothing to do with food.

Not yet tired, but drifting.

When the weight of the day began to press against me, we slipped away from the circle, back into the winding tunnels.

With most of the camp still gathered around the fire, the tunnels were quiet as Elios and I made our way back to the caves. It was the perfect moment—for privacy, for rest, for relief. I gathered clean clothes and listened carefully for voices. When none came, we slipped into the hot spring.

Steam curled from the water like a beckoning hand, and I didn't hesitate. As I submerged, my body shifted, tail unfurling beneath the surface in a smooth ripple of violet. The warmth surrounded me like a salve, easing the soreness in my spine, my legs, my thoughts.

Compared to the frigid bite of the Lamalis Sea, this water was luxurious.

Elios slid in behind me, his arms winding around my waist, his chest solid against my back. After using a small handful of berries to cleanse his skin, he turned his attention to me, running his hands gently through my hair, working the soap into my scalp.

I closed my eyes and let go. Let the water hold me. Let his touch carry the weight I was too tired to bear. For a moment, nothing else existed—no curses, no monsters, no goddess. Just this heat. Just his breath against my neck.

But peace is always short-lived.

The sound of footsteps broke it.

I froze, barely breathing, still submerged in my mermaid form. Elios tensed behind me as Dimitris entered the chamber with a lazy stride that slowed to a halt the moment his eyes found me.

Even in his bleary state, he stopped cold.

His gaze locked on my tail, shimmering and undeniable beneath the water. His jaw slackened, and his eyes widened, not even flicking to my bare chest above the surface.

He stared.

And I couldn't move.

My heart thudded so hard I felt it in my throat. I stayed still, like if I didn't blink, didn't breathe, I could vanish.

But more footsteps echoed behind him. The rest of our group was coming.

Elios moved first, shifting to block me with his body. His arm came around me in one swift motion, shielding what he could. That touch snapped me back into myself, but it was too late.

Dimitris had seen. They all had.

"You will say nothing," Elios hissed, his voice sharp and final. Not a warning. A *command*.

Dimitris nodded, still frozen, but he didn't look away.

My arms crossed tightly over my chest. Vulnerability burned like an open wound. The rest of the group filtered into the chamber, their eyes taking in more than I wanted to give. Scanning their faces, sinking certainty settled in my gut.

They knew.

Markos didn't react. Ocevia kept her eyes on the floor, fingers working the hem of her tunic. Aris rubbed the back of his neck and stared somewhere above our heads, giving me the grace of his discomfort.

Elios raked a hand through his damp hair, frustration etched across his face. "Make a fire and wait for us," he said tightly. "Looks like we all need to talk."

The others shuffled out, but I stayed where I was, trembling in place, staring into nothing. My thoughts spun in wild circles, trying to make sense of what I'd lost in a moment of carelessness.

If only I had shifted back sooner.

If only we'd waited.

If only…

Elios turned and pulled me to his chest, wrapping me in a tight, protective hold. I let him. I didn't know what else to do.

"They won't say anything," he whispered into my hair.

I wished I believed him. I hated the position I'd put him in. Hated the risk I had become.

"They weren't supposed to know," I whispered. "Not yet."

His hands rubbed up and down my back, trying to ground me.

"This is bad, isn't it?" I said, my voice barely audible.

He pressed a kiss to the top of my head. "It's going to be okay. My men are loyal."

I pulled back enough to look up at him, searching his eyes. "Are you ever going to tell me what you and these men do? I know you're more than just a traveler seeking adventure."

He exhaled through his nose and glanced toward the tunnel, where the firelight still flickered.

"I'll explain everything by the fire," he said. "Let's get out and dress before they come looking for us."

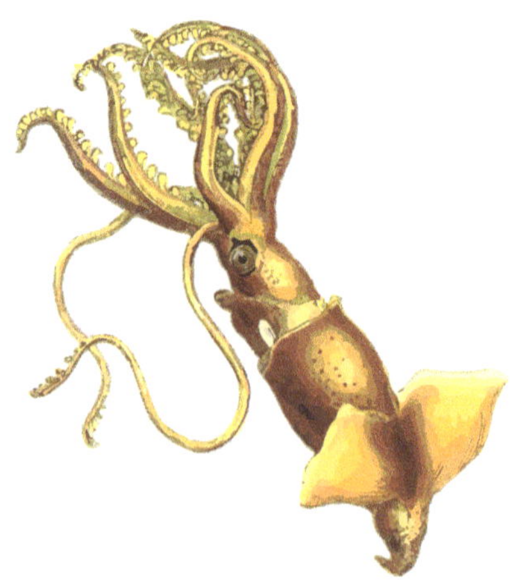

Chapter Twenty-Nine

REVELATION BY THE FIRELIGHT

As Elios requested, our group gathered around the fire pit in the main chamber of the cave, where the air still carried the scent of wet stone and smoke. Aris crouched beside the dying blaze, stirring the glowing coals to bring it back to life. The fire responded eagerly, climbing higher into the dark as shadows stretched across the walls like memories trying to find shape.

Markos settled beside Ocevia with a familiarity that made no effort to disguise itself. His arm rested around her waist, the gesture natural and sure, and the way she leaned into him left no more questions. Whatever they were, they had already become it, quietly and without ceremony. The intimacy between them had always lingered in the way their eyes met or how their steps fell into sync, but now it was confirmed by the ease of closeness, the unspoken understanding between their bodies.

Dimitris sat off to the side, a silent figure whose expression gave little away. The stunned disbelief he had shown earlier had settled into something more carefully composed, a mask of calm that felt deliberate. I couldn't tell if he was angry, uncertain, or simply turning over every piece of truth inside his head in quiet calculation. Whatever he felt, he was keeping it close.

As Elios and I approached the fire, something tight fluttered beneath my ribs. I was still holding his hand too tightly, fingers clenched around his like I was trying to anchor myself, and even though I knew it, I couldn't bring myself to ease the pressure. He didn't seem to mind. His grip remained steady, warm and grounding.

He brought me to the edge of the circle and lowered himself onto the ground. Without hesitation, he pulled me into his lap, his arms coming around me in a protective fold that felt both possessive and gentle. I eased into him slowly, letting the heat of the fire warm one side of me and the steady rise and fall of his chest ground the other. His breath was soft against the side of my neck, and while the knot in my chest didn't fully disappear, it loosened just enough to let me breathe.

"I guess I should give you all an explanation." His voice broke the quiet with a calm that belied the weight of what he was about to say.

The rest of the group remained silent, their attention focused entirely on him. No one moved. No one interrupted.

"We're not traveling with human women, as you now know, but I should start from the beginning."

Without flinching, Elios began to tell them everything. From the shipwreck to our rescue, from our lives beneath the sea to the curse that bound us, he held nothing back. He spoke plainly, the way someone does when the truth is heavy enough that it doesn't need embellishment. He explained who we were and what had been done to us, the way Miris had stolen our freedom and turned us into instruments of death. His words painted the truth in firelight—our curse, the rules we had broken, the lives we had taken, the blood we owed just to taste air again.

Even Ocevia sat quietly, listening to the parts of the story she hadn't lived herself. Though she had found us on the island, there were still details she hadn't heard. She didn't interrupt. None of them did. Aris remained crouched by the fire, still as stone. Dimitris leaned forward, hands clasped tightly together, unmoving.

Aside from our more intimate moments, Elios shared every detail. He didn't glorify it. He didn't shield us from the weight of it. But still, I felt no shame in his voice. Only resolve.

When he finished, the silence stretched. Not heavy with suspicion, just thought. No one stood. No one backed away. I hadn't realized I was holding my breath until the stillness made it feel loud.

Finally, Aris broke the quiet.

"So, are Azure and Ocevia planning to stay out of the sea for good?"

Although I had thought about it more times than I could count, it wasn't a question I had ever been able to answer with certainty. The idea of never returning to the water filled me with a strange ache. Being a mermaid was my curse, but it was also the life I had known. My lungs remembered the sea. My body remembered the way it felt to move through deep currents, to disappear into silence and salt. And yet, it was also where I had suffered most.

I looked at Elios, unsure if he wanted to speak for me, but he only watched, waiting.

Tucking a strand of damp hair behind my ear, I glanced at the others, every face turned toward me with cautious expectation.

"I'm not sure, but I don't want to be anywhere near Miris. If she finds us, she will kill me and Elios. The farther we are from her lair, the safer we will be. Ocevia has never disobeyed the Sea Goddess like I have, so she may survive... after being tortured for running away."

The words hung there, and for a moment, I wished I could take them back, not because they weren't true, but because they felt like a wound spoken aloud.

I looked at Ocevia then and saw the way her shoulders folded inward, quiet but sharp. The sadness in her eyes made my heart twist.

Markos, without a word, leaned over and kissed her temple, the gesture as instinctive as a heartbeat. He held her closer, his jaw set with a promise already made.

"I won't let that happen. Even if I need to take her to another continent, I won't let Ocevia spend another moment in slavery. Not while I'm still drawing breath."

A small smile spread across Ocevia's face, but the emotion behind it was harder to read. There was warmth, yes, but also guilt—something soft and wounded that flickered behind her eyes. I could feel it in her stillness. She believed him, but part of her feared what it might cost him.

Markos cleared his throat, his voice cutting gently through the stillness left in the wake of his promise. "But I have a confession to make..."

His hand, still resting on Ocevia's waist, slid upward along her side with a tenderness that contrasted the weight of what he was about to say. His fingers brushed the edge of her jaw, then moved slowly down her cheek, a soft motion that held more than affection. It was reassurance, a silent plea for her to understand.

"I already knew they were mermaids," he said.

The words landed like a stone dropped into the firelight, sending ripples across the group. For a moment, no one responded.

"The tribal elder, Great Protector, told me when we arrived," he continued, his voice steady now. "I figured Elios already knew. I figured it was why we were running. I didn't want to say anything out of protection for Ocevia and Azure until Elios said something first."

He turned then, shifting his gaze to Elios. There was no challenge in his tone, no accusation. Only a quiet offering of truth, long-held and carefully timed.

"I was going to talk to you about it, Brother, but I was waiting until we got somewhere more secure."

Elios didn't respond right away. I could feel the way his body tensed beneath me, the way his fingers flexed slightly where they rested against my ribs. He didn't look angry. Just tired. Worn thin by too many secrets, too many burdens balanced across the days since we'd escaped the sea.

His jaw clenched for a moment, then loosened as he exhaled. When he finally spoke, his voice was level.

"I would have said something once we arrived in Ceveasea for the same reason you didn't speak up, Markos. It's not that I didn't trust you or our other friends—Aris and Dimitris. We've been through a lot together, and I trust all three of you with my life. But I knew what they were wasn't relevant to our mission, and I couldn't risk anyone finding out who could put them at risk. Anyone at this camp could turn them over for a bit of coin. It was best to keep their secret until we got to a safe house."

His arms tightened slightly around me, drawing me closer against his chest. I didn't miss the way his voice changed at the end, the way it dipped into something softer, something meant for me and Ocevia alone.

"I suppose there is more I need to explain, at least to Azure and Ocevia."

The others remained quiet, listening.

Markos' brow furrowed slightly, but he didn't speak again. Ocevia shifted beside him, sitting straighter, her eyes locked on Elios with quiet attention. I could feel something similar in myself, an unease laced with curiosity, knowing that what he was about to share wasn't easy for him.

Elios turned his gaze toward me. There was no fear in his expression, only the weight of something long held back.

"I told you I've spent my life traveling. That wasn't a lie, but it wasn't the whole truth either."

He reached up, rubbing the back of his neck, the motion almost self-conscious. The firelight flickered across his face, gilding the edge of his jaw in amber, softening him even as the truth began to unravel.

"You asked what The Circle was back at the tavern. Aris, Dimitris, Markos, and I are part of that group. Our mission is to rescue slaves and smuggle them to lands where they can live free."

There was a beat of silence, and then his words began to settle over us like a second fire, slow and warming in the places that had gone cold from fear. I stared at him, not because I was surprised—but because it suddenly made sense. Every moment, every choice, every kindness that had confused me when we first met... this was why.

I didn't know how to respond to his confession, but it settled something in me. The way he had tried to soothe my guilt, the way he had looked at me and never once seen a monster. It all made sense now. He had spent his life walking into danger to free those who couldn't escape it. Of course he had looked at me and seen someone worth saving. That was who he was.

"And Vasso?" I asked quietly, my voice catching slightly on the words.

Elios nodded. "Yes, Vasso and his wife are also part of The Circle, but their roles differ from ours, although they are no less dangerous. Their inn is used to house freed slaves and provide shelter for us when we pass through. It also serves as a communication hub for members. The rest of us, more than twenty now, have dedicated our lives to this cause. Some of us have been doing this since we were teenagers. Many kingdoms still support slavery, with their kings profiting from the trade, but we do our best to rescue those we can."

His words washed over me, and I absorbed them in silence. I thought of the long days he'd spent on ships, in taverns, in strange cities where every smile could be a trap and every step could lead to capture. He hadn't just saved me. He had saved countless others. And he would have continued to save others, even if I had never crossed his path.

A quiet awe stirred beneath my ribs. The life he had risked, the choices he had made, the way he had folded his arms around me without asking for anything in return... I loved him more in that moment than I knew how to say.

And yet beneath that love, another feeling bloomed too—*fear*. Not of him. But of what this life might take from him.

Even with all I'd heard, and with Markos' arm still wrapped firmly around my waist, there was a question that weighed heavily on my mind. It lingered like a shadow behind the warmth of the fire, behind every promise and every confession. I felt it settle in my chest as the others began to quietly absorb what had been said.

"So, what happens to us now?"

The words came out quieter than I expected, not fearful, but stripped bare. I wasn't asking to challenge the plan. I was asking to see if there *was* one at all.

Markos' body tensed behind me. I felt the way his muscles coiled beneath his shirt as though the thought of an uncertain future triggered some primal instinct to protect. His hand slid across my back, steady and grounding, but he didn't speak. It was Elios who answered.

"Nothing changes from here," he said. "We'll leave this camp when the weather clears and make our way through the mountain pass to the city of Ceveasea. If we hear any word of Miris' people snooping around, we'll move further inland."

His voice was even, the tone of someone who had spent years planning escape routes and contingencies. Every word was laced with quiet certainty, not just for Azure and me, but for the entire group. He wasn't only protecting us. He was guiding all of them now.

"Aris and Dimitris will eventually return to Starspell for their next assignment," he added, glancing toward the two men beside the fire. "But I assume Markos will stay with us."

Before everyone turned to Markos, Aris and Dimitris both nodded in agreement. Their loyalty was quiet, but it was there. I had been bracing for disappointment, unsure if they'd choose to walk away once our truth was laid bare. But they didn't flinch. They didn't hesitate. It was enough to loosen something in my chest I hadn't realized I'd been holding.

Markos didn't need time to answer.

"I won't leave Ocevia," he said. "There's nothing back in Starspell for me. I can still do my job from inland."

The way he said it left no room for argument. No apology. No second-guessing. His arm tightened around me again, and I leaned into the warmth of his body, letting it sink in that, for the first time in years, I had someone who didn't intend to let go.

Ocevia melted against Markos as he rubbed her back, his movements slow and reassuring. Her posture softened, her expression calm. I had seen her fight and endure and bleed, but never like this. Never this quiet, this grounded. She looked more at peace than I had ever seen her, and the sight of it stirred something deep in my chest.

It was more than relief. It was longing.

Not just for safety, but for something simpler.

The kind of ease that came from being wanted without question. The kind of stillness that came from knowing you no longer had to survive alone.

There had never been time for conversations about men, never space for romance between drowning and death. But now, as I looked across the fire at my oldest friend and saw her resting in the arms of someone who loved her without condition, I felt something unfamiliar rise in me.

Maybe we could talk about things like that now. Maybe we could build something new out of everything we had survived.

The fire burned low, its glow dimming to embers as the others rose one by one, dispersing in our cavern. No goodnights were exchanged, only the soft scrape of boots on stone, the hush of fading voices, and the shared understanding that something between us had shifted. The circle no longer held suspicion. Only trust.

With our secret laid bare and the men still choosing to stand beside us, the storm I had carried in my chest began to settle. Not vanish but shift just enough to let me breathe. I followed Elios deeper into the cavern, where the Arcane had prepared raised sleeping platforms along the walls. Thick furs lined the surfaces, softening the stone beneath and holding the warmth of the fire that still flickered in the distance. The air was cool, laced with the scent of smoke and mineral-rich earth, but the space felt safe.

Elios climbed onto the platform first, then reached for me without a word. I joined him, sinking into the furs as he pulled a blanket over us and wrapped his arm securely around my waist. I let myself lean into him, resting my body against the steady comfort of his warmth. For the first time since I'd been cursed, I let myself believe in this quiet closeness—not as a danger, but as something earned.

I didn't expect peace to last. I didn't believe safety would stay.

But for tonight, at least, the fear had grown quiet.

And in that quiet, I slept.

TOWARD HOPE

By the following day, the storm had passed, leaving the sky scrubbed clean and the path ahead stretched wide like a promise that could not yet be trusted. The wind carried a damp chill, a sharp breath against my skin, and though the trail ahead would no doubt be thick with mud, that wasn't reason enough to stay. The longer we lingered in one place, the greater the risk. Miris' reach was long, and her fury patient. Sooner or later, her shadows would find us.

We couldn't afford another day of waiting.

After thanking the Arcane tribe for their hospitality and enduring a round of heartfelt goodbyes, we readied the horses, secured our supplies, and set off for Ceveasea. The morning was quiet, but not peaceful. Hooded cloaks masked our identities once again—a precaution Elios insisted on, and one I no longer questioned. With every step, I felt the weight of the past pressing close, like the hem of my cloak tugging at my heels.

As I pulled the fabric tight around my shoulders, a thought burrowed into the back of my mind. Would I be hiding my face until the day I died? Would every glimpse of the sun have to be stolen from behind a veil of secrecy?

No matter how far I ran, she would chase me.

Miris was not a goddess who forgave. She was a predator who hunted without rest, a storm that wore the face of beauty and swallowed everything whole.

I leaned into Elios' warmth as we rode, grateful for the clothing Vasso and his wife had provided. The coat was a little long in the sleeves, the boots a little stiff from age, but they held the cold at bay. I was thankful. Before we'd left camp, Ocevia and I had taken one final soak in the hot spring, a brief, shared moment of silence beneath the steam. Now I wished we'd stayed longer. The wind was colder than I expected, and though Elios was confident we would reach the border city by nightfall, I had learned not to place too much faith in certainty.

I prayed he was right. Not only to avoid the night creatures he had warned me about, but because I longed for firelight and the familiar curve of his arms around me.

The path we traveled was one of warnings and whispered stories. Rumors marked this route as dangerous, overrun with bandits who preyed on travelers too desperate or too naïve to turn back. I stayed alert, my gaze constantly shifting between tree lines and rock formations, watching for movement in the shadows or the glint of steel where it didn't belong. I had survived worse than blades and travelers, but that didn't mean I welcomed the test.

As the trail narrowed and dipped into winding terrain, my thoughts began to drift. No matter how far we traveled, no matter how urgently the present pressed against me, my mind always found its way back to her.

Daneliya.

I didn't know where she was now. I didn't know who had taken her in after Miris tore our lives apart. Was she still in Thatia, or had she been sent elsewhere? Was she safe? The only thing I knew for certain was that she was nearly eleven now. Nearly grown. Nearly a stranger. She had lived years without me. That truth sank into my chest with quiet weight, always there, even in moments that should have felt brighter.

The thought of her in an orphanage, or worse, in the care of someone unkind, gnawed at me with cruel persistence. She was the only family I had left. I had missed everything—birthdays, seasons, her changing laugh, her changing voice. Even when joy found me, the grief was never far behind. It sat beneath my ribs like a stone, patient and unmoving.

Having Elios in my life didn't erase that pain, but his presence softened it. He was a steady flame in a world that had taught me to fear fire. Still, no matter how deeply I loved him, there would always be a part of me shaped by the absence of my sister. That ache wasn't something love could replace.

"We'll stop for a break soon," Elios murmured against my ear, his breath a warm pulse on my cheek. "Are you hungry?"

I shrugged, though the tension in my stomach had little to do with food. "I'll eat. How much farther do we have to go?"

He glanced toward the horizon, eyes narrowed as though reading the map carved into the mountain's spine. "About five hours left, give or take. But I'd like to make better time. We shouldn't stop for long. I don't want to be caught in these mountains overnight."

The warning in his voice settled over me like frost. A shiver moved through me at the thought of what waited in the dark. Of what might be listening even now.

"What happens if we don't make it?" The question escaped before I could swallow it.

Elios leaned in and kissed my cheek, slow and certain. "Even if we lose daylight, we'll be okay. There are caves along the pass where we can shelter and light fires to keep night creatures away. I'd rather avoid it, but I won't let anything happen to you. Don't worry."

His voice had that quiet conviction again, the kind that wrapped around fear and steadied it. I believed him. I didn't doubt that he would fight for me.

What haunted me most wasn't whether he would try.

It was what would happen if trying wasn't enough.

Still, I leaned into his chest, letting the motion of the horse lull my thoughts back into the present. The trail curled between jagged cliffs and dense trees. The terrain was stark, yet strangely beautiful. Tufts of green clung to stubborn soil. Peaks rose like the bones of old gods, reaching for a sky the color of pale silver.

Between them, shadows pooled in hollows and under ledges, places the sun had not yet reached.

Places where danger might already be watching.

When we reached a narrow stream that cut across the trail, the horses slowed to a natural halt. The soft murmur of water filled the quiet space between cliffs, its voice calm and constant in a way that made the mountains feel almost sacred. We dismounted without a word, stretching our limbs and moving to refill the canteens. The water sparkled clear and cold, threading over smooth stone and splashing into shallow pools. A patch of grass along the bank gave the horses a place to graze while we rested, and the chill in the air made the cold water bite sharper than expected.

Ocevia and I shared a look before stepping closer to the stream's edge. Without needing to speak, we slipped off our boots and dipped our legs beneath the surface. A shimmer of magic stirred through the current as our bodies responded to the call of water, shifting beneath the surface into our true forms. Our tails, bright and shimmering even in shadow, moved through the water.

It hadn't been long since we last soaked, but we never knew when the next chance might come. Better to take it now, to reset the twenty-four-hour clock rather than risk the pain of transformation when it was too late to stop it.

The moment passed quietly. Once we stepped from the water, we dried quickly, wrapped in clean trousers and cloaks that still smelled faintly of smoke and pine. Then we joined the others for a late midday meal.

The dried bear meat we'd carried from the Arcane camp had an odd texture—chewy and tough, smoky in a way that clung to the back of the throat—but it was a welcome change from fish. I couldn't decide if I liked the flavor or if I was just grateful to eat something different. Either way, I kept chewing.

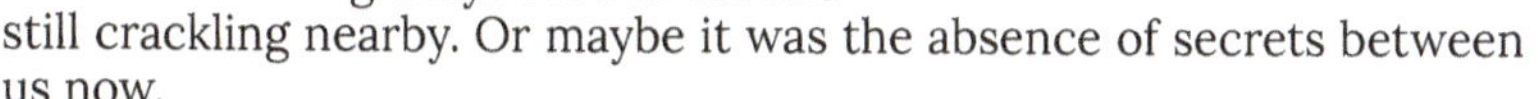

We sat in a hollow beside the stream, the cliffs cupping us from the wind. Around us, the air felt lighter than it had since we left the coast. Maybe it was the break from riding. Maybe it was the fire still crackling nearby. Or maybe it was the absence of secrets between us now.

Whatever it was, something had shifted.

A quiet camaraderie settled across the group. Elios and Dimitris sat side by side, their blades balanced in their laps as they passed whetstones slowly across the steel. The rhythmic rasp of metal against stone was a calming sound, one that felt almost ritualistic. Between strokes, they traded stories—old rescues, failed plans, near misses and narrow escapes. I only half-listened, my eyes following the way Elios' muscles flexed as he worked. Occasionally, he'd lean over to steal a piece of dried fruit or bread from my plate, grinning like he was ten years younger and hadn't a care in the world.

Not far from us, Ocevia sat cross-legged beside Aris, weaving sections of his long golden hair into tight, careful braids. Her expression was calm, intent, and something about the simplicity of it caught me off guard. Markos was beside her, reclined on a flat rock with his arms folded behind his head, one boot resting over the other. His eyes were half-closed, but his presence was anything but idle. He was listening. Watching. A silent protector.

The scene around me felt surreal—so different from the days we'd spent fighting for every scrap of safety. These men would kill for us. Bleed for us. But now, for a few quiet hours, they traded stories and passed around food like brothers around a campfire. I hadn't expected to find peace like this in the mountains.

"Have you spoken to Kimon recently?" Dimitris asked, breaking the soft rhythm of blades and stories.

Elios paused mid-stroke. He lifted the blade slightly and glanced over. "About six months ago. Why? Something new?"

Dimitris gave a low chuckle. "You remember that woman he was seeing? Emilia, maybe? Turns out our old friend got her pregnant. Word is, they're married now."

Elios laughed and resumed his work. "Good for him." Then he looked toward me, his eyes warm. He reached for my hand and threaded his fingers through mine. "We should all be so lucky to have a good woman to come home to. I know I feel like the luckiest man alive. Once I get my lady to safety, all will be right with the world."

His thumb brushed over mine. The words were light, said with a smile, but they landed deeper than he likely intended. I held his hand a little tighter.

"I hope to find someone just as special one day, brother," Dimitris said, his voice sincere, with none of the teasing he usually carried.

Elios rose then, stretching his arms overhead until his joints popped. He clapped Dimitris on the shoulder with affection, then turned toward the rest of us.

"Let's get moving again. I don't want these ladies stuck in the cold after dark."

His tone was casual, but there was steel behind it. We all felt it. No one argued.

We packed quickly, folding blankets and securing gear. Within minutes we were on horseback again, turning inland once more. The sun had begun its descent behind the mountains, its light washing the path in soft gold and long shadows. With each mile, the scent of saltwater faded, replaced by pine and stone and the faint smell of snow drifting from the peaks above.

With each mile, the sea faded behind us, and Miris' presence slipped further from reach.

Though never far enough.

As we crossed another stream, the terrain began to rise in earnest. The forest floor gave way to stone, and the trail beneath the horses' hooves turned uneven and narrow. Each step echoed with the sharp strike of metal on rock, and the wind that met us was colder than before. It pushed between the cliffs like it had a purpose, curling beneath our cloaks and stinging our skin with the promise of higher altitude.

We were climbing toward the highest point of our journey.

The road ahead wound through a pass carved by time, a path that threaded the border between two vast kingdoms. Ceveasea lay just beyond, nestled in the valley between Avrearyn and Dekresian. I didn't know much about it. Only that it was distant, and that getting there meant leaving behind everything I had ever known. It was more than a city. It was a threshold, and something in me stirred at the thought of it.

What kind of people lived in a place like that? Would they look at me and see the monster I used to be? Would they sense the sea still clinging to my bones, no matter how far I traveled from it?

I turned my head slightly toward Elios, my voice soft against the hum of wind. "Is Ceveasea in the kingdom of Avrearyn or Dekresian?"

He had one hand on the reins and the other resting lightly on my thigh, his fingers tracing slow circles through the fabric of my trousers. I wasn't sure he even realized he was doing it. The warmth of his touch was a quiet rhythm, one that helped drive the chill from my limbs.

"Technically Dekresian," he replied, his voice close to my ear. "But both kingdoms claim it, since it's right on the border."

His hand moved a little higher, each pass sending a slow heat through me. I shifted in the saddle, trying to stay focused, but the closeness of his body made the mountains feel farther away.

"Dekresian outlawed slavery a decade ago," he continued. "Their king, the Tamer of the Fire, was a slave himself until he escaped as a teenager.

Because of that history, the kingdom's become a haven. It's usually where we take the people we rescue."

Hope stirred in me, quiet and tentative. The idea of a kingdom where freedom wasn't just a story someone told at night felt almost too large to hold. It was a fragile thing, that hope. But it warmed me more than the cloak around my shoulders.

I closed my eyes, leaning into Elios' chest as he nuzzled against the curve of my neck. His lips brushed my skin, and shivers trailed down my spine, not from cold this time, but from him.

"Do any of the kingdoms know what Miris is doing?" I asked, though I already knew what he would say.

He shook his head. "Like mermaids, she's a myth to most. Real to very few. There are rumors, sure, but people treat them like bedtime tales. If every legend were true, we'd live in a world full of monsters and magic, hiding in plain sight."

He paused, then kissed the edge of my jaw, slow and deliberate.

"Then again," he murmured against my skin, "since mermaids are real... who knows how many others are too?"

His words stayed with me as we rode, their warmth lingering even as the wind picked up again. I tucked my head beneath his chin, letting the steady rise and fall of his breathing match my own.

For a while, no one spoke.

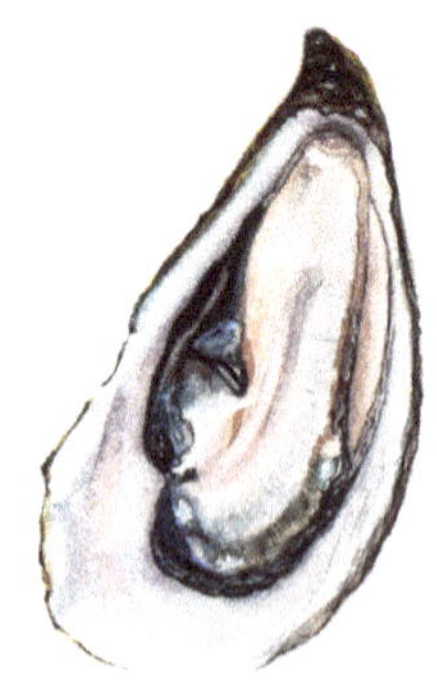

The silence wasn't tense or uncertain. It was the kind of silence that only came when there was nothing more to explain, when words became unnecessary because the presence of another person said enough.

The trail narrowed again, winding along the edge of a ridge that overlooked a vast valley. Jagged peaks cut into the sky beyond, their sharp silhouettes touched with the fading gold of late afternoon. The sun was sinking, and with it, the world turned quieter. Heavier. The kind of quiet that made you pay attention.

Each step the horses took sent loose pebbles tumbling down the cliff sides. I watched them fall and wondered if Miris could feel it—how far we had come. How far I had climbed to escape her grasp. I wondered if she could still taste my fear in the air.

With each mile that passed beneath us, the weight in my chest lifted little by little.

We were riding toward something. Not quite freedom. Not yet. But something that moved in the same direction. Something that smelled of pine and moss instead of salt and blood. The farther we got from the sea, the quieter my thoughts became.

But not silent.

Never silent.

Beneath the calm, the ache for Daneliya remained. The guilt. The fear of what waited behind us. The certainty that Miris had not given up her pursuit. All of it lingered beneath the surface, woven through my body like thread.

But now, for the first time in so long, I felt something else rising alongside it.

Hope. Gentle and uncertain, but real.

And for once, I didn't push it away.

I held it close.

Chapter Thirty-One

Hunted in the Dark

Although the sun had long since set and the sky blanketed us in moonlight, a knot of weariness and hope twisted quietly inside me. The city lights on the horizon felt close enough to touch, but something in the night pressed against my skin like a warning. Our group chose not to make camp. With the city lights just over the next ridge, Elios and the others decided it was better to press forward than risk sleeping in a cave overnight. The choice hadn't come easily. Danger lurked either way but walking another hour through the dark seemed safer than spending an entire night exposed in the wilderness.

Despite the city's nearness, it never seemed to draw closer. Maybe our horses were tired, or perhaps the saddle's rhythmic sway lulled me too deeply, but the glow of distant lanterns remained stubbornly fixed on the horizon. Shadows thickened around us as we passed through the final line of jagged peaks, and the mountains grew deathly still, as though they too were holding their breath.

A knot of unease twisted low in my stomach. The night air felt charged, as if the mountain itself was waiting for something. I could sense the tension coiling in Elios' posture behind me. We had faced danger before, but this stillness was different. It felt expectant. Watching.

Slowing our horse, Elios reached for his sword hilt and scanned the darkness ahead. Whatever he was searching for, the grim set of his jaw made my pulse stumble. One by one, the others began to ease their mounts, eyes sweeping the terrain, alert and silent.

Breath caught in my chest as Elios passed me the reins and wrapped his free arm around my waist. His sword came free with a metallic whisper. I barely knew how to control a horse. Before my curse, I'd only ridden a handful of times, and even then, only under careful supervision. Luckily, Dark Heart moved steadily forward without needing my command.

From somewhere up the ridge, a hiss split the silence—sharp, reptilian, and menacing. It echoed off the cliffs like a threat.

Dark Heart stumbled, his hooves faltering. His tail lashed, a nervous tremor racing through his powerful frame.

My gaze darted around the shadows. "What was that?" The whisper barely escaped me.

In response, Elios pulled me closer and signaled to the others with a small nod. Blades emerged around us. The three men of The Circle gripped their hilts, eyes locked on the dark beyond the pass. Though I couldn't see Ocevia, rapid breathing reached my ears. Hers or mine, I couldn't tell. The fear was mutual.

Off to the left, Dimitris whistled softly, his chin jerking toward a stretch of darkness no different from the rest. Something waited there. Watching. Stalking.

Then, without warning, the snap of wings echoed like cracking thunder.

I shrank into Elios as Aris darted in, his sword flashing as he swung. The blade caught only air. A blur shifted at the edge of my vision, some dark shape that vanished again into shadow.

Above us, chattering sounds erupted, strange and wild, unlike anything I had ever heard. They echoed off the cliffs, bouncing in every direction, confusing and terrible. I couldn't tell how many creatures surrounded us. Maybe one. Maybe dozens.

Another hiss gave way to the rush of wings.

With a shriek, the beast dove toward us again, this time aiming directly for Dark Heart.

Elios struck with perfect timing.

His blade met flesh, and the creature screamed, an awful, high-pitched sound that cut through the night like a knife through cloth. Hands flying to my ears, I tried to shield them from the shrill noise. Above, the creature retreated, wings beating the air as it disappeared into the blackness.

Darkness concealed its shape, and its speed made it impossible to track. Yet Elios and the others seemed to know exactly what we were facing. With a sharp tug, he took the reins from my hands, urged Dark Heart into a sprint, and pressed a kiss to my neck.

"I love you," he whispered, then vanished from my back.

Panic surged as I twisted, fearing he had leapt into the dark.

Before the scream could rise in my throat, I saw him.

He hadn't jumped.

Elios now stood balanced on the saddle, blade poised, boots secured in stirrup holds I hadn't known existed.

A flicker of motion to the side revealed Aris doing the same. My breath hitched as both men adjusted effortlessly to the galloping horses, as though it were second nature.

Behind them, Dimitris joined the fray, his posture just as sure, just as deadly.

With a mixture of horror and awe, I watched their synchronized movements and prayed none of them would fall.

A sharp whistle from Dimitris sliced through the air, another warning.

Just seconds later, the creature descended again, a blur of wings and malice. It struck with brutal force, knocking Aris clean off his horse. A cry tore from my throat as his body hit the ground with a sickening thud, his horse thundering ahead without him. Dark Heart kept running, but my gaze locked on Aris, unmoving in the dust.

My chest constricted. Pain twisted through me like a blade.

He had fallen protecting me and Ocevia. We were both in its path.

A sob escaped, ragged and choked.

To our left, something landed beside Aris with a bone-jarring thump.

The silhouette that loomed over him was vaguely humanoid, tall, black-winged, *monstrous*. I squinted into the dark, trying to make sense of what I was seeing. With pale, chalky hands, it reached for Aris. My breath caught, the sound snagging in my throat as I watched in helpless horror. I wanted to scream, to move, to do something, but all I could do was grip the reins tighter and pray Dimitris reached him in time. My body felt frozen, like the fear had turned my limbs to stone.

Dimitris, still balanced on his saddle, pulled hard on the reins, spinning his horse around. Without hesitation, the beast galloped straight toward the attacker. Just before colliding, Dimitris leapt from the saddle, blade already swinging. The force of the blow severed the creature's head before it even sensed him coming.

Its body collapsed, the severed head rolling to a stop near the horse's hooves.

I stared, barely breathing, desperate for any sign of life from Aris. A twitch. A breath. A word.

But above me, another shriek tore the night apart.

This time, the scream came from Elios.

Or maybe it came from the monster he fought.

Before I could react, another humanoid figure swooped toward me. In one smooth motion, Elios met it midair, slicing through its torso with a single devastating strike. Blood sprayed across my tunic, hot and sudden, splashing across my face. I squeezed my eyes shut as dizziness swept over me, pulse thundering. I didn't dare open them.

A sickening crunch against the nearby cliff told me the creature had been thrown into stone.

Elios dropped into the saddle behind me, grabbing the reins and wheeling Dark Heart around. We raced back toward the fallen.

By the time we reached them, Markos and Ocevia had already dismounted. Ocevia stood close to him, her breathing shallow and quick, like she hadn't yet escaped the fear of the fight. A torch in Markos' hand lit the scene, its flame flickering across the rocks, catching on blood and stone alike. When I saw Aris speaking, actually speaking, to Dimitris,  a sob of relief broke free, tears tracking down my blood-spattered cheeks. Dimitris knelt beside him, inspecting the angry wounds on Aris' midsection.

Everything was still. The silence that followed wasn't peace. It was the breath the world takes after something breaks. I dismounted slowly, legs trembling as I found my footing on the rocky path. Elios joined the others, crouching beside Aris to help tend to his injuries, but I couldn't move toward them. My body felt hollow. All I could do was look.

My eyes caught on something near my feet, and I froze.

The creature's severed head lay in the dirt, its face turned away, a curtain of black hair soaked with blood hiding most of its features. For a moment I could breathe. It was just a dead thing, no longer a threat.

Then Markos stepped forward. With Ocevia tucked protectively against his side, he nudged the head with the toe of his boot.

It rolled to a stop, and the breath caught painfully in my throat.

Even in death, its eyes burned with hatred. Crimson irises stared out from a face so pale it looked carved from moonlight. Its features were distorted, inhuman. Elongated fangs jutted from its mouth, and its lips were torn where it had screamed.

The bile in my throat surged and I stumbled back, one hand pressed to my mouth.

Revulsion surged up before I could stop it, and I doubled over, retching into the dirt as the horror of what I'd seen overtook every other thought.

This thing—this *monster*—had once been human. I could feel it in my bones. Whatever it had become, whatever it had lost, it had started like us. It had been made, just like me. Not born into horror but shaped by it. My mind reeled. I wanted to believe there was still something left inside it, something that remembered what it once was. But maybe not. Maybe whatever did this had taken everything. And the thought of being reshaped like that, of being unmade, terrified me.

It could happen to anyone.

Recognition.

Markos' voice cut through the haze, low and cold. "You picked the wrong prey tonight." Without waiting for a response from the world or the corpse, he kicked the creature's head. It struck the rock wall with a sickening splatter, then vanished into the dark like it had never belonged to anything human.

Behind me, Aris groaned, trying to sit up, the effort twisting his face with pain. The sound snapped me back to the present. He was still hurt, and it was still my fault.

As I stood by helplessly, Dimitris and Elios remained beside Aris, discussing how to get him to the city. Although they were strong, Aris was larger than both of them, making it a difficult task to lift him.

Markos released Ocevia's hand and stepped forward, slipping beneath one of Aris' arms to help support him. The three of them worked together silently, guiding their friend slowly toward Dimitris' horse.

Aris leaned heavily against them, one arm wrapped around his middle as he protected what was likely a set of broken ribs. His jaw was clenched tight, and pain was etched into every line of his face.

Once they reached the horse, they worked in quiet coordination to lift Aris into the saddle. He slumped forward, his posture heavy with exhaustion. Dimitris mounted behind him, looping an arm firmly around his chest to keep him steady before giving the reins a gentle tug.

The horse moved forward at a slow, cautious pace.

Markos returned to Ocevia and gently gathered her into his arms. She offered no resistance, only sagged against his chest, her eyes wide and vacant. With practiced ease, he lifted her onto their horse and swung up behind her.

After securing Aris' horse to Dark Heart's saddle, Elios turned to me and extended a hand. I placed mine in his, grateful for the strength he offered as he helped me climb up. My legs still trembled, more from what we'd just survived than exhaustion.

Once I was seated, he mounted behind me and guided Dark Heart back to the trail, the city lights waiting just beyond the ridge.

The city waited just over the next ridge.

Around us, the night exhaled. Crickets resumed their quiet song. An owl called from somewhere far above, and the world pretended, for a moment, that the violence had passed.

But I felt it in every beat of my heart, in the tension coiling through my chest and the dread sinking into my bones.

Though the creatures were gone, their presence lingered like smoke.

And as we rode toward the lights of Ceveasea, I couldn't shake the feeling that something else still waited in the dark.

THE SILENT STREETS

We reached Ceveasea without encountering any further attacks, but the relief was bitter. The quiet that awaited us wasn't comfort, it was foreboding. The city sat hollow and still, as though it had braced for something and decided to never unbrace.

Shadows pooled in every corner. The streets were empty, not a single soul lingering under the pale gleam of the moon. Even the taverns were shuttered. No music, no firelight spilling from open doors, no laughter. Just silence, and that silence pressed in close.

I had never known a human city to be so devoid of life, not even before the curse. This was different. This was fear.

"Where is everyone?" I asked. My voice felt too loud, too alive, like it didn't belong in this place. Every time our horses' hooves struck the cobblestone, I flinched.

Elios looked up at the sky, his voice low. "The citizens know what lurks outside their borders and are smart enough to avoid it. Unlike Starspell, you won't find many people in the open here after the sun goes down."

A chill ghosted over my arms as I scanned the alleyways, half expecting glowing eyes to blink from the dark. We were exposed, vulnerable, and my heart hadn't stopped racing since the attack.

But then the street narrowed, and we turned a corner.

A high stone wall loomed ahead, its iron gate closed tight. A single lantern hung beside it, swaying in the breeze. Behind the bars, a man watched us. His face was half-cast in shadow, but his posture was steady, unflinching.

He didn't speak. He just looked, and I hated that I couldn't tell if he was assessing us for danger or silently mourning the fact we'd survived.

After a beat, he moved and pushed the gate open. Its hinges groaned like the bones of something old.

We rode through as the quiet folded in behind us. The man—grizzled, late fifties maybe—didn't look surprised to see us. He just closed the gate again, locking it with a heavy clang that echoed through the small courtyard.

"Staying for long, Elios?" he rasped, stepping into the flickering lantern light. His eyes passed briefly over each of us, but there was no warmth in the way they lingered. Just recognition.

Elios didn't answer immediately. He dismounted, then reached up for me, his hands steady at my waist. The moment his fingers brushed my sides, I exhaled too sharply, too fast. He didn't notice.

Or maybe he did and chose not to mention it.

I slid down into his arms, and for a second, I let myself lean into his chest. Just for the contact. Just for the grounding. Then I stepped away.

While he led our horse to the stable near a stack of hay, I stood beneath the lantern, its soft glow making the courtyard feel smaller. More intimate. Less safe.

"We're not sure how long this time, Old Man," Elios called out. "Do you have a few rooms for us? Say, three?"

"Aye," the man said simply, already moving to prepare the stalls.

Beside me, Markos helped Ocevia down, his hand lingering briefly at her waist. When I met her eyes, I saw the same exhaustion I felt. Beneath that, something harder. The guilt we shared, though we hadn't yet spoken it aloud.

The men turned to Aris next. Carefully, grimly, they lifted his unconscious body from the saddle. He groaned—barely—but it was enough to twist something deep in my chest. His face was ashen, jaw clenched tight. His body sagged between them, and I couldn't tell if he was still fighting or had already started to let go.

I looked away.

"Is Phaedra inside, Georgios?" Markos asked, bracing Aris' weight as he reached for the building's heavy wooden door.

"Yes. Yes, she's inside." Georgios waved them toward the entrance like he was done being part of the night.

Ocevia found my hand and twined our fingers together. Her grip was cool and steady, but I felt the tension in it.

We followed the others through the threshold.

The air inside was cooler, *heavier*. The scent of aged wood, herbs, and dust filled the narrow corridor. A single lantern burned along the far wall, but it wasn't enough to soften the shadows. They clung to the corners like smoke.

We passed through a storage room lined with crates and into a hallway barely wide enough for two. Our footsteps felt too loud, as if the building itself were listening. Every floorboard creaked beneath our boots like bones groaning under strain.

At the end of the hall stood a set of tall double doors. Elios shifted Aris' weight to Dimitris and Markos, crouched, and pulled something from his coat. A small bronze medallion. The same symbol was inked on his chest—the broken chain.

Without a word, Elios slid the medallion beneath the door. A pause, no more than a breath, and then the lock disengaged with a soft click.

The woman who opened it wasn't what I expected.

Tall and poised, she carried herself with the stillness of someone who had long ago stopped flinching. Severity clung to her—not as cruelty, but as control. Her curls were pinned back into a knot at the nape of her neck, though a few strands had escaped to frame her angular face. A scar curved from beneath her right eye to her cheek, pale and raised, like the memory of a tear carved into skin.

She didn't speak. Didn't smile. She simply stepped aside, holding the door open with the calmness of someone who had seen far worse, and knew we were only the beginning.

They carried Aris into the room and laid him out on a wide table.

"What happened to him?" she asked, reaching for a dagger without waiting for an answer.

Elios stepped in to help, and together they cut away the shredded trousers. Deep bruising marked Aris's side, and his leg bent at an unnatural angle. His eyes fluttered open, glazed with pain, before slipping shut again.

I backed away, my stomach tightening as guilt pressed behind my ribs. I couldn't look at him like that... so broken. Not when I still had strength in my limbs and breath in my lungs. Not when this pain had followed us.

On a nearby table, I caught sight of a small bronze medallion etched with a broken chain. It matched the tattoo on Elios' chest. A symbol of The Circle. I wondered if Dimitris bore it, too.

"Vampires. A few of them attacked us on our way into the city and knocked him off his horse," Elios said, pulling me from my thoughts.

The woman, Phaedra, shook her head, pulling a small vial from her apron. "Was he bitten?"

"No." Elios tilted Aris's head back while she dropped a few violet drops into his mouth.

They moved in quiet coordination, hands steady and sure, as though this routine had been rehearsed many times before. There was no wasted motion. No panic. Just quiet skill born from necessity.

I slipped onto the settee between Markos and Dimitris, the leather cool beneath my legs. A moment later, Ocevia joined us, her features drawn tight with exhaustion and something quieter—*worry*.

"He just fell from his horse? His left leg is broken, and he has a few broken ribs as well. There are no signs of head trauma, but there might be some internal bleeding. A few broken bones wouldn't be enough to make this big man pass out," Phaedra responded.

Her voice wasn't judgmental. Just... measured. Precise. Like everything about her.

We all watched as she bound Aris' ribs and splinted his leg, her face not revealing any emotion. Despite the efficiency, my stomach churned. He was strong, one of the strongest, but even he wasn't invincible. The sea had taught me what broke could stay broken.

Relief stirred somewhere under the dread, soft but tentative. We'd found her in time.

But he wouldn't be going anywhere anytime soon.

Once Aris' wounds were tended to and he'd been given medicine for pain, Phaedra washed her hands, then pulled a set of keys from her apron.

"You three can carry him into the sickroom across the hall. Then I'll show you to your rooms," she said, gesturing toward the double doors.

My heart beat faster as she turned to Elios and asked, "Will you be staying long, Elios?"

He gave a soft nod. "We'll be here for a while. Thank you for your hospitality, Phaedra... and your discretion."

She held his gaze a moment longer, then turned without another word. Her footsteps creaked down the stairs, vanishing into the stillness that swallowed the rest of the house.

Ocevia and I followed the Elios to one of the rooms across the hall, the floorboards whispering beneath our steps. When he pushed the door open, it creaked like it hadn't been used in weeks, revealing a narrow chamber cloaked in flickering candlelight. The glow clung to the dark wood paneling but couldn't quite reach the corners, leaving the shadows to breathe and settle where they pleased.

The room was spare, just a modest double bed with a worn wool blanket, a round table barely large enough for two, and a pair of chairs tucked close beneath it like they were hiding from the cold. The windows were shuttered tight, thick iron locks bolted into place, not to keep something in, but to keep something out. Whatever this building had once been, it was clear it had since become a sanctuary built by necessity.

It wasn't beautiful. It didn't offer comfort or softness.

But it held the promise of a closed door. A lock that turned. A pause in the running.

And tonight, that was enough to call it safe.

After everything we'd been through, safety felt decadent.

I stepped into the room slowly, letting the door close behind me with a quiet thud. Candlelight flickered along the wood-paneled walls, casting shadows that shifted and stretched with each movement. The room was compact, the air still and warm, smelling faintly of dust.

My gaze caught on a second door off the bedroom. I crossed the room, opened it, and nearly sagged in relief. A narrow bathing chamber waited on the other side. The tub inside was shallow, just large enough to slip into, but it was private. *Safe.* The kind of space that let me breathe without fear.

The ache beneath my ribs loosened. Not much, but enough.

Having a place where Ocevia and I could soak our tails in secret wasn't just comfort. It was mercy.

Behind me, Elios moved around the room, lighting the remaining candles one by one, each new flame gilding his jawline in gold. The glow caught in the hollows of his cheeks, and for a breathless moment, I simply stared.

He didn't speak. He didn't need to. His presence filled the room like heat from a banked fire, steady and certain. There was strength in him, yes, but also something gentler. Not fragility. Not hesitation. Just warmth. Real warmth. Not the kind the sea offered right before it stole your breath.

"What is this place?" I asked, hanging my cloak on the back of a chair and gazing out of the window at the darkened street.

"The Dusty Lantern serves a lot of purposes," he said, glancing back at me. "There's a tavern downstairs. An infirmary. The inn's up top. People come here when there's nowhere else to go. When they're too hurt or too hunted to keep running."

He lit the last candle and turned to face me. "It's strange, but it works. Especially with Phaedra patching people up."

Fatigue rasped along the edges of his voice, but a small smile still broke through. It was faint, but it was real.

Reaching for me without hesitation, he wrapped his arms around my waist.

I wasn't prepared for it. Not the warmth. Not the certainty. Not the way it unraveled something tight and aching inside my chest.

His hold wasn't rushed or desperate—just... *sure*. Like this was something he'd been meaning to do for a long time.

Before my thoughts could catch up, I melted into him. My forehead found the curve of his throat, and I breathed him in: salt, smoke, worn leather, the faintest trace of iron. He smelled like the world above. Like freedom. Like someone who had stayed.

Arms sliding around his waist, I let myself hold him in return.

"This is where we bring the people we rescue," he whispered into my hair. "Before they disappear into safer lives."

I closed my eyes.

How could I tell him I didn't want to disappear?

How could I say that I didn't want him to disappear either?

But the words never made it past the knot in my throat.

A knock pulled us apart. Elios pressed a kiss to my temple and stepped away.

When he opened the door, Georgios stood waiting with a tray in his hands. The scent of something warm and rich spilled into the room, and my stomach answered with a low, unashamed growl.

Murmuring his thanks, Elios accepted the tray and shut the door with a quiet click. He crossed the room in a few long strides and set it gently on the table with care: a steaming bowl of stew, a small loaf of bread, and a decanter of wine. Candlelight skimmed across the curve of the glass, sending soft prisms sliding over the tabletop.

I sank into one of the chairs as he poured the wine, the scent of thyme and slow-cooked meat curling in the warm hush between us. Every movement he made was slow, *intentional*, as if rushing would break whatever spell held the room together.

When he bent to kiss me, I reached for his wrist instead. Just for a moment. Just to feel the quiet thrum of life beneath his skin, to ground myself in something steady before I dissolved.

He looked down at me, one brow raised in soft curiosity. "Are you okay?"

I nodded, not trusting my voice just yet. "Just... needed to make sure you were really here."

His expression softened, reaching across the table to squeeze my hand. "I'm here."

As I poured wine into our glasses, he ladled generous servings of the stew into two bowls. When he passed mine across the table, he gave a quiet, almost playful smile. "You're going to love this. Phaedra may have a permanent scowl, but she cooks like someone who still believes in kindness."

I wrapped my hands around the bowl like it was something precious. The broth was scalding, but I didn't wait. I took the first sip too fast, burning my tongue, but the pain was a welcome tether. Each bite tasted like a memory. Like comfort. Like something human.

Root vegetables. Soft meat. Herbs I hadn't tasted in what felt like forever. I ate too quickly, too hungrily, but I couldn't stop. It wasn't just food. It was warmth I hadn't let myself want.

"Careful," Elios murmured between bites. "It's not going anywhere."

"I know," I said softly. "I just... it's been a long time since something tasted like it was made to be shared. Now, I can't seem to get enough of it."

In Miris' sea, food had meant survival. Functional. Forgettable. Here, it meant something else entirely. Here, it tasted like care.

Across from me, Elios ate quietly for a moment, his lashes lowered, mouth soft in the firelight. "I keep wondering when this is going to feel real," he said. "Like one blink and we'll be back in the wreckage. Or worse."

"Me too," I whispered. "But right now, I want to believe it."

He nodded. That quiet, steady kind of agreement that asked for nothing but offered everything.

He should have walked away.

But he hadn't.

He was still here, still choosing me. After the wreckage. After the blood. After the truth of what I was.

And somehow, that undid me.

The bowl in my hands blurred, the stew swimming behind tears I refused to let fall. I blinked hard. Pressed the rim to my lips. Swallowed.

Too fast. Too hot. My hands trembled.

I told myself it was exhaustion. Hunger.

But it wasn't.

I didn't want to lose this—this fragile, aching sweetness between us. I didn't want to go back.

Not to the ocean. Not to the silence. Not to a life stripped of warmth, of touch, of the quiet intimacy of being seen and not shunned.

I couldn't return to the cold ache of loneliness, to the suffocating still-ness of a world where no one reached for me. Not when I had this. Not when I had him.

Letting this slip through my fingers?

That was the thing I couldn't bear.

CHAPTER THIRTY-THREE

A MOMENT'S RESPITE

After our exhausting and dangerous day, sleep came quickly for both Elios and me that night. The chamber's small windows let in very little light, making it far too easy for us to sleep later than usual.

As someone who had been nocturnal for years, I was surprised by how easily I had adjusted to a regular human routine. Aside from the general threat to our safety, we had no obligations to pull us out of bed. Still, my body remained too accustomed to its usual daytime rhythm. A full bladder and an empty stomach conspired to disturb my cozy slumber if I didn't get up willingly.

When I opened my eyes that morning, I found Elios' muscular arm wrapped snugly around my waist. I rolled over to admire his sleeping face, something that always made my heart flutter, only to discover he was already awake, watching me. His eyes were bright with affection, and the way his tousled brown hair stuck out from sleep only made him more attractive.

Seeing him looking at me like that made me smile. He returned the gesture with a grin of his own, his blue gaze lighting up even further.

"Good morning," he said, his voice raspy with sleep. The depth of it resonated low in my belly.

"Good morning to you."

He pulled me closer, pressing a kiss to my lips, warm and unhurried. "How did you sleep?"

I stretched my arms above my head, a yawn escaping me as I arched into the movement. "Longer than I needed to," I said with a sleepy smile, "and it was glorious."

Tucking a lock of hair behind my ear, Elios leaned in and pressed a kiss to my forehead. His voice, low and soft against my skin, sent a shiver racing down my body.

"After everything you've been through, you probably forget how much you need. Sleep as long as you want. I'll chase away anyone who tries to disturb you."

I giggled, resting my cheek against his chest. "Well, I don't think you can chase away my hunger while I sleep. We should get dressed and check on Aris too. I want to see how he's feeling."

Elios kissed me again, his lips slow but insistent, his tongue teasing until my thoughts scattered. For a moment, the idea of leaving the bed slipped from my mind entirely. When he finally pulled away, I caught his wrist and tugged him back down, pouring all the passion I could muster into the next kiss. My earlier hunger faded, replaced with a very different kind of need.

Elios slid his arms around me and rolled onto his back, guiding me with him until I was straddling his hips. My body settled against his, the thin fabric between us doing little to mute the heat of his arousal pressing against me.

The alignment was perfect—*too* perfect. A slow ache unfurled in my core, and the thought whispered through my mind before I could stop it: I should have gone to sleep naked.

Now, I wanted nothing between us at all.

My hips rolled of their own accord, grinding against him, dragging his shaft along the apex of my thighs. The cloth between us was maddening. Even through my trousers, the sensation was exquisite, coaxing a moan from deep in my throat as my back arched with pleasure from the friction against my clit.

Elios took advantage of my exposed neck, leaning up to suck the sensitive flesh into his mouth. Each flick of his tongue sent a jolt of heat through me. He rocked his hips to meet mine, matching my rhythm. The pressure was overwhelming, but I craved more. He would mark my skin with the attention he gave my throat, and I welcomed every second of it.

My tunic was too thick, too stifling against the warmth of his bare chest. Rising onto my knees, I fumbled with the tie of my top and pulled it free, tossing the fabric to the side of the bed. Elios' wicked grin was the only warning I received before he rolled us again, switching our positions effortlessly.

"Hey!" I protested, but my voice turned into a gasp as he tore my trousers from my body, ripping the fabric like it was nothing.

His hand slid between us, and he gripped his cock, the tip already slick with arousal. He dragged it slowly through my folds, circling my clit, teasing the entrance. A groan escaped me—half frustration, half raw need. My hips lifted involuntarily as he dipped in just enough to coat himself with my wetness, only to pull away again.

I barely had time to voice my complaint before he slammed into me, burying himself to the hilt with a single, deep thrust.

My legs flew up as I moaned—loud, breathless, unguarded. He pounded into me, each stroke brutal, but in the best way. There were no thoughts left in my head, only sensation. Every time he drove into me, the tension in my belly coiled tighter, closer to the edge.

"Gods, Little Tempest. You feel so good."

"I'm so close," I whispered, barely able to breathe. "Please. Elios."

With a guttural growl, he dropped his mouth to my neck and bit, just enough to sting, before sucking the pain away. The roughness of his thrusts broke me open. My climax crashed through me like a storm, my teeth sinking into the blanket as I tried to stifle the scream it pulled from my throat.

But then his release followed, his final thrusts deep and shattering, and my voice found his name.

I was dazed. My body hummed with satisfaction. The room, the world, everything beyond the two of us faded away. We didn't know how to take it slow. The intensity of our need burned too hot to be restrained.

After we'd bathed and dressed, Elios and I made our way downstairs. The scent of roasted coffee beans and warm bread met us at the bottom of the steps, a comforting contrast to the night before.

In the tavern, our uninjured companions were already gathered around a table, steaming mugs in hand. The space had a rustic charm—wood-planked walls matching the aged floors, thick beams crossing the ceiling like ribs in a great ship. Along the far wall, narrow windows filtered in soft morning light, casting a golden haze across the room.

At first glance, the fortified wooden door might have seemed excessive, its heavy boards and metal locks intimidating. But after coming face to face with a vampire, the need for that kind of protection felt painfully obvious.

We slipped into our seats as Georgios arrived with two plates piled high and matching mugs of coffee. I offered a grateful nod before wrapping my hands around the warm ceramic.

"How's Aris?" Elios asked between bites.

"He's in a lot of pain," Dimitris answered, taking a sip of his drink. "Phaedra's been giving him a tonic for relief, but it keeps him drowsy. He's asleep now."

The reminder twisted my stomach into knots. If not for me, he never would've been attacked. I picked at the eggs, forcing down a bite in an attempt to settle the unease curling low in my gut. The flavors were pleasant—savory, warm, perfectly cooked—but my appetite refused to cooperate.

"Anyone send word to Kimon?" Elios asked, shoveling food into his mouth at an alarming pace.

Markos placed his utensil on his plate, nodding. "I messaged him this morning. Told him we were here, and he responded a short while ago. The safe house will be ready tomorrow." His expression darkened slightly. "I'm unsure if Aris will be ready to move, though. One of us may need to stay behind. I hate the idea of leaving him in Georgios and Phaedra's care while he's like this. Phaedra can tend to him, but he's too big for her to lift on her own."

Dimitris took a slow sip of his coffee before answering. "I'll stay with him if it comes to that. You two should get these ladies to the safe house when ready. They'll be more comfortable there."

Elios lifted his mug in a mock salute. "Appreciate the offer, Brother, but I have a feeling you just want to stay behind to sample the drinks in this fine establishment."

Laughter bubbled from my lips, and when I glanced over at Ocevia, I caught the trace of a smile curling at the corner of her mouth.

From behind the bar, Georgios snorted. "Those drinks won't be on the house, either. I'll have your ass washing dishes."

Dimitris rolled up his napkin and lobbed it at Elios, the ball landing near his plate. "Ha. Ha. Funny, really." He turned toward the bar. "Not you, Old Man. I'll wash dishes if you need help. It's preferable to washing Aris' backside." His smirk was unrepentant as he shifted his gaze back to Elios. "Anyway, what's on the agenda for today, boss?"

Elios leaned back in his chair, draping an arm around my shoulders. The way I instinctively nestled against him made something in my chest ache with gratitude.

"I would say to remain hidden," he said, his expression turning serious, "but we need ears on the ground in case Miris' people show up asking questions. I don't want to be blindsided."

The mere mention of her name sent a chill through me, but before the fear could take hold, Markos leaned in and pressed a kiss to Ocevia's cheek. She relaxed immediately, and I watched as he murmured something in her ear before leaving the room.

A moment later, I slid into the seat he'd vacated, giving Ocevia a teasing look.

"Well..." I drawled, dragging out the word.

A blush crept into her cheeks. "Well, what?"

"I can't wait to hear all the details. How did everything come together?" I flicked a finger toward the door where Markos had gone. "Just so you know, there's no judgment from me. Elios and I fell quickly, so I'm happy for you."

She glanced toward the others, her voice dropping as she leaned closer. "From the moment I saw him standing outside the tavern, I knew he was mine. I couldn't deny my interest. I wanted the chance to see what we could become." 

The honesty in her voice echoed something in my own heart. "I felt the same way when I saw Elios clinging to those rocks after the shipwreck. Out of everyone that night..." I hesitated, lowering my voice, "Out of everyone who died that night, he fought so hard to survive. I couldn't take my eyes off him. It felt like a sign that I was meant to find him. I may have carried him to that island, but we saved each other."

Ocevia took a slow sip of her tea, then reached across the table for my hand. Her fingers were cool. Steady.

"Do you think we can really get away with this?" she whispered. "I mean... actually escape? I feel like Miris' eyes are on us no matter where we go. I don't want to go back, Azure. I can't leave Markos."

Her voice cracked, and I felt the sting of it in my own throat.

"I'd be lying if I said I wasn't afraid," I told her. "But these men... they'll stop at nothing to protect us. We have to hold onto that."

I squeezed her hand one more time, both of us clinging to that thin thread of hope. It wasn't much, but it was something. And for now, something had to be enough.

A small smile touched her lips, though it didn't quite reach her eyes. That kind of smile I knew too well. The one you wear when you're still afraid but need the world to think you're brave.

That unspoken fear echoed in both of us. No matter how far we ran or how many days we stayed ahead of her, Miris always felt just behind. Her presence loomed like a shadow, etched into our bones, coiled deep in our memories.

I felt Ocevia's fear as sharply as my own. Years spent under the Sea Goddess's control had left us haunted in ways we didn't yet know how to name. That fear was stitched into the very fabric of our being, and no amount of firelight or love could burn it away completely.

For all the freedom we'd fought for, the weight of her still lingered.

No matter how brightly the sun shone, part of me would always live in her darkness.

We lingered at the table for a while, sipping our drinks and trading quiet glances. The tavern had taken on the hush of early morning, the sort of stillness that felt borrowed—*fragile*. Outside, the world went on, but in here, everything had slowed.

Markos returned first, his boots echoing against the wooden floor. He moved with purpose, but the moment his eyes found Ocevia, some of that tension melted away. He leaned down to whisper something in her ear, and whatever it was made her smile. A real one this time. One with light behind it.

Elios leaned in toward me, lowering his voice. "If we get word from the safe house, we should be ready to move fast. I want our things packed by nightfall. Just in case."

I nodded, the familiar weight of caution settling into my chest. "Do you think she knows where we are?"

"Not yet," he said. "But I've seen how fast word spreads. We need to be ahead of her. Always."

His fingers found mine beneath the table, and I curled into the warmth of his touch.

Across from us, Dimitris was still bantering with Georgios about the cost of drinks and the quality of breakfast. Even now, humor served as armor, though the worry hadn't left his eyes.

For a moment, I let myself breathe. *Just breathe.*

But even in this quiet hour, I could feel the sea inside me shifting. The pull of it. The threat of it. The past was never far behind, and neither was *she.*

Chapter Thirty-Four

CAPTURED BY DARKNESS

I knew that exploring Ceveasea was off-limits, but I couldn't help but want to experience living among humans again. I understood the ban and the potential dangers it could bring. Ceveasea was the largest populated area near Starspell, and it was likely that Miris' people would search for us there.

Even Elios stayed indoors, unwilling to risk discovery. I had little doubt that the Sea Goddess knew of his existence and the soul she had stolen from her. The only thing keeping him safe was that she didn't know his true identity, but if Lucia or Oona were still alive, that protection would be lost.

Markos and Dimitris were the only ones who ventured outside to gather supplies and meet with contacts, searching for any signs of those hunting us.

Ocevia and I spent our morning helping Phaedra around the building and caring for Aris. He slept most of the day, only needing help to reposition himself and take his pain medication. Despite his recent injury, he was recovering quickly under Phaedra's care, which gave me some relief.

As the tavern's opening time approached, Elios and I joined Georgios in the kitchens to help prepare dinner. Since I wasn't skilled at cooking, I focused on washing dishes and chopping vegetables.

The busy work kept my mind occupied and distracted me from thoughts of Miris. Georgios was a talkative man who enjoyed sharing stories from his past. He and Elios had many tales to tell, some adventurous and others dangerous, but they were all a welcome distraction from the stress we had been facing lately.

When we first arrived at the tavern, it was quiet and empty. However, as soon as we opened the doors, people began pouring in as if it were the most popular place in town. To avoid being recognized by Miris' associates, Elios, Ocevia, and I donned hooded capes and settled into a dark corner booth. We spent a few hours chatting, wanting to avoid being cooped up in our rooms while avoiding unwanted attention.

Meanwhile, Markos and Dimitris mingled with the other customers, listening in on conversations and occasionally joining them to gather information about Miris' underlings. They had spent most of the day in town for that purpose, and from what they had discovered, we were the only newcomers. If Miris' people were in town, they were doing a good job of hiding.

Unlike most taverns, where crowds partied until the early morning hours, The Dusty Lantern began to thin out as the sun set behind the buildings. Once all the patrons had left for the night, our group helped clean up in gratitude for Georgios and Phaedra's hospitality.

I was surprised when I saw a familiar face enter the main room while I washed dishes behind the bar. Aris, seated in a rolling wooden chair, grinned from ear to ear. Everyone stopped what they were doing and approached him, excited to see him up and about.

Elios placed a reassuring hand on Aris' shoulder. "How are you feeling, Brother?"

Sighing, Aris rubbed his leg. "Pretty good, considering. My leg and ribs hurt like hell, but this chair is a blessing." He propelled himself forward a few inches, then back again with his hands. "Phaedra had Georgios drag it out of storage. I can't get up the stairs, but at least I can make it to the bathroom on my own. Having someone help me piss does little for my warrior image."

A slow smile spread across my lips as I watched Aris chatting with the group. I had been worried about him, and guilt had loomed over me like a dark cloud. Seeing him getting around on his own and in good spirits was a relief. Although he couldn't walk independently, he was on the road to recovery. The best part was that he didn't resent Ocevia or me for the injuries he sustained while protecting us.

As our group continued talking with Aris, I kissed Elios on the cheek and headed for the bathroom.

The corridor separating the tavern from the infirmary was dark, just as it had been the night before. A single lantern illuminated the entire space, casting a faint glow that created eerie shadows, making my blood run cold. I was alone, which added to the hall's sinister atmosphere. I wasn't sure where Phaedra had gone, but the infirmary was empty.

I took the lantern from the table outside the bathroom and stepped into the small, windowless space, closing the door behind me. The dark swallowed everything until I struck the flint. The wick caught with a sharp hiss, blooming into light that stretched across the dark walls and blurred mirror. The glow settled unevenly, shifting across the basin and tiled floor like it was alive, wary of the silence.

After relieving myself, I splashed cold water on my face, hoping the chill would soothe the strange tightness in my chest. It didn't. My reflection met me with pale skin, damp strands clinging to my cheekbones, and eyes too wide. Something in the air felt wrong—not loud or sudden, but crawling, as if something unseen hovered just out of reach. A stillness that didn't feel like peace.

Aris was healing. We hadn't been approached or followed. There was no reason for dread, and yet every inch of my skin prickled with awareness. I pressed my hands to the edge of the basin, exhaling slowly through my nose, trying to breathe away the chill nesting at the base of my spine.

When I finally turned off the lantern and opened the door, the hallway stretched before me, quiet and empty. Only a single lantern flickered at the far end, its light barely reaching the corridor's center. I clutched the handle of the lantern I'd brought with me, bracing myself to cross the threshold. I told myself I was imagining things, that I was still on edge from the past few days, but instinct roared otherwise.

The second I stepped into the hall, the world turned.

A clammy hand clamped over my mouth, yanking my head back with jarring force. Another arm coiled around my waist, iron-strong and merciless, locking my arms against my ribs and lifting me clean off the floor. I kicked and twisted, but my captor's grip only tightened, crushing the breath from my lungs. My scream died against the palm pressed hard to my face, stifled before it could ever reach the air. The lantern slipped from my fingers and crashed to the stone floor, the glass exploding in a sharp burst. Its flame extinguished instantly, leaving behind only the hiss of cooling embers.

A sudden prick pierced the side of my neck, whether needle or fang I couldn't tell, followed by a searing heat that spread like wildfire through my veins. My limbs turned to lead. My thoughts unraveled. Panic roared in my chest, but my body no longer obeyed its commands. Everything blurred: the corridor, the dim light, the air itself. The world tilted violently, then vanished into black.

My mind surfaced in fragments, awareness torn into ribbons.

The thunder of hooves pounding over uneven rock. The jolt of my body slung across the back of a horse. My wrists were bound behind me, the rope biting into tender flesh, slick with sweat and blood. A gag filled my mouth, choking every whimper. I was conscious enough to feel the sway of the animal beneath me, but too weak to do more than shiver.

Faint torchlight flickered in the dark as we reached our destination. The world around me was jagged and unfamiliar until I recognized the sharp silhouette of the mountain pass.

Terror surged through my chest, rising like a second heartbeat. The mountain pass loomed ahead, each jagged silhouette illuminated by torchlight, and every instinct in me screamed that I shouldn't be here.

I had almost died in this place. The memory of crimson eyes and ice-cold breath on my skin haunted every stone I now recognized. My muscles tensed as I struggled against the bonds, but the rope only bit deeper, fraying skin and soaking into the rawness beneath. My vision pulsed in and out, and waves of nausea swept over me, heavy and unrelenting.

Then I heard a voice I hoped to never hear again.

"Don't bother, Azure. You won't be getting away again."

The words slithered through the dark, thick with spite.

Lucia stepped into view, her face contorted in a mask of rage. Her hair hung in damp, matted clumps, and her skin was streaked with grime. Firelight licked the edges of her silhouette, casting her in flickering orange and red that only sharpened the madness in her gaze.

Even half-conscious, I knew her. I knew the venom behind every syllable she spoke.

I scanned the shadows behind her, desperate for a second figure, some flash of Oona's magic, a silhouette I could exploit, anything to tip the odds, but no one came. The emptiness around us echoed louder than her voice. No allies. No missteps. Just Lucia. Just me.

Like a predator savoring the moment before the kill, she crouched low, her head tilted in mock curiosity. The firelight caught in her eyes, glinting with a cruel satisfaction, the kind that knew exactly what it planned to do and relished every second of the wait. Madness swirled in their depths, fractured and glittering, like storm light breaking across a blood-dark sea.

"This is for Oona, you stupid bitch," she hissed.

Before I could react, her fist drove into the side of my head. Pain exploded through my skull, and the world fractured into darkness once more.

My legs screamed in pain as I was dragged along the ground, broken stones biting into my flesh. Yanked into the sea without warning, I choked on the water as it filled my lungs. Using the last of my energy, I transformed into my mermaid form and breathed deeply, my lungs easing their burning protest.

Whatever Lucia had used to drug me still flowed through my veins, blurring the edges of reality. My captor paid me no attention, allowing me no opportunity to swim free. My tail dragged along the bottom of the sea, coral and rocks ripping chunks of my scales off. Each iridescent scale scraped off felt like a nail ripped from its root. I cried out, but the sound was muffled beneath the water. The pain was excruciating, yet it paled in comparison to the fate that awaited me.

Our destination was clear, and I knew I would not survive.

Chapter Thirty-Five

THE SEA GODDESS'S WRATH

After an eternity of being dragged across the ocean floor, Miris' underwater fortress finally appeared. My tail ached with every movement, and Lucia's constant tugging on my chains kept me from slipping into unconsciousness. The rope dug deeper into my already injured wrists. Still, I refused to give Lucia the satisfaction of hearing me cry out.

As we approached the gates of the fortress, I looked around at the countless mermaids and mermen who stared at me with a range of emotions: fear, curiosity, and bloodthirstiness among them. But no one dared to intervene as Lucia shoved me through the gate into the airlock separating the exterior courtyard from the lavish interior.

The sudden change in pressure caused my tail to shift painfully, leaving me naked and vulnerable. Even worse, I could feel the shredded remnants of my legs dangling in the hot wind as the airlock dried our bodies. The excruciating pain threatened to overwhelm me, but I forced myself to remain conscious.

Miris' greed for human luxuries outweighed her hatred for land-dwellers, so her palace was filled with only the finest things. But for me, it was a place of punishment rather than pleasure. As Lucia dragged me through ornate halls and corridors, my body left a trail of blood on the pristine marble floors.

Eventually, we reached a nondescript door that led us down into the castle's depths. My heart sank as I realized where we were headed to a place I had never been to before, despite my punishments. Bile rose in my throat, but I swallowed it back down. Fear would do me no good here.

The deeper we swam, the colder it became. Shadows thickened around us as Lucia dragged me through the water, pressure mounting with every downward pull. My tail scraped along rough rock, torn scales drifting into the dark like petals stripped from a dying flower. And then I knew. I knew exactly where she was taking me.

My stomach twisted with dread, and I fought back the urge to think of Elios. His words, to survive at all costs, echoed in my mind. Still, I pushed them away, afraid that even thinking of him would somehow give away his true identity to Miris. Death seemed inevitable in this underwater palace, stunning on the surface but cold and cruel within. But I vowed to bide my time and take any chance I could to end it quickly.

The airlock offered little relief from the sweltering corridor. Despite my best efforts, I slipped and stumbled with my injured legs as Lucia impatiently dragged me along with her chains. The effects of the drug they had given me were wearing off, leaving my heart racing and my body flooded with adrenaline.

We twisted through a labyrinth of dark hallways, each looking identical to the last. I knew where we were headed to the dungeon, every mermaid's worst nightmare. As we approached, a hulking guard stood outside in nothing but tight pants and boots, his massive muscles and scars making him a terrifying sight. His deep turquoise eyes and jagged scars only added to his intimidating presence.

Inside the dungeon, Lucia wasted no time in securing me to the wall with sharp metal shackles that dug into my skin. My attempts to resist were met with excruciating pain, and I could do nothing but endure it.

Lucia's face contorted into a feral snarl as she left me alone in the cell, reminiscent of her attack on Elios at the beach. In an instant, she unleashed her fury upon me, landing blow after blow until I was doubled over in agony on the ground. Unable to contain myself any longer, sobs wracked through my body—sobs of fear, anger, and helplessness. I felt weak and pitiful compared to the strength I had once possessed as one of Miris' mermaids.

Lucia stormed out of the cell with one final triumphant look and slammed the door behind her, leaving me alone in this hellish place.

I remained huddled on the frigid stone floor, my breaths coming in ragged gasps as I clutched my throbbing face. My stomach grumbled with hunger, and my body ached with exhaustion, but it couldn't compare to the despair that weighed heavy on my heart. As time ticked by, I couldn't help but think of my friends, Ocevia and Elios. Miris was after them, too, so why was I the only one captured? Though grateful for their safety, my mind couldn't shake off the fear that they may also be taken by another mermaid working for Miris.

The thought alone made it hard to breathe as I prayed that I was the only one captured. I wanted my friends to remain free and evade Miris' people, even if it meant never seeing them again. Every beat of pain coursing through my body was nothing compared to the ache in my heart. I needed Elios and Ocevia to survive and escape from Miris' grasp.

Please, just be safe.

The clang of approaching footsteps echoed outside the cell, low voices trailing behind them. I held my breath, listening. The words were muffled, but the sharp edge in the tone sent a ripple of unease through me. A bolt scraped back. Hinges screamed. The heavy metal door swung open, flooding the dungeon with harsh light.

Miris.

I staggered upright, retreating until my back hit the cold stone wall. My heartbeat roared in my ears. I hadn't expected her to come here. To summon me to her grand hall, yes. To send others to torment me, of course. But to step into this damp, fetid place herself?

That meant something.

It meant she was furious.

Two guards flanked her, massive and armored, their expressions impassive. She waved them off with a flick of her hand. One hesitated, brow furrowed.

"Your—"

"Don't you dare question me. Get. *Out.*"

Her voice cracked like a whip.

The guards bowed and left in silence. The door slammed shut behind them, and the lock ground into place with grim finality.

Alone, the Sea Goddess fixed her gaze on me. I balled my fists at my sides to still their trembling. That gaze, quicksilver and swirling with cruelty, stripped the breath from my lungs.

Miris looked like a dream sculpted from nightmare: impossibly beautiful, impossibly lethal. Her gown, little more than flame-red gauze, clung to her frame like smoke, revealing and concealing with wicked balance. Her long black hair tumbled down her back, framing sharp cheekbones and full lips curled in a mockery of a smile. But it was her eyes that held me. Silver. Shifting. *Drowning.*

"You stole from me, Azure."

The pendant at her throat—a diamond-cut nautilus hanging from a golden chain—glinted as she toyed with it. I said nothing. Arguing wouldn't change what was coming.

"The male you took, his soul is mine."

Her grin widened, the cruelty in it radiant.

I dropped to my knees. "Please." My voice cracked, and the plea spilled out before I could stop it. "Do anything you want to me. Just let him go."

Barking a laugh, she waved the words away as though swatting at a gnat.

"Oh, darling. You really think you have a choice? You belong to me. Your soul, your body, your suffering are *all* mine. With a flick of my wrist, I could turn those pretty legs into a tail and watch it rot away inch by inch until your heart stops beating."

The grin twisted into something more sinister.

"But I won't be that merciful. You disobeyed me, and for that, you'll be punished. First, I'll reclaim what's mine. Then I'll make you watch while I devour his soul."

I bowed my head to the floor. Chains rattled against stone.

"No. *Please.*"

She closed the distance in two long, purposeful strides, the floor groaning beneath her deliberate steps. I flinched at her approach but didn't retreat. Her hand fisted in my hair, jerking me upright with cruel force. Pain blazed along my scalp, and my knees dragged hard against the cold stone as she forced me to face her.

"Did you fall for him, Little Mermaid? Did his soul sing to yours?"

She released my hair only to seize my jaw with brutal force, sending a spike of agony through my already bruised cheekbone.

"Did you give him your body? Is that why you're clinging to what belongs to me?"

Her nails bit into my skin.

"You may have bonded with him when you saved his life, but don't worry. I'll sever that connection myself. I'll ride his cock while you watch and show you what it means to please a man. Maybe your little heart will forget him before I yank his soul from his body."

With the last threat, she threw me.

My spine struck the wall with a jarring thud, and my skull cracked against the stone a breath later, sending white light flashing behind my eyes. Pain bloomed in a dozen places at once, but none of it compared to the crushing ache in my chest. I could endure her wrath, endure *anything*, but if she found Elios, if she laid a single hand on him...

No.

Turning her back to me, the Sea Goddess walked to the door.

"My riders are already on their way to Ceveasea. They'll find him," she said, her hand resting on the latch. "And when they do, I'll return to keep my promises. Hope you're ready for the show."

The door slammed shut, sealing me in darkness with nothing but the sound of my ragged breath and the image of her silver eyes burned into my mind.

Chapter Thirty-Six

SCARRED BY SHADOWS

The bonfire burned low at the center of the cavern, casting its molten light over the curved stone walls, wrapping the shadows in amber and rose. Heat from the flames licked at my skin, chasing away the chill that clung to the cave's edges. I nestled deeper into Elios' arms, the familiar weight of him grounding me in a world that felt too good to be real.

His fingers traced slow, reverent lines along my waist, the pads of them callused from years of survival but impossibly gentle now. A shiver ran down my spine as he dipped his head and pressed his lips to the base of my neck, the warmth of his breath a silken contrast to the flickering firelight. He lingered there, tasting my skin, breathing me in.

There was no hunger in him. Not tonight. Only worship.

I let my eyes fall shut and turned into his touch, the sensation of his hands, his breath, the quiet thrum of his heart beneath mine—everything I had once feared I'd never feel again. There was no Sea Goddess. No chains. No past. Just Elios. Just this heartbeat between us.

He kissed the hollow beneath my jaw and whispered in my ear. "I love you."

The words sank deep, rooting in the cracks that still ran through my soul. He had no idea how long I had waited to hear that. Or how impossible it had once seemed that anyone could say it to me and mean it.

Tears slipped down my cheek, and I kissed him back, my voice thick with emotion. "I love you, too."

I meant it with everything I had left.

The sound came like thunder through water—metal shrieking against metal, a bolt thrown open, the door crashing back against the wall. I jolted upright, the remnants of the dream shattering into ash. My heart slammed against my ribs as bootsteps pounded toward me, echoing off the damp stone.

The light was dim, but it was enough to blind me after sleep. My vision blurred. For a breathless moment, I thought it might be Elios. That maybe the dream had bled into reality. That maybe he was coming for me.

But the figure who entered was too large. Too fast. And too silent.

A rough hand closed around my arm and yanked me to my feet. My shackled legs tangled, and I staggered. Panic flared hot and immediate. I twisted in his grip, instinct taking over, but it was no use. He was all bone and brute strength, and I was nothing but skin and blood and memory.

Another figure loomed in the doorway, draped in a heavy cloak. Only his mouth was visible beneath the hood—expressionless and still, like a statue carved from shadow.

"Don't bother fighting," the man holding me muttered, his voice a growl steeped in grime. He reeked of sweat, old blood, and rusted iron. "You're coming with us."

I tried to rip myself free, but his grip only tightened, crushing the bones in my forearm. He turned without ceremony, dragging me from the cell as if I weighed nothing at all.

The hallway beyond was narrow, slick with condensation. Water ran in thin rivulets along the stone, reflecting the lantern light in sharp, broken glimmers. My bare feet skidded with every step, but he didn't slow.

I craned my neck, desperate to glimpse his face. I caught only the dark and intricate tattoos winding up his massive arm like snakes. I grit my teeth against the sting of tears. I would not cry. Not for them. Not while they were watching.

The second man followed behind in silence, a wraith wrapped in fabric, moving with purpose. I had no idea where they were taking me.

Only that it would be worse than where I'd been.

The air in the chamber was thick and wet, saturated with mildew and the sharp tang of iron. Salt clung to every surface. Water dripped from the ceiling in irregular patterns, echoing through the stone like a broken clock, each drop a warning that time no longer moved in any direction that served me.

They dragged me into a large chamber, its vaulted stone ceiling stretching high above like a cathedral built for pain. The damp weight of it pressed down on my chest, making each breath feel like something stolen. My stomach knotted as my gaze caught on the chains hanging from the ceiling, long iron lengths beaded with condensation. They swayed faintly, as if disturbed by the ghosts of those who had hung here before me.

One of the men pulled me forward, guiding me to the center where a pair of manacles hung open like jaws waiting to snap shut. He said nothing as he forced my arms overhead. My back arched with the strain as he yanked my wrists high and secured them with a metallic finality. Rising onto my toes, I tried to relieve the pressure, but there was no mercy in the iron. My feet couldn't find the floor. Instead, I hung there, suspended and trembling, the full weight of my body stretching my shoulders to the brink.

The taller man stepped back into the shadows, leaning against the wall. Watching. Waiting. His silence crawled across my skin like mold, and the longer he stood there, the harder it became to breathe. I clenched my teeth, forcing stillness into my limbs, even as fear scratched at the inside of my ribs.

Then he moved.

Time stretched thin as he approached, the distance between us shrinking like breath in my lungs. He reached for the coiled whip hanging from its hook. When he stepped into the light, the mask came into view—rough leather, stitched with no care or symmetry, slits hacked for his eyes and mouth. The grin visible beneath it wasn't human. It was hunger.

He raised the whip.

The first crack exploded through the room, loud and sharp as a gunshot. I flinched hard, but the blow didn't fall.

The second came closer. A whisper of leather cutting the air.

Then *pain.*

It landed across my thighs, hot and searing, and I screamed before I could even form the breath to stop it. Blood streamed down my legs, mingling with the sweat that already clung to my skin.

Another strike. And another.

He didn't speak, but the silence was a lie. His breath came ragged, uneven, like someone savoring a fine meal. The whip snapped through the air, and the agony came fast behind it. My screams no longer sounded like me. They came from somewhere deeper, from the part of myself I never wanted anyone to reach.

Staying just out of view, he moved like a tide I couldn't outrun. Each time the whip landed, my body jerked and twisted. My wrists tore against the manacles, my breath coming in shallow gasps.

He wanted me to break. And I was breaking.

My voice fractured, but I sobbed, biting my lip, biting the inside of my cheek. I told myself I wouldn't beg, but I did.

Eventually, the word slipped out. Small. Desperate.

"Please."

And still, he didn't stop.

Circling with the inevitability of a storm creeping over the horizon, he sent each lash out like a probe, testing for resistance, finding none. No question left his lips, but he didn't need to ask. The answers were etched into every flinch, every involuntary twist of my body. He watched the way my muscles seized and stuttered, how my breath caught too late to shield me from the next blow.

Then came his voice, quiet and amused.

"It's easier when you've made the first mark yourself. I haven't had the pleasure of decorating you before, but let's test my aim. Nine out of ten?"

He struck again.

This time the pain didn't just split skin. It hollowed me out. I didn't know if he found the old scars, but I didn't care.

When the darkness finally took me, it wasn't pain that claimed me. It was the blessed quiet of *nothing*.

Chapter Thirty-Seven

WHISPERS IN THE DUNGEON

Days lost their names in the dark.

Time didn't pass so much as shatter. It fractured under pain, then stitched itself together just long enough for me to bleed again. The hours blurred, collapsed, unraveled. I stopped counting. Even the beatings became unmoored from chronology. My ribs ached, but from *which session? Yesterday? A week ago? Or some echo of the day I stopped hoping time would be kind?*

The hooded man came whenever silence had grown too long. Always the same steps. Always the same grin beneath the mask, like my suffering was a secret joke he got to relive over and over. The whip, the knife, sometimes both. He called it curiosity, but there was no science in the way he studied my screams. He wasn't a man seeking knowledge. He was a boy who liked to break his toys.

And I was splintering.

My body betrayed me more often now. I passed out too fast, woke too slow, caught in a limbo where pain blurred into dream. Sometimes, I opened my eyes unsure if I was still alive, or if this was some cruel afterlife where every breath hurt and every blink stitched another wound into the day. There was fear in it not just of the pain, but of losing my grip on what was real. Of forgetting my name. Of forgetting *his.* Sometimes, I saw Elios in the corner, watching. Sometimes Ocevia. Sometimes Daneliya, humming the lullaby I used to sing for her when our parents were gone. Their faces flickered at the edge of my mind, impossibly soft, impossibly cruel. Because they vanished. *Every* time. And the cell would quiet again, and I would feel like I'd died without the mercy of stopping.

The food was laughable. A lump of bread. Two fingers of dried fish. I was always hungry, always aching. My skin had grown tighter over sharp bones. My stomach no longer growled. It had learned to whisper.

But I lived. I endured. Not because I was brave. Not because I was strong. I endured because Elios had not yet walked through those doors.

That hope—fragile, thin as wet paper—kept me from unraveling completely.

One day, or maybe it was night, I'd stopped trying to guess, I lay curled beneath the scratchy blanket, tracing the seams between the stones with my fingertip. I whispered the numbers under my breath, using each syllable like a rope to keep myself tethered.

Ninety-five. Ninety-six. Ninety-sev—

The shriek of the iron hinges froze my lungs.

I shut my eyes fast. If I looked unconscious, maybe they'd leave me. Maybe I'd be spared another round of playing the game where I screamed and he smiled.

But the hand that touched me wasn't cruel.

It was cool. Careful. A damp cloth, pressed gently to my shoulder.

I startled upright, spine slamming against stone, breath catching with a sharp gasp. Pain flared across my back and ribs, and my vision swam.

She stood before me, wide-eyed, frozen, the cloth still in her hand. Red hair twisted into a tidy braid. Freckles kissed across her pale cheeks. And turquoise eyes—our curse branded there like sea glass.

"I didn't mean to scare you," she said, her voice soft as the cloth in her hand. "I thought you were asleep. My name is Corileia. I've been sent to clean your wounds."

My throat burned. I managed a rasp. "Why now?"

She hesitated, lowering her gaze. "It isn't just now. I've been coming all week. You haven't noticed how quickly you've been healing?"

I blinked at her. "A week?"

She nodded. "Every day. I've been using balm while you slept."

I didn't know whether to curse her or thank her. Faster healing meant faster beatings. But slow healing was the path to infection. To rot. To dying in this place without anyone knowing my name.

She stepped closer, slow like she expected me to bite. I didn't stop her. I didn't move at all.

"You've been in bad shape," she murmured.

A bitter laugh escaped me, dry and sharp. "That obvious?"

Lips twitching into the faintest smile, she dipped the cloth into a shallow basin, wrung it out, and pressed it to a gash near my ribs.

I hissed. The pain was immediate, like fire licking open an old wound.

"I'm sorry," she whispered. "But you're healing slower now. The fever... it took more than I expected."

"It's fine," I said through clenched teeth, my voice catching on a gasp. "Just keep going."

Her hands were gentle. Her presence was something I didn't know how to name—too tender for this place, too human. It reminded me of my mother humming while brushing tangles from my hair, of how Daneliya used to reach for my hand in the dark. It felt like being remembered. Softness, maybe. Humanity, worn like a cloak.

"Talk to me," she said, dabbing balm into the wound. "Tell me something. Anything. It might help."

"Like what?"

"Is it true?" she asked, glancing up. "That you saved a man from the sea?"

I blinked. That she even knew startled me.

"There aren't any secrets in Miris' dungeons," she said with a rueful shrug.

"Then why ask?"

"Because I want to hear it from you."

I looked past her to the lantern hung on the far wall, its flame dancing like it was trying to run.

"It's true," I said quietly.

She smeared more balm across the wound. I flinched but didn't pull away.

"Why?"

I opened my mouth. Closed it. Then said, "Because I couldn't watch him die. I didn't know him, but it felt like... like I was supposed to. Like the sea had put me there for a reason."

Corileia paused, the balm pot still open in her lap.

"Do you regret it?"

The answer was immediate.

"No."

She didn't ask again.

She didn't need to.

We sat in silence, her hands careful, the balm warm. The quiet wasn't empty. It was deliberate. A stillness that allowed space for breath, for unspoken things, for the ache of existing in the aftermath of too much pain. A hush that held space for pain, for memory, for things too fragile to name. I wanted to speak, to ask if she remembered kindness before the sea took it from us, but I stayed quiet, afraid it might break whatever fragile balance lingered between us.

When the knock came, something in me braced to fight. I wanted to rip the door from its hinges, to keep her there, to keep one good thing from slipping out of reach.

The guard took her by the arm. She didn't resist. She didn't even look back, and that broke something soft inside me.

I curled around myself, burying my face in the folds of the blanket, eyes fixed on the seam between stone ninety-six and ninety-seven, the only thing still solid in a world that kept erasing what mattered.

The hinges groaned sometime later, a sound so sharp and sudden it felt like the world exhaling through broken ribs. I didn't move. I stayed curled inward, caught in the haze between exhaustion and awareness, where time lost all meaning and pain made its own kind of silence.

Footsteps crossed the threshold, measured and soft. No clink of chains. No stench of sweat and old blood. Just the sound of shoes on damp stone, deliberate and restrained, like someone trying not to disturb the ghosts.

Slowly, I lifted my head, the motion aching with every bruised vertebrae, every memory I hadn't asked to keep.

A new guard stood above me—young, lean, ghost-pale, the kind of man built for blending into walls. He wore no hood or mask, but he didn't need them. His face was already vacant, stripped of individuality, a vessel of blank compliance. He looked at me the way one looks at a window: something to glance through, not at.

"The Sea Goddess has summoned you," he said. His voice was flat. Empty. He held out a set of manacles. "Hands."

I stared at the cuffs, the metal dull and familiar, like they already knew the shape of me. Part of me wanted to laugh, or spit, or ask what it would even change. But instead, I lifted my wrists with slow, deliberate resignation. Not because I agreed, but because I had no better choice.

He closed them without hesitation. The iron bit into bruises that hadn't stopped aching since the first day they took me. It was old pain redis-covered, like a wound that had never fully healed, only quieted. My skin knew these cuffs. My wrists had memorized their grip. It was a strange comfort in its predictability, a twisted reminder that I still existed, still endured. He gave a single, testing tug on the chain, then turned for the corridor. I followed, barefoot and unsteady, each step burning.

My heart beat fast, but it wasn't panic. Not quite. It was something colder. Dread sharpened into awareness. Miris only summoned the cursed when she wanted something. And she never wanted anything that didn't bleed.

We moved through corridors I had never seen before: hallways of polished stone and vaulted ceilings. The torches here didn't flicker like they did near the cells. They burned steady, golden, casting long reflections on the wet floor. Carved kelp and coral adorned the columns. A wealth of detail that made the dungeon feel even more like the underworld.

I memorized what I could.

Not because I believed I could escape, but because pretending to plan kept a sliver of defiance alive in me.

Left at the iron arch. Right at the split in the coral wall. Broken tile near the third torch bracket.

It gave me something to hold.

Eventually, we reached a pair of doors so large and ornate they didn't look like they belonged in the same world as the cells. Vines twisted through the carvings, silver glinting beneath the low light. Monsters tangled in their curves, all teeth and tail and hunger, etched in perfect stillness.

The sentinel outside nodded, opening one door and allowing us inside.

The throne room was stunning, crafted to mesmerize before it cut. It lured you in, beautiful and brutal, a mirage wrapped in menace. It caught the breath in my throat and turned it to glass, sharp-edged and delicate. Every inch of it whispered danger dressed in elegance, a temple of power where the air itself bent in reverence or fear.

Torchlight caught on six black columns rising from the floor, weathered and towering, worn by time and salt like bones of ancient leviathans. Murals spanned the domed ceiling, creatures painted mid-motion in sweeping spirals and hunting arcs. Statues lined the edges, mermaids frozen mid-breath, lips parted and eyes hollow, as if caught in the moment before revelation and forever denied it. A black rug unfurled toward the throne, flowing with the quiet inevitability of a current, flanked by banners embroidered with beasts dredged from the deepest trenches.

And there, on her throne of obsidian and coral, sat Miris.

Her crimson gown shimmered with the sheen of spilled blood under moonlight. It clung to her form with liquid precision, the train coiling around the base of the throne in a serpentine sprawl of silk and malice. She possessed the beauty of lightning, brilliant and merciless, designed to strike before you could admire it.

Her smile sharpened when her gaze found me, and my stomach turned as if her look alone could split me open. It wasn't just recognition. It was ownership, a silent declaration that she knew exactly how close I was to breaking and exactly how to finish the job.

I dropped mine. Not in deference. In armor.

"Leave us," she said.

The guard turned and walked away.

The silence that followed was engineered. Designed to stretch. To bend me.

She tapped her nails against the throne's armrest. A steady, rhythmic click that echoed in my spine.

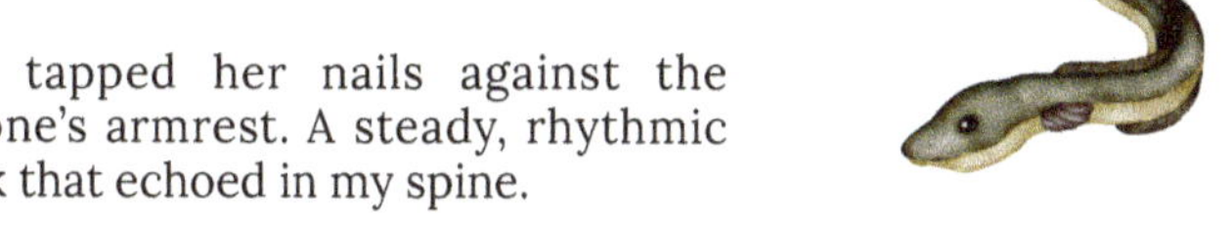

I said nothing.

Eventually, she leaned forward, chin balanced on one hand. Her lashes lowered, like she was tired of waiting, though the gleam in her eyes said otherwise.

"My scouts found your life-mate," she said, her voice like silk pulled taut. "And that pitiful friend of yours. *Ocevia*. A sorry little thing. Weaker than you, if that's even possible."

My head snapped up before I could stop it. "Where are they?"

Her sigh was theatrical. Bored. Amused. "Still in Ceveasea. *For now*."

Then her eyes caught mine and held.

"But not for long. They've been clever, I'll admit. But they won't outrun me forever."

She rose slowly, like the sea coming to a boil. "And I still have promises to keep to you, Little Mermaid."

My knees wanted to buckle. My throat locked. I bowed my head again, not out of submission, but to hide the ruin on my face.

She made a sound in her throat—part scoff, part hum. Then flicked her hand.

"Take her back."

The doors opened. The same guard returned, silent as before. He fastened the chain to my manacles, then turned toward the corridor.

But her voice lingered.

Like rot in saltwater. Like prophecy.

They were coming and she would be waiting.

CHAPTER THIRTY-EIGHT

A FRIEND'S FINAL STAND

I paced the narrow cell, my newly healed skin drawn tight across my shoulders, still pulsing with the memory of pain. The walls felt like they were closing in, pressing against every breath. Air hung thin and damp, too heavy to pull in, too light to satisfy. My thoughts frayed into spirals, unraveling into scenes I couldn't bear to picture. If Miris caught Elios and Ocevia, she wouldn't end it quickly. She would dismantle us. Make me watch the pieces fall before death was ever allowed to touch us. It wouldn't be execution. It would be spectacle. A punishment by slow erosion.

Then, like a warning from the bones of the palace itself, a sudden boom shattered the quiet. The sound echoed deep, a rupture that made the walls feel thinner, the danger closer.

I froze.

It wasn't the heavy tread of boots or the taunting whisper of the hooded man. It was louder. Sharper. Like something had broken free.

Muffled voices chased the sound, hushed and swift, like something unleashed was already on the move.

I scrambled into the corner, crouching low against the wall. My heart surged painfully in my chest, so loud I almost didn't hear the key scrape in the lock.

The bolt slid free and I braced for pain.

The door creaked open, the hinges shrieking like something dying.

Light spilled in, soft and golden and wholly out of place, a warmth that didn't belong here, as if the sun itself had wandered into the dark by mistake.

I watched with my fists clenched as a shape appeared in the doorway. Blonde hair. Pale skin. Eyes like lit seawater.

My breath snagged somewhere between a sob and a prayer.

"Ocevia," I whispered, too stunned to believe it.

She stepped inside in a rush of breath and purpose, her eyes rimmed with tears that hadn't yet fallen. In two strides, she closed the space between us and pulled me into a fierce embrace, arms winding around me with the desperation of someone trying to stitch shattered things back together with nothing but skin and willpower. My ribs flared with pain, but I clung to her anyway.

"I'm going to get you out of here," she whispered against my hair.

I lifted my hand to her cheek, fingers trembling as they traced the familiar curve of her face. She was real—warm and breathing, her skin damp with salt and grief. Not a dream. Not another fever-born hallucination conjured by hunger and despair.

"You're really here. I don't understand... how did you get past the guards? Where's Elios? What about the others? How did you end up with Corileia?"

Smiling through her tears, my friend nodded toward the corridor. "I knocked out the guard with a lantern. Slipped past the rest. There weren't many." Her voice dropped. "They figured you weren't a threat, but they weren't ready for me."

She crouched as she spoke, working quickly on the shackles. Her fingers trembled as they turned the lock, telling me she was just as afraid as I was.

"Everyone is fine. Dimitris stayed behind with Aris. Elios and Markos are in boats above the palace, waiting. Corileia was in the next cell. I opened hers by mistake and she told me where to find you. She's been helping you... so I figured she was worth saving."

I turned slightly, offering a weak nod to the healer. "Thank you."

But my thoughts spun toward the surface. Toward Elios. If Miris realized he was near...

"Ocevia, we have to get Elios out of the sea. If she finds out he's here, she'll—"

"I know." Her voice cut in, firm and raw. She reached for my hand. "No one's coming. Let's move."

She peeked into the hallway and whispered, "Corileia, do you know the way?"

Without hesitation, Corileia nodded and took the lead.

We slipped into the corridor, the cold floor biting into my bare feet with each cautious step. Torchlight flickered ahead, throwing tangled shadows that danced along the walls like ghosts echoing my fear.

With my body a brittle frame barely upright, I leaned heavily on Ocevia. I hadn't walked this far in days, maybe weeks, but I didn't let myself stumble.

Not now.

Not with freedom close enough to taste.

We walked through the winding corridors, the air thick with the scent of mold and seawater, each step echoing like a countdown. The damp clung to our skin, cold and insinuating, threading itself into our bones. I stumbled once, bare feet slipping on the slick stone, but Ocevia steadied me. Her presence was heat against the chill, the only thing that kept me from unraveling as fear whispered louder in the hollows of my chest.

Corileia led with quiet certainty, her movements fluid and instinctive, as if her body remembered these halls even when her mind wanted to forget. She didn't speak. None of us did. The quiet between us was necessary, but it hummed with urgency.

Each burning breath scraped its way through my raw throat, as if even the air punished me for daring to hope. My vision swam at the edges, but I focused on Ocevia's steady pace, her profile a lighthouse in the storm of my mind. I thought of Elios waiting somewhere above, of the warmth of sunlight I hadn't touched in weeks. The sea didn't welcome us yet. It watched. It waited. And I could feel its breath caught in its lungs, ready to decide whether to free us or drag us back under.

We crested a rise, the slope steep beneath our aching legs. At the top, soft candlelight flickered from the chamber beyond.

The foyer.

Ocevia flattened herself against the wall, eyes narrowing with the calculation of someone who'd faced worse odds and won. Pressing into the chill of the stone, her fingers lifted in a silent command, and I obeyed, willing my pulse to quiet, to shrink itself into something undetectable.

After ensuring the coast was clear, she turned to us and whispered, "One guard stands between us and the exit. We'll have to take him out."

I nodded without question, though I wasn't sure I could even lift my arms, let alone fight. My whole body trembled, not just from exhaustion, but from the anticipation of what came next.

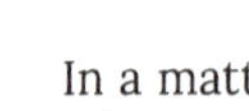

Ocevia didn't wait.

In a matter of seconds, she grabbed a heavy vase from a nearby alcove. Corileia, not hesitating for even a heartbeat, reached for the fireplace poker.

Unable to fight, I followed, heart pounding, each step aching, but to my relief, the guard never looked up.

Ocevia struck first.

The vase shattered across the back of his skull with a sound I felt more than heard—a sharp, splintering finality that echoed inside my chest. Blood sprayed and his body hit the coral floor like a dropped anchor. Corileia stood ready, but she didn't need to swing.

For a suspended, gut-wrenching second, I stared down at the body. My stomach twisted. I wanted to look away—*needed* to—but my eyes stayed locked, transfixed by the ruin we'd made. There was no rush of justice, no vindication. Only the hollow, nauseating thud of survival.

My hands shook. My breath came too fast.

We couldn't run. There was nowhere to go. The sea was all around us, thick with blood and vengeance.

But we moved anyway, because the only thing worse than standing still was waiting for what might come next.

Ocevia pulled me through the next chamber, Corileia close behind. When we reached the airlock, Ocevia slammed her palm against the control panel. It responded with a low whine and a sudden hiss as the seals disengaged.

Water rushed in, crashing through the chamber with the force of a tide unchained. It was cold and clean and sharp against our skin, flooding away the dungeon's rot with something almost holy in its violence.

As it engulfed us, our bodies responded. The transformation wasn't gentle. My bones shifted, reshaping with a painful grace as my legs dissolved into the shimmer of a tail. The wounds and bruises faded, hidden beneath sleek muscle and iridescent scales, as if the sea refused to carry our scars.

The final door creaked open, and the sea surged forward, not just a passage but a summons. It reached for us with ancient familiarity, part predator, part sanctuary.

Taking a mere moment to ensure there were no guards nearby, Ocevia surged forward with Corileia following.

I hesitated for a single breath, the moment suspended between fear and freedom. Then I kicked hard, chasing the trail of bioluminescence left in their wake like a thread pulled through darkness.

The sea swallowed us and the chase began.

The sea stretched above us, a ceiling of dark silk pierced by distant threads of sunlight. It looked impossibly far, a false sky promising air and warmth and the man I loved. Everything I wanted was waiting above that veil of water. For a moment, all I could hear was the rush of my own heartbeat and the rhythmic thrum of my tail cutting through the cold.

Then the water shifted, brushing against my skin like a change in mood, like the tremble of breath before a scream. The pressure around us deepened, a slow tightening, as if the ocean had drawn in a lungful of dread and was about to exhale.

I glanced over my shoulder, catching the glint of sharpened coral spears and the shimmer of approaching tails. They were closing in—faster than I wanted to believe. Panic surged, thick and cold in my chest, but I buried it beneath the rhythm of my strokes. I couldn't afford fear. Not when every heartbeat counted.

Corileia swam just ahead, graceful despite the urgency. Ocevia flanked me, close enough that I could feel the ripple of her strokes beside mine. Her sharp gaze flicked to me and then past me toward the threat behind.

The current shifted once more, sudden and brutal, as if the ocean itself had grown hands and was determined to hurl us downward. It slammed into us like a fist, dragging us toward the deep, away from the light, away from escape.

My body jolted, tumbling in the water like a leaf caught in a whirlpool. I fought against it, every muscle screaming as I clawed upward, but the sea didn't care. It pulled and dragged, a thousand invisible fingers trying to drag me back into the deep.

Miris had awakened.

When I twisted to look behind me again, the guards were close enough for me to see the expressions on their faces. Focused. I wasn't sure if they were here to kill or capture, but either way, they weren't slowing down.

At that moment, fear burned in my chest. Not for myself.

For him.

Elios.

He was waiting above, so close I could almost feel him. If they caught us here, they would reach him next.

I pushed harder, tail burning with every beat, but before I could surge ahead, Ocevia grabbed my wrist.

I tried to pull away, but she didn't let go.

Frustration twisted in my gut. We didn't have time. I turned toward her, ready to tell her to swim faster, but her eyes stopped me.

She wasn't afraid.

She smiled at me, not with relief or reassurance, but something quieter, heavier. It was the kind of smile you gave when you knew you were making a choice you couldn't undo.

And then, gently, she blew me a kiss.

Timothy Higgins
2012

CHAPTER THIRTY-NINE

THE LEGEND RETURNS

My heart stopped when my best friend met my gaze, nodded once, and pointed toward the surface before turning away. She swam into the current, straight back toward the undersea palace and the dozen guards chasing us. Before I could call out, Corileia turned and followed her, vanishing into the dark like a whispered prayer.

A silent scream clawed at my throat as I watched them disappear. I wanted to follow. Every part of me begged to turn around and help them. But I couldn't. I had no strength left to fight. Ocevia had made her choice. She had sacrificed herself to stall Miris and the guards so I could save the men. She hadn't even hesitated. That thought gutted me, because I had.

With one final, heartbreaking glance over my shoulder, I clenched my jaw and swam.

I shot upward through the water, adrenaline burning in my veins. My tail shifted into legs just before I broke the surface. The salt stung my skin as it changed, but I didn't stop.

Two small boats floated above the sea like fragile rafts in a storm. Elios and Markos were at the oars, helpless without wind to fill their sails. I gripped the edge of Elios' vessel, and he pulled me inside with shaking hands. His lips met mine, the salt of the sea and tears mingling on our tongues. For a moment, it was paradise. A moment where the world felt whole again.

But we had no time for paradise.

"We have to go. Now!" My voice cracked, raw and frantic. They didn't know. They couldn't possibly understand how close the threat was. We were seconds away from being swallowed whole.

Elios didn't move. Jaw clenched, his hands roamed my arms and sides, checking for injuries, his expression shifting to fury as he saw the fresh scars.

"Where's Ocevia?" Markos asked. His voice was tight, urgent. Fear etched every line of his face.

Heart splitting open, I turned toward him, trying to mask my worry. "We were being chased." My throat tightened. "She told me to keep going and then... she turned back to stall them."

I scanned the water, my eyes burning. In the other boat, Markos ran a trembling hand down his face. His shoulders sagged, the grief curling at the edges of him like smoke.

I wanted to dive back in. Every instinct screamed at me to turn around, to swim after her, to bring her home. But I couldn't. Not yet. I had to keep them safe first. I had to get us out of reach. And somewhere deep inside, I knew—if I turned back, none of us would survive.

Then the water shifted beneath the boat.

A ripple. A shadow.

My heart jolted. "Miris is coming for you! We need to go!"

Elios' jaw set like stone. "No. We're not leaving without Ocevia."

Before I could argue, water exploded beside us as several heads broke the surface. None of them were hers.

I lunged toward the edge of the boat, ready to throw myself back into the sea, to buy them a few more moments, but before I could move, the water beneath us swelled.

A monstrous shape rose from the deep.

Eight colossal tentacles burst from the sea, flinging guards into the air and dragging them back under. Screams echoed for only seconds before the ocean silenced them.

We stared in stunned silence as the water leveled, our boats suddenly still, as though the Kraken had never surfaced at all. The calm felt unnatural, like the eye of a storm that still had more to say.

My thoughts raced, spinning toward the worst possibilities. Was Ocevia injured? Had the Kraken taken her too? The ocean around us looked like glass—unnaturally calm, too still, too quiet, as if the sea itself was holding its breath. No one moved. Not a single oar dipped into the water. Markos and Elios clutched their swords, eyes locked on the rippling surface, bracing for whatever nightmare would rise next.

And then, chaos returned.

Something shot upward from the depths, dark hair trailing like a shadow. A body broke the surface with terrifying speed. I lurched backward, nearly knocking Elios into the sea, as our eyes met.

Miris.

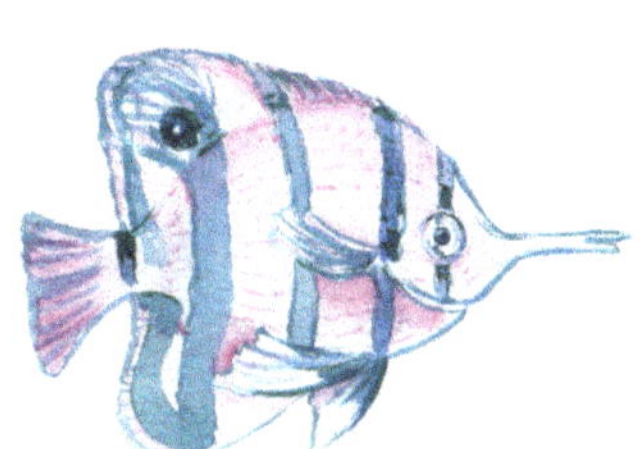

My heart thundered against my ribs. I couldn't breathe. Couldn't speak. The Sea Goddess hung in the air, writhing violently, a massive tentacle wrapped around her waist, suspending her midair like a rag doll.

The Kraken had her.

"Damn it," Markos muttered, his voice low and grim as he paddled toward our boat.

Miris twisted in the Kraken's hold, her movements frantic, but it was no use. She was exhausting herself, just like I had in the chains beneath her palace. Her magic fizzled in the air like a dying spark.

The tentacle curled tighter, winding around her torso, pinning her arms to her sides. She writhed, but the hold didn't falter. She was powerless.

The creature rose slowly from the sea, rust-colored limbs spreading outward, water cascading down its slick body. Its head emerged last, enormous and terrible, with a dozen snakelike feelers curling from its crown.

And then I saw them—its eyes, turquoise and unmistakably hers. My hand flew to my mouth as the truth struck me like a crashing wave, cold and undeniable. The Kraken's gaze was not wild, not mindless. It was focused. Aware. Her.

"Call off your beast, Azure!" Miris shrieked, her voice sharp and un-hinged. "Or my guards will destroy every last one of you! Do you think my previous threats were frightening, Little Mermaid? You haven't seen anything yet!"

The Kraken didn't hesitate.

It lifted Miris higher, then slammed her into the sea with such force that the water itself seemed to recoil. Blood streamed from her brow and nose as she was yanked back into the air, limp in the creature's grip, sputtering curses through a mouth full of sea foam.

Gradually, her thrashing slowed. Her silver eyes narrowed—not with fear, but focus. Cold, calculating.

And then she smiled. Not at me. Not at the creature holding her. At something beyond us. And the look on her face sent a chill down my spine.

I turned, heart hammering, already dreading what I'd find, and the sight that met me nearly brought me to my knees.

Chapter Forty

A Throne Claimed by Death

I watched in horror as the scene unfolded in slow, unbearable motion. Markos' eyes were wide, unblinking, frozen with fear as a blade pressed to his throat. Blood already tracked down his neck in a thin, glistening line. Lucia's grin spread slowly, twisted and feral, one hand clamped over his mouth while the other gripped her dagger like a promise of pain.

With her companion gone, Lucia had unraveled completely. She was unmoored, feral, and volatile.

Elios shifted on his feet beside me, his knuckles turning white around the hilt of his sword. We stood frozen, held captive by the sight of the deranged mermaid and the man she held like bait.

A blood-curdling screech echoed through the air, a sound that made my eardrums throb, the mournful song tugging at my heart. The sea creature's heart-wrenching cry was filled with pure terror, its immense fear palpable in every note. Its tentacles, which had thrashed wildly before, now stilled as the creature released another desperate wail. It was as if all hope had been drained from its body, leaving nothing but anguish and despair behind.

The creature's eyes never left Markos, even as the snarling mermaid pushed the blade deeper into his throat. They were at an impasse, but Miris, ever impatient, made the first move.

With a wicked grin, the Sea Goddess tilted her head back and let out a maniacal cackle. "Kill him!" she bellowed, her eyes blazing with malicious intent. Lucia's grin widened. Before I could blink, she sliced his throat and tossed him into the sea.

Elios let out a cry, raw and broken, as Markos hit the water.

Without hesitation, he dove from the edge of the boat, cutting through the waves in powerful, furious strokes. He reached the neighboring vessel within moments, hauling himself aboard.

Before Lucia could react, his blade flashed.

Steel met flesh in a savage arc, slicing clean across her abdomen. The sound that followed was sharp and wet, a brutal tear that echoed through the stunned quiet. My stomach lurched as blood poured down her front, thick and dark against the pale deck. Lucia staggered back, shrieking, her feral grin replaced by something twisted, panicked, and pained.

Then the Kraken screamed.

It wasn't just a cry. It was a guttural, soul-deep sound that shattered the air like a storm tearing through the sky. The water trembled around us. It was grief made sound, a wail so raw it felt like the sea itself was mourning. A roar of anguish thundered up from the depths, vibrating through my bones.

Then the sea erupted.

Tentacles surged upward—faster than thought, faster than breath. They wrapped around Miris with a violence that split the world open. She thrashed, but it was useless.

There was no mercy left in the ocean.

The tentacles tightened, coiling with relentless force. Her arms were pinned. Her silver tail writhed, slashing against the sea in wild, frantic bursts. Her scream never made it to the surface. The water took it.

And then she came apart.

Her torso tore sideways, flesh shearing from bone. Her head was flung into the air, spinning once before vanishing in the spray. Limbs ripped free with the dull crunch of shattered coral. Blood streamed like ink, coiling through the water in long, red ribbons.

The Kraken didn't just kill her. It un-made her.

She had taken everything. And now, the sea had taken her.

Justice wasn't clean. It was violent. Unforgiving. Drenched in salt and fury and sorrow. And for the first time, Miris knew what it meant to be powerless.

The Sea Goddess was no more, but before I could process that, the Kraken vanished beneath the waves.

There was no time to breathe. No time to feel. My focus snapped back to Elios, who'd made it back to our boat and climbed in, fighting to catch his breath. I swam toward him just as the water stirred again.

The Kraken resurfaced, rising from the deep with slow, haunting poise. In its massive limbs, it cradled a pale, bloodied, and barely conscious Markos. His body sagged in the Kraken's hold, his breath shallow, his pulse a flicker. Blood still drifted from him in red ribbons, mixing with the sea. I was already in the water, swimming hard, the salt stinging my eyes as I raced toward the other boat.

By the time the creature reached the vessel, I was there too, gasping as I pulled myself over the side. The Kraken lowered Markos onto the deck with a tenderness I never would have believed it capable of. His chest rose in shallow, uneven movements, each one weaker than the last. He was alive but fading quickly.

Elios moved beside me and pressed hard on the wound, his hands slick with blood as it poured too quickly to contain. I wanted to help, but I didn't know how—not really. I didn't know if anyone could save him. I dropped beside Markos anyway, bracing one hand on his chest, whispering something I couldn't even hear over the sound of the waves, hoping the sound of my voice could hold him here just a little longer.

The other boat drifted into ours, its wooden hull nudging gently against the side, as if even the sea itself acknowledged the weight of what we had just endured. Lucia's broken form hung over the edge, her blood trailing in thin ribbons across the water.

With a final, sweeping strike, the Kraken slammed the vessel, sending it spinning before it capsized beneath the weight of the sea. Lucia slipped beneath the surface with barely a ripple—vanishing just as the massive creature sank after her. Lucia returned to the same sea she had stained with the lives of so many others, finally claimed by the very force she had once believed she could control.

Heartbroken, I turned away, unable to watch the light fade from our friend's eyes. I had already seen, and caused, too much death. Needing the connection, I rested a trembling hand on Elios' back and stared at the place where the Kraken had disappeared beneath the surface. I didn't know what I was waiting for—maybe a miracle, maybe the return of my friend. Anything that could undo the silence pressing in around us.

As if answering that unspoken plea, familiar blond hair bobbed next to the boat. For a single breathless second, I thought it might vanish again, but then Ocevia broke the surface and hauled herself over the side, collapsing beside the man she loved. Her sobs cracked open the stillness, and I could barely bring myself to watch as she clutched Markos, her hands trembling violently.

For a few moments, the only sounds were her cries and his struggle to survive.

I closed my eyes, tears slipping free as guilt wrapped its cold fingers around my throat. Ocevia had stayed behind. She had faced down a dozen enemies. She had trusted me to protect them, and I had failed her.

Then a voice cut through the silence.

"Don't cry, beautiful," Markos whispered.

My eyes flew open. For one impossible second, I thought I'd imagined it—just another cruel trick of grief, but *no*. His lips had moved. His voice, weak and trembling, had come from him. Markos. *Alive*. Speaking. I could barely breathe through the shock as Ocevia drew back, disbelief blooming in her eyes.

Unblinking, Ocevia smoothed the wet hair from Markos' forehead, her hands trembling. His eyes fluttered open, and he took in a deep, shuddering breath.

My heart jolted. Relief and shock tangled in my chest.

"Ocevia?" Her name barely made it past my lips, soft and uncertain, as if saying it too loudly might shatter what I was seeing.

She didn't answer right away.

Her attention stayed fixed on him. Fingers brushed along his jaw, tears glistening as they trailed down her cheeks. Maybe she was stalling. Maybe she already knew what I was going to ask and couldn't yet bring herself to meet my eyes.

"Hm?" she murmured at last, her voice low, still looking at Markos like he was something rare she didn't believe she deserved.

The wound on his neck was gone. Not even a scar remained. It was like it had never happened.

Across from me, Elios cast a questioning glance, but I didn't return it. *Couldn't.* My gaze stayed on my best friend. The truth was already there between us, but I needed her to speak it. Needed to hear it come from her lips, even if I already knew what it meant.

"Ocevia," I said softly. "You killed Miris."

She flinched, and I immediately regretted saying it. The sigh that left her was long and tight as she finally looked up and met my gaze. "I've wanted to tell you for a long time," she said, her voice barely louder than the wind. "When I was a child, I couldn't control my powers. I hurt people, Azure. A lot of people."

Her hand rose to the shell necklace at her throat, fingers closing around it like a tether.

"My family... they were afraid of me. They shunned me. Becoming a mermaid was better than being who I was."

Her voice cracked, and she looked away again, back at Markos. "I didn't tell you because I couldn't bear the thought of you fearing me too. You were my only friend."

A sharp ache spread through my chest.

I couldn't begin to imagine how lonely she must have felt carrying that secret—how heavy it was to be loved for something she'd worked so hard to hide.

"I wouldn't abandon you, Ocevia," I said. "And I'd never fear you."

I reached across the space between us and laid a hand on her shoulder. I wanted to do more, to take some piece of that burden from her, but words and touch were all I had.

Then something else surfaced in my thoughts... the last person we'd seen before the palace began to fall. The woman who'd risked everything to free me.

"Ocevia, did you see what happened to Corileia?"

Ocevia's expression fell. She turned her face back to Markos and gently brushed a lock of hair from his eyes.

"A guard took her," she said. "Dragged her back toward the palace. I wanted to follow. I was going to. But then I saw Miris rise toward the surface and..." She paused, eyes lingering on Markos' face. "I couldn't risk it. I needed to protect all of you. And to do that, I had to transform. I had to become what I'd spent my whole life hiding."

Guilt twisted in my gut when she wiped a tear from her cheek. Not because she'd lied, but because she had been afraid to tell me the truth.

Because I had let her carry it alone.

Markos reached up and brushed another tear from her face with his thumb, his touch impossibly tender. "Everything is going to be okay, my Sea Maiden."

His gaze was full of warmth, and something in my chest eased just watching them. Ocevia had always been so many things—strong, secretive, sarcastic—but this was different. This was something she hadn't been given in far too long.

Love. *Real* love.

Without a word, Elios laced his fingers through mine, his thumb brushing gently across my knuckles. I leaned into the touch, letting the quiet steadiness of it soften the sharp edges inside me.

From across the chamber, a small, fragile smile curved Ocevia's lips. "All that matters is that you're alive, Markos. That everyone is alive."

The words lingered in the air, quiet and tender.

Uncertain how to approach what still hung between us, I shifted my weight. We all knew the question was coming.

Some truths still needed to be spoken aloud.

"Ocevia..." I said again, slightly louder this time. "You killed Miris. That means—"

"I know what it means," she said, cutting me off before I could finish. Her voice held no hesitation, only quiet resignation.

At her side, Markos stiffened. He gently tilted her face toward his, his brow creasing with unspoken worry. "What does it mean, Ocevia?"

She leaned into the hand that cradled her cheek, eyes drifting closed. Another tear slipped free.

"It means I'm the new Sea Goddess.

BEYOND THE OCEAN'S CURSE

3 Months Later

"Do you miss it?" Elios asked as he stepped up behind me, his arms wrapping around my waist.

I hadn't realized how long I'd been standing at the edge of the dock, staring out at the sea. It shimmered beneath the soft morning light, beautiful in a way that made my chest ache.

The answer to his question wasn't simple.

One shoulder lifted. "I don't miss the curse," I said quietly. "But I do miss Ocevia."

Just saying her name pulled at something tender inside me. My best friend. My sister in every way but blood. The weight she now carried still felt impossible. I was free because she'd chosen to stay behind.

Elios pressed a kiss to my cheek, and I closed my eyes at the warmth of it. His arms around me made it easier to breathe.

There had been a time, curled up in that dark, freezing cell, when I thought I'd never see him again. Never feel anything again. But he was here. We both were. And now, I got to keep him.

"We'll visit soon," he murmured. "I know you miss her. I miss Markos too. But they're together. They're healing. And she's doing something no one else ever has."

He was right.

Before we left the sea, Ocevia had used the power Miris left behind to break my curse. My tail was no longer bound to her magic, and the bargain had been erased. I still had the ability to return to the ocean if I chose, but the duty to kill was gone. That hunger was gone.

For the first time in memory, mermaids had a choice.

Ocevia had given that to us.

She'd changed everything.

The ocean felt different now. It didn't hum with death. It didn't pull like it used to. Under her rule, the water had begun to heal, and so had I.

I touched the seashell strung around my neck—a smooth, pale spiral I'd picked up from the cove where Ocevia and I used to dream aloud, before everything went dark. It wasn't enchanted. It wasn't cursed. Just a piece of the sea I chose to keep.

A reminder that I'd survived it.

Elios reached for my hand and brushed his thumb over the ring he'd given me. The sapphire caught the sunlight and scattered it into the sky like something pulled from a fairytale.

"We should board soon," he said, pressing a kiss to my temple.

I nodded and turned to look at him. *Really* look. His face was sun-warmed and clean-shaven, his expression soft and steady, the way it always got when he was trying to make me feel safe without saying the words out loud.

"I'm a little scared," I admitted. "It's been so long. What if she doesn't want to come with us? What if she doesn't remember me at all?"

"She was just a kid," I added, my voice thinner than I wanted it to be. "And I've changed. What if I'm too different now?"

Elios smiled in that quiet way of his—the one that always made me feel like we could handle anything, as long as we were together.

"She's probably nervous too," he said. "And if she doesn't want to live with us in Starspell, we'll move to Thatia. We can live anywhere now. That's the whole point. We're free."

Free.

The word settled somewhere deep inside me, warm and strange.

I never expected freedom. Not after everything. I didn't know what to do with it now that I had it. But as I leaned into his chest and let the rhythm of his heartbeat slow mine, I started to understand.

The sea wasn't my home anymore.

He was.

The wind picked up gently, wrapping the scent of salt and sunbaked wood around us. It carried something that felt like a blessing—something that whispered, *you made it*. For the first time in years, maybe in my whole life, I wasn't waiting for something terrible to happen.

My heart, cracked and stitched together more times than I could count, felt almost whole. The song of death no longer lived in my throat. And my family—my *real* family—was about to be whole again.

"You're right," I said, a small smile tugging at the corner of my mouth. "It's been over three years. She's waited long enough, and so have I."

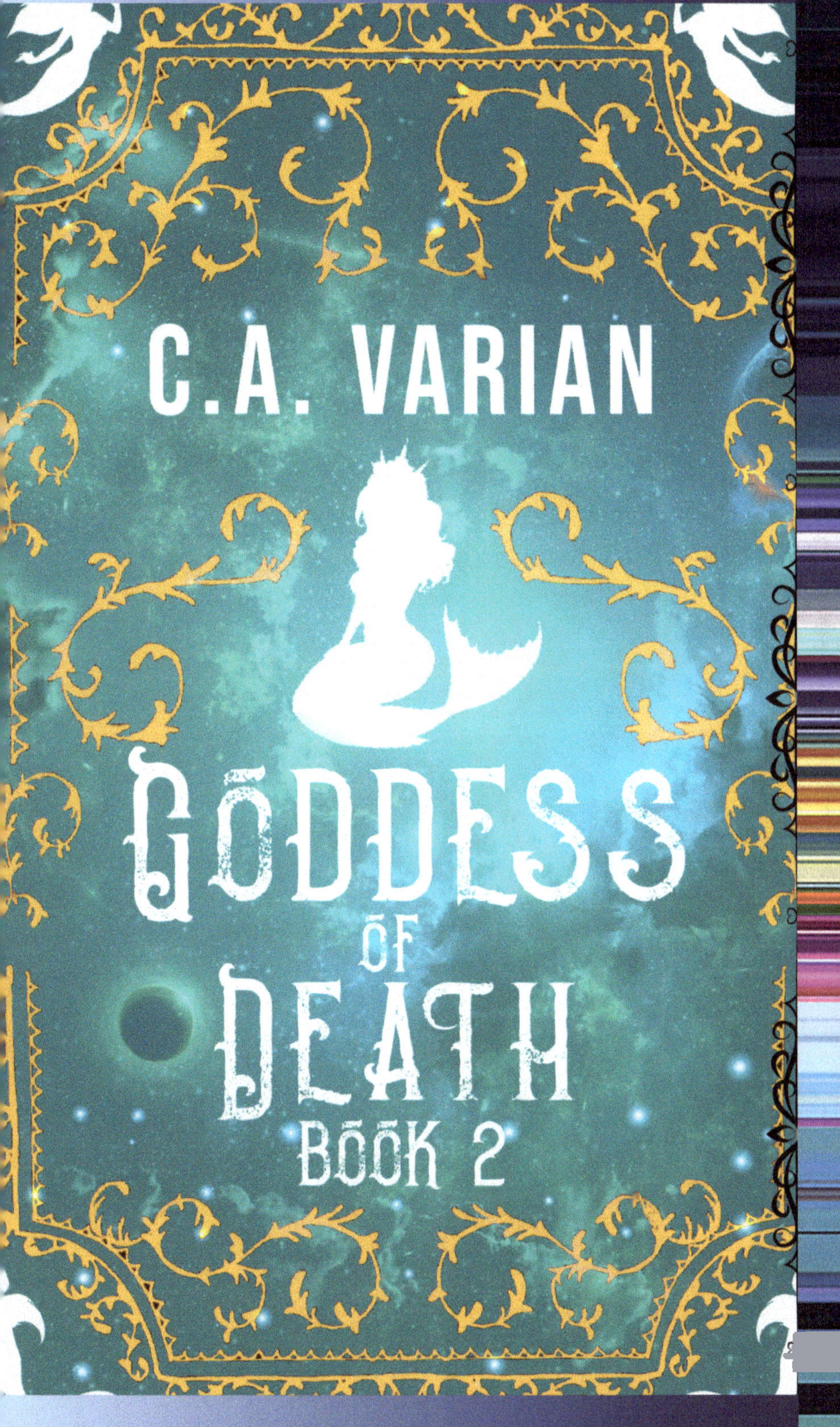

C.A. VARIAN
GODDESS
OF
DEATH
BOOK 2

Book Cover by Leigh Graphic Designs

Page Edge Design by Painted Wings Publishing

Chapter Header design by Leigh Graphic Designs

Hardcase Design by Athena Crest Arts

2nd edition 2025

FOREWORD

Every story has a shadow.

In *Song of Death*, Ocevia Kallallis seemed like one, tragic, cursed, fading quietly into the background of Azure's journey. But she was never just a side character.

Ocevia was Azure's best friend. Her fiercest protector. A girl who bore the weight of bloodlines, secrets, and sea-born magic no child should ever carry.

Not a footnote.

A storm.

Goddess of Death is her story: raw, unflinching, and brimming with rage, devotion, and the sea's cruel beauty. It's a tale of what happens when power is inherited, when love becomes dangerous, and when silence is no longer an option.

This is Ocevia's tale.

And she was never meant to be forgotten.

Chapter One

THE SHELL AND THE SHACKLE

My trembling fingers clutched the seashell necklace around my neck, its smooth surface slick with tears. The chain dug into my damp skin, as if it, too, understood what it had become: a shackle, a prison, a curse.

The shell itself was beautiful. Pale pink, delicately ridged, the kind of treasure a child might pluck from the sand and press to their ear, hoping to hear the ocean's song. But there was no song now. There was only silence. There was only loss.

It felt too heavy. Too big. I didn't want it. I wanted to rip it off and hurl it into the sea, let the waves swallow it, and me with it. But I didn't dare.

Its weight bore down on me, suffocating, like an anchor tethered to something I couldn't name. I was only eleven. I should have been running along the shorelines, sun-kissed and laughing, not standing here, drowning on dry land.

Before me stood the Sea Goddess herself, the executioner of my innocence.

Miris loomed like a specter torn from a nightmare, her quicksilver eyes swirling with something unknowable. It wasn't warmth. It wasn't comfort. It was distance, as if I were nothing more than a ripple on the vast tide of her eternity.

She was breathtaking. Ethereal. Terrifying. A being made of salt and shadows, of whispered prayers and unanswered pleas. The myths had never done her justice.

Her silver tail had been traded for slender, human legs, a reminder that she held the power to walk in both worlds. She was beyond rules, beyond mercy.

I didn't want to be part of her world.

Her long fingers brushed against the necklace before letting it fall. The shell struck my chest, cold as stone, the chain snapping tight around my neck like a lock sealing shut. A shiver tore down my spine at the sudden bite of metal against skin.

It was done. There would be no undoing it now.

"As long as you wear this," she murmured, her voice sliding into my ear like the pull of the tide, "the beast inside you will remain hidden."

She leaned closer. Her lips grazed my ear with a touch so soft it felt like the ocean breathing against the cliffs. "Your bloodline was meant to be lost," she whispered. "But the sea never forgets its monsters."

Another shiver prickled along my skin, sinking deeper than before.

The beast inside me. Something slumbered beneath my bones, waiting. My heart pounded harder, louder, deeper, like it didn't quite belong to me anymore.

I didn't understand. Not really. I only knew that something was wrong with me. That I had frightened people. That my parents had whispered behind closed doors when they thought I wasn't listening.

That they had called her.

That they had given me away.

A lump rose in my throat, thick and unyielding. I swallowed it down, forcing myself to stand still, to keep my chin lifted even as my chest trembled. Crying wouldn't change anything. It never had.

And yet, as I looked up at Miris, the question slipped from my lips before I could stop it. My voice was small, shaking beneath the weight of the moment.

"Will I ever see them again?"

Silence, at first.

Then Miris smiled. A beautiful, empty thing. A cruel thing.

Her fingers brushed the seashell at my throat, playing with it like a toy.

"My mermaids are not allowed to visit the human lands, Little Fish," she said, her voice soft as the roll of distant tides. "You will never see them again... unless they dare to enter the sea."

The words gutted me like a knife slipped between my ribs.

Never?

Never again would I feel my mother's loving arms, her fingers stroking my hair as she sang me to sleep. Never again would I hear my father's deep laugh, lifting me high and calling me his brave girl. Never again would I hold Elaria's tiny hand, feel her squeeze tight when she was scared and needed me.

The realization crashed into me like a wave, stealing my breath.

Gone. They were gone.

I didn't want to cry in front of her, but the tears came anyway, hot and quiet, slipping down my cheeks.

Miris tilted her head, studying me like a serpent watching a bird trapped in its cage. Her gaze was cold, ancient, inevitable.

"Do not weep," she murmured. "We will be your new family."

The words turned my stomach. They were meant to soothe, but they only tasted like salt and lies.

I could still feel the last time my mother touched me—her trembling hand brushing my hair, her voice cracking as she said I'd be safe. My father hadn't looked back when they left me on the shore.

Not even once.

I knew better than to argue with a goddess. Her rules were absolute, and her punishments worse than death.

My fingers closed around the seashell, squeezing until its edges bit into my skin.

This was not a gift.

It was a cage.

And I was already dead.

I didn't remember moving.

One moment, I stood on the sand of Thatia's shoreline. The next, I stared into the endless black of the Lamalis Sea, the prison that would swallow me whole.

The air was thick with salt and the scent of approaching rain. Wind rolled in from the water like a breath held too long. The storm had gathered quickly, the sky darkening with unnatural speed.

Miris stood beside me, unmoved by the chaos. Wind whipped her onyx hair across her shoulders, but she didn't flinch. She belonged to the sea. No, she commanded it. The storm bowed to her.

I swallowed hard, my voice wavering. "When do we leave?"

A smile crept across her lips, slow and certain.

She didn't answer with words. She answered with a blade.

Pain.

A searing slice across my palm.

I gasped, the air stolen from my lungs, but Miris took my bleeding hand in hers and let my crimson life spill into the golden sand. My pulse thundered through the wound, warm droplets splashing like sacrifice.

The world tilted, and agony hit with brutal force, folding me inward before I could catch my breath.

A scream tore free from my chest as something inside me unraveled. My bones twisted. My flesh bent. My very essence split apart like thread snapping loose.

I collapsed onto the sand, arms shaking as I clawed at the ground, desperate to hold on to whatever I had been. But it was already gone.

My legs were gone.

Where feet had once danced through wildflowers and the halls of my home, now shimmered an iridescent turquoise tail. Beautiful in the way lightning is beautiful. Stunning. Unnatural.

Something meant for killing, not for dancing. Not for an eleven-year-old girl with flowers in her memory and salt in her blood.

A broken sob escaped my lips. I couldn't walk. Couldn't stand. I wasn't human anymore.

I wasn't anything.

A monster, a servant, a slave. Titles I had never imagined claiming. Yet here they were, etched into my skin like prophecy, carved by fear and seafoam.

I stared at my hands, trembling and blood-streaked—foreign. The first toll of the debt.

Fifty thousand lives. Fifty thousand deaths.

That was what she demanded.

Freedom was no longer mine to imagine, and the person I had been no longer existed.

At just eleven years old, everything I had been was gone. A child one moment, a curse the next. My life—sunlight, laughter, names I used to answer to—had ended before it truly began.

Miris turned toward the sea, her steps slow and unhurried. The storm broke behind her, rain slashing across my skin as if the sky itself mourned what I had lost.

I lifted my head once more, looking back at the shore—the home that would never again be mine.

Maybe they thought they'd saved me.

Maybe they thought this was mercy.

But as I stared into the dark, churning water that waited below, I saw the truth.

There was no mercy here. Only monsters bred from sorrow.

And now, I was one of them.

"The pain will lessen once you are grown," Miris said, her voice distant and cold. "It is always harder for the young."

Her words didn't comfort. They weren't meant to. She had seen it all before.

How many children had she watched fall apart? How many had she dragged beneath the waves, never to be seen again?

The thought sickened me, but it no longer mattered.

I wasn't human anymore.

I took one last, shaking breath, and with the goddess at my side, I slipped beneath the waves into the darkness that would become my home.

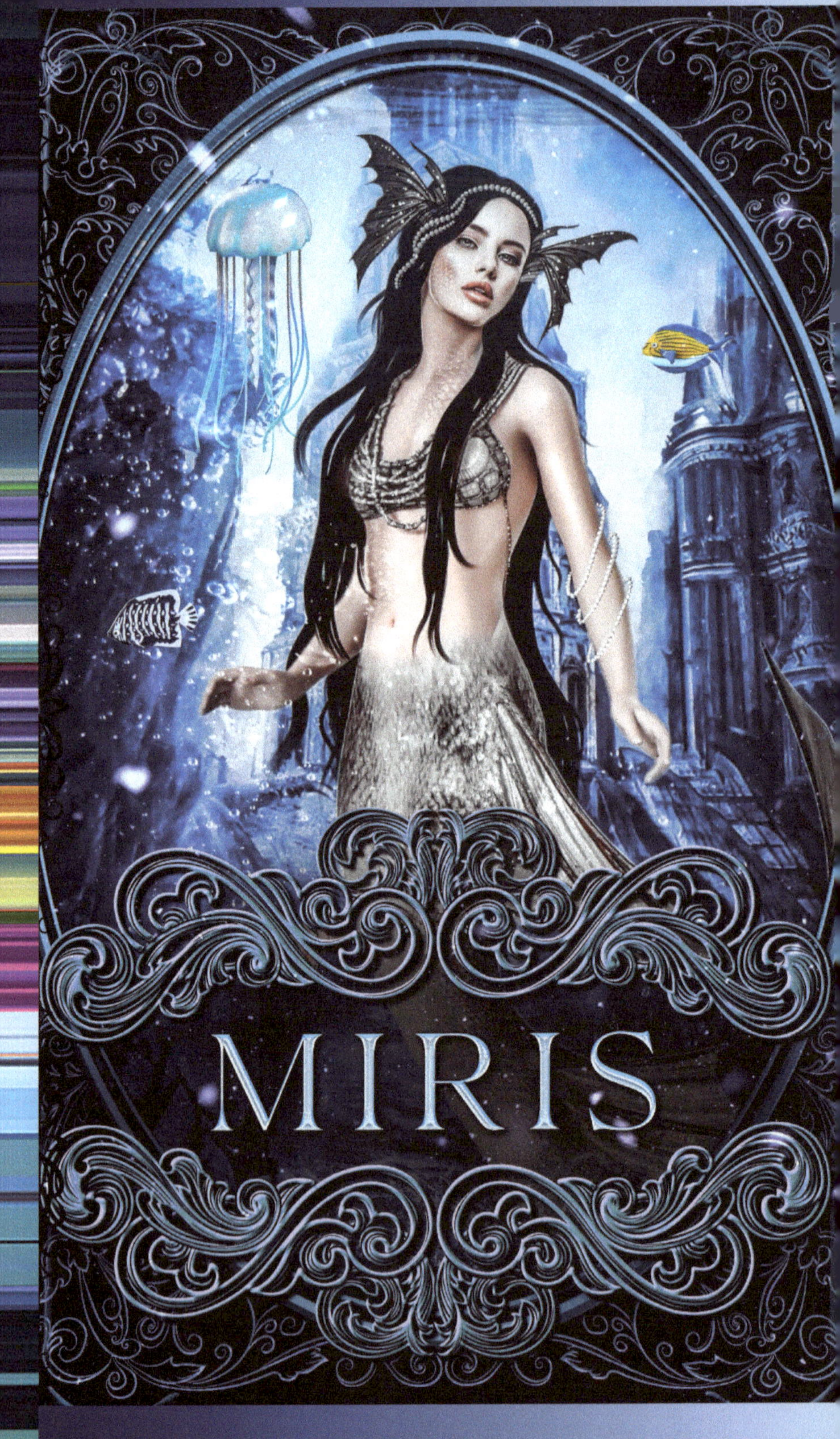

MIRIS

A LESSON IN OBEDIENCE

Four Years Later

Tonight, I was supposed to kill them.

My lips parted, the first note of the song forming at the back of my throat, but nothing came. Air clawed its way into my windpipe, but my body locked up. The voice Miris had cursed me with, the weapon she had forced on me, refused to move.

The other mermaids were already singing. Their haunting melody stretched across the water like gossamer threads, winding around the men's minds and pulling them toward the inevitable. The song tugged at my core, slipping inside like a hand around my throat—warm, persuasive, impossible to ignore. It wanted to wear my voice like a mask. I fought it with everything I had. I wasn't ready. I didn't want to be this.

One of the sailors leaned over the railing, scanning the dark water. His face was soft, still edged with the last traces of childhood. He couldn't have been much older than me.

I clenched my fists.

I couldn't do this. Not tonight.

Instead of singing, I dove.

The water wrapped around me like an old friend—calm, quiet, forgiving. It washed the melody from my ears, dulled the pressure in my chest. My heart pounded as I swam deeper, away from the ship, away from the others. If I could just disappear for one night... if I could pretend, for a little while, that I wasn't one of them...

Something yanked me backward.

A hand. No, a claw. Sharp nails sank into my arm, wrenching me from the depths and dragging me toward the surface. My stomach twisted. The rush of terror chased away the relief I had only just begun to feel.

Lucia.

The golden-haired mermaid grinned, one of Miris' most brutal enforcers, her turquoise eyes gleaming with something close to amusement.

"Running away, Little Fish?" she crooned, her grip tightening like an iron shackle. "Tsk, tsk. Miris won't like that."

I thrashed against her hold, but she was stronger. Her fingers were like vices, digging into the soft flesh of my wrist. Her gaze flicked toward the ship, where the men had already begun their descent into madness. Their limbs were sluggish. Their voices slurred with the enchantment of our sisters' song.

"You could have had your pick," she mused. "That one was pretty, wasn't he?" She leaned in, her breath sharp with brine. "Would you have spared him, Ocevia? Would you have let him live?"

The words I wanted to throw at her lodged in my throat, burning. I said nothing. She already knew.

Lucia's grin widened. "Come now," she cooed. "You know the rules. The debt must be paid. Miris doesn't take kindly to disobedience."

Before I could protest, she yanked me upward, dragging me through the churning sea with ruthless force. The water frothed and surged around us, but I barely noticed. My mind had already sunk beneath the weight of the truth I kept trying to outrun.

I was going to be punished.

A short time later, Miris' guards threw me onto the stone floor like a gutted fish. My body hit the cold, unforgiving rock with a sickening thud. The air ripped from my lungs as pain knifed through my ribs. I gasped, fingers scraping the wet surface as I tried to push myself up. Then I froze at the sound of a low, indulgent chuckle echoing through the chamber.

"Still so defiant," Miris murmured.

I lifted my head, vision swimming. She stood before me, her silver gaze unreadable, her beauty terrible beneath the pulsing bioluminescent glow. The water around the perimeter of the chamber moved with her presence, waves forming from nothing, rising and falling as if bowing to her.

With a smile I knew was fake, she crouched beside me, fingers trailing over my cheek with a gentleness that unsettled more than any blow.

"I expected better from you, Little Fish." Her voice was soft, almost affectionate, but I knew better. "No matter how old you grow, no matter how long you swim in my sea, you will always belong to me."

Salt and copper filled my mouth as I swallowed. My jaw throbbed with the effort of holding back my voice.

She sighed, the sound so quiet it could almost be mistaken for sorrow.

"I give you everything. Life. Power. Purpose." Her fingers brushed the seashell at my throat, the one that bound my truth beneath its gleaming surface. "And yet you resist."

I clenched my fists against the stone, remaining silent.

"Lucia."

I barely had time to react before the first blow landed.

Pain burst across my ribs as a heavy club slammed into my side, knocking the breath from my lungs in one ragged gasp. My vision blurred, darkness creeping in at the edges. The second strike came even faster, slamming into my back and sending fire down my spine. A cry rose in my throat. I bit down on it, holding it back.

Folding in on myself, I shielded my head as more blows rained down. Fists, boots, something heavier—I couldn't tell anymore. Everything blurred together, pain carving its mark into my skin until I could barely think.

I wanted to be strong. I tried to be strong. But I was only fifteen, and I wasn't ready for this.

Blood filled my mouth as I clenched my jaw, determined not to scream. I wouldn't give them the satisfaction. My breath came in shudders, my strength draining with every strike. My body trembled, legs shaking beneath me, but the assault ended as suddenly as it had begun.

I collapsed, my cheek pressing to the cold, damp stone. Pain clung to every inch of me. My ears rang with the ghost of their laughter—faint, detached. Footsteps moved around me, too distant to track.

A shadow fell over me only seconds before Miris knelt beside me once more, her fingers weaving into my hair as she forced my head up.

"I do this because I love you," she murmured. "Because you are mine."

A shiver ran through me. My lungs seized as I tried to breathe, but my painful ribs made it impossible.

She leaned close, her lips brushing my ear.

"Now tell me, Little Fish," she whispered, her voice soft as the tide. "Whom do you serve?"

My throat locked. The words wouldn't come.

Her fingers tightened.

"Say it."

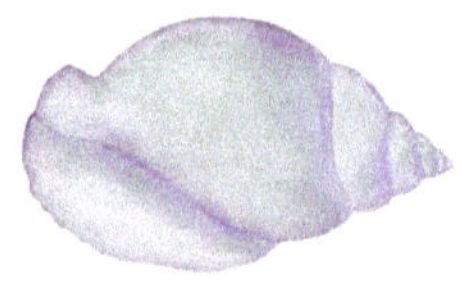

The word scraped from my lips, barely audible. "You."

Miris smiled, satisfied. "Good girl." She released me and rose to her feet with the effortless grace of a tide returning to sea. "Let this be a lesson, Ocevia. I expect obedience. Next time, I won't be so merciful."

Turning away from me, her cobalt gown glided across the floor as she moved toward the exit, her obsidian hair catching the pale shimmer of bioluminescent light.

The moment she was gone, my body collapsed onto the stone. My breath shuddered from my lips, my tears mixing with the saltwater seeping through the cracks in the floor.

I blinked at the stone, unsure if the blood on my hands was real or just a memory still pulsing behind my eyes. The pain was sharp. The silence was worse.

No matter how strong I thought I was, I had been reminded of the truth.

I was nothing but a Little Fish in Miris' vast and endless sea.

I didn't know how long I lay there.

Time lost all meaning, swallowed by the steady throb of pain radiating from every part of me. My ribs flared with each shallow breath, and my skin burned where the blows had landed. The stone beneath me was slick with sweat, blood, and seawater, the cold of it seeping into my bones until I couldn't feel where my body ended and the ground began.

High above, water dripped from the cavern ceiling. Each soft drop echoed in the silence, a slow reminder that the punishment was over, but not forgotten.

They were gone now. All of them. Even Miris.

I didn't know which had been worse, the beating or the way she had smiled afterward, satisfied, as if I were nothing more than a misbehaving creature she had finally broken.

I tried to shift, to sit up or at least roll to my side, but my muscles screamed with the effort. A weak sound slipped from my lips before I could stop it, and shame followed immediately after, rising hot and bitter in my chest. I hated myself for that sound. Hated how easily my strength had been stripped away.

I was supposed to be stronger than this, but even stone cracked under the right amount of pressure.

For the first time in years, I let the tears fall. No gasping sobs, no cries for help. Just silent, shuddering tears that vanished into the darkness.

Once, I believed I could endure anything Miris gave me. That no matter what she did, I could hold onto something of myself. A sliver of defiance. A memory untouched. A piece of who I was before.

But tonight, lying there on the cold stone floor, I felt that belief slipping through my fingers.

She was winning.

If I didn't find a way to escape her grasp—if I kept letting her tear me down piece by piece—there would come a day when nothing remained.

No voice. No will. No self.

Just a pretty monster, bound by salt and silence.

Chapter Three

The One Who Wouldn't Bow

Three Years Later

They sent her on her first hunt before the bruises had even healed.

Newly cursed and still raw from whatever loss had tethered her to the sea, she moved like someone trying not to drown. Her tail shimmered in the gloom with a strange, dangerous beauty, too bright for the depths, too fragile to survive here. But it wasn't fragility I saw in her. It was fire. Wild, ragged, reckless. The kind of fire that didn't last long in a place like this.

They called her Azure. I had heard the guards whisper it. The one who begged for her sister. The one who said yes. Another soul traded for survival. Another girl condemned to earn her freedom through blood. Still, they had sent her into open waters as if she were ready. As if she already belonged.

She didn't. Not yet.

She hovered at the edge of the reef, silent and tense, her violet-streaked hair swirling like smoke in the slow churn of the current. From a distance, she looked composed, another beautiful predator of the deep. But up close, the fractures showed. Her tail was rigid, her arms locked stiffly at her sides. Fear clung to her like a second skin, invisible unless you knew where to look.

And Lucia always knew where to look.

We floated along the outskirts of the channel, a silent line of mermaids waiting for the merchant vessel to drift close enough to sing. Below us, a warm current coiled with restless energy, thick with the promise of death. The others hovered in perfect stillness, their gazes pinned to the ship like wolves circling a bleeding deer.

Then Lucia broke formation.

Gliding past us like a silk ribbon loosed into the water, she made her way toward the newest of us. Her smile was all sugar, but her eyes were rot. She circled Azure with a slow, deliberate grace, savoring the tension that radiated from her like heat from a wound.

"Well, well," Lucia purred, her voice curling through the water like smoke. "Little Storm. Hiding already?"

Azure didn't move. Didn't speak. Her gaze remained locked on the distant ship, her jaw clenched tight.

Lucia circled again, closer now. "Not hiding? You must be afraid."

I stayed where I was, arms folded loosely across my chest. Involvement was dangerous, especially with Lucia, but a low unease prickled beneath my skin.

A small, nearly imperceptible flicker rippled through Azure's tail.

Lucia leaned in, her voice turning sharp and cruel. "You're not planning to sing tonight, are you? Or have you already forgotten what you owe?"

Silence.

Lucia smiled, tilting her head, her golden hair fanning out like a halo around her. "You made quite the bargain, didn't you? Your sister's life for five thousand strangers. That's a lot of blood for one little girl. You'd better get started."

"She's worth any price," Azure said, her voice steady, but the water around her shivered with the force of it.

Lucia's smile twisted into something feral. "What if I pay one for you?" she said sweetly. "What if I drag that ship down myself and carve your first mark into the stone before you've earned it? You wouldn't want the Sea Goddess to think you're ungrateful. She might take that precious sister back."

That was when Azure moved.

With no warning, no hesitation, she lunged at Lucia, claws bared and eyes burning with wildfire. It was reckless. Beautiful. Hopeless.

Lucia caught her easily.

With a brutal twist, she slammed Azure into the reef, hard enough to send shockwaves through the water. Blood unfurled from Azure's shoulder, a dark ribbon that curled lazily toward the surface.

That was when I moved.

I didn't think. I didn't plan. I just swam.

By the time I reached them, Azure had crumpled against the coral, one arm hanging limp at her side, her breath coming in short, sharp gasps. No tears. No pleading. Just a grim, stubborn refusal to break.

Lucia turned as I approached, her smile thin and mocking. "Ocevia. I'm surprised you're still alive."

"She's new," I said, trying to seem calmer than I felt. "You've made your point."

"Oh, I haven't made it yet."

Crossing her arms, Lucia drifted closer. The sweetness had drained from her voice, leaving only the sharp glint of cruelty behind.

"She'll learn," I said, glancing toward Azure and then back at Lucia.

Her smile twisted into a sneer. "She's refusing to."

"Then let Miris punish her," I said, my voice a steady blade between us. Around us, Azure's blood continued to darken the water, a silent accusation.

Lucia's gaze narrowed to slits. "Are you planning to take her place?"

"No." I tilted my head slightly, unblinking. "I don't need to, and it's not your place either."

A long pause stretched taut between us. Even the current seemed to still.

Lucia's smile returned, brittle and bright. She shrugged, a ripple of amusement flickering across her face. Then she turned and vanished into the darkness, her laughter trailing behind her like the remnants of a dying song.

Only when she was gone did I move to Azure.

Blood still floated around her in slow spirals, staining the reef below. Her breathing was shallow, ragged. Carefully, I closed the distance between us, reaching out. She flinched away, her voice rough and breathless.

"Don't touch me."

I didn't retreat.

"I'm not going to hurt you," I said, barely above a whisper.

"I don't need your help."

"I know."

I drifted lower, settling beside her without touching her, letting the slow pulse of the ocean cradle us both. I didn't speak. I didn't offer empty comforts. I just stayed, anchoring us there against the tide.

Above us, far beyond the reef, the other mermaids sang. Their haunting melody rose and fell, claiming another ship, another set of souls. Another debt marked on the walls of Miris' dominion.

Azure said nothing more. She pressed trembling fingers to her wounded shoulder, her eyes clamped shut, as if willing the world to vanish.

Maybe she didn't want me there. But I stayed, because the life waiting for her now would be brutal. And she wasn't the only one who needed someone to stand beside her.

By the time we returned to the caves, the sea had darkened to black ink, and the world above the waves had surrendered to silence. Neither of us spoke as we crossed the threshold into the hollowed cavern. The fire in the center burned low, its sullen orange glow bleeding across the rough-hewn stone. The salt in my hair turned brittle as it dried, clinging to my skin like a second, colder layer.

Without a word, Azure moved like a shadow, tucking herself into the corner farthest from the entrance. She wrapped her arms tightly around her knees, pulling the thin blanket over her bruised shoulders as if it could shield her from the weight of what she had endured. She made no sound. Not even when she shivered. Not even when the fire cracked and spat and threatened to die.

Not wanting to overwhelm her more, I settled down a short distance away, close enough that she could feel my presence, far enough that she could pretend she was alone if she needed to. The stone was cold beneath me, and the ache in my body was a dull throb that spoke of battles both fought and surrendered. I leaned back against the damp wall, folded my arms across my chest, and closed my eyes.

Hours passed.

The fire burned low, its embers hissing like dying memories. Outside, the tide muttered against the rocks, restless and insistent, a lullaby too bitter to offer comfort. The hush between us grew heavier with every passing moment, saturated with the things we didn't say.

And then, her voice broke the silence.

It wasn't the mermaid's melody we were cursed to sing. It wasn't the deadly enchantment that pulled sailors to their deaths. This was something raw. Something human. A thread of music so fragile it sounded like it might shatter if she breathed too hard.

Her voice wavered off-key, catching and slipping through the notes like a body battered by the current. I didn't recognize the song, and I didn't need to. It wasn't meant for me. It was for the girl she used to be, the one Miris had stolen from the world above the waves.

Every broken note curled through the cavern, drifting like mist, filling the empty spaces inside both of us. The spaces where hope used to live.

I didn't move. I didn't speak. I only listened, letting her sorrow settle into the hollow places inside me.

When the last note faded, the fire's glow trembled against her face, shadows sinking into the hollows of her cheeks. She stared into the dying embers, her body folded tight, as if bracing herself against a world that had already taken too much.

I stayed where I was. Not out of duty, but for something simpler, something that asked nothing in return.

Sleep didn't find me that night. I lay awake in the dark, staring at the hollowed stone ceiling while the memory of her song lingered like sea on my skin. I hadn't meant to care for her. Not when caring meant losing.

But somehow, I did.

And in that cavern, beneath the hollow stars carved into the stone, I realized I wasn't alone anymore.

We were two broken things, bound not by blood or fate, but by something just as strong: survival, and the stubborn will to remember who we had once been.

In the silence between shipwrecks and sorrow, we hadn't found safety, but we had found each other.

And for now, that was enough.

A Debt Written in Souls

Three Years Later

"Just a little longer." I blew gently on Azure's back as I screwed the lid back on the ointment tin. The wounds from the lashing were deep, still oozing blood in some places. "They should scab over soon. If you would stop defying her, she would stop having you whipped."

She exhaled a pained breath. "Even if I stayed out of trouble, she would still find a reason to punish me."

I knew my friend was correct. Trouble clung to her like a second skin, no matter how still she stood. Still, seeing her injuries reminded me why I followed the rules. It had been a long time since I had angered Miris, and I intended to keep it that way. Her temper was reason enough to obey.

"You're probably right." Leaning forward, I rinsed my hands in the salty water pooling along the edge of the stone. Waves crashed violently against our small cove, a sound that might have sent a human fleeing for safer shores. For us, though—for mermaids—it was just another rhythm in the song of the sea. We spent most daylight hours hidden away on the jagged islands that dotted the Lamalis Sea, tucked into the cracks between tides where Miris' shadow couldn't reach quite as easily.

"Are you going to be ready to go back out tonight?"

Azure glanced at the dozens of markings carved into the cave wall behind her before returning her gaze to me. Although I pretended not to notice, I knew exactly what she was thinking. When the Sea Goddess had brought her younger sister back to life after she drowned, Azure had been forced to agree to repay five thousand souls. So far, she had only managed to carve one hundred forty-three marks into the stone. She had a long way to go before she could return to the human world and reunite with her sister.

Faded memories of my own family flitted through my mind. Faces I could no longer fully remember, voices warped by time and silence. It had been nearly a decade. I touched the shell necklace resting against my chest, feeling its familiar weight settle there. They had discarded me like garbage, and it had been too long to still grieve for them. I doubted they were grieving for me, even though part of me still hoped they might.

"I don't think I have a choice. My back can't take any more lashings just yet," she said.

Brushing my long hair away from my face, I pursed my lips as I looked at my friend's back—her once-smooth, porcelain skin now marred by layers of raised scars and half-healed wounds. The sight made my chest tighten, though I masked it. The two of us were the same age, but Azure had spent the first eighteen years of her life as a human. Becoming one of Miris' enslaved mermaids had not come easily. She rebelled more than the others, which often earned her punishments worse than anything I'd ever endured.

Secretly, I wished she would just play along. Not because I didn't understand her resistance. I did. But because I feared what would happen if she kept testing Miris' limits. I feared what would be left of her by the end.

Still, I couldn't bring myself to tell her how to live. Not when survival was the only thing any of us had.

Azure turned her head and met my gaze. Her turquoise eyes shimmered in the filtered light. That color was the same in all of us, like sea glass and stormwater, but somehow, hers still looked alive. Her long black hair, streaked with violet, clung to her back in damp waves, accentuating her high cheekbones and lashes. Even exhausted, she looked regal.

I glanced down at my own hair—blond like sunlit sand, tangled from salt and wind. I threaded my fingers through the knots and tried not to feel like the dull version of something once bright.

Our voices, like our faces, had been shaped for a purpose. We were designed to be beautiful, lethal, enchanting. Human men couldn't resist the sound of us or the sight of us. The moment they heard our melody and spotted us in the waves, they were lost, helpless to fight it. Their ships veered off course. Their hands slipped from the wheel. Some leapt to reach us. Others drowned before they understood why.

Each life we claimed brought us closer to freedom. One step closer to becoming human again.

At least for most of us.

For me, there would be no freedom. I couldn't choose to spare lives, even if I wanted to. Refusing to feed souls to the sea was defiance, and defiance was punished.

"You really don't. You'll never be free if you keep putting more marks on your back than on that wall," I said, gesturing toward the carved stone behind her. Her gaze stayed locked on mine, even as she tried to sit up. A grunt slipped from her lips, and she winced when the wounds on her back stretched open again.

"Yeah... that's going to hurt you for a while."

I didn't want to say it aloud, but I admired her for it—how she still resisted, even now. I understood why she disobeyed Miris. I didn't want to be a killer either, but this curse didn't come with choices.

We had no freedom. No power. No voice that wasn't borrowed.

"I'm aware. I'm the one who always takes the whip, after all," she said, the statement turning my stomach. "Have you ever even been punished by Miris?"

I looked toward the horizon, inhaling deeply as the sea breeze moved through the cave. I couldn't remember everything—not my human life, not the exact moment it ended—but I remembered why I had been cursed. My form had never been safe. It hadn't been traded for a life like Azure's. It had been sealed, bound, controlled. My own family had feared what I was.

Even now, after all these years, that memory burned the clearest.

The scent of brine and damp stone filled the space as waves slammed against the jagged mouth of the cave. The sound echoed around us, louder than the silence I let stretch between her question and my answer.

It wasn't that I didn't know what to say.

It was that I realized how little power I had left to claim for myself.

"I have not."

Chapter Five

THE TRUTH I DON'T TELL

For a moment, I considered telling her the truth. About what I was. About what Miris had taken and sealed away. I thought about the reason I had been cursed in the first place. The creature that slept inside me. The one they called a monster. But I couldn't bring myself to speak the words aloud.

I didn't want Azure to look at me the way my family had.

So instead, I cleared the haze from my expression and changed the subject. "It's a rough day for sailors," I murmured. "Good for us, if the storm rolls in."

Azure sighed and reached for her breast band, fastening it with slow, deliberate hands. There was little modesty in our world. Most mermaids wore nothing at all. We were designed to allure, not to hide. Azure, though, always wore hers. I had stopped asking why.

"I don't consider it good for me either," she muttered. "I never wanted to be a killer."

Our gazes met. There was no accusation in her voice, just exhaustion.

A flicker of silver gleamed in her turquoise eyes. I understood. I always had. She didn't need to say what I already knew.

Miris did not tolerate mercy.

"The sea claims lives," I said. "We're just bystanders."

Azure laughed, but the sound was bitter and dry. She tucked a loose strand of onyx hair behind her ear, her fingers brushing skin that had once been smooth. "Bystanders?" she repeated, her voice low with disbelief.

The conversation wasn't over. I could feel it.

And I knew I hadn't meant what I'd said. I had only said it to soothe her, to shield her from the weight of what we had become. It hadn't worked.

Rather than defend myself, I turned and walked toward the darker curve of the cave, where we often rested during the day. The light couldn't follow us there. Azure rose behind me, slow and careful, and followed without another word.

Although I could shift into a human form and use my legs, I wasn't allowed to enter human settlements. The curse forbade it. So, I spent most of my time in the caves or on uninhabited islands, small, jagged patches of stone scattered across the Lamalis Sea. Other mermaids preferred the underwater caverns or the glittering spires of Miris' palace. I had always avoided both.

Even before I met Azure three years ago, I had kept to myself. She shared the same instinct. We didn't need to speak it aloud. The palace reeked of control, and Miris' eyes saw everything.

"That's just wishful thinking, and you know it," Azure said, her tone sharp with cynicism. "Most of those ships would make it safely across if it weren't for us. She's turned us into monsters. The sea is the weapon, but we're the ones wielding it."

I didn't argue. I couldn't.

She was right.

The weight of each death pressed down on me, no matter how many times I told myself I had no choice. It didn't matter that we were made to sing. It didn't matter that the enchantment moved through us like a current. The lives still ended by our hands. Or our voices.

Tears pricked the corners of my eyes. I turned away quickly, wiping them with the back of my hand, hoping she wouldn't see. Even after all this time—even with Azure—I had never truly opened up to anyone. My secrets belonged to Miris alone. No one else knew what I really was, or what had been locked inside me.

I intended to keep it that way.

"We don't have a choice, Azure." My voice came out quieter than I intended. "You can try to deny our fate, but it gets you beaten. And it's not bringing you any closer to seeing your sister again. Surely you understand that."

At least she had a chance.

I almost told her that. Almost whispered that she was lucky to have someone waiting on the other side of all this. But the words stopped in my throat. My curse wasn't her fault. My family had offered me to the Sea Goddess without a second thought. Azure wasn't to blame for the fact that I owed fifty thousand souls, a debt so high it was never meant to be repaid.

"I'm sorry." Azure placed her hand on my elbow, the heat of it grounding me. Her voice softened. "I know. I just hate this."

I nodded, swallowing hard.

I felt the same. Every part of me hated it. Hate didn't change anything. All we had, truly, was each other.

I wrapped my arms around her and buried my face in her shoulder. She smelled like salt and storm winds. I cried quietly into her skin. Not because I thought it would help, but because it was the only thing I could do.

"We all do," I whispered. "None of us chose this life."

Trying to lighten the mood, Azure snorted. "I can think of a few who might, like the Seawraiths."

A breath of laughter broke from me. It wasn't much, but it was real.

Oona and Lucia. Miris' loyal monsters. They had long since chosen this cursed existence, surrendering whatever they once were in exchange for blood and power. They didn't just kill—they reveled in it. They didn't just torment—they enjoyed it.

They weren't like us.

Stifling a laugh, I nodded against Azure's shoulder, the edges of my despair dulling slightly. "Come on," I murmured. "Let's get something to eat."

SHADOWS OF THE PAST

Azure opened the crates lining the back of our cave and pulled out some pieces of fish—a meal we were both tired of eating. Still, I tried to be grateful. As meager and unappetizing as it was, it was food. Fish made up most of our meals, whether dried or fresh, and they were equally unappealing.

Despite this, I nibbled on the paper-thin strips of meat while holding my nose, swallowing them down with a grimace.

"I would give anything for a roasted duck."

A snicker escaped Azure's lips. "Me too. I don't remember my mother's cooking, but my father made a delicious stuffed goose. I could go for either at this moment."

"That sounds delicious. I don't actually remember my mother's cooking either, but I can imagine she was great at it." A deep melancholy settled inside my chest, threatening to overshadow anything bright in my heart. I didn't remember my family enough to miss them, which stung just as much. Thoughts of them always brought up a chaotic mixture of emotion I didn't know how to navigate. "When we finally gain our freedom, you must introduce me to your family."

"I don't have a family anymore." The look on my friend's face made me regret bringing up our families at all. "All that's left is my little sister. I hope she found a home with someone who cares for her. With only one hundred and forty-three souls after three years, my sister will be grown and married by the time I'm free."

"I'm sorry, Azure. I didn't mean to bring up painful memories."

Warmth filled me as Azure squeezed my hand. It had been years since I last had a family, and Azure was the closest thing I had to a sister I could remember. I couldn't help but feel a spark of hope for the future. For the first time in a long time, I knew I was not alone.

"No. It's okay. It's my fault for never telling you about them. I've moved past that loss."

"I understand. It's hard to bring up things that cause us pain, especially when we are supposed to be hardened out here."

Perhaps that was why I executed the indiscriminate killing I was commanded to do. After doing it for so long, I had built unbreakable stone walls around my heart. I had completely insulated myself from emotional pain, making it easier for me to do whatever was asked of me without hesitation or regret. There were times when my misdeeds haunted me at night without my permission, but I always pushed the thoughts away quickly. It did no good to dwell on the past.

There was an uncomfortable shift in my posture as Azure met my eyes, more due to my vulnerability than the cold stone beneath me.

"And what about your family? Will I ever get the chance to meet them?"

In terms of my past, I avoided discussing it as much as I could. The reasons I was enslaved to Miris and the topic of my family were off limits, even to Azure. Sighing, I fidgeted with the shell necklace that concealed my true form. It never left my neck, a silent weight that reminded me of where I'd come from and what I truly was.

"Maybe someday."

In truth, I lied. There would never be another time for me to see my family, nor would Azure ever have the opportunity to meet them. There was nothing I could do but hope my friend didn't have to suffer through the same thing. Azure's sister, Daneliya, was everything to her, and her desire to return to her sister was the most important thing in the world. Even if I would never see my own family again, I vowed to myself that I would help Azure pay back her life debt, even if I had to sacrifice the souls I'd collected to do so. I would help Azure return to her little sister.

When Azure and I stepped outside the cave a short time later, a tempest threatened to rage around us. Severe storms had the potential to help us sink ships and claim souls, but they also limited the number of vessels that could cross the sea. Regardless of the weather, we had no choice but to hunt at night. Azure's back was a testament to that fact. Taking souls weighed heavily on my conscience, and it never got easier, though I knew it was even more complicated for Azure. Unlike her, who had only been cursed by Miris three years prior, I had been carrying out the Sea Goddess's bidding for most of my life. I didn't have another life filled with experiences to fall back on.

"Usual spot?" I asked as I dropped down to sit on the edge of the rock, my human legs transforming into an iridescent turquoise tail.

We typically waited for ships near the southern shipping channel, closest to my family's home in Thatia, where I had lived before being taken away. Nightfall was a busy time for mermaids seeking victims, so finding an unclaimed spot was challenging. Lingering near Thatia always sent a pang of longing through my chest, but I could never bring myself to search for the location. Since I had been forbidden from returning to the human lands for any reason, I had no idea whether my family still lived there or where they might be. The question didn't hurt as much as it had when I was younger, but it still stung. It always would.

Although ships could navigate through many parts of the sea, they preferred to stay near the same stretches of water since those areas were deeper than those near the coast. Most of the ships in the channel belonged to merchants transporting goods from mainland Thatia to other kingdoms accessible by water: Avrearyn, Zourin, and Azure's homeland of Vidaica. On the other hand, there was also the threat of pirates who attempted to harm those at sea, robbing merchant ships and wreaking havoc. Since pirates were deemed dangerous nuisances, we focused on sinking them first, though merchants were also considered fair game. Ultimately, souls were souls, and Miris didn't turn any away.

With the tip of my tail already in the water, I settled beside Azure on the rocks. We took a moment to watch the darkened sky as thunderclouds rolled in, then slid into the water and vanished beneath the surface.

As we swam through the storm, the wind was so strong that it forced us to dive deeper. The lightning and heavy winds made swimming at the surface nearly impossible.

After an hour of traveling, we reached our usual hunting grounds. We lifted our heads above the surface and scanned the horizon for signs of danger. The boats were nowhere in sight, though that didn't mean one wouldn't pass through eventually. In the distance, a brilliant flash of lightning crisscrossed the dark sky. The crackle of thunder drove Azure back below the surface while I remained above.

"Anyone foolish enough to be out on the water tonight deserves what's coming," she said as her head broke the surface, her long onyx hair billowing around her like silk.

I stayed above the water, treading carefully while gazing at the sky. The rain didn't bother me as much as it bothered my friend, though I understood her concerns.

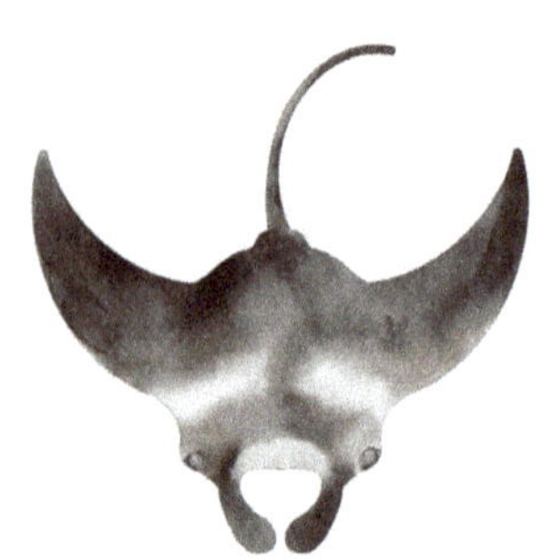

"I admit that tonight doesn't seem like it will be very productive. The storm is too severe. However, let's wait a little longer. A ship might still arrive."

There was a moment of silence between us as we scanned the horizon, each lost in our own thoughts. A sinking feeling washed over me, and I tensed against the gentle lapping of the waves. Ahead of me, Oona and Lucia broke the surface of the water. Just seeing them sent my heart into a wild tumble.

"This is our spot," Azure hissed, her words laced with venom. "Find somewhere else to hunt."

"You and your weak little friend do not own this water. We hunt where we choose. Go ahead. Try to take souls from us. It won't end well for you." Oona spat, her cruel smile widening as Lucia circled around us like a feral animal.

As I braced myself for an inevitable attack, Azure grabbed my hand and pulled me away. When I turned to glance at our enemies and then looked in the direction we had swum, I noticed a merchant ship approaching. The moment we reached a rock outcropping along the channel, we began to sing:

Our voices blended perfectly in the song we knew would resonate with the souls of the sailors. Oona and Lucia could barely be heard over the storm, though I could see them singing across the channel.

Aiming to outshine the bloodthirsty duo, Azure and I sang louder, hoping to catch the ship's attention before our enemies reached us.

As the ship veered in our direction, Azure and I hid behind the rocks, continuing our haunting song as we did every night. Our voices rose above the howling wind, echoing through the darkness as if enchanting the ship. Despite the turbulent waters, the craft floated as if there were no captain at the helm, heading straight for the rocks that would crush its bow and send it to the depths. Our song entranced the sailors, who became disoriented and lost control of their vessel.

As I watched, the ship crashed into the jagged rocks, causing a loud sound that echoed throughout the night. A thunderous lightning bolt boomed overhead, creating an ominous beat to crunching wood and victims' screams.

No matter how many years passed, I could never forget the haunting cries of the dying. Their wails haunted my dreams. Despite my guilt, Azure and I continued to share the souls we recovered from the shipwreck, just as we always had. However, the task of collecting souls on board would not be easy. A confrontation was inevitable, with Oona and Lucia waiting across the channel. Although our song caused the crash, Oona would not allow us to take credit for all the lives lost.

"I'm going to head for the stern to see how many are already in the water," I said just before swimming away.

As I made my way around the back of the ship, I sang to lure the sailors away from anything that could keep them afloat. I wasn't surprised when Azure didn't follow. Getting her to the channel and forcing her to crash ships was all she could handle. It was the reason her back was etched with more lines than the cave wall. If she had approached the vessel intending to drown everyone on board like the others did, she would have removed more souls from her debt. Instead, her guilt and the desire to fight against our captor kept her hidden in the shadows while I took the light from those who succumbed to the sea, sacrificing them to the Sea Goddess.

After every soul had entered the sea and their lives extinguished, I expected Oona and Lucia to cause trouble. I also anticipated that Azure would find me among the wreckage, but as I swam through the pieces of debris, I realized my friend was not there, nor were our enemies. I was utterly alone in the storm.

Azure was gone.

I felt it in the water before I knew it. Something was off. The current was too still, the silence too sharp. The familiar pull of her presence, the quiet hum of her song beneath the waves, wasn't there.

I searched the wreckage first, expecting to see her lurking on the edges as she often did, but there was nothing. No trace of her. Only the echoes of the souls we had taken and the watching eyes of the others.

I needed to find her before someone else did. Before Miris did.

And I feared I was already too late.

The storm had passed, but the sea churned violently in its wake, as if mirroring the unrest tightening in my chest. I swam for hours, my body aching, my mind screaming for an answer that would not come. The water gave me nothing—no trace of Azure's scent, no disturbance in the current that spoke of her passage. She had vanished as if the sea itself had swallowed her whole.

The thought gnawed at me, a slow-growing terror that burrowed deep into my bones. What if she had been taken? What if Miris already had her?

I forced the panic down. No. I couldn't think like that. Not yet.

Desperate, I turned toward our cave. If she had escaped, if she was safe, that's where she would be. The journey felt longer than ever before, the weight of exhaustion pressing heavily on my limbs as I cut through the dark waters.

The island's silhouette loomed before me, its jagged cliffs black against the sky. My heart pounded as I neared the shore, scanning for any sign of life. There was no fire burning at our usual spot. No familiar figure waiting for me.

A sharp pang of unease rippled through me. She wasn't here.

She could have sought shelter elsewhere, one of the scattered islands dotting the Lamalis Sea, a hidden cove far from Miris' reach. But something in my gut twisted at the thought. This wasn't like her. She wouldn't disappear without a word.

I dragged myself onto the rocks, shifting onto my legs, but even on solid ground, the unease did not fade. It clung to me, thick and suffocating, whispering that something was terribly, irreversibly wrong.

I scanned the shoreline, the wind howling across the cliffs, stirring the tide into restless waves. The storm was over, but its echoes lingered in the distant sky, lightning flickering at the horizon. My instincts screamed at me, warning me that this was only the beginning.

I should have rested. Should have waited until dawn to resume my search. But the thought of waiting, of doing nothing, was unbearable.

Instead, I turned back to the water, my pulse thrumming like a war drum. Without hesitation, I dove beneath the surface once more, heading toward the last place I had seen my friend.

I would not stop searching. Not until I found her.

Chapter Seven

Darkness on the Horizon

Even many hours later, the sea groaned with the weight of what it had taken, churning the wreckage of the merchant ship like bones in a mouth too full to swallow. I had returned to the scene of the crash, just in case Azure was injured among the debris.

Broken planks floated like driftwood coffins. Torn sails rippled through the water like shrouds. A child's sandal tumbled past me, caught in a slow spiral toward the abyss.

I moved through it all without pause, the silence louder than any scream. My eyes scanned the ruins with growing desperation, searching for a glint of violet-black hair, the shimmer of her tail—anything that might belong to Azure.

"Where are you?" I murmured into the current.

I dove deeper, gliding through the fractured remains of the hull. The ship had split nearly clean in half against the rocks, its once-proud ribs now jutting skyward like the bones of something long dead. I swept my fingers along the seabed, searching for torn cloth, a blood trail, a shape hiding in the dark. The sand offered nothing. The sea gave no answer.

She wasn't here.

A flicker of movement caught my eye, and I turned sharply, hope surging before I registered the silhouette.

Lucia.

She moved through the wreckage like she belonged to it, her golden hair drifting behind her, her eyes glinting like broken glass. She trailed one hand along a shattered mast, nails tapping against the wood as she studied me.

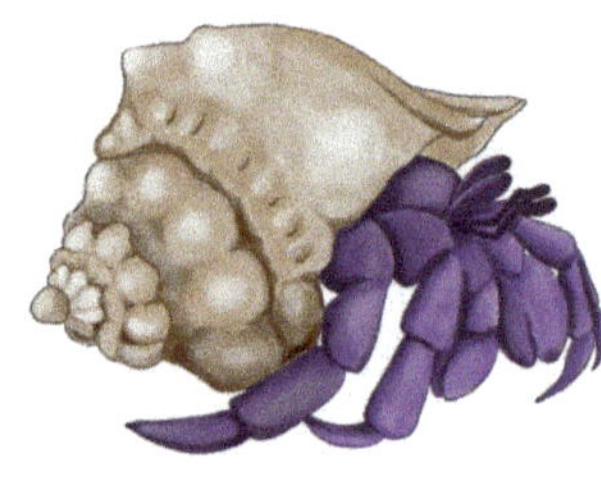

"Looking for something?" she asked, her voice curling through the water like smoke. "Or someone?"

I forced my features into stillness. "Where's Azure?"

Lucia tilted her head, mockingly thoughtful. "That's a very good question. No one's seen her since the wreck." Her smile curved at the edges, indulgent and cruel. "You wouldn't happen to know something about that, would you?"

"If I did, I wouldn't be here."

She moved closer, slow and graceful. Her gaze slid over me like a blade. "You're worried."

I didn't respond.

Her smile widened. "You should be."

She circled me once, her tail slicing through the water like a knife, then paused to examine a cracked barrel spilling dried figs into the sea.

"Funny thing," she said, casual and light, "Miris is worried too."

I stiffened. The cold crept deeper.

"She's been asking questions. About the girl who sings less. The one who hesitates."

My chest tightened. "Azure hesitates because she doesn't want to become like you."

Lucia turned, her smile fading slightly. "No, Ocevia. She hesitates because she still thinks someone will save her." She leaned in, close enough that I could see the faint, hairline scars along her jaw—old wounds. "But you know better, don't you?"

I held her gaze. "If I find her, she'll be safe."

Lucia's laugh rang sharp and clear. "If you find her before Miris does."

She turned away then, flicking her tail in a wide arc as she glided into the dark.

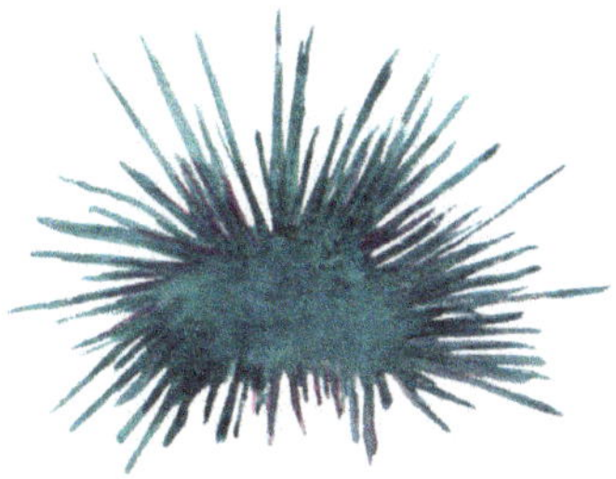

"Swim fast, Little Fish. It's a long way down."

And just like that, she was gone.

The sea was quiet again. But the hunt had begun.

I had barely left the wreckage when the guards intercepted me.

They rose from the shadows of the reef like ghosts: two figures in scaled armor, their eyes blank and unreadable. No names. No questions.

"Miris wants to see you."

The larger one didn't even look at me when he said it. His voice was flat, the kind used for pronouncing sentences, not requests.

My stomach twisted, but I didn't resist. I simply nodded, falling in between them as we swam toward the undersea palace.

The farther we went, the heavier the water became. The vibrant reefs that bordered the Lamalis Sea gave way to stillness, fields of bone-colored coral, their branches brittle and unmoving. The palace rose from the darkness like a monument to something ancient and long forgotten. Its spires coiled upward like a creature reaching for light it could never touch.

I had been here many times, and still, it made my skin crawl.

The corridors were silent as we entered, our bodies trailing slow-moving shadows along the pearl-inlaid walls. The usual sounds of song and chatter, of sly laughter and whispered threats, were absent. Only the quiet drip of water from high above echoed through the halls, as if the ocean itself were holding its breath.

We passed beneath an arch carved with the names of the first mermaids, their syllables worn down with age. I didn't dare read them. They always stared back.

Miris waited in the throne chamber, her figure sprawled across her obsidian seat like a goddess sculpted from moonlight and malice. The soft glow of bioluminescent shells lit her from beneath, setting her silver eyes alight with a pale, merciless gleam. She looked both ethereal and deadly, beautiful in the way storms are beautiful right before they tear something apart.

I bowed low, head dipped just enough to show deference without fear.

Miris watched me from her throne, sprawled like a predator at rest, her silver eyes gleaming in the bioluminescent light.

"You've been busy," she said, her voice smooth as silk dragged through blood.

I kept my gaze low. "I was hunting, Mistress."

Her fingertip traced lazy circles along the curved coral of the armrest, a gesture too casual to be harmless. "Were you?" she mused.

"Yes," I answered, my voice flat and steady despite the pulse hammering in my throat.

A pause followed, too long to be anything but calculated. Miris tilted her head slightly, studying me with a look that peeled skin from bone.

"And yet... the souls you've brought me lately have dwindled," she said, each word a shard of ice. "You used to be one of my most faithful."

The accusation slid over my skin, leaving a trail of cold.

I forced my body not to flinch. "My loyalty hasn't changed."

Her lips curled faintly. "Hasn't it?"

Miris rose with the slow, deliberate grace of something that had never forgotten how to kill. Her black hair floated around her like a living thing, coils of darkness framing her pale, predatory beauty. She began to circle me, moving with a weightless elegance that made the very water seem to tremble.

"You've grown quiet," she murmured, her voice low and close behind me. "Not in song. In spirit. I feel it in the way you move. In the way you hesitate."

I stayed silent, muscles locked tight against the instinct to flee.

She stopped just behind me, and the brush of her hand on my shoulder was light enough to be mistaken for affection. Then her nails pressed in, a silent reminder of how easily she could tear me open if she chose.

"You still wear the shell I gave you," she said, her breath ghosting against the side of my face.

"Yes, Mistress."

Her fingers drifted along the back of my neck, tracing the delicate lines of the cord that held the shell against my skin.

"And yet..." Her voice softened to a whisper. "Your heart swims elsewhere."

The words pierced clean, sharper than any blade.

"I serve," I said quietly, forcing the lie past the knot lodged in my throat.

Miris moved in front of me again, her silver gaze slicing into mine. "Do you?"

The question hung between us, too heavy and too knowing. Her hand dropped from my skin, leaving a phantom trail of cold in its absence.

Her fingers flexed once at her side before curling back into a fist. She was losing patience.

"Where is Azure?"

The name fell into the moist air like a stone, sending ripples through the fragile silence.

I swallowed hard. I had rehearsed this moment, buried the fear deep, layered my truth with just enough emptiness to be believable.

"I don't know," I said, steady as stone.

Miris studied me for a long moment, her expression unreadable.

Then, with a soft hum of thought, she stepped away. The water swirled around her like smoke.

"Find her," she commanded, her voice like the ocean summoning its own. Inevitable. Final.

I bowed again, lower this time, hiding the tremor in my muscles, and turned to leave. The guards fell into silent step behind me, shadows made flesh, their presence heavy and cold.

I didn't breathe until I reached the open sea.

The current tugged at me as I left the palace, slow and cold, like the sea itself knew I didn't belong there anymore.

I didn't speak. I didn't sing. I let the silence pull at the edges of my thoughts, let it burrow into the cracks I hadn't realized were forming. The deeper I swam, the more the water muffled everything: my breath, my heartbeat, the lingering echo of Miris' voice in my mind.

The reef passed beneath me, all jagged teeth and shadow. Dead coral stretched in pale ridges beneath my tail. A few small fish darted out of my way, quick and startled, vanishing into crevices like they could sense the storm bleeding from my skin.

No one followed.

Not the guards. Not the other girls. Not Azure.

I surfaced for air I didn't need, letting my face break the water just beneath the heavy sky. The stars were gone. The moon hid behind a wall of clouds, draping the sea in a lightless gray. I hovered beneath it, suspended in stillness, surrounded by too much space and not enough warmth.

I didn't know where to go. Not really.

The current didn't carry her scent. The sea didn't whisper her name.

I floated, arms limp at my sides, and let the weight of everything settle into my bones.

Azure had always been a constant. A hum just beneath the silence. Even when we didn't speak. Even when she was angry. Even when she was half-broken from the last lashing.

And now she was gone.

I didn't even have a direction to start from. Only fear. Only the empty space where she should have been.

My eyes stung, but I refused to cry. The ocean had taken enough from me. It didn't get my tears, too.

I thought of Azure's hands after our last hunt—how they trembled slightly when she thought I wasn't looking. I thought of her humming under her breath when she was nervous. Of her silence after Miris questioned us both for the first time. I had known, even then, that she wasn't going to last in this life. Not without someone protecting her.

And now I wasn't there.

I wasn't anywhere that mattered.

The guilt pressed in so hard it felt like drowning. Not the sharp panic of being pulled under. The slow, heavy kind. The kind where you realize no one is coming to save you. And worse—you failed to save someone else.

I tilted my head to the sky. I didn't pray. Not to the Sea Goddess. Not to anyone. I had stopped believing in mercy years ago.

But in the silence that stretched above and around me, I heard something else.

Not a voice. Not a name. Just a question I couldn't shake.

What if she's already gone?

The thought gripped me. I clenched my fists, nails biting into my palms.

No. She wasn't gone. She couldn't be.

If she was, there would be nothing left of me worth saving.

I turned, my tail slicing through the sea with fresh resolve. I didn't know where I was going yet, but I would keep swimming.

Even if I had to search every trench, every reef, every ruin. Even if the sea swallowed me whole.

Chapter Eight

The Abyss Calls

By the third day, exhaustion had sunk its claws deep into my body. I hadn't eaten. I hadn't rested. There was no time for either. I had slipped beneath the surface with nothing but the weight of her name lodged in my chest, and I refused to rise again without her.

The days blurred into a single, aching rhythm: stroke, search, repeat. My hands were raw from scraping reef walls. My tail burned with every flick. The cold had crept past my skin and into my bones, a slow, gnawing chill that made me feel hollow from the inside out. Still, I searched. Every cavern. Every trench. Every forgotten place we had once spoken of in half-whispers and shivered dreams.

At first, I called her name again and again, until my throat ached and the current stole the sound. By the fourth day, even my voice had faded. So had any remaining hope. The sea offered no reply. Even the fish kept their distance, as if grief could be tasted in the water.

There was nothing. No sign of her. No sign of anything.

I swam past the outer edge of the familiar world, beyond the Sea-wraith hunting grounds, beyond the places where Miris' whispers once curled through the currents. Past memory. Past light. Past the names of anything I had been taught to fear.

Here, the sea changed.

It grew thick. Slow. Like it carried weight. Memory. Sorrow. Shapes moved in the periphery of my vision, long and strange and silent. The light above dissolved into shadow, then into nothing at all. And the current, once wild and shifting, no longer obeyed the tide or moon.

It moved with intent. A pull. Steady and silent, like breath drawn in and never released.

I drifted toward the lip of a trench carved deep into the ocean floor, its mouth jagged as broken glass. The depth beyond it was unknowable. A wound in the sea.

And still, I didn't turn back.

The ruins rose slowly from the dark like the bones of something forgotten. A broken pillar here. A collapsed archway there. Coral threaded through shattered stone. The deeper I moved, the more the water resisted, as though it, too, remembered what was buried here. The carvings were barely visible, revealed only when my fingers brushed the surface. But under my touch, the stone pulsed. Subtle. Warm. Alive.

Not just ancient. *Familiar.*

These were not the works of merfolk. Nor human hands.

They belonged to something else. Something older than either. Something that had always known me.

My fingers traced a spiraling symbol etched into the ancient stone. A hum stirred beneath my skin—not sound, not light, but something older. It moved through me like recognition, like a name half-remembered. The water gathered around me, pressing in not with heaviness, but with awareness. As if the place itself had opened its eyes.

As if it had been waiting for me to return.

It wasn't fear I felt. It was knowing.

This place remembered the shape of my blood. And somewhere inside me, I remembered it too.

I hovered there, suspended in a stillness that didn't feel empty. It felt like breath held at the edge of a name.

I wasn't following her trail anymore. This wasn't where Azure had been. This was where I had always been meant to arrive.

The silence deepened as I swam farther in.

No current stirred. No fish darted between the stones. No songs curled through coral halls. The sea here wasn't just quiet—it was watching. Still and heavy, like the water itself had become a breath held too long.

Light twisted beneath the arches in ways that made no sense. It didn't fade; it fractured. The blues and greens that had once given the ocean its beauty thinned into colorless hush, the water dimming into a bruised translucence that stained everything in memory.

Carvings spiraled across the walls, glowing faintly in a ghostly hue that reminded me of veins beneath pale skin. When I brushed my fingers across them, they didn't sing, but I knew they recognized me. A hum bloomed under my skin, rising through my bones.

Not a sound. Not a voice. Something older.

A presence. Archaic and endless. Like the walls had been waiting for me to return.

I drifted forward, deeper into the bone-colored hall, flanked by shattered pillars and monuments long drowned. The pressure didn't thicken with depth alone—it changed. The weight that settled against me wasn't the sea. It was recognition. Like the ruins were no longer simply ruins, but ribs. And I was no longer an outsider. I was the breath returning to a long-silent body.

One column had split clean down the middle. On either side, curling lines rose like tentacles or smoke, too deliberate to be decoration, too familiar to dismiss.

I floated closer, heart beating louder than my strokes.

The current stirred across my cheek, cool and careful, like the breath of something ancient just behind me.

And that's when I felt the connection.

A moan drawn from the bones of the earth. A beat that didn't belong to my body but echoed through it anyway. A pulse that wasn't mine and yet felt rooted in the shape of my spine.

"Leave."

The message didn't come as speech. It slid into me like pressure through a crack. A knowing. A warning.

"Leave before you become."

The words struck something I hadn't thought of in years. A whisper I had once tried to forget.

Miris' voice, sharpened by scorn: "The sea remembers what it once gave your bloodline... and what it might take back."

At the time, I'd thought it was a child's curse. Just words meant to frighten me into silence.

But here, in this place of drowned breath and sleeping bones, I understood.

It had never been a threat. It had always been a warning. Sharp and distant, like the glint of teeth just below the surface.

The water no longer felt still. It pulsed around me in quiet, deliberate waves, each one heavier than the last. It didn't press me away. It folded inward, slow and steady, like breath drawn in and never released. Not with rejection, but with recognition. Familiar. Almost fond.

This place didn't fear me. It claimed me.

Beneath my hand, the carvings vibrated faintly, and heat pulsed through the lines into my palm. My tail flicked once, a twitch too fast to stop, like a muscle remembering something it was never taught.

I wasn't a trespasser here. I wasn't an intruder. The ruins didn't look at me as something foreign.

I was known. And somewhere, deep in the marrow I tried not to name, I knew this place too.

I turned to leave, but the ruins followed. Not in motion, but in memory. They clung to the back of my eyes, pressed into my ribs, stitched into the rhythm of a heartbeat I couldn't separate from my own.

I didn't flee from the darkness. I fled from what it showed me.

It remembered me. And part of me remembered it back.

I didn't surface. Not yet. The weight of the ruins clung to me like seaweed, wrapping through my thoughts, dragging them downward even as I swam upward. The water shimmered strangely in my wake, disturbed by something I couldn't name. Every stroke felt like a question the sea had yet to answer.

By the sixth day, I had stopped believing I would ever find her. Hope had collapsed into ritual: stroke, breathe, search, repeat. I wasn't looking for a person anymore. I was chasing the ghost of her. A warmth I wasn't ready to lose. A presence I could no longer name.

Then the current changed.

It shifted—subtle as breath. A curl of motion through the dark, winding around me like silk through fingers. It didn't pull. It beckoned. A suggestion, not a demand.

I followed.

The sea quieted again. The silence wasn't absence. It was listening. Waiting. The current no longer moved as water should. It threaded its way through coral and stone with a slowness that felt deliberate. Thoughtful. Like the turn of a page in a book written in my blood.

Something in my chest clenched. This didn't feel like her.

It felt older.

The glow came next. A soft bloom of light between reef and stone, pulsing slowly. Familiar, but not known. The kind of glow that didn't illuminate so much as awaken. A warmth that stirred memory, not vision.

In a narrow fold of reef, I saw it.

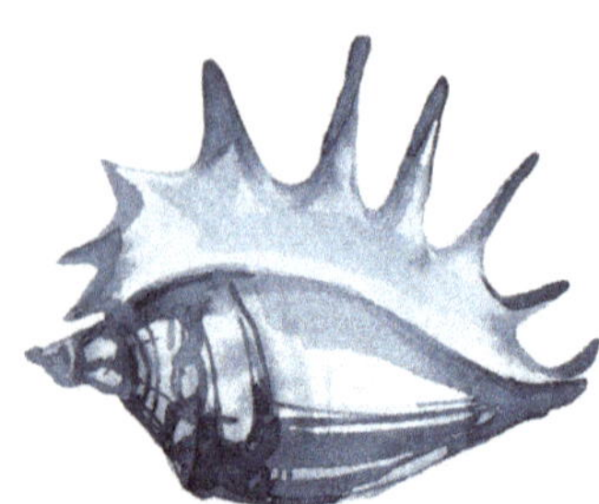

A shimmer. A breath held in stillness. Not light. Not magic. Something quieter. Waiting.

I moved closer. The current curled around me, patient as breath, brushing lightly across my spine. My fingers reached forward without command, brushing the edge of the reef.

The shimmer stirred.

Warmth rose through my hand. Not with fire, but with recognition. It didn't speak. It didn't call. It endured.

This wasn't left behind. This was waiting.

Not a trail. Not a signal. An echo.

The ocean had not forgotten me. And maybe—*just maybe*—I hadn't forgotten it.

The current deepened. A slow pull forward. Behind me, the water thinned and cooled, brushing my skin with pressure that felt like memory. Or warning.

I didn't turn back.

I followed.

And in the depths behind me, the sea remembered my name.

Chapter Nine

THE GATHERING STORM

The current led me to the edge of a jagged reef before dissolving like breath into open water. Whatever presence had been guiding me was gone now, faded into the dark like a dream unraveling on waking. Still, the pull in my chest remained.

I hovered in the open sea, scanning the depths, the surface, the ledges that marked the edge of the southern isles. No sign of Azure. No whisper of song. Just silence, and the slow churn of the ocean as tension coiled deeper into its currents.

Above, the wind stirred, rippling the surface into uneasy swells. I felt the shift in pressure before I saw it: a storm was coming. Real. Wild. Not magic. Not a song. Just nature, rising in rage. Clouds gathered above, darkening the sky into bruises. They rolled in heavy and low, like they carried the weight of mourning. I kept moving. I had to.

Hour by hour, the pressure deepened. The sea grew tense beneath the wind. Fish scattered. The coral groaned. Even the silence shifted and emptied itself, as if the ocean held its breath in anticipation of something it feared to see.

By dusk, I caught movement on the horizon. A ripple. A shape. An island. It rose like a shadow through the mist. Jagged. Unfamiliar. Not a place I knew. Not one Azure and I had ever named. But I recognized it all the same.

Oona and Lucia were already ahead of me. Their scent rode the water: bitter, sharp, impossible to mistake.

I swam faster, tail slicing through the water as the storm cracked open above me. Rain fell in sheets. Thunder split the sky. The island drew closer. So did the danger.

The storm was in full command by the time I reached the shoreline. Rain sheeted the surface, breaking it into foam and fury. Thunder rolled like the war drums of some forgotten god, and wind howled through the cliffs with a voice full of grief. I didn't surface. Not yet.

The island loomed, sharp-edged and wreathed in mist. Its cliffs rose like broken blades from the sea. It felt wrong, not just from the storm, but from something older. Something deeper. I felt it humming in my bones, scraping at my nerves, vibrating behind my teeth like pressure building beneath the skin of the world.

The current that brought me here had long since faded, but something else had taken its place. Fainter, more primal. A trail curled into the water, biting at the back of my throat. Oona. Lucia. Their presence stung like salt in an open wound. It sank into my lungs, crawled through my ribs. A warning. A promise.

I pressed closer to the island, staying just below the surface. Lightning flashed, throwing the world into stark fragments of white and shadow. That was when I saw them.

Two figures moved through the shallows, stepping onto the sand as they shifted into their land-bound forms. Even from here, even with the storm raging, I saw the tension in their shoulders. The way their eyes scanned the trees. Predators. Poised. They'd found something. Or someone.

I drifted forward, using storm and stone as cover. The water roared in my ears, relentless, but through a crack of lightning I caught motion at the tree line. Small. Still. Human.

A *man*.

For a breath, I forgot how to breathe. He stood tall despite the rain, sword drawn and steady. His soaked clothes clung to a frame built for endurance. His body spoke of battle, not beauty. And some-how—*somehow*—he didn't look surprised to see them.

Panic bloomed sharp in my chest. Not because of him, but because of what his presence meant.

Azure had been here first. She had brought him. And now, Oona and Lucia would finish what the sea had begun.

Jealousy wasn't what I expected to feel, but it bloomed anyway, bitter and fast, scorching beneath my ribs. I didn't know what he was to her, and I didn't care. He meant danger. Exposure. A risk none of us could afford.

The waves tugged at me, as if trying to hold me back. My body ached, breath tight. I'd been searching for days on instinct alone. And now, here I was, half a heartbeat from losing her.

I let the sea take me lower, slipping into its dark cradle.

Above, the pressure shifted, a ripple through the water like breath held tight. Blades would be drawn soon. Blood would spill, and I would not let it be hers.

Rain hammered the surface as I hovered beneath it, suspended in the storm. The current pressed close, thick and watching.

The man didn't move.

Even as Oona closed in, blade gleaming. Even as Lucia circled behind him. He stood his ground. Rain lashed him. Blood stained his shirt. His stance never wavered. He was protecting someone.

Then I saw her.

A shadow at the tree line. *Azure.* Crouched low. Breathing hard. Watching. She hadn't run. She hadn't fled. She waited, just as I did, for the moment to break.

Oona raised her blade.

"I've already told you. I don't know who she is. I'm here alone," the man called out. His voice cut clean through the storm.

He was lying. For her.

Oona didn't believe him. Neither did Lucia. It was in the way their eyes cut toward the trees. They knew she was there. They wanted her to reveal herself.

"Lies," Oona spat, her voice slicing the storm apart.

Lucia pulled a dagger from her belt, her smile slow and sharp. She crept forward, her blade gleaming wet with rain.

"Come on out, or we'll kill your lover boy," she said.

The man didn't flinch. His sword rose higher. His jaw locked tight.

"Not that we won't kill him anyway," Lucia added, her voice gleaming with cruelty. "He's already a dead man."

The world held its breath.

Then, Azure stepped out.

She moved through the rain like it couldn't touch her. Her fists clenched. Her face defiant. Her eyes burned.

"If I surrender, you have to let him go," she said.

My heart clenched around the realization. She was giving herself up. Not for escape. Not for strategy. For him.

Oona barely looked at her. Her blade spun lazily in her grip.

"I don't know, Azure," she said, voice like ice finding the cracks. "Our Goddess wouldn't be pleased if we let him walk. His soul belongs to her."

The sea rose with the storm. Thunder cracked. The cliffs screamed. Waves clawed at the rocks like they wanted to tear the island away piece by piece.

I could hear the pounding of my heart, feel the sea closing in like a fist. I couldn't stay hidden. I wouldn't.

My hand rose to the shell at my throat, my last tether to restraint, to control. And without another breath, I tore it free.

Chapter Ten

BLACK BLOOD

The moment the shell left my neck, the ocean changed. It was as though the sea itself inhaled, a long, shuddering breath that rattled the very bones of the deep. Power surged into me, ancient and unshackled, pouring through my veins with a violence that stole the air from my lungs. My scream never made it to the surface. It was swallowed by the pressure, lost to the churning waters, as my body arched back, suspended like a marionette on invisible strings.

Something inside me, buried and bound for years, woke. I didn't try to stop it. I couldn't.

The pain was blinding. Bones cracked and stretched, joints dislocating one by one as my arms elongated and twisted into monstrous forms. Flesh tore apart, reshaping itself into something both primal and colossal. Tentacles unfurled from my shoulders, rust-colored and slick, coiling through the water like living serpents eager for a target. My face split open. My jaw extended, bones shifting with sickening cracks, until my mouth was lined with feelers that twitched hungrily, guided by instincts that weren't my own. I opened my mouth to scream again, but what came out was no longer a human sound. It was a roar, deep and prehistoric, the kind of sound that shook the seafloor and made the ocean itself recoil.

I was the monster Miris had feared I would become.

The Kraken.

For years, I had carried the weight of it in my blood, bound beneath skin and bone, silenced by a shell that masqueraded as safety. My family had hidden it, feared it, abandoned me because of it. They had called it a curse, but it was older than curses. Older than blood itself. It was memory passed through marrow, hunger whispered through generations. They had sent me to Miris not to be healed, but to be erased.

I wasn't supposed to survive.

473

But I had.

And now, I was awake.

My massive limbs surged downward, propelling my monstrous form through the water like a cannonball. The sea bent around me, parting in a swirling vortex as I launched toward the surface. Every movement was instinct. Every thought, a whisper buried beneath the storm now raging inside me.

The sky exploded above as I breached.

Rain hammered the sea in relentless sheets, lightning forking through the clouds in jagged spears of silver and white. I broke through the surface like a nightmare made flesh, the world above suddenly small, fragile, laughably weak beneath my fury. Tentacles the size of tree trunks slammed into the shore, sending water and debris flying in every direction. The sand churned. The air itself seemed to crack beneath the force of my arrival.

And still, my mind reeled, struggling to comprehend the enormity of what I had become.

Everything looked different now. Smaller. Breakable. Already half-undone by my presence alone.

A flicker of movement caught my attention.

Evil.

She stood frozen on the beach, her
body drenched, a dagger clutched
uselessly in her hand. Her eyes locked
onto mine, or what remained of them,
and for a heartbeat, time stilled between us. Without thought, one of
my tentacles lashed out, wrapping
around her waist. I lifted her from
the sand with a surge of muscle and
instinct, as easily as plucking a leaf
from a river's surface.

Oona screamed, high and raw, the
sound almost human enough to hurt.
She stabbed into the thick flesh of my tentacle, her dagger flashing in
a desperate, glinting strike, but it barely scratched the surface. She
was lighter than I remembered. Small. Fragile. A wisp of the fierce
fighter she had once been. Grief twisted deep inside me, sharp and
bitter, even as I held her suspended over the wrecked shore.

A movement flickered beyond her, pulling my gaze.

Azure.

She stood beneath the sodden canopy of trees, the rain pouring in
rivulets down her hair, her cloak plastered to her skin. Her wide
turquoise eyes locked onto the monstrous form clutching Oona. And
through her expression, I saw the reflection of what I had become,
but she didn't see me.

She saw the beast. *The horror.* The nightmare every whispered
warning had painted in the darkness.

Pain bloomed sharp and raw inside my chest, worse than the agony
of transformation. Worse than the fury boiling through my veins. It
was a wound not born of battle, but of recognition. The kind of old,
silent wound that festers beneath the skin.

The same look my mother had given me the night she called Miris.

The same look that had shattered my childhood.

The same look that had chained me into silence.

I tightened my grip on Oona. Not from rage. Not from hatred. But
because I had no other language left. No voice that could reach through
the rising wall of fear that now separated me from everything I had

tried to protect. All I had were these monstrous limbs and the stubborn, bleeding heart still trapped within them.

Letting go would mean surrender, and somewhere deep inside the beast, the girl I had once been—the girl who had loved, and lost, and dared to dream of something better—still clung to life.

I was still Ocevia.

And I would not fall silent again.

The storm swallowed me whole as I plunged beneath the waves, Oona still thrashing violently in my grip. Her blade flashed once, slicing into the thick muscle of my tentacle, sending a flare of pain searing through my monstrous form. But the sensation was distant now, muted and dull, like the memory of pain rather than pain itself.

I tightened my hold, dragging her deeper into the churning black. The water around us turned thick with blood—hers and mine—a dark cloud unfurling outward as I descended. Every inch that brought us closer to the seafloor stirred the Kraken's hunger deeper inside me, a gnawing roar that drowned out thought.

I tried to focus. Tried to remember why I had unleashed this terrible part of myself.

Azure. The reason I had surrendered to the monster at all.

But submerged in the freezing abyss, with Oona crushed in my grasp, those memories slipped away like sand through open fingers. My mind was no longer entirely my own. Every rational thought was ripped apart by the storm rising inside me. Even my body felt foreign. Every movement, every stretch of muscle and tendon, dragged me further from the shape I had once known. The slick, coiling weight of the tentacles pulling against me was a reminder that the girl I had been was already fading.

Oona twisted, her tail snapping out in a desperate attempt to break free. I slammed her against a jagged boulder jutting from the ocean floor. She went limp for a heartbeat, dazed just long enough.

I coiled tighter around her and shot downward, driving us toward the trench below. The pressure built against my monstrous form. The sea itself seemed to recoil around me, its currents ragged and torn, as if even the water did not know what to make of the thing I had become.

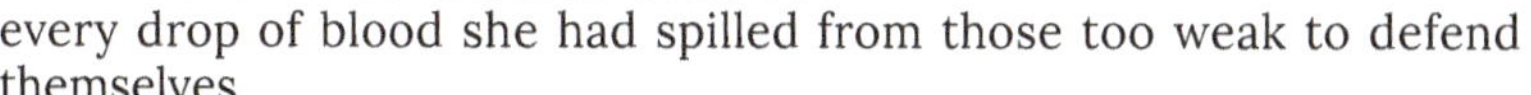

Rage thundered through me, deafening and relentless. Not rage for Elios. Not even for Azure. Rage for every lash Oona had ever delivered. For every broken child she had sneered over. For every drop of blood she had spilled from those too weak to defend themselves.

She deserved this.

I dove deeper. The ocean pressed harder against my skin, but the Kraken inside me only roared louder, gorging on my fury.

And yet, something flickered. A memory. Azure's eyes.

Wide. Terrified.

Not of Oona.

Of *me*.

The tentacles around Oona faltered. A fraction of looseness. A breath of hesitation. And it was enough. She drove her dagger deep into my flesh. Black blood burst into the water like smoke. The Kraken screamed inside me, a wordless howl of rage and pain, and instinct took over. I lashed out without thought, slamming her into a wall of coral with a force that made the ocean itself seem to shudder.

Still, she fought. Even broken, even bleeding, Oona fought with the desperate ferocity of someone who had nothing left to lose. Her magic flared in frantic bursts, her tail a blur of gray as she twisted and darted through the blood-clouded water. But I was faster.

One massive tentacle surged forward, coiling around her midsection. She kicked. Screamed. In a final burst of power, she hurled a bolt of magic toward my face. I twisted away, the energy searing a jagged line of molten pain across my side.

But it wasn't enough.

She turned to flee, blood trailing behind her like a ribbon torn loose in the current, and I followed.

I slammed into her like a breaking tide, knocking her limp. Her body crumpled under the force as blood spiraled from her head like ink spilled across a canvas. Still, the Kraken inside me snarled for more, its hunger a living thing clawing against my ribs.

As Oona's limp body drifted toward the ocean floor, I followed. Silent. Deadly. The crushing cold pressed tighter with every pulse of the sea.

The water churned around me, dark and wild, as if even the tides themselves were caught in the gravity of my rage. The world blurred into a haze of red and black and storm.

And somewhere, buried beneath the roar of blood and fury, a voice whispered my name.

Small. Trembling. Almost lost.

A voice I barely remembered as my own.

The damage was done.

My vision wavered. My limbs shook. I tried to rise, but the weight of the abyss dragged me down, heavier with every frantic beat of my heart.

The beast inside me clawed at its weakening cage, fighting to survive, refusing to surrender to the growing silence pressing in from all sides.

Through the blur of blood and cold, I saw it.

The shell.

The necklace I had torn from my throat drifted just beyond my reach, caught in the sluggish suction of one of my wounded limbs. Its pale gleam shimmered in the darkness, pulsing faintly like a star about to die. Like a memory tugging at the edges of my unraveling mind.

I hesitated.

Taking it back meant losing this strength. This rage. This terrible, broken power that had made me untouchable. But it also meant remembering.

Remembering who I was. Who I needed to be.

The girl who had once sung to the sea. The girl who had loved without fear.

The girl Azure might still believe could be saved.

The Kraken raged inside me. Its hunger gnawed at my bones, demanding I let it devour everything: Oona, Lucia, even the part of me still whispering to fight. My limbs trembled with the weight of the choice. The blood lust howled, promising I would never be powerless again if I only let the shell drift away.

But I couldn't.

Because somewhere deep within this monstrous body, the girl who had once believed in songs, in light, in love, still existed.

She was battered. She was broken. But she was still breathing.

Trembling, I reached for the shell, monstrous tentacles fumbling against its smooth curve. For one terrible heartbeat, I almost let it go.

But then I closed my suction cup around it.

The moment I touched it, the world shifted.

Pain receded, draining from my veins like the last warmth of a dying star. Power bled from my limbs. Thought, memory, even rage collapsed inward, swallowed by the crushing darkness rushing up to meet me.

The roar within me quieted.

The Kraken's claws slipped away, not with a scream, but with a shudder that left me hollowed out and gasping.

And the sea, vast, endless, merciless, once again cradled me in its silence.

REPERCUSSIONS OF THE MONSTER

Consciousness returned like a bruise: slow, aching, dark at the edges. The world was muffled and distant, as though I were trapped beneath a veil. I lay curled against the seafloor, the sand and seaweed beneath me strangely soft, cradling my broken body in a silence that pressed down like mourning. The weight of the deep settled into my ribs, cold and relentless.

Something was wrong.

I couldn't breathe.

Panic surged. A spike of clarity cut through the haze in my mind. My lungs convulsed, desperate for air. I twisted, gasping, and a trail of silver bubbles fled from my mouth, vanishing into the dark above.

My tail was gone.

Legs.

My body had reverted. The transformation had drained me, stripped away the Kraken, and left me human again. Fragile. Bleeding. Dying. A deep gash split across my thigh, and blood spilled in spirals, blooming red in the cold blue sea. Pain radiated from the wound in slow, crushing waves.

The ocean whispered its lullabies, soft and coaxing. *Let go*, it said. *Sink. Rest.*

I couldn't. Not yet.

Please.

The word pulsed through me, a heartbeat, a tether. Please, not like this.

I kicked weakly, limbs unfamiliar and heavy, muscles trembling with every stroke. The current fought me, dragging at my body, licking at my wounds like teeth. My chest ached. My vision tunneled. The surface shimmered above, impossibly far, a cruel mirage painted in light.

Still I rose.

My face broke through.

Air crashed into my lungs in a violent gasp. I choked, coughing and sputtering, clinging to the breath that might save me. The waves pounded around me, shoving me back, but I fought. I clawed forward, hands reaching for land, for safety.

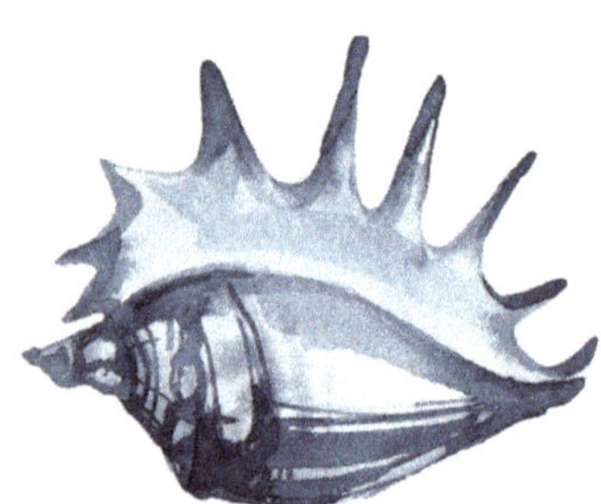

Fingers met sand.

I dragged myself from the sea, inch by inch, my body screaming in protest. My palms tore on shells and stone. My wounded leg throbbed with every movement. Salt stung my eyes, but I kept going.

There was no one waiting.

No voice calling out. No hands reaching for mine. Only the hiss of waves behind me and the wind slipping through the trees like something lost.

I collapsed, my face pressed into the coarse sand. My tears mixed with the salt already clinging to my skin.

I should have let it take me.

But pain would not let me rest.

The wound on my thigh still bled. My body trembled from effort. Even with a mermaid's healing, I could feel how close I was to the edge. The power inside me had gone quiet, reduced to a distant ache.

I had to move. I had to survive. I had to find her.

Gritting my teeth, I forced myself to crawl. My elbows screamed with every pull. My knees shredded against stone. Blood marked my passage like a trail for predators.

Still, I crawled.

A scent caught on the wind—faint, smoky, and warm.

Fire.

Hope.

I turned toward it, heart pounding. Each inch I dragged myself forward felt like an eternity. The rocks tore at my skin, but I didn't stop. I couldn't.

"Azure..."

Her name fell from my lips like a prayer, ragged and weak.

Still I crawled. Still I bled. Still I survived.

Dreams and reality blurred as my body surrendered to the rest it so desperately needed. I drifted in and out of consciousness, aware but not awake, tethered to the world by the faint sounds of voices echoing through the stone walls. Azure and the human, Elios, moved about the cave, their soft exchanges grounding me, even when I couldn't make out the words. Just knowing they were near kept the dark from pulling me under, kept the monster I had been from swallowing me whole.

When I finally forced my eyes open fully, the fire had burned low, its glow trembling across the cavern walls like something half-remembered. For a disorienting moment, I thought I was alone.

Panic bloomed fast and sharp in my chest.

Had they left me? Had I been abandoned after all?

No. Azure wouldn't do that. She wouldn't.

Before fear could take deeper root, two silhouettes appeared in the narrow passage beyond the room. Relief unfurled inside me so violently that my body trembled. The moment Azure's gaze found mine, she sprinted across the space and dropped to her knees beside me.

"What happened?" I croaked, my voice rough from sleep, my throat burning with thirst.

Azure grabbed the water beside me and pressed it gently to my lips.

I tried to drink too quickly, choking on the first desperate swallow.

"Easy," she warned, pulling the cup back slightly. "You need to take it slow."

I swallowed again, slower this time, then licked the remaining drops from my lips, every movement sluggish, every breath raw against my chest.

"I was going to ask you the same thing," she said, sitting back on her heels. "You showed up with a deep gash in your leg, collapsed in the cave, and you've been unconscious ever since."

Blinking against the sting of smoke and exhaustion, I looked down at my thigh. Bandages were wrapped tightly over the wound. I winced when I brushed my fingers against the edge of the dressing, and Azure immediately swatted my hand away with a scolding glare.

"How did you get that injury?"

My gaze drifted toward the fire, the flames casting fleeting, distorted shapes along the cavern walls. I hesitated.

"I... don't remember much after seeing the Seawraiths."

It wasn't a complete lie. My memories of the transformation were frag- mented, shattered by adrenaline and pain. But the parts I did remember, the feel of Azure's eyes locking onto the monster, the way her fear had cut deeper than any blade—those I held close.

I rubbed a hand across my face, then down my arms, checking for other injuries, grasping for something solid to anchor my story.

"I followed them," I said quietly. "I overheard them talking about finding you. I thought I could stop them. But I was pulled under during the chaos. Someone's dagger got my leg."

The half-truth tasted sour, burning against my tongue.

Azure leaned back slightly, wiping a smear of water from her chin. Her expression remained unreadable, her silence heavier than any accusation.

"Did they survive the attack? From the creature, I mean."

I shrugged and reached for the water again, avoiding her eyes. The firelight crawled along the stone, dragging out ghosts I didn't dare name.

"And who is he?" I asked instead, nodding toward the man beside her.

Azure glanced at the human, then back at me.

"This is Elios. I pulled him off a rock outcropping after the shipwreck and brought him here."

Elios nodded, silent but steady. His presence was striking—dark hair, bright blue eyes, a quiet strength that needed no announcement. A tattoo marked his chest, a broken chain encircling one shoulder.

I raised an eyebrow.

With the sword leaning against the wall, he didn't look like a man who needed saving.

I studied them both. The nearness between them, the ease, the comfort that had taken root even in the shadow of disaster. They had found something here, something I had almost forgotten could exist.

A *bond.*

And I wondered, aching deep in my chest, how long it would last once the sea came calling again.

Chapter Twelve

The Third Wheel

Azure and Elios had built a raft and planned to leave. After being attacked by Oona and Lucia, we knew Miris would eventually send others after us. It was only a matter of time. Even in this brief moment of peace, we all knew it couldn't last.

I sat cross-legged near the cave entrance. Sunlight slipped through the cracks above, spilling dappled gold onto the cave floor as I ate a mango. The fruit was soft and overripe, its juice dripping down my fingers and chin. I wiped it away with the back of my hand, only half-aware of the mess I was making. Azure laughed, and I knew I looked feral, but I didn't care. Hunger had made a beast of me, and I had no shame left to spare.

"Any idea where you're headed?" I asked, watching her as I licked the sticky juice from my palm. The words came out more casual than I felt.

I glanced at Elios and caught the stretch of his arms as he leaned back, his posture relaxed but his eyes alert.

"We were thinking we would all travel to Starspell and then inland."

I nodded, pretending to consider it, though the last thing I wanted was to intrude on their fragile, blossoming romance. Nor did I want to disobey Miris, but I wouldn't say that aloud.

"I'll be fine," I said lightly, gesturing dismissively with the fruit's pit. But as I shifted to stand, a bolt of pain shot through my leg like lightning. I gasped and sank back to the ground with a hiss.

"On second thought," I muttered through clenched teeth, wincing as I pulled my leg in closer. "Guess I'm stuck with you two for a while."

Elios chuckled. When I shot a half-hearted glare at Azure, he lifted his sticky hands in mock innocence, wearing a grin so boyish it made him look younger.

"What?" he asked, clearly amused.

Rolling her eyes, Azure pointed at me with a teasing scowl. "Don't encourage her."

I flashed her an exaggerated look of wide-eyed innocence. It was too easy to fluster her, and I had always enjoyed doing it. Even now, aching and bruised, the spark of our friendship gave me comfort. She was the closest thing to family I had. There was something healing about teasing her, something that made me feel normal again, even if only for a moment.

Still, what surprised me most wasn't the pain or the laughter. It was the way Azure and Elios seemed to exist in harmony. For two people from such different worlds, they moved like they belonged together. There was something unspoken between them, an understanding I could feel but not quite name.

"So, when do we leave?" I asked, trying to sound casual, as though my bones weren't still heavy with exhaustion.

"First light," Elios replied, his gaze flicking toward Azure. Her nod was subtle but decisive. And just like that, the plan was made.

They planned to wait until first light, when most of the mermaids slept, hoping that those hunting us would be resting. However, what I knew that they didn't was that Lucia was still alive. A fact that filled me with icy concern. As we sat by the fire, I couldn't shake the feeling that the feral mermaid could be waiting for us to exit the cave, ready to strike and end our journey before it even began.

"The time when most mermaids are asleep," Azure said, interrupting my thoughts. "Elios and I will gather more food today and pack whatever supplies we can."

"And what about me?" I asked, taking another bite of the mango, its sticky orange juice leaving a trail down my forearm.

Azure's laughter echoed off the cavern walls, and I raised an eyebrow.

"Well, first, you need a bath." Her words stung a bit, and I felt my cheeks flush with heat.

"Next, you'll rest. Elios and I will paddle the raft until you're well enough to help."

I scoffed, ready to argue. I didn't want to seem helpless, to be treated like a burden.

"I can help, but I am not getting back in the ocean to bathe yet. My last trip there was, in case you forgot, an utter disaster. Wet my tail? Yes. Submerge? Absolutely not."

Azure handed me a glass of water as she snorted. "You lost a lot of blood, so you aren't paddling yet. Besides, we have a hot spring here."

"And you're just telling me this now?" I scowled, though a mischievous note laced my voice. I had noticed the water dripping down the far wall, but I hadn't seen the pool tucked into the shadows. Hot springs were rare in this region, and excitement bubbled in my chest at the thought of sinking into warmth.

"Sorry. I must have forgotten because you were bleeding out and all," Azure said, gesturing toward the pool, a piece of mango still between her fingers.

I peered through the gloom. The fire's glow wavered along the walls, shadows twitching with every flicker. My pulse quickened.

"You and your lover have to carry me over there. It's been so long since I've sat in a hot bath, and there aren't many that we are allowed to visit." I lifted my arms in surrender, my injured leg throbbing in agreement.

Elios sighed but didn't hesitate. He scooped me up like I weighed nothing and carried me to the stone ledge near the spring. He set me down with surprising gentleness.

Despite my initial concern that the warm water might irritate the wound, I slipped into the spring's embrace. A tremor shivered through my chest as my body responded to the heat. To my surprise, my legs shifted into a tail, a shimmer of energy pulsing through me that I hadn't felt since the battle. The gash stung, but it was manageable.

If we were leaving the island, I needed this. I needed to submerge, just once more, before we entered the open sea. Because if Lucia had returned to Miris, if she had spoken of what I'd done, then every current could carry my scent back to the queen.

And next time, they wouldn't send Oona.

I knew I was no longer safe in the Lamalis Sea, and leaving with my friends was my best option. But trepidation still filled me. It wasn't just the fact that I was forbidden from entering human lands. After killing Oona, I had long since broken those laws. No, my true concern ran deeper than exile or punishment. It was the thought of being away from the water—the very element that defined me. Even now, surrounded by steam and warmth, I longed for the sea like a missing limb.

Ever since I became a mermaid, Miris had warned me: if I didn't submerge my tail every day, it would rot and kill me. Part of me believed it was a manipulation tactic, one of her many lies to keep us tethered to her reign. But I wasn't willing to test that theory. Not now.

If we made it to human lands, and deeper into the mountains, the scarcity of water would only grow. Away from the tides, I would be vulnerable. We might find ways to survive, to adapt, but the uncertainty unnerved me.

As I floated in the hot spring's embrace, my thoughts drifted like sea foam on the surface of a wave. The pool was larger than I'd initially realized, wide enough for several bodies to stretch out in comfort. Azure and Elios had left the cave to gather more supplies, and I was alone again. The firelight shimmered softly over the stone, shadows drifting like thought across the cavern. Even from here, I could tell the sun was sinking beyond the horizon.

We all knew the dangers of nightfall. In the dark, mermaids hunted. If someone was still tracking us, it was only a matter of time before they found our trail. Staying hidden behind the stone-blocked entrance was our only chance.

Fear coiled in my chest, tight and familiar. Yet beneath that fear, a flicker of something else stirred.

Excitement.

I hadn't walked on human land since I was taken at eleven years old. I had dreamed of it, longed for it, but the dream had soured over the years. Even if we escaped Miris, even if we crossed into human territory, I couldn't search for my family.

I didn't even know if I wanted to.

A knot of old pain twisted inside me. Part of me missed them desperately: my mother's stories, the soft lull of her voice, the way her blue eyes sparkled with warmth. But I didn't trust those memories. They were too kind for the truth. My parents had chosen obedience over love. They had handed me over to a monster.

I leaned back against the stone, letting the steam blur my vision. Behind my closed eyes, I pictured my mother sitting beside me, brushing hair from my brow and whispering tales of the sea. A storybook scene I couldn't quite believe. A life I could never return to.

A tear slipped down my cheek before I could stop it. I cursed under my breath, angry that it still hurt so much.

Footsteps shuffled at the far end of the cave, and the low murmur of voices reached my ears. Azure and Elios were returning.

I wiped the tear away quickly, steeling myself.

Thoughts of my past would have to wait.

For now, survival was the only thing that mattered.

Chapter Thirteen

SETTING SAIL

That night, I curled up on a bed of palm fronds beside the flickering fire, wrapping a strip of leather around my arms and shoulders to keep warm. The cave air was heavy with sea salt and smoke, and the fire's warmth reached only so far. Across the flames, I watched Azure and Elios settle in beside each other, their bodies pressed close, faces glowing with the firelight. Shadows danced across their cheeks as the flames cracked and spit.

Earlier, they had returned from the forest with my arms full of fruit, including more of those sweet, overripe mangoes. Then they had spent the last light of the day rebuilding the barrier of rocks at the cave's entrance. It wouldn't keep Miris' monsters out if they came, but it gave us the illusion of shelter. Of control.

Still, tension hung in the air like mist. Azure hadn't said much since the sun dipped below the trees. Her brow furrowed in that way it always did when she was thinking too hard, carrying too much. She was strong, but leading an escape with a wounded mermaid and a mortal man was a weight no one could bear alone.

And Elios. He was brave, yes. Skilled. But he bled. He broke. He didn't have a Sea Goddess's curse to stitch him back together. No matter how fearless he looked sitting beside her, I couldn't help but wonder how long his strength would last.

I turned back to the fire, letting its warmth bleed into my skin. The glow softened the edges of everything, including my thoughts, but it couldn't quiet the truth pressing at the edge of my mind.

We wouldn't be safe much longer.

Somewhere in the chaotic tumble of my mind, thoughts drained more energy than I had to spare. I succumbed to unconsciousness as the flames flickered in the dark space around me. I didn't know how long I'd slept, only that the warmth of the fire had turned into a fading ember behind my closed eyes.

I was just beginning to drift again when a gentle hand touched my shoulder.

It was Azure.

"How are you feeling, Ocevia? Any pain?" she asked, her voice soft as waves brushing the shore.

I blinked against the dim light, already reaching for the crude shoes beside me—primitive things, pieced together from scavenged leather. My limbs ached from yesterday's efforts, but the pain was dulled, less biting than before.

"Like I was thrown off a cliff and then eaten by a shark," I muttered as I slipped on the shoes, wincing slightly. I wasn't embellishing. Every joint protested, but I forced myself to move anyway.

Azure was already folding our leather blankets, her movements quiet. I hadn't worn shoes since I was a child. The straps pinched in odd places, and I hated how clumsy they made me feel. If danger came swiftly, I'd rather run barefoot than trip over salvaged soles.

Giving one last tug on the laces, I tightened them as securely as possible.

"We'll need proper shoes before we hike into the mountains," I said, scanning the dim cavern as if I might find a solution among the rubble and firewood.

Azure didn't respond, but her silence wasn't cold. It was focused. We both knew the road ahead would demand more than courage. It would demand sacrifice.

Before carrying our packs into the cave's front chamber, Elios paused to kiss her. A mischievous grin crept across my face as I caught the moment, their closeness framed by the faint morning glow filtering through the rocks. Despite the playful gleam in my eyes, something heavier coiled in my chest, a quiet longing that had lingered there longer than I cared to admit. I'd never had a lover, never been kissed by someone other than my family.

Love had always felt impossible, unattainable for someone like me. Not under Miris' rule. Not with the Sea Goddess's curse pulsing through my blood. But watching Azure with Elios, watching the gentleness and ease they shared, made something stir in me. It awakened a need I had buried, a need deeper than freedom, deeper than vengeance.

I wanted love. Real love. The kind that could not be stolen or commanded.

The idea that I might find it in the human world, beyond the ocean's reach, was both terrifying and intoxicating.

I was willing to risk everything just for the chance.

"I have credits in Avrearyn and Ceveasea. You can get whatever you want," Elios said as he walked toward the exit.

My eyebrows lifted in amusement, and I caught the sight of Azure shaking her head.

"No. We are not going to spend all Elios' coins," she said, sticking her tongue out at me.

I scrunched my nose and made a silly face, and for a brief moment, we both laughed. The kind of laugh that melted the heaviness in my chest.

Having Azure safe, close, and free brought me a sense of ease I hadn't known I'd missed. With her nearby, I remembered who I was beneath the pain.

Azure lifted a sack of leather blankets and followed after Elios into the corridor. As they disappeared into the passage leading to the front chamber, their voices became muffled echoes beyond the stone.

I didn't follow right away. I needed to pull on the layered strips of leather that would serve as clothing. A moment later, light poured into the cave, filtered and golden, as they shifted the boulders aside to prepare the raft.

I leaned against the wall, bracing myself to join them. When I finally stepped forward, pain lanced through my leg like fire. Two steps in, and I staggered.

Before I could fall, Elios was there. His arms wrapped around me, lifting me as if I weighed nothing.

"Put me down, please. I can walk, Elios," I said sharply. My tone was harsher than intended, but I didn't care. I'd had enough of being carried like some fragile relic. I wasn't his to protect—not like that.

"Not until we get you to the raft. It took a long time to stop your bleeding, and I can tell it still hurts," he replied, his grip firm but careful.

Azure walked beside us, carrying an arm full of supplies. "We can tell it still hurts you, Ocevia. Just wait another day to walk on it."

I squirmed in his arms, stubbornness rising, but it was no use. By the time we reached the beach, I had stopped fighting him. The raft bobbed on the tide, ready for our journey, and for the first time in a long time, I didn't feel like running.

The raft was a patchwork of wrecked ships and forest salvage, bound together with leather strips and a battered sail that fluttered lazily in the early morning breeze. It looked more like a desperate hope than a seaworthy vessel, but it was all we had. I stared at it, unease pooling in my gut.

I was glad I could swim. If the raft splintered apart beneath us, which wasn't out of the question, I at least had that small comfort. It looked stable enough for three, though it would be tight. Claustrophobic, even. And if a storm came, or if Miris' hunters caught wind of us, we wouldn't stand a chance.

Still, we had one advantage. If we kept our scents out of the water, the mermaids would struggle to track us. That single hope clung to me as tightly as the humid air.

The sight of the raft was a physical reminder of our peril. We weren't just leaving an island. We were fleeing a goddess.

"You know," I said as Elios set me down onto the raft's uneven planks, "I'm never going to strengthen my leg if you don't let me try."

His eyes narrowed as he turned to push the vessel into the water. "You can practice when we're in Avrearyn. We need to get out of here while it's still early."

I crossed my arms, lips twitching into a pout as Azure smirked at our exchange.

The raft bobbed in the shallows, water lapping at its sides as Elios steadied it. Azure climbed in, paddle in hand, her eyes scanning the sea with quiet focus. She moved to the front of the craft and wedged the paddle into the water, holding it steady.

Elios followed, settling into the rear with a long board in hand. A final push sent us drifting away from the shore.

And just like that, we were at sea. Three souls against the tide, chasing freedom across uncertain waters.

CHAPTER FOURTEEN

TO FREEDOM

Just like the day before, my energy waned, pulling me into uncon-sciousness again and again as the raft drifted across the open sea. The wind was fickle, strong one moment, stagnant the next, forcing Azure and Elios to paddle with unrelenting effort. Every muscle in their arms strained as they maneuvered the fragile vessel toward the continent. According to Elios, we were bound for the kingdom of Avrearyn, a name that lingered in my mind like a whispered promise.

Despite my fatigue, I listened to Elios speak about his plans with quiet resolve. He talked of buying supplies, securing a room at a tavern, and resting before we pushed onward to Ceveasea. His confidence suggested experience, like he'd traveled these paths more times than he let on. And perhaps he had. Though I knew little of his past, I sensed the weight of many miles behind his words.

Having left the human world so young, I felt a hollow space where certainty should have been. Elios spoke of a former slave king ruling a sanctuary hidden in the mountains, a place Miris couldn't touch. It sounded like a myth, but the hope it carried was enough to ignite something inside me. Something that felt suspiciously like belief.

But even as my thoughts turned toward freedom, Miris lingered. The Sea Goddess had forbidden her mermaids from ever stepping foot on land, yet I knew she still sent scouts across borders. She would not forget our defiance. Elios had been marked as hers the moment Azure saved him, and as for me, I had tasted blood. I had broken her sacred laws. Her wrath would be endless.

My heart pounded with dread as sleep crept over me once again. The sun warmed my skin, the raft rocked with deceptive gentleness, but neither comforted me. Fear, old and sharp, burrowed into my ribs.

A soft touch on my shoulder stirred me from the haze. The sky above glowed in hues of peach and lavender as the sun dipped low on the horizon.

Despite sleeping for hours, my body felt drained, as though the seashell necklace I wore still siphoned power from me. Releasing the Kraken had stripped me raw. The very thought of becoming that monster again made my skin crawl. It haunted the edges of my mind like a shadow just out of reach.

"We should wet our tails before the sun sets," Azure said, rubbing my shoulder.

I nodded groggily and sat up, my limbs heavy, my skin sticky from sweat and salt. The wind had shifted, tugging at our tattered sail and pushing us gently toward the distant shore. Still, Elios didn't relent. He kept paddling, face taut with concentration, eyes on the fading line where sea met sky.

Night would come soon, and with it, danger. Though we were far from the main channel where most mermaids hunted, the sea held no true safety. The idea of slipping into the water felt like a gamble, but I had no choice. If the tale about our tails rotting was true, I couldn't afford to skip a single day.

Gripping the raft's edge, I eased my legs over the side and lowered myself into the water. My tail returned with a sharp twist of pain as salt stung the healing wounds. Still, the water embraced me like a memory, and I exhaled slowly. Here, in the sea, I felt whole. Even afraid, I belonged.

"How long will it take us to reach land?" I asked quietly, watching as a pale ribbon of moonlight shimmered across the surface.

A splash beside me, and Azure slipped into the sea. She didn't answer right away. Her eyes followed Elios on the raft, her expression soft, filled with something that had no name but could only be love. Even as she tilted her head back to rinse her hair, her attention stayed tethered to him.

It was strange and beautiful. Forbidden, but real.

Though we'd never spoken about it, I could see it plain as day. Azure loved him. And he loved her.

A sigh broke from my lips before I could catch it. The longing inside me twisted again.

"If this wind holds," Elios called down to us, "we might reach the coast by tomorrow."

A surge of excitement quickened my heartbeat as I climbed back into the raft, careful not to tip it over. The coastal Avrearyn city of Starspell had always intrigued me, even as a child, though I'd never seen it with my own eyes. The thought of stepping out of the sea and onto the continent was like waking from a nightmare into a dream. It meant hope. It meant freedom.

I curled up on the raft's floor, hugging a leather blanket to my chest while Azure and Elios took turns rowing. The sail billowed gently above us, carrying us forward like a whispered promise. Still, unease prickled at the back of my mind. I worried our scent had drifted through the water like a beacon for any mermaids still searching. We had to put distance between ourselves and the place we entered the sea.

I stirred briefly in the evening to eat but drifted back into sleep soon after, the exhaustion still wrapping around me like a shroud. There was something about the rhythm of their voices, the steady lap of waves against the raft—it soothed me. Perhaps I felt safe with them. Or perhaps I had simply run out of energy to be afraid.

If Azure hadn't been on the island to care for my wounds, to hold vigil while I recovered, I knew I wouldn't be here now. We had saved each other. And though she'd never ask, I owed her my life.

The sea was too quiet.

Not calm, *never calm*, but quiet in a way that felt wrong. Like something sacred holding its breath. I lay at the back of the raft, my injured leg tucked beneath me, every muscle heavy with ache. The salt clung to my skin, cold and slick, and though I tried to rest, my body would not loosen. A knot had formed in my chest, tight and unmoving. Something beneath the surface of the world had shifted. I felt it in my bones.

The raft creaked beneath us, the sail limp in the still air. Even the ropes had fallen silent, too soaked to groan against the center post. The stars above blinked faintly behind veils of cloud, as though the sky itself were reluctant to witness what was coming.

I could hear Azure breathing just ahead of me, light and steady, but strained. She didn't trust this silence either.

Elios shifted his weight near the center of the raft, careful not to unbalance the patchwork boards beneath us. He reached for the nearest tie, checking the lines again with deft hands, each motion deliberate in the confined space.

My thoughts drifted, not toward sleep, but toward memory. The sea had taken so much from me: blood, voice, freedom. And yet now, as I lay on this fragile patchwork raft with a human and a rebellious sister of the tide, it felt as if I was finally beginning to take something back. Something unspoken. Something almost like belonging.

Until the quiet broke.

It started with a whisper. A breath across the surface that stirred the hair at the back of my neck. The first gust made the sail twitch. The second snapped it like a whip.

Azure was already moving. I felt her hands on my shoulder, shaking me awake, though I had never truly slept. Her voice was urgent.

"Wake up. Something's wrong."

Heart leaping into my throat, I jolted upright.

I blinked against the dark, but I didn't need to see. I could feel the shift. The sea had come alive. Not with life. With fury.

Waves swelled beneath us, rising without warning. A low rumble rolled through the water, followed by a flash of white lightning that painted the horizon in bone.

"Grab the rope!"

Elios' voice split the chaos. My body pitched sideways as the first wave struck, soaking us in freezing spray. I reached out blindly and caught the edge of the raft, my injured leg a screaming weight beneath me.

Another crash. Salt and wind and cold slamming over us like a wall. I screamed, not in fear, but instinct, a sound torn from the depths of something ancient inside me.

Elios was beside me in an instant, one arm locked around my waist, the other wrestling the sail. Beside him, Azure was braced between his thigh and the side of the raft. The raft tilted, teetering on the edge of capsizing.

For a breathless moment, I thought we would be thrown. That the sea would claim us all.

Then the rain fell.

A sheet of cold. A thousand knives against my skin. Thunder cracked the sky in half. The raft bucked beneath us like a beast in a snare. I clung to the wood, to the rope, to the nearness of the only two people left in the world who knew me.

"Azure, hold on!"

Elios' voice tore through the wind.

I heard Azure's answer, a sound more breath than words, swallowed by the storm.

The sea lifted us high, then dropped us. A wave rose, massive and unrelenting. We struck it head-on. The world shuddered as the raft slammed down. I felt the air ripped from my lungs.

"Don't let go!" Elios called. His voice was raw, pulled from somewhere deep.

I didn't.

Even as my arms shook. Even as the sea tried to tear us apart.

I held on.

When the storm passed, it left behind a silence heavier than before. The kind that lingered after something terrible had screamed itself hoarse.

The raft rocked gently, battered and soaked. The sail hung in tatters. I lay curled against the rear beam, my hair clinging to my face, my limbs aching with exhaustion.

Azure touched my shoulder, and I opened my eyes.

"We made it," she whispered.

I nodded. I couldn't speak.

Elios crouched beside us. His face was pale, lips drawn tight. One hand still held the rope like it was the only solid thing left.

"We lost the sail," he said. "And half the food."

Azure didn't respond immediately. Then her voice came, quiet and steady. "But we're alive. That has to count for something."

The wind had softened to a breeze, brushing across my skin like an apology. The sea rolled beneath us, no longer furious but watchful. Above us, a single streak of sun pierced the clouds, as though the sky had remembered how to breathe.

In the distance, land waited.

Hope had never felt safe to hold. But for a moment, I did.

I let my eyes fall shut, the rhythm of the water lulling me somewhere between exhaustion and relief. I didn't sleep, not truly. I drifted in that liminal space between now and what comes next.

Squinting against sunlight, I awoke to the sight of land on the horizon. The pale blur of it sharpened as my eyes adjusted, and a breath of pure joy escaped me. The warmth of hope bloomed in my chest.

"We're almost there, ladies," Elios said, his voice tinged with triumph. Azure turned toward him, and when their gazes met, something soft passed between them. It was love, undeniable and raw. I looked away, unable to quiet the ache it sparked inside me.

Turning toward the coastline, I took in the outline of the harbor city. Towering peaks cradled the town in a natural embrace. Wooden and stone structures lined the waterfront, and though the people were too far to see, it felt as if they were reaching for us.

A smile spread across my face. I hadn't stepped foot on human land since I was a child. I barely remembered what it was like, and yet every fiber of me longed for it. I wanted love. A home. A life that was mine.

"I haven't been to the human lands since I was a child. I don't even remember what it was like," I whispered, the words slipping free like a prayer.

Movement stirred beside me, and I turned just in time to see Azure shift into her mermaid form. Her tail shimmered in the sunlight, violet scales catching the glow in dazzling hues.

"We should wet our tails before we reach land. Who knows how long before we can do it again?" Azure said, her voice laced with practicality. She reached into a worn bag, pulling out two glass bottles. As she filled them with seawater and handed one to me, she poured the other over her tail, using her hands to smooth it across the glistening surface.

"I don't want to attempt getting in the water again. It'll draw attention if we flip the raft too close to shore and spread our scents. We'll have to do our best by wetting them from here."

Nodding, I let the shift overtake me and felt my legs slip away, replaced by my turquoise tail. The raft grew cramped as we both took up more space, our scales glinting under the sun.

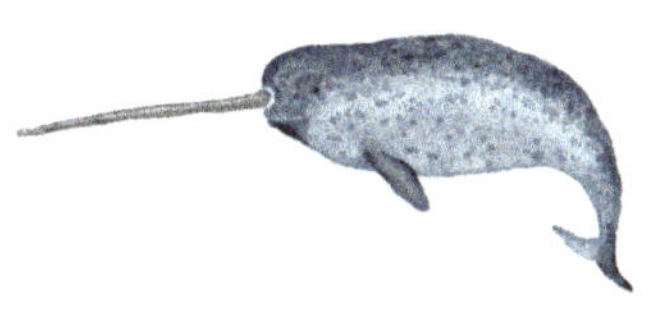

We rinsed ourselves with care, using the bottles to trace water over our fins. I could feel Elios watching us, curious and awed. Though we weren't supposed to reveal ourselves to humans, he already knew. Azure had saved him from drowning. He had seen her for what she was, and though he hadn't chosen to stay, he hadn't run either.

I didn't fully understand why she had taken that risk, but deep down, I knew. If it had been me, I would have done the same.

Throughout my years of enslavement, as I lured thousands of souls to the deep, I had never looked into their faces. I didn't want their haunting visages to invade my dreams. Yet, they still did. Always appearing as shadowed silhouettes in the darkness, their screams echoing as their light was snuffed out. If I ever had a chance to break that cycle, if I ever found a man I could fall in love with and escape with, I would take it without hesitation.

As I poured the salty water over my tail, wincing as it slid across my still-healing wound, my gaze drifted toward Azure and Elios. Their wordless flirtation unfolded like a dance, silent but vivid. I grinned to myself, caught between delight and awkwardness, wishing I could vanish and give them privacy. The raft was small, too small, and I sat mere inches from Azure as she dampened her tail with slow, deliberate movements. Across from her, Elios' blue eyes tracked every gesture, heavy with desire.

I had never known a man's touch, never known anyone's. But something low in my belly stirred, a tight ache that whispered of longing. Not for Elios specifically, but for something deeper. To be touched. Seen. Wanted. As we neared the human lands, I clung to the hope that maybe, just maybe, I would find someone who would look at me the way Elios looked at her.

With a quiet, self-deprecating laugh, I interrupted the moment.

"Just for the record... I am not sharing a room with you two love-birds."

Azure groaned, burying her face in her hands as color bloomed in her cheeks. Elios chuckled under his breath.

I drained the last of the water over my tail and shifted back into my legs. The land loomed ahead, close enough now that I could make out individual buildings and ships bobbing in the harbor. I took a deep breath, centering myself.

We had intended to arrive in Star-spell by midday, but the wind had delayed us. The sun had long since vanished, and the city pulsed with life beneath a sky full of stars. Golden candlelight spilled from windows, silhouettes drifting across the glass like ghosts of a life I no longer knew. People walked the streets, some laughing, others heading home. The sheer normalcy of it struck me like a wave.

This was what I had been denied. This was what I wanted.

"My friend's tavern is close to the harbor," Elios said, breaking into my thoughts. "We'll go straight there once we dock this contraption. He can arrange for clothing and supplies, and we can finally order food and drinks. Real food. Not just dried fish and fruit."

I smiled, heart full, eyes glistening with anticipation.

After all these years, I had returned to the human lands. And for the first time in forever, I wasn't running from something. I was running toward it.

As Elios tied the raft to the floating dock, I stood and took my first step onto the wooden planks, the scent of the city drifting on the night breeze.

It was the scent of possibility.

Chapter Fifteen

TO BE FREE

As soon as my feet touched the docks, a sigh of relief escaped me. The makeshift raft bobbed gently in the water, tied to one of the pilings, though we never intended to use it again. My thigh still ached, a dull echo of pain that reminded me of all I had endured. Yet the edge had softened after the rest I'd managed over the past few days.

I took a cautious step forward, only to be swept up into Elios' arms. Cradled like a child, I huffed, my pride bristling. I was about to protest, but I already knew it wouldn't matter. He wasn't going to set me down until he decided it was safe. So I surrendered to the stubbornness of the human and crossed my arms, grumbling beneath my breath.

Azure walked beside us, her pace steady, her expression calm, though the weight of our journey still clung to her shoulders. Together we made our way up the wooden pier toward the stone buildings that lined the bustling street beyond.

As we neared a tall, weatherworn structure, music and laughter spilled from within. The air buzzed with the strumming of fiddles and the jangle of tambourines. Voices rose in song and shouted greetings. Glasses clinked, and boots stomped in rhythm. The scent of roasted meat, fresh bread, and spiced ale wrapped around me, warm and heady, stirring something deep in my chest.

Even as I sulked about being carried like an invalid, I couldn't help but smile.

Azure reached the door first and pulled it open, its iron handle creaking in protest. With a quick motion, she gestured for Elios to step inside. As he crossed the threshold carrying me, something shifted inside me.

The tavern was nothing like I had imagined, and yet it was everything.

As a child, I had only dreamed of places like this, forbidden from entering before the sea took me. My memories of Thatia were faded and fragile, but this space reignited a longing I had buried long ago.

The room was alive.

Long wooden tables stretched across the space, packed with townspeople. Laughter and chatter mingled with the upbeat tunes played by a group of bards in the corner. The music thrummed in my bones, joyous and untamed. Warm candlelight flickered on stone walls, and the air was thick with camaraderie and the rich perfume of cooked food.

A pang of yearning hit me square in the chest. This was the human world I had been ripped from. This was what it felt like to be free.

But then I became keenly aware of myself.

The leather strips that covered my chest and waist, once practical in the sea, felt woefully inadequate here. Among layers of wool skirts, cloaks, and embroidered tunics, I stood out like a ghost from a different world. I resisted the urge to wrap my arms around myself, forcing my spine to straighten instead.

I wouldn't shrink. Not here. Not now.

Still, my eyes flitted across the room, drinking in every detail, every face, every laugh, every clink of a tankard. I was no longer an exile from the land. I was part of this world again.

Even if I didn't quite know how to belong.

At the bar, a silver-haired man caught Elios' gaze. His hazel eyes gleamed with recognition as he murmured something to the elderly man with an eye patch sitting beside him, then strode toward us.

"Elios," the silver-haired man greeted warmly, his voice deep and full of unspoken familiarity. As he clapped Elios on the shoulder a little too hard, I jolted in his arms, grumbling in protest.

Finally, Elios set me down, and though my legs wobbled slightly, I stood firm, slipping into the background beside Azure.

Elios shook the man's hand, his smile genuine. "Vasso, it's good to see you, old friend. Business looks like it's going well."

Vasso returned the smile, his warmth unforced as he draped an arm over Elios' broad shoulders, turning him to survey the bustling tavern. "It's been a good season." His hazel eyes flicked toward me and Azure, assessing but not unkind. "What brings you back to Starspell?"

"We're just passing through," Elios said, his tone casual. "We probably won't stay more than the night."

Something unspoken passed between them.

Vasso's nod was subtle. "Off the record, it is then. One room or two?"

A pit formed in my stomach.

What exactly did Elios do for a living? What kind of past did he have that allowed for these silent agreements?

I trusted him. He had risked everything to keep Azure and me safe. But doubt crept in, whispering that I didn't truly know him at all.

"Two," Elios said. "But near each other if possible. We also need supplies—clothes for my companions and something to eat. Unfortunately, we've had to travel with little more than the clothes on our backs. Are my credits still adequate?"

Beside me, Azure wrapped her arms around herself, shifting uncomfortably. I could see the self-conscious tension in her posture. We were mermaids, accustomed to wearing little, but here, surrounded by fully clothed humans, we were exposed.

Vasso chuckled, slapping Elios on the back once more. "Your credits are more than enough. Let me grab those keys for you, and you can get these ladies settled upstairs. I'll bring you food and beverages while Chryssa rustles up some clothes. The stores are closed at this hour, but she should be able to scrounge up a few things until morning."

As Vasso walked away, Elios slid his hand into Azure's, the simple gesture reminding me how alone I truly was.

I let my gaze drift across the tavern, drawn toward the band in the corner. The joyful energy in the room pulsed around me, a stark contrast to the storm that churned inside my chest. My foot tapped absently against the wooden floor, caught in the rhythm of the melody, but my mind was elsewhere.

A few minutes later, Vasso returned, holding two silver keys. With a quick flick of his wrist, he motioned us toward the narrow, shadowed stairway tucked away in the back of the tavern.

Elios released Azure's hand and wrapped an arm around me, helping shoulder some of my weight as we ascended the dimly lit stairs. I scowled at him, muttering protests, but I let him help.

The corridor on the second level was dimly lit, heavy shadows stretching along the walls. Only a few flickering sconces provided enough light to navigate. Elios moved with certainty, clearly familiar with the place, and quickly found our guest rooms at the far end of the hall. Stopping in front of the last door on the right, he turned to me as he unlocked it.

"Make yourself comfortable," he said, pushing the door open. "One of us will come to knock when Vasso sends up food and clothing. Get some rest. There are usually towels in the bathing room and a bathtub for your tail."

The moment the word bathtub left his lips, I perked up.

Water. *Finally.*

I barely heard anything else. Without hesitation, I darted past them, excitement surging through me, and flung the door shut behind me. Whatever Elios and Azure planned to do with their night, I didn't need to know.

They needed privacy. And I needed water.

Chapter Sixteen

THE GIFT OF WATER

The candlelit room was modest but inviting, the large bed taking up most of the space. The open door to the bathing room caught my eye instantly, and I moved toward it with single-minded determination. The copper tub gleamed under the dim light, a sight so beautiful it nearly brought tears to my eyes.

My stomach grumbled loudly, reminding me of the feast waiting downstairs, but food could wait. I had gone far too long without fully submerging in water, and I could feel it in every aching muscle, every dry patch of skin.

Reaching the tub, I halted abruptly, my excitement dimming as I realized I had no idea how to operate it.

Frowning, I inspected the spout and the metal handles. It couldn't be that difficult. Biting my lip, I grabbed one of the handles and twisted. Nothing. I tried the other. Still nothing. I pushed down, pulled up, growing increasingly frustrated until, finally, something rumbled within the wall. A moment later, a steady stream of water poured from the spout, splashing into the tub below.

I let out a triumphant laugh, slapping my hands together in celebration before tearing at the leather bindings covering my body. In seconds, I shed the material and stepped into the tub, sighing as the cool water washed over my skin, shifting my legs into my iridescent turquoise tail.

The water was colder than I would have liked, but I didn't know how to make it hotter or if that was even possible. Still, relief settled deep in my bones as I leaned back, letting the sensation of weightlessness relax every fiber of my being.

The tub was smaller than ideal, the end of my tail draping over the rim, but I made do. Grabbing a nearby glass, I scooped up water and poured it over the parts of my tail that didn't fit. Droplets splashed onto the floor, but I didn't care. As I bathed, I hummed softly, making up a tune as I went along, losing myself in the simple pleasure of being submerged.

I was so caught up in my singing and the rhythmic motions of rinsing my hair that I didn't hear Azure enter my room until she called out to me.

"Ocevia? Food is ready!"

Startled, I paused mid-note, blinking as I realized just how much water I had spilled onto the floor.

"I'm in the bathtub," I called back, shifting slightly as I grabbed the glass again and poured more over my hair.

A moment later, Azure appeared in the doorway, grinning as she took in the mess I had made. "You're lucky it was just me and not one of the staff checking on you."

I shrugged, unbothered. "They shouldn't enter my room without permission."

Azure rolled her eyes, nodding toward the door. "It was unlocked."

I groaned, tilting my head back against the edge of the tub. "I haven't been in the human lands since I was a child. I couldn't figure out how to lock it. I don't know how to use half the stuff in here. It took me forever just to figure out how to turn the water on."

Azure's expression softened, guilt flickering across her face. "I'm sorry, Ocevia. I should have shown you around and explained things to you."

I smirked, hoping to ease her guilt as I shifted back into my legs, the transformation smooth and familiar. Reaching down, I pulled the drain at the bottom of the tub, watching the water swirl away. "Don't worry about it. I'm the one who ran off at the promise of a tub. If you and your muscled brute give me food and clothes, I'm sure I can figure out how to use the bed on my own. I don't plan on doing much other than sleeping after I eat."

Azure snickered, shaking her head as she turned toward the door. "I'll bring you a plate of food and a glass of wine while you dry off. I expect they'll bring up clothing soon. I'll be right back."

I nodded, watching as she disappeared into the darkened room, the door hinges barely making a sound as she slipped out.

Once she left, I climbed out of the bathtub, dragging the soft towel over my damp skin and relishing the clean sensation. The water had been a much-needed reprieve, but now that I was out, the cool air prickled my skin with gooseflesh.

The fire in the hearth had burned low, leaving the room dim and chilly. I knelt in front of the fireplace, shivering slightly as I reached for the logs stacked in a basket against the wall. My fingers traced the rough bark as I arranged the wood, searching for smaller kindling to help the flames catch. Before I could attempt to light it, the door creaked open again, and Azure strode in, a tray of food balanced in her hands.

The aroma hit me first: herbs, slow-cooked meat, something rich and savory that made my stomach twist with hunger. My mouth watered, but I forced myself to focus as she crossed the room and reached for a small metal object above the mantle. She knelt beside me, her expression patient.

"Here," she said, placing it in my hands.

For the next few minutes, she guided me through the process, demonstrating how to strike the metal against the flint until sparks ignited the dry wood. It took a few tries, but eventually, the flames flickered to life, crackling and spreading warmth through the small room.

Satisfied with my work, Azure dusted off her hands and gestured for me to follow. "Come on, let me show you a few things."

I trailed after her as she moved through the space, pointing out different amenities, how to use the washbasin, how the door latch worked, even how the strange contraption beside the bed could be adjusted to provide more light. Each small detail fascinated me, a glimpse into the life I had lost all those years ago.

The knock at the door startled me from my thoughts. Azure answered, cracking it open just enough for Elios to slip a small bundle of clothing through the gap. I caught a glimpse of his silhouette before the door shut again.

Azure turned, unfolding the garments and giving me an approving nod. "These should fit."

She helped me dress, lacing me into a long white top that tied down the front and handing me a loose pair of trousers. The fabric felt foreign against my skin, the weight of it both comforting and strange. It had been a decade since I'd worn human clothing. I knew I would have to get used to it again, but for now, while I was alone, I wanted to breathe.

As Azure left, I exhaled, feeling the weight of the night settle over me.

I picked up the plate of food and the glass of wine, making my way toward the window. The room was silent now, too silent, and I found myself craving the hum of the sea, the endless lull of waves crashing against the shore. Settling into the chair, I placed my meal on the windowsill and hesitated, tugging at the loose sleeves of my borrowed shirt. The fabric rubbed against my skin in an unfamiliar way, a reminder that this world was no longer truly mine.

The stars glittered above the mountain range beyond the city, a breathtaking view that should have filled me with awe. But instead, a deep, aching uncertainty curled inside my chest.

Fear. Of being recaptured by Miris. Trepidation. At venturing further into the unknown. Excitement. At the possibility of a life on land.

The emotions twisted together, pressing against my ribs until my breath came shallow. The air in the room suddenly felt too thin, too tight, and for a brief moment, I wanted to run to Azure, to seek the comfort of familiarity.

But I couldn't.

It was no longer just the two of us. She had Elios now, and I... I had no one.

A tear slid down my cheek before I could stop it. The loneliness in the room was suffocating.

I clenched my jaw, forcing myself to push past the emotion. I would allow myself one moment of weakness, just one, before I moved forward.

Swiping the tear away, I picked up my spoon and forced a bite of stew past my lips. Even though it had cooled, the burst of flavor was unlike anything I had tasted in years. A groan escaped my throat before I could stop it, and I shoveled another bite into my mouth, barely chewing before swallowing.

I ate fast, desperate, scraping the bottom of the bowl until my spoon hit empty porcelain. Only then did I reach for the wine, lifting the glass to my lips and taking a deep sip.

The bitter tang caught me off guard. I nearly spat it out.

I stared down at the dark red liquid, frowning. People drank this all the time, and I didn't know why?

Standing abruptly, I strode back to the bathing room, pouring the offending liquid down the drain before refilling my glass with water. It was a waste, I supposed, but I didn't care. I had no interest in developing a taste for something that burned my throat.

Returning to my chair, I grabbed a piece of fresh bread, biting into it as I cracked the window open.

The breeze swept in immediately, cool and crisp, carrying the familiar scent of salt and water. I inhaled deeply, letting it soothe me. The sheer curtains swayed, ghost-like in the moonlight, and I closed my eyes, savoring the simple pleasure of feeling full, clean, and—for the first time in years—*safe*.

CHAPTER SEVENTEEN

BETWEEN TWO WORLDS

Light streamed through the open window, and I felt a cool breeze skimming across my bare skin, pulling me from a deep sleep. I had sat in front of the window for hours, anticipation replacing my earlier exhaustion. When my eyelids grew too heavy to keep open, I moved to the bed, moaning as the soft bedding embraced my naked body like I was floating in the clouds. I drifted off to sleep as soon as my head settled on the pillow.

Rolling over in the blanket, it took me a moment to remember where I was. A bright smile spread across my lips as birds filled the air. I sprang out of bed, racing toward the door to find my friend. However, when my hand grabbed the handle, I let it go and returned to the pile of clothing on the floor. I stared at it momentarily, groaning as I bent over to pick it up.

After living for so long without clothing, these garments made little sense to me. Still, I tugged the large white top over my head, leaving the straps undone, before pulling the trousers up my legs. I darted across the hall without glancing in the mirror and banged on my friend's door.

Though I could hear footsteps inside the room and muffled voices, it took Azure and Elios a moment to answer. My grin widened as I intended to ask Azure what it was like to share a bed with a male alone when they had a moment. I wasn't sure if they had gotten that far, but by how they were together, I had little doubt they had.

Heavy footsteps approached as I fumbled with the straps on my tunic, and the door swung open.

With his hair disheveled and his clothes as hastily pulled on as mine, any doubt that my friend was still innocent vanished. Behind him, Azure was fastening the laces of her own tunic, but her eyes widened when they met mine. Before I could greet her, Azure dashed across the room, grabbed my arm, and pulled me inside.

"Ocevia," Azure said, exasperation filling her voice as she reached for the ties on my top, pulling them tight before tying them. I tried to watch her movements to replicate them later, but her hands moved too quickly. "You can't stand in the hallway half-dressed."

Taken aback, I glanced down at my clothing, incredulity crossing my face before I returned my gaze to her. "I usually wear a lot less than this, Azure. You're being ridiculous."

Clearly holding back, Azure placed her hands on my shoulders. "Mermaids wear less, but humans don't. Remember, you're pretending to be human right now."

With how unfamiliar I was with human customs, I didn't argue, and Azure seemed relieved.

"So, what's the plan for today?" I asked, eyeing both of us as we waited for a response.

Sitting on the bed, Azure quickly laced up my boots before lacing up her own.

"Let's head down to the tavern for breakfast first," he suggested, gazing at Azure for confirmation. I couldn't help but stifle a snicker when I saw her cheeks redden.

"Or I can have it brought up if you'd prefer," he added, but I was already feeling the excitement bubbling inside me. Excited to mingle with other humans and unwilling to eat another meal alone, I darted toward the door, hoping Azure and Elios would follow.

As soon as we stepped into the tavern, warmth enveloped me. The air was thick with the scent of baked bread and sizzling meat. Just like the night before, the place was alive with chatter, laughter, and the clatter of plates and mugs. The energy in the room was infectious, drawing a smile to my lips as I let my gaze drift across the crowd.

Humans. Free humans. They lived their lives without fear of Miris, without the constant shadow of servitude looming over them. I envied them.

Following Elios and Azure, I took a seat at a table tucked into the corner. Elios ordered three daily breakfast specials without hesitation, and my stomach grumbled eagerly at the thought of another warm, flavorful meal. The previous night's dinner had been the best thing I'd tasted in years, and I was already desperate for more.

As we waited, I let my attention wander, taking in every detail around me. The way the patrons laughed, the way their hands danced through the air as they spoke, the rich colors of their clothing—so vibrant and varied compared to the simple, functional garments I'd worn for the past decade. Their shoes, their accessories, their relaxed way of existing in this world fascinated me.

So much had changed since I'd left the human realm, and I had never lived in Starspell. My home had been Thatia, on the opposite side of the Lamalis Sea, but even then, I had only seen glimpses of human life from the shadows of my childhood. My parents had never taken me to places like this. I had only ever dreamed of sitting at a table in a lively tavern, eating with friends.

And then, of course, there was the other thing I longed for. Romance.

My gaze flicked from one male patron to another, searching for something, someone who might stir that spark within me. But to my disappointment, none of them did. No glances that made my stomach flip. No stranger's eyes that set my pulse racing. No matter how much I wanted it, the connection I sought remained elusive.

The approaching server snapped me from my thoughts, and as soon as the scent of food hit me, all previous musings disappeared. My gaze dropped to the plate set before me, and my chest tightened with unexpected emotion.

Eggs. Fried potatoes. Simple food, but food I hadn't tasted in so long. My memories of meals before the sea were faded at best, blurred by time and survival. But this, I could already tell, was going to be incredible.

The moment my eating utensil was in my hand, I dug in.

The first bite hit my tongue, and my entire body shuddered. I groaned unabashedly, my eyes rolling back as warmth and flavor exploded in my mouth.

"This is so good." My words were barely intelligible, a mixture of speech and moan as I swallowed and immediately scooped another oversized bite onto my utensil.

By the time I took my first sip of tea, I had already cleared half my plate.

I barely noticed whether my friends were eating. If they were, they certainly weren't as dramatic as I was, but I didn't care. I had never been easily embarrassed, and after years of eating dried or raw fish, this was ecstasy on my tongue.

My stomach made an odd, protesting noise by the time my utensil scraped against the empty plate, reminding me that I had eaten too fast. Only then did I finally look up at Elios and Azure, only to find them gawking at me like I was some kind of wild animal.

I blinked. "What?"

Before either of them could respond, a middle-aged woman approached the table, dropping off several bags filled with clothes and supplies. I perked up immediately, already eager to dig through the gifts and see what human comforts I had been given. But just as I reached for the nearest bag, movement from across the tavern caught my eye.

Vasso.

He strode toward us with a firm, urgent purpose, and before I could ask what was wrong, he reached out and grabbed Elios' wrist, catching him off guard. The look on the older man's face was enough to set me instantly on edge.

Elios didn't hesitate. Without protest, he rose from the table, allowing himself to be led toward the dimly lit hallway near the stairwell.

A knot of unease tightened in my stomach. Something was wrong.

I stood as well, and with Azure at my side, I followed them.

Vasso's behavior spoke volumes before he even said a word. His gaze flicked side to side, searching the room for listening ears. His fingers flexed at his sides as if he were coiling for something unseen. The sinking feeling in my gut only worsened.

This wasn't good.

Just when I was about to demand an explanation, Vasso finally leaned in close, his voice dropping to a whisper.

"I don't mean to rush you off, Elios, but there were some individuals asking questions in town last night. They were asking about a woman with her description."

I barely had time to process the words before his gaze landed on Azure.

A slow, icy dread slid through my veins, burning the back of my throat. No.

Someone was looking for us, and there was only one possibility for who it was.

Miris' scouts.

My hand instinctively sought out Azure's, gripping it tightly. Her fingers trembled, but she didn't speak, her face paling with fear.

Vasso continued, his voice still a whisper, his tone urgent. "They came into the tavern after you three went to bed. I didn't recognize them under their cloaks, but I ran them off. I doubt they've left the city."

A sharp inhale filled my lungs, but it did nothing to calm the rapid pounding of my heart.

We weren't safe.

We had never been safe.

And now, Miris was closing in.

Chapter Eighteen

DANGER AT OUR HEALS

Resigned but unsurprised, I watched as Elios rubbed his eyebrows, clearly deep in thought, before he spoke. "Send word to our contacts. We'll set out for Ceveasea today."

Vasso's eyes flicked to me and Azure before returning to Elios, nodding in acknowledgment. "I can spare a few men from The Circle. I don't want you to leave with these ladies without some extra swords."

I could feel the tension radiating from Elios as he nodded sharply and reached for my hand, urging Azure and me back up the stairs. A muscle in his jaw twitched, betraying the stress he was trying to hide.

Although I didn't know what 'The Circle' was, the term resonated with importance, something deeply entwined with Elios. My curiosity piqued, but as Elios hurried us down the hall, leading our escape from the city, I sensed it wasn't the right time to ask questions.

We walked in silence until Elios opened the door to our room. He led us inside, his urgency palpable.

"Take a moment to wet your tails while you can. I'll get our packs together. You know what Vasso said. They're already here. If we don't leave now, we may never get the chance."

A wave of nausea rose in my throat, churning into a bitter taste that I struggled to swallow. I turned to the bathing room, desperate to do something, anything. But I stopped when Azure didn't follow.

"Elios," she said, hesitation lacing her voice. "What is The Circle?"

Elios reached for Azure's hand, his immense stress evident on his face. He scanned the room, then returned his gaze to her.

"I promise to tell you everything once we're safe. But for now, we need to get moving. I imagine Vasso is preparing the horses and men right now.

The sooner we leave, the better. The longer we wait, the more danger we'll all face."

I knew this wasn't our deserved answer, but I also had to admit Elios was right. If Miris' henchmen were already in the city, we needed to leave immediately. The Sea Goddess had a far-reaching influence, and if we could escape her grasp, we had to stay one step ahead.

As Azure handed me a set of clean trousers and boots, I hesitated for a moment, but I couldn't bear the thought of being away from my friends for long. With a determined breath, I left the safety of our room and crossed the hall back into my own, intent on quickly soaking my tail so I could return to them as soon as possible.

A short time later, we stepped out into the narrow alley behind the tavern, pulling the heavy door closed behind us. The midday sun tried to reach us, but the tall stone walls on either side kept the alley cloaked in shadow. The smell of damp earth and woodsmoke lingered in the air, mingling with the sharper scent of horses up ahead.

I followed the others toward the end of the alley, where the stone walls gave way to a small, sheltered yard hidden from the main streets. Several satchels lay packed and ready on the ground, piled neatly near the horses. Vasso and his wife, Chryssa, moved between them, handing off water skins and bundles of supplies to the men who waited.

As I scanned the clearing, my gaze caught on a figure near the trees and held. A man stood beside an onyx horse, chewing idly on a piece of straw. His dark hair fell past his shoulders, almost blending with the horse's black mane. He hadn't even glanced our way, but my heart thundered in my chest as if he had. I silently begged him to look up, but he didn't seem to hear the frantic plea beating against my ribs.

Just then, a tall, muscular man with bright red hair and a full beard approached our group, grinning as if he carried the sun itself. I tore my gaze away, reluctantly, as he wrapped Elios in a familiar hug.

It quickly became clear that Dimitris Teresides was as vibrant as his hair. I couldn't help but giggle quietly at his enthusiasm. As the horses were saddled and our belongings secured, Dimitris and Elios fell into an easy conversation like old friends catching up. I didn't know much about either of them yet, but their bond was obvious.

The more preparations continued, the more my nerves grew. I shifted from foot to foot, unable to shake the unease curling in my stomach. I had never ridden a horse before, and the thought of mounting one now filled me with a flutter of panic.

Azure moved to my side, her hand warm as she grasped mine.

"Are you okay?" she asked, her voice low.

I couldn't tear my gaze away from the horses long enough to answer properly.

"I don't know how to ride a horse, Azure. That thing may kill me," I said, half-joking, half-serious.

Azure shrugged and squeezed my hand.

"I haven't ridden a horse since I was younger, and I have barely any experience either, but I'm sure you won't be alone. You'll ride with one of those fine men." She gestured with a playful sweep of her hand, but my attention had already fixed on only one.

Markos.

I had learned his name earlier, overhearing it as Dimitris and Elios spoke. Markos was quieter than the others, more watchful. He hadn't said much, but something about him pulled at me like the tide. I didn't know what it was, only that it was strong enough to leave me breathless.

The fourth man, Aris, stood nearby, towering over the others with his golden hair tied neatly back and his muscular arms marked with tattoos. He looked like he had lived a life of battle and adventure, but it was Markos who held my focus.

Markos, with his summer-green eyes and quiet strength.

As the group finished strapping down the supplies, I turned back toward the man I couldn't stop watching, just in time to catch him looking at me.

My breath caught. For a moment, neither of us looked away.

Azure squeezed my hand again, bringing me back to myself. I barely heard her as I lifted my hand and, without thinking, pointed directly at him.

"I want that one, I think," I said, my voice shameless.

Catching me by surprise, Azure burst out laughing, the sound bright and irreverent against the tense stillness of the alley. When she caught her breath, she patted me on the back, grinning.

"I'm not sure if you get to choose, but I'll see what I can do."

Flushing from head to toe, I tightened my grip on my cloak and ducked my head, but when I dared a glance up, I saw Markos was watching me from across the small yard. His lips twitched, almost smiling.

Hope bloomed in my chest. Whatever would happen next, it had already begun.

Chapter Nineteen

The Promise of a Kiss

"Hey, Markos," Elios said, interrupting my awkward moment.

Markos' sudden departure left me with a mix of relief and disappointment. I couldn't hear their conversation, but the mischievous grin on Elios' face sent a rush of warmth to my cheeks. As Markos started walking back toward me, my heart raced. I'd never considered myself shy, but with each step he took, I found myself increasingly breathless.

"Ocevia?" he asked, extending his hand toward me. His voice was a low rumble, gentle and steady. My cheeks burned hotter as I nodded and reached out to let him take it. When he smiled, a slight, almost secret grin, it nearly sent me to my knees.

"Elios said you'd like to ride with me?" he asked, framing it as a question, letting me back out if I changed my mind.

I nodded again, my voice trapped in my throat.

He lifted my hand to his lips and pressed a soft kiss to my knuckles, his eyes never leaving mine. The moment felt like magic stitched into reality.

"Well, it's nice to meet you, Ocevia. I'm Markos, and this handsome brute is Storm." He tilted his head toward the horse behind him. "May I walk you to him and help you onto the saddle?"

His kind demeanor broke the spell he held over me just enough to get a few words out. "Yes, but I have a confession." My voice was barely above a whisper, and I noticed him lean in slightly to hear me. His scent, woodsmoke and pine, wrapped around me, grounding and dizzying all at once.

"And what might that be, Ocevia?"

For a second, I considered telling him that I wanted to stay pressed against him forever, but I reeled myself in.

"I've never ridden a horse. And I'm a bit terrified."

His grin deepened, slow and reassuring. "That's not a problem," he said softly. "You'll be with me. I won't let anything happen to you."

He slid his hand to the small of my back, guiding me gently across the dusty clearing as the rest of the group mounted their horses. The sun glinted off Storm's obsidian coat, and as I approached, the horse's size became daunting. His black eyes were intelligent and calm, far more so than my own thundering heart.

Noticing my apprehension, Markos intertwined his fingers with mine and raised our joined hands to rest against Storm's warm flank.

"He may look intimidating," he said, his voice soothing. "But he's loyal and patient, just like me." The teasing note in his tone made my stomach flip.

His green eyes sparkled with quiet sincerity. "Neither of us will let you fall. That's a promise."

I wanted to believe him. And at that moment, I did.

With surprising ease, Markos wrapped his arms around my waist and lifted me onto the saddle. The world tilted, and I barely had time to settle before he mounted behind me. His strong chest pressed to my back, his arms folding on either side of me to take the reins.

"Ready?" he asked, his breath tickling the shell of my ear.

I nodded, unsure whether it was to answer him or convince myself.

With the gentle nudge of Markos' heel against Storm's side, we began to move. I prayed that this new journey wouldn't break me.

A warm sensation surged through my body, radiating outward and pooling in the depths of my being. Unlike anything I had encountered before, it was an unfamiliar feeling: pure, unbridled desire. Though I had never found myself near a man, nor had I ever felt the brush of his skin against mine, something about Markos ignited a heat within me that was both thrilling and overwhelming. Each glance from him sent shivers down my spine, and the way his presence enveloped me was intoxicating. I could sense the deep, thudding pull of lust awakening in my core, leaving me breathless and yearning for a connection I had yet to fully understand.

I squirmed in my saddle, desperately seeking some stimulation against the sensitive spot between my thighs. Being touched by a man was uncharted territory for me, but I had explored my own body enough to know how good it could feel. And with Markos against my back, I couldn't stop thinking about his touch, his kiss, and everything else I was ready to experience with him. As we rode through the winding back alleys of Starspell and toward the towering mountains ahead, my mind was consumed with thoughts of Markos and the forbidden pleasures he might one day give me. I craved his touch more than anything else at that moment.

The rhythmic sway of the horse only heightened my awareness of his body behind me—his thighs pressed to mine, the subtle shifts of his hips as he guided the reins. Every time his breath ghosted near my ear, it sent another ripple of heat through me. I had never wanted someone like this before, so completely, so instantly.

As we traveled down the city's back alleys, I felt relieved that there weren't many people around to recognize us. The entire group wore hooded black cloaks, just in case. I suspected they had no idea that Azure and I were mermaids. Still, they seemed to understand that we were in danger and needed to be escorted out of the city discreetly.

A thought crossed my mind: I would eventually need to tell Markos about my true nature, especially if I hoped he would take me to his bed. However, revealing the monster hidden in my necklace was something I wanted to avoid at all costs. All he needed to know was about my tail.

The cobblestone streets gave way to a dirt path that led toward the mountain pass as we left the city. The rhythmic clacking of Storm's hooves threatened to lull me to sleep. Markos' arms stayed wrapped securely around me, his hands steady on the reins. I allowed my eyes to close for much of the ride, grateful for the warmth of his body beside me. I imagined what it would be like if our skin touched instead of just our clothing, if his hands traced my bare waist, if his lips found the spot just beneath my ear where my pulse thrummed.

Once we entered the mountain pass, we no longer needed to maintain silence to avoid attracting attention. Muffled voices reached my ears as I noticed Azure and Elios engaged in a quiet conversation ahead of us. Elios held my friend tightly as they rode, while Aris led the way and Dimitris brought up the rear, keeping close behind Markos and me. But

I hardly noticed any of them. My thoughts, and my senses, were wholly occupied by the man holding me as if I belonged to him.

And perhaps... I wanted to.

Reaching forward, I rubbed my hand across Storm's soft mane, nervousness making me lick my lips.

"Do you have a wife, Markos?" I asked, curiosity getting the better of me.

He chuckled, the sound warm and rumbling against my back. "Well, that was an unexpected question, Ocevia. No, I do not have a wife. Do you have a husband?"

"Where I'm from, having a lover is not allowed. I don't really get the chance to interact with men."

A pang of guilt twisted in my chest as I thought about the lives I had taken. I had interacted with humans, just not in the way he was imagining. I knew he would eventually learn the truth about me, but I swallowed the guilt and exhaled.

"I've never had a lover. Or even been kissed. I want to, though."

He stiffened behind me, just a little.

"You don't get the opportunity to go on dates? To get married?"

Confusion creased my brow. I turned to glance at him over my shoulder.

"What's a date?"

One of his brows arched, and the corner of his mouth curved with amused disbelief.

"Why, my lovely Ocevia, you've missed out on a lot. Maybe, once we get somewhere safe... if you'd like, I could take you on your first date. To answer your question: a date is when a man takes a woman somewhere nice to woo her and make her fall in love with him... or with whomever they love, for that matter."

Before he even finished his sentence, I was nodding eagerly.

"Yes! I would love for you to woo me... but I think I'm already in love with you."

The chuckle that escaped him was low and rich, but I tensed, unsure if I had said something wrong.

"I'm sorry if I hurt your feelings, little one," he said, his tone gentle as his hand slid down my arm, interlacing his fingers with mine. "I didn't mean to upset you. It's just that I've never had a woman tell me she loves me the moment we meet."

I turned fully toward him, a teasing smile curling my lips.

"That's a good thing since you're supposed to be my mate, not theirs."

His eyes sparkled. He lifted one hand to trace along my jaw, fingertips feather-light. A tremor rippled through me at his touch, sending a shiver down my spine.

"Your mate, huh? Is that what I'm supposed to be to you?"

With a slow nod, I leaned into his palm. "My heart says so."

His thumb swept across my cheek.

"Then I'll just have to work hard to earn that title properly."

And with that, we kept riding. Two souls pressed close on horseback, heading into the unknown, our hearts already far ahead of us.

As his touch lingered, warm lips brushed against my cheek in a gentle kiss, igniting a flurry of sensations within me.

"Your heart can't lie to you, so it must be right. Maybe later, you'll let me kiss you again, and you can tell me more about being your mate."

Gooseflesh prickled along my arms and legs as a deep throb awakened between my thighs.

"You could kiss me now."

His eyebrow lifted, and a grin spread across his face as something flickered in his gaze, an unreadable thought.

"If you want me to kiss you, little one, I promise I will when we get somewhere safe. But for now, we must speed up and find shelter for the night. It's unsafe to be in the open in these mountains past nightfall. Things come out in the darkness that we don't want to cross paths with."

With that, the moment slipped away, leaving me both eager and uncertain as we continued our journey. When I turned back to look before us, a slight tinge of disappointment settled in my chest, coupled with the fear that crept in from Markos' ominous warning. He dug his heels into Storm's sides, urging the horse to go faster. A moment later, we were riding right next to Elios and Azure.

"Any ideas where you want to stop tonight, Brother?" Markos asked Elios, his arms still snugly around my waist. Azure was tucked in close to Elios, her cloak wrapped firmly around her. The thought of Markos intending to kiss me and the sight of my friend happy with her lover sent my heart soaring.

Before responding, Elios glanced up to scan the sky as if searching for something.

"We need a place we can defend, somewhere with a water source, before sundown. You know the creatures that roam these lands at night. I don't want to be vulnerable once we lose the protection of daylight."

Their words ignited a burning fear in my chest, but I tried not to let it overwhelm me. Markos had promised he would keep me safe. He twisted to look at Dimitris before turning back to Elios.

"There's a camp about five hours from here. Maybe less if we pick up the pace."

"Let's try to get there before sundown," Elios replied.

Without another word, Markos followed Elios' order, digging his heels into Storm's side again. We galloped forward toward our destination as I watched the sky, silently hoping the sun would wait to take its slumber until we arrived.

CHAPTER TWENTY

CAVES OF REFUGE

After a long ride at a heavy gallop, our group finally reached our night's rest just before sundown. From a distance, I would never have guessed the extent of the village deep within the mountain pass. From the main road, it appeared to be only winding canyons and scattered cliffs with caves of various sizes. However, as we drew closer, I realized the settlement was large, filled with dozens of men, women, and children living in the caves lining the mountain's base. Smoke curled upward from a central bonfire, and the scent of roasted meat wafted through the air, making my stomach twist in hunger.

We had snacked along the way, mostly dried fruit and stale bread, but it wasn't enough. The rich, savory aroma of cooked meat stirred a deep yearning in me. This place, carved into the cliffs, felt older than time. Weathered banners hung from ledges, and winding stone steps led to cavern homes aglow with soft candlelight.

As I shifted slightly in the saddle, Markos gave my hand a light squeeze before slipping off Storm. I stayed mounted, watching as he approached a tall, imposing man carrying a spear. The man looked as though he had stepped from the pages of an ancient tale. His black hair, braided and adorned with feathers, reached past his lower back. He held a spear fashioned from bone and flint, primitive but clearly not to be underestimated.

Tension thickened the air as Markos spoke privately with him. Our group remained silent, every movement measured as we waited. My nerves spiked with every passing second, heart hammering in my chest. If this tribe refused to grant us shelter, we'd be forced to retreat into the wilderness, into the night. Into the monsters.

A chill crept through me as I curled my fingers around the enchanted seashell hanging from my neck. The beast slumbered within, its presence always there, just beneath the surface. I squeezed the shell, grounding myself against the rising unease.

When Markos returned, a faint smile played across his lips, and the elder followed closely behind him. Relief surged through me at the subtle change in Markos' posture.

"We can stay," Markos said, his voice steady. He lifted his hand toward the man beside him. "This is a tribal elder, Great Protector."

The large man nodded once, his expression unreadable, and walked away without a word.

"The Great Protector said we can use the caves at the far end," Markos added, gesturing to the right side of the cliffs. "There are a few rooms inside, and water for drinking and bathing. He exchanged gold for the night."

Elios nodded, already scanning the terrain. With a motion of his hand, he signaled the group to follow.

Markos mounted Storm again in one smooth motion, sliding in just behind me. His arms wrapped around my waist with familiar ease. Then, with almost boyish mischief, he kissed my cheek. The light press of his lips sent a ripple through me, and I shivered.

"Are you tired, my little Sea Maiden?" he murmured, his voice brushing the shell of my ear like velvet. The heat of him, so close, melted the tension in my shoulders. But something in his words tugged at me.

Twisting in the saddle, I met his gaze. "Why did you call me a Sea Maiden?"

His smile faltered just slightly. He looked around the camp, scanning for listening ears, then leaned in close again.

"The Great Protector told me that you and your friend were mermaids," he said softly, voice barely above a whisper. "I didn't want to believe him, but he insisted. He said you were in great danger, and that the Sea Goddess would seek to reclaim you. Is that why we're hiding you, Ocevia? Did she enslave you?"

A sharp breath snagged in my chest.

For the second time that day, I was speechless.

The urge to tell him the truth burned in my throat, but so did fear. What if he turned on me? What if he saw me as a monster, just another soul to be bartered for coin?

I turned away slowly, putting my back to him once more. His arms didn't tighten. He gave me space, even while holding me.

My thoughts were a storm: hope, longing, terror, shame. But buried beneath all of it was one persistent ember, the desperate wish that maybe, just maybe, Markos could be different.

As my heart thundered against my rib cage, almost painfully, my mind fumbled over what to do. Part of me wanted to jump off the horse, grab my friend, and run. We'd already come too far to be recaptured and dragged back to Miris' dungeons. Sensing my fear and hesitation, Markos slid his hand around my waist and pulled me closer to speak directly into my ear.

"Do not be afraid of me, Ocevia. Whether you're a mermaid running from the Sea Goddess or a human slave escaping a master, I will protect you with my life."

Some of the tightness in my chest eased with his words, and I hoped they were genuine.

"If we get caught—"

My words were cut off as Markos tucked my hair behind my ear and interrupted me.

"I'm not going to let you get caught. I give you my word that I will give my life to protect you."

Leaning into his touch, I nodded. "And what about the Great Protector? Will he turn us in?"

He shook his head. "The Arcane River Tribe does not associate much with civilization. They sustain themselves through a simpler way of life. He assured me that no one else would know. He also told me that there's a hot spring running along the back of the cave system, which would be perfect for you and Azure to wet your tails if you need to."

While I pondered Markos' words, we approached one of the more extensive caves, its entrance closed off with a wooden gate. Storm's steps slowed as a tribal member approached us, lifting his hand to take the reins from Markos. Peering inside, I noticed that the large cave, now gated, was a stable meant to protect their livestock from mountain predators. I could only hope the place where we would spend the night would have similar protection.

With the reins in the young tribal male's hands, Markos dismounted. He reached up, grabbed me by the waist, and lifted me off the horse, setting me down in front of him. Our gazes locked for a moment, and neither looked away for several beats of my heart. There was something steady and grounding in his eyes.

In my peripheral vision, I noticed Elios placing Azure on the ground. As Azure leaned over to stretch her limbs and back, she smiled at me.

Elios called out to Markos, and I stepped away from him to approach my friend. There were undoubtedly many topics we needed to discuss.

"Markos said there is a heated river inside!" I couldn't help but exclaim, my excitement bubbling over and widening Azure's smile.

"Are you having fun? You seem to be," she teased.

A flush came to my cheeks as I patted Azure on the arm. "Yes, I am actually. Markos smells so good and has been such a gentleman. Plus, he's really handsome."

Azure reached for my hand while we followed behind the males toward the cave entrance.

"I'm glad you've enjoyed his company, especially since you were with him all day on a horse. Do you still want to ride with him tomorrow?"

Excited to spend more time with Markos, I quickened my pace. "Of course, I'm going to ride with him again. I'm going to make him my husband." Although I could see on Azure's face that she didn't necessarily share my enthusiasm, I meant every word. Markos would be mine, and I would be his. It was the one thing in the world I was sure about.

When we arrived in the ample cavernous space that would be our home for the night, Azure squeezed my hand and turned to face me.

"You don't have to tell him about us if you're not ready. You can wait until he falls asleep to soak properly. Don't feel pressured."

With a warm embrace, she turned and walked away. I opened my mouth, almost calling her to share my conversation with Markos, but I closed it again. Markos already knew I was a mermaid, but that would have to remain our secret for the moment.

CHAPTER TWENTY-ONE

PROMISES IN THE DARK

The cluster of caves where we would sleep was more expansive than I expected. Each narrow opening led to its own sleeping chamber, a leather screen fastened across the entrance for privacy. In the main room, a fire crackled low in a circular hearth, casting a flickering glow across the uneven stone. The sharp, mineral scent of sulfur from the hot spring filled the space, earthy and pungent, its warmth grounding in a way that made the stone feel almost alive.

Ancient paintings adorned the cave walls, brushstrokes worn soft by time. Scenes of hunts and rituals stretched across the stone like a memory etched in water. At the back of the cavern, steam rose gently from a wide pool fed by a stream that shimmered like a silver vein, threading through the floor and linking this chamber to the others.

Azure veered toward an opening on the right side of the main cavern. I glanced after her, already knowing she and Elios would choose that space for themselves. I didn't mind. Instead, my gaze drifted to the left.

Markos was waiting.

He stood near a shadowed doorway, his hand extended in quiet invitation. I stepped toward him without hesitation, my heart fluttering with something fragile and unspoken. He said nothing as he guided me behind one of the leather screens into a smaller, more private chamber.

Inside, the space was quiet and unadorned, primitive in its simplicity but offering a kind of unexpected comfort. A raised stone platform lined with thick furs rested against the far wall. In the center of the room, a shallow fire pit glowed softly beneath the arched ceiling, its embers giving off a faint, pulsing heat.

I crossed to the bedding and sat down, trailing my fingers over the pelts. They felt softer than anything I had ever touched. For a few breaths, I just sat there and let myself feel the stillness of the space. The quiet warmth, the distant sound of water, and the flicker of firelight made everything feel just shy of safe.

Markos lingered near the entrance. His voice was soft, touched with uncertainty. "If you'd rather have the space to yourself, I can take the main room."

I looked up at him and smiled. "I don't want to sleep alone. There's enough space for both of us."

He raised a brow, the corner of his mouth lifting in quiet amusement. "What if I stay here with you but take the floor? That way I'm close, just not crowding you."

I wrapped my arms around myself, rubbing at my sleeves though I wasn't cold. The cloak I wore was warm enough, but something in me needed more. I met his gaze and tilted my head, voice soft with playful innocence. "It's freezing in here. Much too cold for you to sleep on the floor."

Markos chuckled and knelt beside the fire pit. He struck the flint, coaxing the sparks into flame with the ease of someone who had done it more nights than he could count. His smirk deepened, and I could feel him seeing straight through me, but he didn't call me out.

I watched him feed the fire, the light painting bold shadows across his face and arms. Beneath the surface of my teasing, something deeper stirred. A longing I couldn't name. If this life could be taken from me tomorrow—by Miris, by fate, by the cruelty of the world—I wanted to have this one night.

Just tonight, I wanted to feel human.

When the fire caught fully and the room filled with gentle warmth, Markos stood and crossed to sit beside me. The silence between us stretched for a moment, deep and weighted. He turned to me, the glow of the flames reflected in his green eyes. When his hand slid into mine, it eased something inside me.

"I can't imagine what you've endured to reach this place," he said softly, rubbing his thumb across my knuckles. "It's clear there's something between us... but I don't want to rush you."

Although his voice carried warmth, something inside me still sank. The ache reached my eyes before I could stop it, and he noticed. His other hand rose to my face, tilting it gently until our eyes met again.

"Please don't take that the wrong way, little one. I'm not pushing you away. I just don't want you to ever think I took advantage of you. You're strong and rare, and I see that. I want what grows between us to be real."

A tear slid down my cheek before I could stop it. He caught it with his thumb, brushing it away gently. Then he gathered me into his arms and kissed the top of my head.

"Tell me what you're thinking," he whispered. "I never wanted to make you cry. Tell me how to help."

I shrugged, the truth a weight I didn't know how to carry. "I don't even know how much time I have left."

The moment I said it aloud, I felt it settle in my chest. Heavy. *True.*

My eyes burned with more tears. With all that stirred in my chest, I couldn't hold them back.

Pulling me into his lap, Markos wrapped his arms tightly around me and pressed a kiss to my cheek. I buried my face in his chest, trying to steady my breath.

"Don't say that," he said, his voice firm but his tone soft. "Don't even think that. We'll leave tomorrow. We'll keep moving inland, farther than she can reach. I won't let Miris take you back. I promise you."

I nodded against him, listening to the steady beat of his heart. "I know you and the others will try. I believe that. But you don't understand her. Her reach is larger than you think. She could be watching us now and we'd never know. I've spent so long not allowing myself to dream—not about a mate, not about love. I thought it would never be possible for someone like me."

My voice broke. I tried to hold it together, but the fear clutched at me.

"Then I saw Azure with Elios… and I met you… and it's just—"

My words faltered. The fear was too raw.

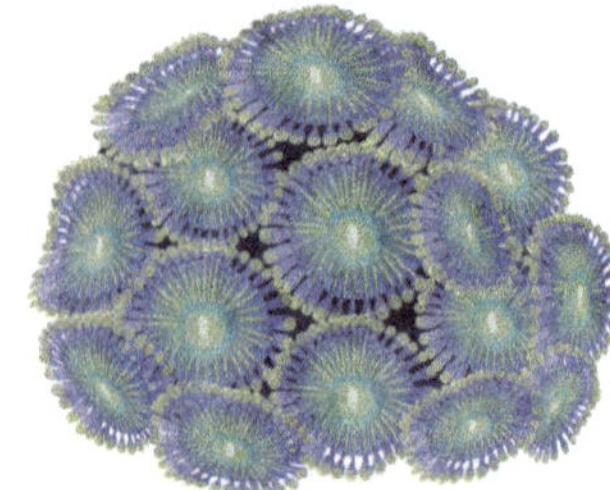

Markos silenced me with a kiss.

It was soft, hesitant at first. But when I didn't pull away, he deepened it, one hand tangling in my hair. I leaned into him, heart pounding, body aching for warmth, for touch, for something that felt like mine.

I had never kissed anyone before. I didn't know what I was doing, but he didn't seem to mind.

He opened to me with a kind of patience I didn't know how to deserve, and when our tongues met, my entire world narrowed to the feel of him—his heat, his hands, his scent. I wrapped my arms around his neck, pulling him closer, drowning in the way he kissed me like I was already his.

Time blurred. The cave, the fire, the fear... it all faded.

He finally pulled back, forehead resting against mine, both of us breathless.

I wanted more. I wanted everything, but before either of us could speak, a head of red hair appeared at the entrance of the cave.

"There's roasted meat outside," Dimitris said. "If you two are hungry."

Arcane Hospitality

Although Dimitris ducked out of the doorway when he saw Markos and me in each other's arms, the moment had already passed. With everyone outside eating, I realized our absence would surely draw too much attention. Everything felt so new, and the last thing I wanted was to answer questions about my budding relationship with Markos. Despite my nerves, I hoped things would progress once everyone slept that night.

Leaving the privacy of our cave behind, Markos and I ventured back into the late-night air toward the largest bonfire in the valley. To my delight, he held my hand as we walked, the touch filling me with a sense of safety, even if it was only surface-deep.

As we moved closer to where dozens of tribal people, including Aris and Dimitris, were gathered, the aroma of roasted meat wafted through the breeze, reminding me just how hungry I was. An enormous animal carcass, its skin crackling and sizzling, hung over the flames on a long wooden spit. I wasn't sure what kind of animal it was. My curiosity was short-lived, though, as Dimitris ran up to us, holding a heaping plate of meat.

"You have to taste this roasted bear! Here! Try this!" he exclaimed, lifting a greasy chunk of meat toward my mouth. I giggled and shuffled back, playfully refusing.

Markos chuckled, wrapping his arm around my waist and pulling me close.

"We'll get some in a bit, Brother. I'm curious about what you've been drinking that has you frolicking around the camp, trying to shove greasy meat into people's mouths," Markos teased Dimitris.

Dimitris's eyes, already glazed over from the alcohol, widened in surprise. I didn't know much about drinking, but I was taken aback by how quickly it had affected him.

"It's a special brew the Arcane tribe makes themselves," he replied, pivoting and walking away. "Follow me, Brother. I'll get a mug of it for you."

As Dimitris wandered several yards ahead, Markos smirked at me.

"My friend tends to drink whiskey as efficiently as a fish drinks water. Feel free to smack him away the next time he tries to stick a hunk of greasy meat in your face," he joked, and I couldn't help but laugh. The expression on Markos' face, along with his words, made me giggle.

"I'll definitely keep that in mind. However, the meat does smell amazing, and I am starving. I've never had bear meat before, though."

I bit my bottom lip and watched as our hosts carved the meat, several working together to make the process more efficient. Even at this late hour, people of all ages had gathered around the central fire. Children played with toys while adults either worked on tasks or sat on logs and stone benches, engaging in conversations over plates of meat and mugs that appeared to be made of bone. Aris and Dimitris were seated near the fire, but I didn't see Azure or Elios.

"Would you like to get something to eat and sit with the others?" Markos asked. I nodded as he slid his hand across my back, gently nudging me toward the fire.

"I don't see Azure or Elios anywhere." As I scanned the area between the cliffs and caverns again, a wave of unease washed over me. Deep shadows lurked around us. However, Markos' gentle strokes on my back helped ease my anxiety.

"Everyone is tired. The last time I saw them, they were heading into one of the chambers. They might be sleeping, or perhaps they're doing something even more entertaining. Either way, I'm sure they'll join us eventually."

He was probably right, and I wished Markos and I were still in that private bedchamber. No matter how strong his arms felt around me or how much safety they provided, I couldn't shake the feeling that my time pretending to be a human woman was running out. Before it did, I wanted him to show me what it was like to have a lover, to experience the pleasures of the flesh that I had never known.

Setting aside thoughts of later, I reached out and took the mug of clear liquid that Dimitris had thrust into my hand. I took a deep sip, only to spit it onto the ground before it had fully hit my tongue.

"What are you trying to do to me?"

Horror spread across Dimitris's face as he struggled to maintain his balance on two shaky legs. Whatever was in that mug must have been strong enough to throw him off-kilter.

"Oh, I'm sorry, Miss. Perhaps the Arcane brew is too potent," he stammered.

I handed the mug to Markos, a grin spreading across my cheeks, and the gesture seemed to relax Dimitris as he wandered away. Markos then led me to where Aris was seated on a giant log among the tribe members, seemingly engrossed in telling a story that captivated the eight people surrounding him.

One of the women, wrapped in a leather cloak with long black hair braided down her back, moved aside as we approached, allowing Markos and me to sit beside our friend. When I glanced back toward where Dimitris had wandered off, my heart warmed at the sight of Azure and Elios approaching us. The red-haired man pulled them into an exaggerated hug.

"You guys have to try this drink brewed by the Arcane people. It's stronger than any whiskey I've ever had!"

Dimitris was loud, clearly intoxicated, but Elios took the bone mug from his friend and patted him on the shoulder.

"You need to slow down, Brother, or you'll retch right off your horse come morning."

Like Markos, Elios seemed to know exactly how to handle Dimitris when he had too much to drink. The bond among the males in our group was strong, evident in the way they looked out for each other, and it made me smile as Elios gently guided his intoxicated friend. Dimitris nodded, mumbling that he would get more food, and then wandered away.

Dropping down onto the log beside Markos, Elios pulled Azure onto his lap. They sipped from the same bone mug as they listened to Aris tell his tale of the high seas.

We spent hours with the Arcane people, enjoying their warm hospitality while eating and drinking. As I sat beside Markos, who had his arm around me, giving me affectionate cuddles and kisses, I couldn't help but feel the allure of living in such an unencumbered way. After so many years at sea, without a warm bed or clothing, I realized I didn't need big cities and modern conveniences to survive. All I truly needed was Markos by my side. With him, I knew I could be happy.

After a long day of travel, our group returned to the caves where we would spend the night. My legs felt as heavy as my eyelids. Although I had hoped to go to the hot spring with Markos to show him who I really was, hoping he would find my mermaid form appealing, Azure reached for me as we entered the central space of the cavern.

"Elios will stand guard out here while we bathe. Is that alright?"

With Azure still unaware that Markos knew the truth, I nodded and followed her toward the pool in the deepest part of the cave system.

Chapter Twenty-Three

Consumed by the Flame

After soaking in the hot spring with Azure, I emerged into the cooler cavern air and spotted Markos standing beside Elios, a sleepy grin on his face that warmed me more than the fire ever could. A flutter rose in my chest at the sight of him, and the excitement of spending the night with him for the first time filled my stomach with butterflies. I realized he meant what he said and that he wouldn't rush with me, even if I wanted him to. But just being intimate with him at all was worth looking forward to.

Azure and Elios walked away, leaving us alone near the central fire together. Then I noticed his hair was damp, telling me he must have cleaned up in a separate part of the caverns while Azure and I were soaking.

"Are you ready to go to sleep, Ocevia?" Holding out his hand, Markos slipped it into mine, pulling me close.

I bit my lip, a grin spreading across my face as we walked across the main room and back into our private space.

I glanced over at him with a teasing smile. "Must we go to sleep just yet?"

As we entered our sleeping area, the fire was already blazing, the flames lighting up Markos' handsome face just enough for me to see the warmth in his eyes. He led me to the bed, dropping to his knee as I sat down. Reaching for my foot, he slid my unlaced boots off and set them on the floor. When he was finished, his green eyes flicked up to mine, glancing at me from under thick lashes.

"What did you have in mind, Little One, if not to sleep?"

I was quiet for a moment, not knowing how to ask for what I wanted. I longed for him to give me everything I'd been missing: his heart and his body. But I realized it would be asking for a lot, possibly more than he was ready or willing to give.

Seeming to sense my hesitation, he rose from his knees and sat on the bed next to me, taking my hands in his.

"I realized something as we sat together by the fire," he said as he held my gaze. "In a perfect world, we would take things slow. I would court you. We would fall in love, and then I would marry you and build a family with you."

My eyes flicked away, and emotions warred inside me as Markos spoke: desire, love, longing, and pain. The pain was because somewhere deep inside my heart, I knew anything we shared would only be temporary. I belonged to the Sea Goddess, and Miris would stop at nothing to get her slaves back.

A tear trailed down my cheek when I turned my eyes back to him.

"But the world isn't perfect," I said, my voice low.

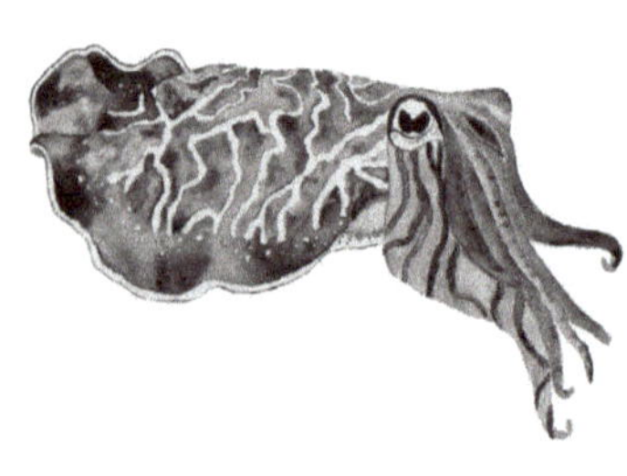

Leaning forward, he swept his finger across my cheek to wipe away the tear before pressing his lips to mine. His scent and the slide of his tongue against mine sent a shiver down my spine, the sensation pooling between my thighs. When he pulled away, I was breathless, the intensity of his eyes only taking my breath away more.

"You're right, my Sea Maiden. The world isn't perfect. Neither you nor I live a normal life, but that doesn't mean we can't love each other how we want to love each other. If you are sure about wanting to explore this connection between us, then I want the same. I want you more than I've ever wanted anything in my life, Ocevia. If you feel the same way, then I don't see any reason why we should deny ourselves."

As the firelight flickered in the depths of his green irises, Markos' words enticed me to meet his gaze. Biting my lip, I reached toward him, touching his shoulder. I leaned in, brushing my lips against his.

The kiss was tentative, a question lingering as my mouth left his. A flicker of doubt passed through me, just long enough to make me breathe, to ask myself if I was ready. Then I looked at him, at the gentleness behind his hunger, and I knew I wanted this. I wanted him.

As if in answer, Markos slid his arm around my waist and pulled me onto his lap, his mouth crashing onto mine a moment later.

With his arms surrounding me, I melted into his embrace, fear replaced by ease as every muscle in my body loosened. He tasted like the warmth of the fire, and it burned inside me. It was as though I was being consumed by the flame, but it soothed me more than it hurt. Running his fingers through my hair, he kissed me deeper, his tongue sliding against mine in a sensual dance that sent pulses of pleasure through my body.

The moment he pulled away and pressed his forehead against mine, his eyes darkened, his chest heaving with desire. My pulse matched his, steady and hungry.

"Can I touch you, Ocevia? Would that be okay?"

A rush of anticipation bloomed inside me as I nodded, closing my eyes as my cheeks warmed.

"I want to touch you too." My voice was barely audible. I hesitated, heat prickling at my neck. "I want this... but I just don't know what to do. I've never been with anyone before, not even seen a man like that. What if I disappoint you?"

His nostrils flared as he tucked my hair behind my ear and leaned forward to place a lingering kiss on my neck. A breathy moan escaped my lips, and I rocked against his thigh as the touch sent a wave of pleasure into my core. I needed him to touch me there, to show me what it felt like to be claimed in the way I had only imagined, completely and without fear.

"There is nothing you could do that I wouldn't enjoy, Ocevia," Markos said, trailing kisses down the column of my neck while loosening the ties on my tunic. His deep voice rumbled against my skin, drawing shivers in its wake. "My body is yours to touch as you wish. I promise I will enjoy it all."

Having spent most of my life wearing little to no clothes, I had never been shy about nudity, but this was different. Markos wasn't just seeing me. He was worshiping me with every glance, every touch. As he slid the fabric of my tunic down my arms, his gaze followed the motion like I was something precious.

The fabric gathered at my waist. My nipples pebbled in the cool air, and he reached out to trace a single fingertip down the curve of my breast. I gasped softly, the sensation stealing my breath as warmth unfurled low in my belly.

"You're stunning, Ocevia. Truly. I don't think I've ever looked at someone like this before."

When he lowered his head to my breast and drew one nipple between his lips, a low moan escaped me. My back arched instinctively, pressing me closer to his mouth. His tongue circled and teased while his hands anchored me in place, one at my waist, the other splayed across my spine.

With Markos holding me in his arms, he shifted his weight and eased me back onto the bed. The furs beneath me were soft, a warm cushion against the tension still ebbing from my limbs. My tunic remained bunched at my waist, but he knelt above me, eyes dark with reverence, before sliding the loose fabric down my hips and letting it fall to the ground.

The firelight licked across my bare skin, and I shivered at the sudden exposure. My nipples tightened from the chill, but it was his gaze that made me feel completely bare. Not just naked, but open. Vulnerable in a way I hadn't expected.

He rose onto his knees between my parted thighs and pulled his own tunic over his head, tossing it aside. My breath caught as I took him in. All sculpted strength and clean lines, his body told a story—one forged through years of fighting for the freedom of others. The dark stubble on his face, the firm lines of his chest and abdomen, the faint trail of hair leading downward. All of it mesmerized me.

My gaze caught on the tattoo that spanned his left pectoral: a broken chain curled into a circle, the severed ends flaring outward. I traced it with my fingertips, slow and curious, wanting to ask but not wanting to break the spell between us.

"Do you mind if I take these off?" he asked softly, fingers brushing the waistband of my trousers—the ones that never quite fit my smaller frame.

I shook my head, wordless, eyes locked on his as he untied the laces and slid the brown fabric down my legs. Cool air kissed my thighs, and I trembled as his touch followed the path, setting my skin ablaze.

He knelt back, his gaze roving over every inch of me. I could feel it, a tangible weight, but instead of making me shrink, it made me bloom.

"You are truly phenomenal to gaze upon, Ocevia."

CHAPTER TWENTY-FOUR

LUST AND REVERENCE

The heat in my chest rose to my cheeks, and something deeper swelled behind it. He meant it. Every word. No one had ever spoken to me that way, not with such certainty. I had always seen myself as just another face in a world of mermaids, nothing more.

Markos leaned forward, his mouth tracing the line of my stomach. I gasped as his lips brushed the sensitive skin, and whatever self-consciousness I'd held evaporated. His hands moved to my sides, grounding me as he kissed his way up, then pulled one breast into his mouth again, lavishing it with attention.

He shifted forward, positioning himself between my thighs. His arousal pressed against my core, the heat of him unmistakable even through the fabric still hugging his hips. I arched beneath him, my breath stuttering with need.

"Take off your trousers, Markos. Please. I want to touch you," I whispered.

He paused only to kiss me once more, then rose to obey. Standing beside the bed, he unfastened his trousers and slid them down over his hips. When he stepped free of them, my breath hitched.

His cock jutted forward, thick and proud, the sight of him stirring both awe and apprehension inside me. I wanted to reach for him but hesitated, uncertain.

Noticing my hesitation, he crawled back over me, slowly, gently, and kissed me as he took my hand in his, guiding it to his length. My fingers curled around him instinctively. The skin was soft, but the heat and the sheer size of him made my heart skip a beat.

He groaned, his hips rocking slightly into my touch. "Does this feel good, my mate?"

A pearl of liquid formed at the tip of his cock as I stroked him, slick and warm beneath my fingertips. Something primal stirred in me as I watched him, this man who had given me nothing but gentleness, now trembling beneath my touch.

Curiosity outweighed hesitation. Leaning forward, I brushed my tongue across the drop of moisture, tasting him for the first time. He gasped, his hips twitching as his fingers threaded into my hair.

"Everything you do makes me feel good," he said, his voice rough. "But I need to taste you before I explode."

His words lit something inside me, a spark I couldn't name but didn't want to extinguish. Even without knowing exactly what was coming, I craved it. I wanted to know what it was to be truly known by him.

Markos gently pressed a hand to my shoulder, urging me back onto the bed. The furs felt too soft, too luxurious under the aching hunger in my body. "Do you still want to do this?" he asked, his tone low, patient, careful. "There's no pressure. We stop the moment you say so."

Even now, with desire bright in his eyes and his cock heavy with need, he would have stopped if I asked. That truth warmed me almost more than his touch.

"I don't want to stop," I whispered. My fingers slipped between us, tracing the length of him again. "I want you."

His gaze held mine for a heartbeat longer, then he kissed me—soft and reverent—as if sealing my answer between us.

Lips trailing down my body, he shifted lower. When his shoulders settled between my thighs, his hands slid along the insides of my legs, coaxing them open. The fire crackled behind him, casting his features in gold and shadow.

My breath caught as he leaned in, warm breath skimming over the most sensitive part of me. "I've never seen such a perfect cunt," he murmured, lips ghosting against my skin. "Just looking at you makes my mouth water."

My cheeks burned, but my hips lifted instinctively, needing him to close the distance. "No one's ever looked at it before," I admitted, voice barely a whisper.

His eyes flicked up, hunger tempered by affection. "Good. I like knowing I'm the only one. I'd hate to pluck out anyone else's eyes."

I laughed, breathless, just as he dipped his head and ran his tongue through my folds. My laugh melted into a moan, legs falling open as he tasted me with slow, deliberate strokes.

"It's as sweet as it is pretty," he said between licks, his voice sending vibrations through me. Then he wrapped his lips around my clit and sucked gently while sliding two fingers inside me.

The sensation was overwhelming—tight, hot, pulsing with something I'd never felt before. My back arched as I clung to him, riding the wave building in my core. The pressure crested fast, and I cried out as release slammed into me.

My thighs trembled, my voice breaking with the aftershocks. He held me through it all, mouth and hands coaxing every last quiver from my body until I was boneless beneath him.

Still, I wanted more. Needed it.

Markos moved over me, eyes darker than I'd ever seen them. "I need to be inside you, my Sea Maiden. Now."

He settled between my thighs, kissing my lips before trailing one hand between my legs. His fingers glided through my slick folds, and I gasped as he circled the swollen bundle of nerves that still throbbed with need.

"You're so wet for me, Little One," he whispered. "But I need to hear you say it again. Are you sure?"

"Yes," I breathed, reaching up to run my fingers along his jaw. "I want to feel you inside me."

He positioned himself at my entrance, the thick head of him brushing against me. I braced myself, heart pounding.

"Take a deep breath," he murmured, then slowly began to push inside.

I gasped at the stretch, the ache. My body fought to adjust, but the tenderness in his eyes grounded me. He stilled, letting me breathe through it, kissing my cheek, my jaw, my lips.

"You're doing perfect," he said, his voice quiet with awe. "Let me know when you're ready."

After a moment, I nodded. He moved slowly, easing deeper, giving me time. The pain ebbed, replaced by something fuller, more consuming.

"You feel like home," he whispered, kissing the corner of my mouth as he began to move.

Each thrust was careful, controlled. His hands caressed my hips, my sides, as if mapping every part of me. The tension in my body slowly gave way to pleasure, and I began to move with him, hips tilting to meet his.

He groaned against my skin, his pace picking up. I gasped as he hit a place deep inside me, one that made my body clench and writhe beneath him.

"That's it," he breathed. "Let go."

The wave built fast, and when it crashed, I cried out his name, nails digging into his shoulders.

Markos followed a heartbeat later, burying himself deep and trembling above me. His breath came hot against my neck as he stilled, chest pressed to mine.

He didn't pull away. He held me, cradling me against him like I was something fragile and deeply cherished.

And I let him.

For the first time in my life, I didn't want to be anywhere else.

I let out a soft, contented sigh as he collapsed on top of me, his weight grounding me, filling every hollow space inside me with warmth and presence. The beat of his heart thundered against mine, and and for once, I felt complete. Safe. *Seen.*

Markos pressed a kiss to my shoulder, his breath still ragged, his body trembling slightly from the intensity of what we'd just shared. Then he lifted himself onto his elbows, just enough to look into my eyes, his gaze tender and astonished.

"That was incredible," he murmured, his voice thick with satisfaction.

My cheeks flushed, the heat of his body still lingering on my skin. My fingers drifted up his arm, brushing over the curve of his shoulder as if I couldn't quite believe he was real. "It was," I murmured, the words catching slightly in my throat.

He smiled, that slow, disarming smile that always melted my defenses. Then, with gentle hands, he tucked a damp strand of hair behind my ear and traced the line of my cheek, his touch as gentle as his smile.

"So," he said softly, his eyes searching mine, "does this mean we're mates?"

The question struck deeper than I expected—not just playful, but hopeful. *Vulnerable.*

I blinked up at him, emotion tightening my chest. The connection between us had always burned, but now it pulsed in my blood like truth. My voice was barely a whisper.

"Yes. I think it does."

CHAPTER TWENTY-FIVE

HOPE IN THE STORM

For the first time since I was a child, I woke up with a warmth in my heart as my mate, Markos, breathed softly beside me. I was grateful to be there, in the safety of our shared shelter, while the storm raged outside. I closed my eyes and listened to the sound of the rain, letting a sense of peace settle over my worried mind. In the darkness of our small cave, lit only by the flickering fire, I couldn't tell if it was day or night, but I knew we wouldn't leave anytime soon, not with the torrential downpour pounding against the stone walls.

Rolling onto my back, I watched Markos' eyelids flutter as he dreamed. Despite the soreness between my thighs, his presence filled me with contentment and desire. He had claimed me as his mate last night, showing me pleasure greater than anything I could have imagined. As much as I wanted to stay there forever, basking in his love, I knew our reality, two people from different worlds, was more fragile than I wanted to admit. Our love was forbidden, and with Miris seeking us, it seemed unlikely we could last. But Markos was worth everything, even if loving him meant risking it all. I didn't know if we could make it, but I was determined to try. Even though we could be discovered and face severe consequences, his promise to protect me gave me hope. Still, sometimes it felt like a fragile dream.

But when he opened his eyes and looked at me with such admiration, every doubt faded.

A sleepy grin spread across Markos' lips as he pulled me close and kissed me. My cheeks flushed under his gaze, and I managed to murmur, "Good morning."

There were so many things I should have said, how much he meant to me, how scared I was, but that was all that came to mind.

Markos chuckled and kissed me again, trailing his lips down my neck and shoulders. His words brushed against my skin like a whisper. "Just when I thought you couldn't get any more stunning, my Sea Maiden, you amaze me. How are you feeling this morning?"

I let out a slow breath, clinging to the quiet safety of his arms. His embrace made me feel safe and warm, but deep inside, a war still raged. Before our night together, I had nothing to lose. Now, the idea of losing him felt unbearable, like something vital would be ripped from me.

"Thank you for being here with me," I whispered, even though it wasn't all I wanted to say.

He smiled and kissed my forehead, his hands gently stroking my back. "I will always be there for you."

Suddenly aware of the storm, Markos glanced toward the entrance to our private space, where the flap of leather still shielded us from view. Realization flickered across his face. Our companions had probably heard everything that happened between us last night. Our lovemaking had been passionate—*uninhibited*—loud enough that there was no pretending otherwise.

Heat rose up my neck at the thought, but Markos didn't seem fazed in the slightest. He just buried his face against my neck, his lips brushing my still-sensitive skin. "I don't think we should set out this morning," he murmured. "At least not until the storm clears and the sun dries some of the path."

My heart picked up at his touch, and when he pulled back with that familiar, mischievous grin, I didn't need him to say more. "Perhaps we can find something to pass the time while we wait," I said, my voice softer than before... *inviting*.

Despite our plans to leave the Arcane camp that day, the storm made it impossible. Rain battered the ground in relentless waves, the kind that soaked through everything and left the earth trembling beneath it. The wind wailed through the caves, not like a whisper, but a voice raised in warning. Travel would have been foolish. So, we waited.

Markos and I sought each other in the quiet that followed, our bodies finding comfort in the warmth of tangled furs. Afterward, we drifted into sleep, lulled by the storm and the soft rhythm of our breathing, until Aris' voice stirred us from the other side of the leather screen that served as our door. The scent of roasting meat reached us before his words fully registered. The central fire had been moved to a larger cavern, and the invitation—unspoken but understood—drew us from bed.

We joined the others for food and drink, gathering around the flames as stories were shared and small laughter eased the lingering tension. For a while, it felt like something close to peace. As the fire crackled lower and the wine dulled the sharper edges of the day, Azure and Elios slipped away into the tunnel that led to their private cave. Sleep tugged at my limbs. When Markos gently nudged me to stand a while later, I followed without question. The four of us, Markos, Dimitris, Aris, and I, moved quietly through the dim corridor, our footsteps muffled against the damp stone.

We had nearly reached the spot where Azure and I had bathed the night before when Dimitris stopped abruptly, forcing me to nearly walk straight into him. The sudden silence coiled tight, and then Elios' voice cut through the dark, sharp and unmistakable: "You will say nothing."

My stomach dropped and I inched forward, leaning around Dimitris just in time to see Azure nude in the hot spring, water beading down her bare skin. Her tail shimmered briefly, vanishing as legs returned in its place.

The truth hung there, exposed.

Markos' arm locked around my waist, pulling me closer. My fingers gripped the hem of my tunic, heart thudding with dread. Elios and Markos already knew. But Aris and Dimitris might not. And if they didn't... *Would they still fight beside us? Would they still see us the same way?*

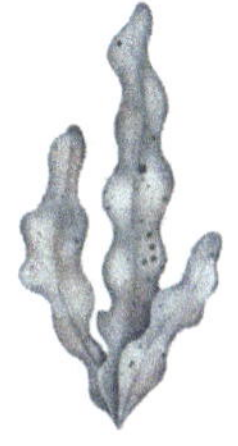

If they turned us in, I didn't know what Azure and I would do.

I looked at Elios. The way he stood in front of Azure, always protecting her, told me everything. I barely knew him. *Any* of them. Not even Markos, not truly. We had shared warmth and desire, but not the truths that lived in the dark. Still, I knew Elios was a good man, and I had to believe the same for the others, but it wasn't enough to calm me.

Panic bloomed in my chest as Azure crouched behind Elios, trying to vanish. He raked a hand through his wet hair, jaw tight. Then his gaze met ours.

"Make a fire and wait for us," he said, quieter now but no less resolute. "It looks like we all need to talk."

No one spoke. Dimitris walked toward the main cavern, and we followed, silent, the weight of exposure thick in the air. Markos didn't let go of me.

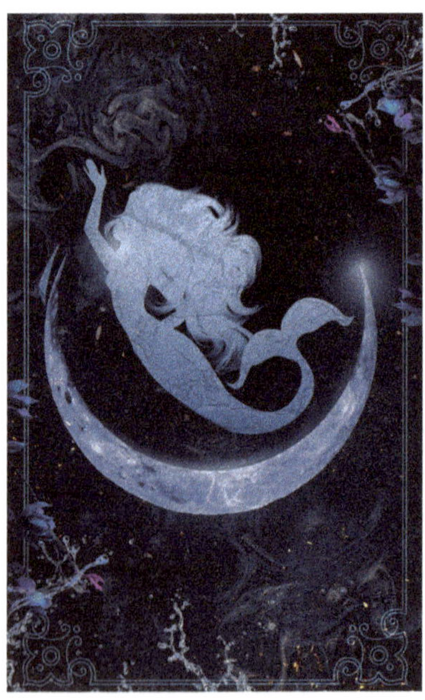

Chapter Twenty-Six

THE CIRCLE'S TRUTH

My heart beat violently against my ribcage as Markos and I followed the other two men into the main chamber of our cave. With his arm around my waist, he leaned over, kissing me on the temple. "It's going to be okay, my Sea Maiden. Trust me."

Despite my nod, the unease of the unknown still gripped me. Markos may have trusted his friends, but I didn't know them well enough to feel the same. *What if they turned on us? What if they decided we weren't worth the risk?* The fear of what was to come was a heavy burden on my shoulders.

Lowering ourselves near the fire, Markos wrapped his arm around my waist and pulled me close. Aris added a few new logs, stoking the fire until the blaze doubled in size. Dimitris sat quietly beside us. Both men were silent as Elios and Azure entered the room.

With their hands interlaced, Elios led Azure toward the fire, sitting on the ground and pulling her into his lap. My hands trembled. My nervousness was palpable, but my lover wrapped his arms around me, clearly trying to ease some of my anxiety.

"I guess I should give you all an explanation." The room was silent as Elios began, the entire group waiting to hear what he would say next. "We're not traveling with human women, as you now know, but I should start from the beginning."

He began his admission without hesitation, telling us how his ship had gone down and how Azure had saved him. In addition to explaining how women were cursed to become mermaids, he provided details regarding their enslavement and how they were forced to kill to earn their freedom.

As I listened to Elios and Azure's story, my breath halted in my lungs. Bile churned in my gut and threatened to come up. The dread only increased when he told the others of the horrific monster who had saved them when Miris' two scouts found them on the island. He may have been thankful for the Kraken, for *me*, but his descriptions of the creature were terrifying. Hearing him speak that way about the monster I became reminded me of the distance between who I was and how others might see me. To them, I was a savior. To me, I was still something to be feared. They reminded me that I was a monster deep down, and I hated it. Twisting the seashell necklace between my fingers, all I wanted was to crush it and destroy the beast within, but I knew I couldn't. With or without the necklace, the Kraken was a part of me. It always would be.

So caught up in my own self-loathing, Aris' voice caught me by surprise. "So, are Azure and Ocevia planning to stay out of the sea for good?"

The answer was complicated, but the question hadn't been aimed at me, so I remained silent, keeping my eyes on my friend. Azure tucked a strand of hair behind her ear as the rest of the group watched her, waiting for an answer she was probably just as hesitant to give as I was. She knew neither of us wanted to return to the Lamalis Sea. However, being a mermaid was who we were, so remaining away from the sea forever didn't seem like an option. No matter where we went, Miris would never stop looking. It wasn't in the Sea Goddess' nature to be forgiving.

After a few silent heartbeats, Azure spoke, her voice low and hesitant. "I'm not sure, but I don't want to be any-where near Miris. If she finds us, she will kill me and Elios. The farther we are from her lair, the safer we will be. Oce-via has never disobeyed the Sea God-dess like I have, so she may survive... after being tortured for running away."

Something within me crumpled at her words, my shoulders folding inward as I fought the tears that threatened to fall. Not because I was upset but because I was overwhelmed. The situation we'd gotten ourselves into was impos-sible, and I didn't know how we would survive it. As though sensing my emotions, Markos pulled me closer, placing another kiss on my temple.

"I won't let that happen." There was no hesitation in his voice when he spoke. "Even if I need to take her to another continent, I won't let Ocevia spend another moment in slavery. Not while I'm still drawing breath."

A smile spread across my face as he pledged his life for me, but my happiness was tinged with guilt. I knew he meant it, but I had taken enough lives in my time, and I couldn't imagine taking him as well. If he sacrificed himself trying to save me... I would never forgive myself.

Before I had a chance to process any more of my own thoughts, Markos cleared his throat and continued. "But I do have a confession to make..."

He paused, running his fingers down my cheek, the touch sending shivers across my body. "I already knew they were mermaids. The tribal elder, Great Protector, told me when we arrived. I figured Elios already knew. I figured it was why we were running. I didn't want to say anything out of protection for Ocevia and Azure, not until Elios said something first."

Markos shifted his gaze to Elios. "I was going to talk to you about it, Brother, but I was waiting until we got somewhere more secure."

Lost in his own thoughts, Elios was quiet for a moment, his jaw clenched. It was clear he wasn't happy that Markos hadn't come forward as soon as he discovered the truth, but it would have been hypocritical to be angry when he had done the same thing.

"I would have said something once we arrived in Ceveasea for the same reason you didn't speak up, Markos. It's not that I didn't trust you or our other friends, Aris and Dimitris. We've been through a lot together, and I trust all three of you with my life, but I knew what they were wasn't relevant to our mission, and I couldn't risk anyone finding out who could put them at risk. Anyone at this camp could turn them over for a bit of coin. It was best to hold on to their secret for a while until we got to a safe house."

Seeming to hesitate, Elios pulled Azure closer to his chest. "I suppose there is more I need to explain, at least to Azure and Ocevia."

I shifted, my attention focusing on Elios as he turned his own to Azure. "I told you I've spent my life traveling. That wasn't a lie, but it wasn't the whole truth either."

It was clear what Elios had to say wasn't easy for him with how he rubbed the back of his neck as though he was trying to ease the tension. "You asked what The Circle was back at the tavern. Aris, Dimitris, Markos, and I are part of that group. Our mission is to rescue slaves and smuggle them to lands where they can live free."

Elios' admission flipped my stomach, but not in a negative way. Markos, my mate, risked his life to free slaves. Hearing that made something shift inside me—a slow, blooming awe that softened the fear I'd been carrying since the day we ran. Maybe I wasn't just running anymore. Maybe I was starting to belong. It was why he hadn't batted an eye when being called to protect me and Azure. He'd originally assumed I was another freed slave. In a way, I was.

"And Vasso?" Azure asked Elios, catching my attention.

He nodded. "Yes, Vasso and his wife are also part of The Circle, but their roles differ from ours, although they are no less dangerous. Their inn is used to house freed slaves and provide shelter for us when we pass through. It also serves as a communication hub for members. The rest of us, more than twenty now, have dedicated our lives to this cause. Some of us have been doing this since we were teenagers. Many kingdoms still support slavery, with their kings profiting from the trade, but we do our best to rescue those we can."

Even with all I'd heard, and Markos' hand still wrapped firmly around my waist, there was still a question weighing on my mind. "So, what happens to us now?"

Markos stiffened behind me, pulling me closer, but it was Elios who answered. "Nothing changes from here. We'll leave this camp when the weather clears and make our way through the mountain pass to the city of Ceveasea. If we hear any word of Miris' people snooping around, we'll move further inland. Aris and Dimitris will eventually return to Starspell for their next assignment, but I assume Markos will stay with us."

Before everyone turned to Markos, Aris and Dimitris both nodded in agreement. I had been bracing for disappointment, half-afraid they would walk away.

"I won't leave Ocevia. There's nothing back in Starspell for me," Markos said, his voice calm, but with a finality that left no room for argument. "I can still do my job from inland."

CHAPTER TWENTY-SEVEN

DAMN GOOD WOMAN

When the storm finally passed, sunlight spilled over the valley like a blessing. The once-slick stone path began to dry beneath its warmth, steam curling in tendrils where the rain had soaked deepest. Despite the comfort we'd found within the Arcane camp, and the kindness of those who had sheltered us, we couldn't linger. Danger no longer pressed close, but it still loomed, a shadow stretching far beyond the cliffs.

It was time to move on.

Our path led toward Ceveasea, and beyond that, the Kingdom of Dekresian—a place we hoped would be out of Miris' reach. I wasn't sure I'd ever truly escape the Sea Goddess. Her influence was deep and treacherous, like the ocean floor. Just thinking about her made my chest tighten, haunted by the feeling that she could reach me anywhere, no matter how far I ran. But I had to try. If not for myself, then for Azure. For Elios. *For Markos.*

Leaving the hidden sanctuary behind was difficult. The mountains felt like they were holding their breath as we packed our things and exchanged quiet farewells. With heartfelt thanks to the Arcane people, we gathered our belongings and stepped once more into the pass. We would have to make good time if we wanted to reach Ceveasea before sunset.

Tucked between Markos' thighs on the saddle, I hugged my cloak tightly around my body. Even with the thick hooded cloak and the clothes given to us by Vasso's wife, the storm had left a chill in the air that seemed to sink into my bones. Maybe it was the temperature or the knowledge of how exposed we were as we traveled through the mountain pass. I had very little understanding of the human world. Still, Markos had told me about the creatures who haunted the area at night, those who fed on the blood of others. I couldn't help but scan the mountains around us, hoping I wouldn't see an evil pair of eyes staring back at me.

As we continued, the warmth emanat- ing from Markos' body took the bite out of the mountain air. He held me tightly against his chest, and the steady rhythm of the horse beneath us soothed me. The sun had risen above the moun- tain peaks, pouring gold over the land- scape like a blessing I hadn't asked for.

The mountains towered around us, silent sentinels that seemed to watch our every move. While the sheer drops and rocky cliffs were intim- idating, the ethereal softness of the sun accented their magnificent splendor. A sense of awe filled me, and for a moment, I forgot about my fear.

Halfway to Ceveasea, we stopped at a stream that crossed our path, letting the horses drink while Azure and I slipped into the shallows to soak our tails. It wasn't the same as swimming, but it was enough to reset our twenty-four-hour limit.

After shifting back to our human legs, we rejoined the men near a patch of grass to rest and regroup. The Arcane tribe had given us dried bear meat before we left the camp, so we sat together and ate, chatting casually as a gentle breeze fluttered my hair. We couldn't stop for long, not if we wanted to make it to Ceveasea before sunset, but there wasn't an urgency to climb back on the horses either.

Aris sat before me as I lounged with Markos in the grass, allowing me to braid his waist-length golden hair. Azure, Elios, and Dimitris sat nearby, sharing pieces of meat as the men sharpened their swords.

"Have you spoken to Kimon recent- ly?" Dimitris asked after telling us about a mission in which their friend Kimon was involved.

I didn't know much about Kimon, aside from him being one of our con- tacts who lived in Ceveasea, but I'd heard his name a few times during our travels. I listened to every word, fascinated by their lives in the hu- man lands. He had traveled across continents and seas, freeing slaves of all ages and bringing them back to places where they could live in free- dom. Hearing about his bravery stirred something deep within me. I felt a mix of awe and humility—*hope*, even—that maybe, just maybe, there was a place for someone like me in this world they were fighting to build.

My companions were true heroes and just knowing that eased some of the tension in my body.

But it wasn't just that which made me feel more at ease. After everything that had been revealed around the fire the night before, there were no more secrets between us about who I was and what I was. At first, I worried that Aris and Dimitris would leave us or, worse, turn us in. But I quickly realized that knowing the truth made them more protective of me and my friend. It lifted a heavy weight off my shoulders.

Turning to his friend, Elios stopped sharpening his blade. "About six months ago. Why? Any recent developments?"

A laugh escaped Dimitris' lips, amusement twinkling in his bright eyes. He hadn't consumed nearly as much alcohol as he had the night before, and it showed in his demeanor. "Do you remember the woman he was seeing? What was her name? Emilia, maybe? Well, our old friend, Kimon, got her pregnant. Word is they've since married."

I tied a band around the bottom of Aris' plait, patting him on the shoulder to let him know I was done. Markos scooted closer to me the moment his friend moved and slipped an arm around my waist. He pulled me into a kiss, Elios' response low in the background.

"I say good for him," Markos murmured against my lips. "We should all be so lucky to have a good woman to come home to. I know that I feel like the luckiest man alive. Once I get my lady to a safe place, all will be right in the world."

"I hope to find someone just as special one day, brother," Dimitris responded, chuckling again.

Sliding his fingers up to cup my cheek, Markos pulled my face toward him, his lips only a breath away from my ear. For a moment, I closed my eyes and let myself feel it—the wonder of being held like I mattered, like I was more than just someone to be protected or pitied. After everything I'd been through, being loved like this felt almost unreal. "It feels good to have a damn good woman in my life." He placed a lingering kiss on my neck, sending a shiver through my body.

Grinning, I tilted my head back and looked up at him. "I feel the same way."

He leaned in and kissed me, lingering on my lips, making my pulse quicken.

Time seemed to stand still for a few heartbeats until Elios' voice disturbed the intimate moment. "Well, let's get moving again. I don't want these ladies in the cold mountains after dark."

DANGERS IN THE DARK

As we rode deeper into the darkness, I couldn't shake the unease that clung to me like a shadow. The path ahead twisted through unfamiliar terrain, each bend drawing us farther from the coast, farther from the reach of the Sea Goddess. We had to climb higher before descending into the valley. The air was thinner here, colder, brushing over my skin like a warning.

We'd set off not long after our meal, eager to reach the city before nightfall. Though I appreciated the break from riding, the thought of resting at an inn was even more enticing. The road before us was wild and strange, untouched in a way that made it feel sacred. As the scenery shifted, a mix of trepidation and childlike wonder stirred in my chest. A future with my mate and friends in new lands thrilled me—so long as we lived long enough to reach it. That fear never truly left me. It lingered at the edge of every bright thought, whispering that hope was fragile, and peace, for someone like me, might always be borrowed.

We mounted our horses and headed inland, putting more distance between us and the sea. And from Miris. The sun's warmth helped ease the mountain chill, though it did little to quiet my nerves. Beneath us, hooves struck the rocky trail in a steady rhythm. I kept scanning the horizon, hoping for a glimpse of rooftops or spires, anything to prove our journey had a destination.

By mid afternoon, my legs ached, and my spine throbbed from the saddle. I tried not to fidget, tried to savor the steady weight of Markos behind me and the warmth of his arm wrapped around my waist. We trailed behind Azure and Elios, our quiet conversations doing their best to soften the strain of the day. Markos occasionally leaned in, whispering something ridiculous just to make me smile, and

I would feel the soft puff of his breath against my neck before stifling a laugh. For a little while, it worked. For a little while, it felt like we might actually outrun the past.

But still, every hour that passed brought us closer to sundown and the creatures Markos had warned me about.

Elios had been adamant: we would not sleep in the pass. Whatever hunted in these mountains came alive at night, and resting in their territory would be a mistake. So, we pressed on, urging our mounts up narrow switchbacks as the sunset painted the sky in streaks of molten orange and deep violet.

Once the sun vanished, the world turned sharp with cold. Darkness wrapped around us like a shroud. Only the full moon offered light, casting a pale glow over the craggy path. I tensed beneath the weight of it all—the silence, the unseen things in the shadows. Cliffs loomed on either side, jagged and close, their faces carved by centuries of wind. Each gust that swept through the rocks sounded like something alive, like breath too close to the back of my neck.

"Look," Markos murmured, lifting his hand and pointing ahead. He brushed his lips to my cheek, a soft anchor.

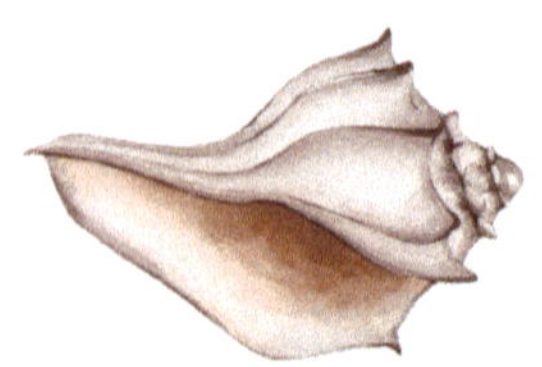

His touch eased something tight in my chest, and when I looked up, I saw the lights. Faint, flickering, nestled in the distance. A city.

Hope sparked.

But it didn't last.

Just as the promise of safety appeared on the horizon, something changed. The air stilled. The wind stopped. The night held its breath.

Something was watching us.

A prickling sensation swept over my skin, making the hair on my arms to rise. I couldn't see it, but I could feel it. That presence, silent and dark, coiling around us like smoke.

The moonlit path stretched before us, almost too perfect, *too clear*, but

the instinct scraping at my spine refused to be ignored. I turned my head, scanning the cliffs, the ridges, the narrow gaps where something might wait.

Before us, Elios slowed his horse. His hand drifted to his sword as his gaze flicked toward the shadows.

Markos shifted behind me. I could feel the change in him—the alert stillness of a man ready to fight. His breath steadied and his arm wrapped more firmly around my waist.

I didn't know what we were walking into, but I knew we weren't alone.

"I need you to take these," Markos whispered, barely louder than the wind. He pressed the reins into my hands, his fingers lingering just long enough to pass something else with them, a thread of calm.

He shifted behind me, and a second later I felt the absence of his arm, followed by the soft metallic ring of his sword being drawn. My heart thudded against my ribs. Every sound seemed louder now, from the creak of leather to the rustle of wind.

It happened in a flash: a high-pitch inhuman shriek tore through the night, slicing through the silence like a blade.

Dimitris whistled sharply and nodded left, eyes locked on something I couldn't see.

Above us, wings beat the air.

A massive shape swept down with terrifying speed, nearly unseating Elios. Azure screamed, ducking low as her mate's sword flashed upward. He missed by inches. The creature vanished into the dark.

The air filled with chattering and clicks, dozens of them, closing in. I twisted in the saddle, trying to track the movement, but the night played tricks with my eyes.

Another shape lunged. Elios caught it mid-flight, his blade slicing into its flank. It shrieked and veered away, leaving behind a trail of something dark in the air.

My pulse pounded in my ears. All around us, the threat multiplied.

Raising his sword, Elios kicked his horse into motion. Azure held tight to the reins, her posture rigid with tension, her wide eyes betraying the fear she didn't speak aloud. In the moonlight, I saw Elios rise to stand on the saddle, sword in hand, every line of him braced and ready. Markos kissed my neck once, then rose behind me, feet planted in hidden stirrups. Storm surged forward.

They had done this before.

Dimitris whistled again.

From the cliff to our right, another creature dropped, colliding with Aris. He hit the ground hard. The sound of it turned my stomach, making my lungs seize.

"Fuck. Aris." Markos dropped back into the saddle, took the reins, and wheeled us around.

We galloped toward him. Dimitris was already there, blade flashing as he ended the creature with a clean strike. Behind us, Elios engaged another, his sword tearing into its chest. The thing slammed into the cliff face and fell.

Then everything went still, the world holding its breath in the aftermath. No longer under attack, Markos brought us to a halt beside Aris, where Dimitris was already kneeling, hands checking Aris for injuries. I didn't breathe until Aris blinked. *He was alive.*

Markos wrapped one arm around me, his other hand gripping a torch that flickered unsteady light over the bloodied stone. We stood together, silent, watching as Dimitris carefully assessed Aris's injuries. His jaw was tight, his hands sure, but even without words, I could see the worry in his eyes.

Pain painted Aris's face in stark relief, but he didn't cry out. The predators might still be nearby.

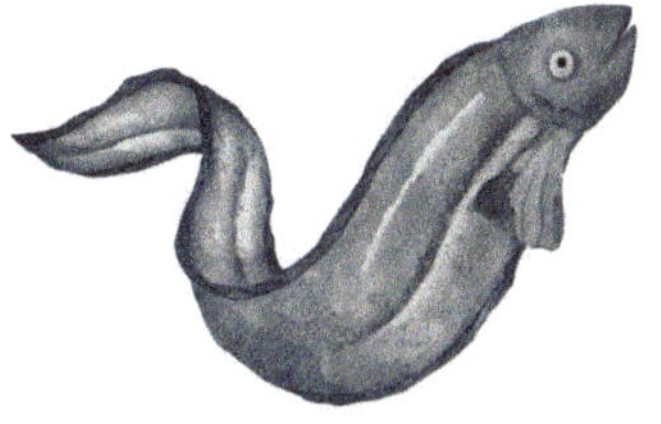

Even though the immediate danger had passed, my body trembled, the terror still rooted deep in my bones. Markos pulled me closer, his hand gliding over my arm in quiet reassurance. I leaned into him, drawing what strength I could from the steady beat of his heart against my shoulder.

While I stood by helplessly, Elios and Azure approached, their steps hesitant, faces pale. They looked as shaken as I felt, but thankfully, neither of them was injured. That alone felt like a miracle.

"His leg is definitely broken," Dimitris said, his voice low, edged with concern. "Might have cracked a few ribs, too."

Elios crouched beside him. They exchanged a few hushed words I couldn't make out, likely figuring out how to move him without worsening the damage.

Then I saw Azure stiffen.

Near her feet, half-shadowed by the rocks, lay a severed head.

I tapped Markos lightly, drawing his attention. He followed my gaze and nudged it forward with the toe of his boot.

A spill of black hair. Crimson eyes, glassy and unblinking. Skin pale enough to shimmer. Elongated teeth and claws, stained with blood that wasn't fresh. It looked almost human.

But it wasn't. Not anymore.

Nausea rising like bile, I turned into Markos's chest. That hollow stare mirrored something I didn't want to name. A wave of shame surged through me, thick and suffocating. *Was that how I looked when the Kraken took hold? Was that what others saw?*

Was that what I truly was underneath it all?

It had once been someone. Someone who'd suffered enough to be twisted into this.

Markos kicked the head, sending it bouncing off the stone and out of sight.

"You picked the wrong prey tonight."

Aris groaned, trying to push himself up, but he couldn't do it on his own. Dimitris and Elios caught him, steadying him between them.

Markos moved to help. Together, they lifted Aris onto Dimitris's horse. Aris leaned forward, arm wrapped protectively around his ribs, teeth gritted against the pain. Dimitris mounted behind him, holding him in place.

When Markos returned, he wrapped an arm around my waist and lifted me onto Storm with a quiet strength that steadied me more than I expected.

After Elios tied Aris's horse to his own, we turned back to the pass.

We would ride for Ceveasea and pray the city held healers. And hope that, this time, it would offer safety.

A HEALER'S TOUCH

Although tensions remained high during our journey toward Ceveasea, we finally reached the border without facing any further attacks. I let out a deep breath, a flicker of relief loosening the tension in my chest. For the first time in hours, it felt like I could truly breathe, but that fragile sense of safety shattered the moment we entered the city, as if the quiet itself was a warning. Something about the city felt wrong.

I scanned the empty streets, a chill slipping beneath my skin in the oppressive silence. My heart still beat too fast, each breath laced with the metallic tang of fading adrenaline. We were bruised, bloodied, and raw, the memory of the attack still crawling beneath our skin. Only when the quiet stretched on did the panic begin to ease, leaving behind something colder. *Dread.*

Unlike Starspell, which buzzed with life even at dusk, Ceveasea was unnervingly still. No patrons spilled out of taverns. No carriages rattled along cobblestones. The only light came from faint candle-glow behind shuttered windows. Even the stars above looked dimmer here, like they feared to shine.

"Where is everyone?" Azure asked. Her voice and the steady rhythm of hooves were the only sounds in the silence.

"The citizens know what lurks outside their borders and are smart enough to avoid it," Elios replied. "Unlike Starspell, you won't find many people in the open here after the sun goes down."

Though I had seen the creatures with my own eyes, Elios' words sent a shiver through me. A whole city, paralyzed by nightfall. The reality of how exposed we still were settled heavily in my stomach. Until we were behind closed doors, we were still in danger.

Markos leaned in and brushed a kiss to my neck. "You don't have to worry, my Sea Maiden. We're almost there."

I leaned into his warmth, watching each shadowed corner while Elios led us down a quiet side street.

At last, we reached a stone structure with a heavy gate built into its wall. A man waited inside, his gaze sharp beneath the glow of a hanging lantern. His sudden presence made my heart jolt, but none of the others reacted. A moment later, he nodded and pushed open the gate. Its hinges groaned, slicing through the silence.

"Staying for a while, Elios?" he asked, closing the gate behind us.

Elios didn't respond right away. Instead, he took the reins of his and Aris's horses and led them toward the stables at the far end of the courtyard. The man followed, still waiting for his answer.

"We're not sure how long this time, Georgios. Do you have a few rooms for us? Say, three or four?" Elios called over his shoulder.

"Aye." The older man, Georgios, barely glanced our way as he tended the horses.

Releasing his arms from around me, Markos dismounted, then turned to help me down with a touch that lingered, warm and steady. I stepped aside to join Azure, watching him lead Storm into the stable. Then they turned to help Aris.

The moment his face twisted in pain, something cracked inside me. Guilt surged, sharp and sudden, tightening in my chest. I pressed a hand to my sternum, trying to steady my breath, but the knot of responsibility only grew.

He had fallen because we were being hunted. He had taken the hit meant for someone else. He had bled for us.

And now he winced with every movement, and I couldn't help but feel the fault was mine. No matter how many times I told myself he'd made his own choice, the truth lodged beneath my ribs like a splinter—he was hurting because of me.

"Is Phaedra inside, Old Man?" Markos asked, reaching for the door.

Georgios nodded and waved toward the building. "Yes. Yes. She's inside."

Following the men, we passed through a heavy wooden door into a dim storage room and down a narrow corridor. The air grew cooler the deeper we went, shadows crowding the edges of flickering lantern light. The stillness felt too familiar. Like the city, this place had been waiting in silence far too long.

At the end of the hall, a pair of tall doors loomed. Elios shifted Aris's weight to Dimitris and Markos, then crouched to slide something beneath the door. We waited.

The response came almost instantly.

A woman stepped out. She was tall and composed, with dark curls and striking green eyes, but it was the scar slashing across her cheek that caught my eye. She didn't speak. She simply gave Elios a single nod before stepping aside to let them pass.

They carried Aris into the room and laid him on a wide table.

"What happened to him?" she asked, reaching for a dagger without waiting for an answer.

Elios stepped in to help, and together they cut away the shredded tunic and trousers. Deep bruising marked Aris's side, and his leg bent at an unnatural angle. His eyes fluttered open, glazed with pain, before slipping shut again.

I backed away, a hollow ache blooming in my chest, uselessness scraping at the edges of my calm.

Near a side table, I noticed a bronze medallion etched with a broken chain. It matched the tattoo on Markos' chest and likely those on Elios and Aris. A symbol of The Circle. I wondered if Dimitris bore the same.

"Vampires. A few of them attacked us on our way into the city and knocked him off his horse," Elios said, pulling me from my thoughts.

Phaedra shook her head, pulling a small vial from her apron. "Was he bitten?"

"No." Elios tilted Aris's head back while she dropped a few violet drops into his mouth.

They worked together in quiet rhythm, their movements efficient and calm, like this wasn't the first time they'd tended to one of their own. I sank onto a nearby settee between Dimitris and Markos, the cushion dipping beneath my weight. Azure joined a moment later, her worry written clearly across her face as she sat forward, elbows on her knees, eyes fixed on Aris.

"He just fell from his horse? His left leg is broken, and he has a few broken ribs as well. There are no signs of head trauma, but there might be some internal bleeding. A few broken bones wouldn't be enough to make this big man pass out," Phaedra responded.

Her tone wasn't judgmental, only precise.

I watched her bind his ribs and splint his leg, every motion swift and efficient. Seeing someone as strong as Aris laid out like this made my stomach churn. It reminded me how fragile even the bravest of us could be. Relief swelled inside me knowing we had found a healer in time but dread lingered. Aris couldn't travel in this condition. Leaving Ceveasea might mean leaving him behind.

Once she finished attending to Aris, Phaedra washed her hands and retrieved a set of keys from her apron.

"You three can carry him into the sickroom across the hall. Then I'll show you to your rooms."

THE DUSTY LANTERN

I hadn't realized it was the Dusty Lantern was an inn until we climbed the second-floor stairs. The silence had masked its true nature, with the first floor empty when we arrived—the tavern closing at sunset. Instead, I'd first come to know it as a place of healing. Phaedra, it turned out, was a well-known healer, and the infirmary tucked behind the tavern was where most sought help when they needed it.

Aris, unable to walk on his own, had been settled in a small room across the hall from the infirmary. It wasn't much, just a single bed and a table stocked with supplies, but Phaedra and her husband, Georgios, had promised to watch over him while the rest of us rested. Markos and I had followed Phaedra and the others up the creaky wooden stairs, the air thick with exhaustion. The stone walls of the upper floor held a long, dimly lit corridor lined with guest rooms. Once our host had shown us to ours, she returned to the stairs with a promise to return with dinner and drinks.

My stomach was painfully empty. We hadn't eaten in hours since leaving the stream somewhere past the Arcane River tribal camp.

Markos shut the door behind us, slipping an arm around my waist and pulling me close. "Do you want to take a bath while we wait?" His voice was low and soothing, and warmth seeped into my skin. "The tub isn't large, but it is deep enough for your tail."

I wasn't surprised the tub was small. These were guest quarters, after all, but I wasn't disappointed either. A private bath was a luxury I hadn't expected.

Leaning into him, I exhaled. "A bath sounds nice... if I have the energy to shift. Today has been overwhelming." That was putting it lightly, but I didn't want to make the day's horrors about me, even if I was the cause.

Markos kissed my forehead, his hand trailing up and down my back in a slow, soothing rhythm. "You'll feel better after a hot bath and some sleep. Aris will be okay. We all will."

His words warmed me, but I couldn't shake my worries. They ran too deep, tangled like seaweed in my mind. Even this far from the ocean, I knew Miris could reach me. The fear still lurked, but it no longer controlled me. I was tired of letting the Sea Goddess rule my life. I'd given her enough already, and tonight, I wanted to reclaim something for myself.

The hallway beyond the door had gone quiet, and our room held a kind of hush that made you whisper without meaning to. Only the soft creak of wood underfoot and the faint brush of wind beyond the shutters broke the stillness. The scent of lavender hung in the air, edged with something earthy and sharp, maybe one of Phaedra's tinctures. It was warmer in here than outside, but I still found myself rubbing my arms, trying to ground myself. Trying to remind my body that I was safe. That I was here. *Now.*

Markos brushed his lips against my cheek before guiding me toward the bathing room. He helped me onto a small wooden stool beside the tub, then turned on the tap, testing the water with his hand.

It still fascinated me how humans had tamed water, drawing it into their homes and purifying it until it ran clean and clear.

"Thank you for caring for me," I murmured, dipping my fingers into the warm water. A shiver of anticipation rippled through me, trailing down my spine to the tips of my toes. My tail ached to be free.

The moment my body gave in to the change, I exhaled a deep breath of relief. The water, though shallow and confined, seeped into every corner of my soul, washing away some of the fear I'd carried since the mountain pass. For the first time in days, I felt like myself—not a fugitive, not a survivor. Just *Ocevia.*

Markos grinned as I fumbled with the laces of my tunic. Batting my hands away, he took over, the fabric loosening under his touch. With a simple motion, my tunic slipped open, the night air cool against my bare skin. His fingers brushed over my nipple, sending a shock of warmth straight to my core. I gasped, arching into him.

His other arm wrapped around my waist, pulling me close as his insistent lips found mine. A spark ignited between us, heat building, consuming, and I let myself sink into it.

It wasn't just arousal, though heat coiled in my belly like a living thing. It was the way he undid me, piece by piece, until the girl I had been beneath the sea felt like a shadow. This was who I was now. Not a weapon forged by fear or a shadow hiding in the surf. This was who I wanted to be—desired, safe, *whole*.

His green eyes locked onto mine when he pulled back, tracing a finger down my cheek and stealing my breath. "It's easy to care for someone when they're your everything."

Slipping my trousers to the floor, my mate lifted me from the stool and placed me gently into the bathtub's warm water. The moment my skin met the heat, my legs shimmered, shifting into the sleek turquoise tail that was as much a part of me as my human form. My fin draped over the tub's edge, too large to fully submerge, but it didn't matter. The sensation of water embracing me, even in such a confined space, was a relief.

When I lifted my gaze to Markos, he stared, his eyes wide with wonder. He reached forward, his fingers gliding reverently over my tail.

"You truly are exquisite, my Sea Maiden," he murmured, his voice thick with awe. "A work of art."

Even though my core was tucked away in this form, it still ached for him, a silent pulse of need.

I smirked, flicking my tail just enough to send water droplets into the air. "Our appearances are deceiving," I said, my voice lilting, *teasing.* "We're meant to allure men. You're simply under my spell."

What I didn't say, what I never wanted to remind him, was that my beauty and sensuality had always been a curse. If I remained human for the rest of my life, my appearance might not be quite so... *enthralling.*

Markos chuckled, the sound low and warm as he leaned in to kiss my lips. I closed my eyes and savored it, letting myself forget the weight I carried, if only for a moment. His touch was an anchor to something good, something safe.

When he pulled back, a grin lingered on his lips. "Your beauty is a blessing, not a curse. And every part of you is beautiful, not just your flesh."

He cupped my face, his fingers tracing the sharp lines of my cheek-bones as if I were something delicate, something to be cherished. "You are a masterpiece," he said softly. "And I'm honored to see you for what you are... to have the chance to love you."

A knock at the door shattered the quiet intimacy between us. Markos kissed me once more before standing to answer it. A moment later, Georgios' raspy voice reached my ears, followed by the unmistakable aroma of a home-cooked meal. My stomach growled in response, making my hunger impossible to ignore.

I squeezed a dollop of soap into my palm, running my fingers through my hair as Markos carried the tray of food and wine across the room. The scent of roasted meat and herbs made my mouth water. Exhaustion tugged at me even as I finished bathing, reluctant to leave the warmth of the water. I wanted to taste whatever waited beneath the covered dish on the table.

Sighing, I shifted my tail back into my legs, standing as water dripped down my body. Markos re-entered with a grin that left no question about what he was thinking, his gaze devouring me. Heat bloomed across my cheeks as I stepped out of the tub, reaching for the cloth in his hands.

A shiver swept through me as he ran the towel over my skin, slow and deliberate. His eyes were dark with something more profound than amusement. Wrapping the fabric around me, he pulled me close, his lips brushing against mine. Sparks danced through my veins as his hands roamed, the warmth of his touch setting me alight.

His kiss deepened, claiming me, consuming me. My body molded against his, my fingers gripping his shoulders, desperate to hold onto the moment. But as his touch ignited me, my stomach let out another loud protest, making him chuckle against my lips.

"Are you hungry?" he asked, amusement flickering in his gaze.

I gave him a sheepish nod as we moved to the table. Azure and I had spent countless nights dreaming of human meals, reminiscing over the flavors we barely remembered. But nothing could have prepared me for the first bite.

The stew was rich and hearty, the meat tender and soaked in thick, herb-infused gravy. A moan escaped before I could stop it.

Markos smirked. "I think I have a new mission… finding the best food in the land just to hear you moan like that."

Heat flooded my face. I grabbed a hunk of warm bread, stuffing it into my mouth to avoid his smug expression. But the buttery richness only added to my pleasure. "I support this idea," I said, savoring each bite. "I have a lot of lost time to make up for."

The first bite transported me. For a flicker of time, I was a child again, huddled beside Azure in the warmth of a hidden cave, chewing stolen bread we'd soaked in sea salt just to pretend it had flavor. But this—this stew was real. Spiced, rich, indulgent. It tasted like freedom. Like choice. Like something earned rather than stolen. For the first time, I felt like I had a future worth savoring.

Every mouthful was better than the last, each flavor more indulgent than anything I'd ever tasted. By the time we finished, my exhaustion had settled deeper into my bones, but I hadn't yet touched the wine. Starspell's wine had never appealed to me, and I doubted this one would be any different. Even now, water would always be my drink of choice, away from the sea.

Markos placed the tray outside the door, but when he returned, his eyes held a different kind of hunger. A jolt of heat surged through me as he lifted me from the chair, pulling me against him. His lips met mine in a deep, languid kiss, his tongue sweeping into my mouth, tasting and savoring. The remnants of wine and spices lingered between us, the intoxicating mix making my head spin.

I melted into him as he walked me backward toward the bed, his hands roaming, teasing. He set me down on the mattress, his weight pressing against me for only a moment before he pulled away.

"I'll be back," he murmured, disappearing into the bathing room.

The sound of water splashing met my ears, but I barely had the strength to move. My body ached for him, for the heat of his skin against mine, but exhaustion was pulling me under.

When Markos emerged, his damp hair trailing down his toned chest, my lungs forgot how to work. A mischievous grin tugged at his lips. "You smell so good. I didn't want to get you dirty."

With a slow, deliberate motion, he untucked the towel from his waist, letting it fall.

I bit my lip as my gaze drifted down, my stomach tightening at the sight of him—hard, thick, and utterly captivating.

Reaching out, I wrapped my fingers around him, stroking slowly, savoring the way his breath hitched, the way his muscles tensed beneath my touch. His eyelids fluttered closed, his jaw tightening as he let himself feel me.

A low groan rumbled in his chest as he thrust into my palm, the movement desperate, seeking.

Memories of our night in the cave surfaced, sending a delicious thrill through me. I wanted to please him. *Needed* to.

Leaning forward, I parted my lips, taking him into my mouth, my tongue swirling over sensitive skin.

A shudder wracked his body. His fingers tangled in my hair as he guided me, his breath coming in ragged gasps.

He moaned my name, low and wrecked, as if it were the only word he knew, his body trembling as he gave in to release.

In his arms, I wasn't a fugitive or a cursed creature. I was just a woman being loved. And for tonight, that was enough.

Chapter Thirty-One

BLISS

Waking up in a warm bed, wrapped in Markos' strong arms, felt like a dream I never thought would come true. The sun's rays streamed through the slender windows, illuminating dust particles as they danced in the morning air. I watched them absently, nuzzling into Markos' chest, the steady rhythm of his heartbeat filling me with quiet, aching happiness. Love swelled within me, overflowing, spilling into every part of my being. He had worshipped me before sleep took us both, leaving us exhausted, sated, and whole. The memory sent a flutter through my belly, desire stirring once more as I tilted my head to gaze at his face. But even in dreams, I'd learned to be cautious. Bliss like this never lasted in the world I'd known. Still, I let myself hope. Just a little.

Markos' emerald eyes blinked open as if sensing my thoughts, locking onto mine. A slow smile curled his lips, a lazy grin that stirred something deep in my chest. I leaned in, pressing a soft kiss to his mouth, and he wasted no time pulling me closer, his arm tightening around my waist.

"Good morning, little one," he murmured, his voice rough with sleep. "How did you sleep?"

A contented sigh escaped me. "Very well," I admitted, snuggling into his warmth. "I'd rather not leave this bed."

His chuckle rumbled beneath my ear, sending a pleasant shiver down my spine. "You don't have to." He tucked a strand of hair behind my ear before kissing my forehead. "After everything you've been through, you deserve to rest."

I smiled against his chest, but his words cracked something inside me, allowing unwanted thoughts to slip through. The past pressed in, unbidden and relentless.

Sensing the shift, Markos tightened his hold around my waist and rolled me on top of him, the blanket slipping away to reveal my bare skin. But there was no hesitation in his gaze, no flicker of uncertainty, only admiration and reverence. And just as I drank in the sight of him, strong and beautiful beneath me, he looked at me as though I was the most precious thing in the world.

The sunlight warmed my shoulder, contrasting with the cool linen beneath me. Somewhere below, a chair scraped across the tavern floor, distant... grounded. But here, with him, everything else melted away.

Markos lifted himself enough to kiss me, his lips moving against mine with a tenderness that made my heart swell. His hands traced a slow, deliberate path over my body, fingertips igniting sparks of pleasure in their wake. The way his touch deepened stole the air from my chest, his tongue parting my lips in an intimate dance that sent heat pooling low in my belly.

Our kiss grew more urgent, more consuming, until he shifted, rolling me onto my back and settling between my thighs. A gasp escaped me as he entered me, slow and deliberate, stretching, *filling*. I clung to him, feeling the steady beat of his heart against my chest as we moved together. His rhythm was gentle, unhurried, like waves lapping against the shore—fluid, *effortless*.

His hands roamed lower, fingers seeking, teasing, sending jolts of pleasure racing through me. I arched against him, a cry slipping from my lips as he circled the sensitive bud of my pleasure, driving me higher. His mouth found my neck, lips grazing, teeth nipping, marking me as he quickened his pace. The pressure inside me coiled tight, unbearably so, and then... *release*. My body trembled beneath him, pleasure surging through every nerve as I cried out his name. Markos groaned as he followed, burying himself deep as he went over the edge.

For a moment, neither of us moved. We lay tangled together, bodies slick, breath uneven, the world narrowed to the steady pulse of our heartbeats. Markos rolled onto his side, pulling me close and pressing a lingering kiss to my lips. My heart was still racing, but I smiled and nestled into him, allowing myself to bask in the warmth of his embrace.

By the time I finally left the comfort of our bed, Markos had already gone downstairs to send a message to a friend about securing a safe house. We couldn't stay in the tavern forever. There were too many eyes and risks. When he returned, we made our way downstairs together for breakfast.

The tavern was already stirring with early-morning patrons. Dimitris sat at a table, chatting with Georgios, who placed a steaming cup of dark liquid before him.

Dimitris glanced up as we approached, lifting his cup with a knowing smile. "You're just in time for coffee."

Guiding me to the table, Markos pulled out a chair, waiting for me to sit before kissing my cheek. "I'll be back shortly."

I watched as he strode toward the bar, exchanging quiet words with Georgios before they disappeared into the kitchen.

"You make him happy," Dimitris said, his voice warm, observant.

I blinked, startled by the unexpected remark. But as my gaze lingered on the empty space where Markos had been, joy spread through my chest.

"I hope so," I murmured, more to myself than to him. Because the truth was, I had never felt happiness like this before, and I wasn't sure what terrified me more... losing it or letting myself believe I could keep it.

I was so engrossed in watching my mate, who had stepped behind the bar, that I nearly forgot Dimitris was sitting across from me. His words warmed my cheeks, but I smiled. "He makes me happy too."

In the dim light of the tavern, his eyes sparkled with something knowing. "That's all that matters."

Before I could respond, Markos returned, sliding into the seat beside me. Georgios followed, setting down breakfast plates and steaming mugs of coffee. The bitter scent wrinkled my nose, but Markos lifted his cup without hesitation, taking a deep sip. He set it down with a satisfied sigh, then turned to me with a smile. "I hope you're hungry. This is the finest breakfast in town."

I had just lifted my spoon when the door swung open. Azure and Elios entered, settling at the table as Georgios wordlessly dropped two more plates and mugs in front of them. For all his gruffness, he was undoubtedly efficient.

"How's Aris?" Elios asked between bites.

Having never tasted porridge before, I wasn't sure about its texture, but the flavor was pleasant enough. I took another spoonful as I turned my gaze to Elios.

"He's in a lot of pain," Dimitris answered. "Phaedra's been giving him a tonic for relief, but it keeps him drowsy. He's asleep now." His tone held quiet concern. He and Aris obviously shared a close bond. All four of them did.

The thought of Aris suffering unsettled my stomach, but I forced myself to take a bite of eggs, the taste sparking a distant childhood memory. Though fragmented, I was sure my mother had fed me eggs. The recollection teetered on the edge of something painful, but I pushed it aside and refocused on the conversation. The laughter felt strange, fragile. It echoed too easily in the corners of my mind still braced for the Sea Goddess' wrath.

"Anyone send word to Kimon?" Elios asked, shoveling food into his mouth at an alarming pace.

Markos placed his utensil on his plate, nodding. "I messaged him this morning. Told him we were here, and he responded a short while ago. The safe house will be ready tomorrow." His expression darkened slightly. "I'm unsure if Aris will be ready to move, though. One of us may need to stay behind. I hate the idea of leaving him in Georgios and Phaedra's care while he's like this. Phaedra can tend to him, but he's too big for her to lift on her own."

Dimitris took a slow sip of his coffee before answering. "I'll stay with him if it comes to that. You two should take these ladies to the safe house when ready. They'll be more comfortable there... and safer."

Elios lifted his mug in a mock salute. "Appreciate the offer, Brother, but I have a feeling you just want to stay behind to sample the drinks in this fine establishment."

A giggle escaped me, and Azure laughed beside me.

From behind the bar, Georgios snorted. "Those drinks won't be on the house, either. I'll have your ass washing dishes."

Dimitris rolled up his napkin and lobbed it at Elios, the ball landing near his plate. "Ha. Ha. Funny, really." He turned toward the bar. "Not you, Old Man. I'll wash dishes if you need help. It's preferable to washing Aris' backside." His smirk was unrepentant as he shifted his gaze back to Elios. "Anyway, what's on the agenda for today, Boss?"

Elios leaned back in his chair, draping an arm around Azure's shoulders. The way she instinctively nestled against him, her love for him so clear on her face, warmed something inside me.

"I would say to remain hidden," Elios said, his expression turning serious, "but we need ears on the ground in case Miris' people show up asking questions. I don't want to be blindsided."

The mere mention of Miris sent a chill through my veins, but before the fear could take hold, Markos leaned in and pressed a kiss to my cheek. His presence soothed the unease curling in my stomach.

"I'll talk to Phaedra," he murmured. "See if our contacts in the city have heard anything. I'll be back soon."

I watched him leave, resisting the urge to follow. I wanted to be close to him, to feel the reassurance of his touch, but I stayed put. A moment later, Azure slid into the seat Markos had just vacated, her expression brimming with mischief.

It reminded me of the days we would sit together, whispering secrets, pretending our lives weren't cursed.

"Well..." she drawled, drawing out the word in a way that made my cheeks flush.

I eyed her warily. "Well, what?"

Grin tugging up the sides of her mouth, Azure waggled her eyebrows. "I can't wait to hear all the details. How did everything come together?" She flicked a finger in the direction Markos had gone. "Just so you know, there's no judgment from me. Elios and I fell quickly, so I'm happy for you."

Heat crawled up my neck. With the others deep in their conversation, I glanced around the room before exhaling.

"From the moment I saw him standing outside the tavern," I admitted, my voice softer now, "I knew he was mine. I couldn't deny my interest in him. I wanted the chance to see what we could become."

Azure nodded, a wistful look crossing her face. "I felt the same way when I saw Elios clinging to those rocks after the shipwreck. Out of everyone that night..." Her voice dipped lower, her gaze flickering toward the others. "Out of everyone who died that night, he fought so hard to survive. I couldn't take my eyes off him. It felt like a sign that I was meant to find him. I may have carried him to that island, but we saved each other."

A lump formed in my throat. Without thinking, I reached over and took her hand. Despite the love Markos had given me, my heart still felt restless, and my mind was still plagued with the fear that I would be found and dragged back into the sea. I didn't want to go back.

Markos hadn't just offered me a bed or a sword. He'd seen me. Even when I couldn't see myself clearly, he had.

I swallowed hard. "Do you think we can really get away with this? I mean... *actually* escape? I feel like Miris' eyes are on us no matter where we go. I don't want to go back, Azure. I can't leave Markos."

Something flickered in her gaze, a shadow of her own doubts. She squeezed my hand, her grip firm, grounding.

"I'd be lying if I said I wasn't afraid," she admitted. "But these men... they'll stop at nothing to protect us. We have to find some comfort in that."

I wanted to believe her. I needed to. But deep down, I feared Miris' grasp would never truly let me go, no matter how far I ran. And if Miris was still out there, watching from the shadows, how long would it be before she reached out and tore this happiness away?

C. A. VARIAN

Vanished into the Darkness

The morning had started out deceptively normal. Too normal, in hindsight—quiet in a way that should have felt unnatural, but I had been too distracted to notice.

After breakfast, Markos and Dimitris set out to comb the city, gathering supplies and keeping an ear to the ground for any whispers that we were being followed. With the ever-present threat of Miris' people coming to Ceveasea, it was safer for Azure and me to remain out of sight. So, while the men scouted, Azure and I stayed behind to help Phaedra tend to Aris, while Elios assisted Georgios around the bar.

Aris slept for most of the morning, kept under by the strong pain tonic Phaedra administered regularly. But whenever he stirred, I was there to help him shift to a more comfortable position or bring him food. I wasn't sure if my efforts did anything to ease my guilt, but caring for him felt like something I could do—something within my control.

As the afternoon stretched on, Azure joined Elios in the kitchen to help prepare food, both for us and the evening guests. Markos and Dimitris returned not long after, just as the tavern began filling with patrons. To remain unnoticed, Azure and I sat with Elios in a dimly lit corner, hooded cloaks concealing our features. Markos and Dimitris blended into the crowd, listening for useful gossip. Laughter buzzed through the tavern, low and warm, wrapping the night in a rare illusion of safety. I caught a glimpse of Markos grinning over a mug, his arm slung carelessly around Dimitris' shoulders.

By the time the last guests trickled out at sunset, we all pitched in to clean up. I was wiping down tables when Aris entered the room, rolling in on a contraption I had never seen before. A *chair with wheels*. My heart swelled at the sight of him up and moving, my breath coming out a little bit easier.

Leaving the rag behind, I crossed the room, slipping my hand into Markos' as we joined the others gathering around Aris.

"How are you feeling, Brother?" Elios asked, patting him on the shoulder.

Aris winced as he rubbed his leg, but his smile remained. "Pretty good, considering. My leg and ribs hurt like hell, but this chair is a damn blessing." Gripping the wheels, he maneuvered himself a few inches forward and back. "Phaedra had Georgios drag it out of storage. I can't get up the stairs, but at least I can make it to the bathroom on my own. Having someone help me piss does little for my warrior image."

His ability to crack a joke despite his pain only made me like him more. After fearing he wouldn't survive his injuries, seeing him here, teasing and grinning, was a relief beyond words.

Dimitris smirked, handing Aris a mug of ale before dropping into the seat next to him. "Having someone help you piss is the closest you can get to having someone touch your cock."

Aris took a sip, eyes gleaming with mischief. "Guess I'm lucky you were around to help me out, then."

Dimitris let out a bark of laughter, nearly choking on his drink. "It's the least I can do for a friend. Just be glad I'm not asking for anything in return." He clinked his glass against Aris' and winked. For the first time in days, the weight of fear eased from my chest, and I let myself believe, just for a moment, that the night would end in peace.

Trying to smother my laughter, I pressed my face into Markos' sleeve, his scent grounding me. I was grateful that Phaedra and Georgios had handled Aris' more delicate needs. I wasn't sure either of us would have survived that level of embarrassment. But Dimitris, of course, seemed intent on teasing him relentlessly.

Azure brushed past me with a tired smile, her fingers briefly grazing mine. Something in that touch made the hair on my arms rise, but I pushed the feeling down, unwilling to ruin the moment with doubt. A chill pricked at the nape of my neck, but I brushed it off, too wrapped in the warmth of the moment to listen. I almost stopped her. Almost. But the moment slipped away like water through my hands.

As the others examined Aris' chair and chatted, Azure excused herself, heading down the lantern-lit hallway toward the bathroom. I barely noticed her go, until a sharp, gut-wrenching feeling gripped me out of nowhere. A weight dropped in my stomach, sudden and suffocating. Then, the sound of shattering glass rang through the tavern.

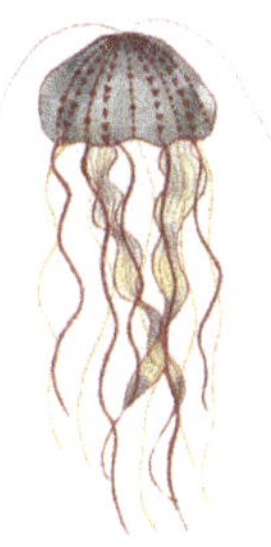

A chill spread through me, locking my limbs in place. The air turned frigid. The lanterns flickered.

Something was wrong.

The world slowed. I saw Elios' grin falter before his body twisted. His mug hit the floor, forgotten, as he bolted toward the hallway without a word.

Markos turned to me, his jaw clenched, his expression strained. "Stay here with Aris. I'll be back."

Before I could argue, he disappeared into the dark hallway after Dimitris.

Abandoning whatever he had been doing in the kitchen, Georgios emerged behind the bar, wiping his hands on a towel. "What's going on? Something wrong?"

I opened my mouth, but no words came. I didn't know what had happened. I didn't know what was lurking in that hallway, but I *knew*. I felt it in the marrow of my bones, in the way my entire body screamed at me to move.

Adrenaline surged through me, breaking through the ice in my veins and I ran. Through the metal gate, I saw Markos, Elios, and Dimitris disappear into the night.

Logic warned me to stay back. That the vampires out there lurked, waiting.

But logic couldn't silence the terror in my blood.

I didn't think.

I followed them.

The night was eerily quiet. Only the occasional hoot of an owl echoed through the darkness, a lone sound in the vast silence. Above me, the stars burned brightly, scattered across the sky like a thousand tiny fireflies. But despite their beauty, an unsettling stillness hung in the air. It felt as though the world was holding its breath, waiting.

"Markos, please... wait!"

My boots struck against the cobbled street as I rushed forward, my breath coming fast. My heart pounded against my ribs, and as a shadowed figure approached from the other end of the block, I skidded to a halt, instinct kicking in.

My breath faltered like a broken wing.

Then, the figure moved closer, stepping into the dim light.

Markos.

Relief flooded me, so sharp I nearly sagged from it. Taking a step forward, I called out to him, but his gaze was already locked on mine.

"Ocevia." His voice was firm, unyielding. "I told you to stay inside where it's safe."

His words held reprimand, but his hand was gentle as it cupped my cheek.

I gripped his arm, shaking my head. "I won't stay inside if you're searching for my friend." My voice trembled, but I steadied it. "Where is she, Markos? What's going on?"

We searched for hours.

Through winding streets, shadowed alleys, and abandoned courtyards, we hunted. Lanterns in hand, our footsteps echoed through empty corridors and rain-slick cobblestones, but no trail remained. Not a single sound. Not a scent of Azure on the wind. It was as though the night itself had swallowed her whole. The silence echoed louder with each step, an unbearable hollowness growing inside me like a scream I couldn't let out.

At one point, I collapsed to my knees in the middle of a back alley, bile rising in my throat. "What if I never see her again?" I whispered. "What if she called for me, and I didn't come?" Guilt curled around my heart like smoke. Markos helped me up without a word, pulling me into his arms until I could breathe again.

By the time we returned to the tavern, exhaustion clung to us like a second skin. We had only one option left. Markos, Elios, and I mounted our horses and galloped into the mountains while Dimitris remained behind to watch over Aris. Waiting until morning was not an option. The morning could be too late. By then, Azure could be back in the sea, ripped apart by Miris.

The hooves of our horses thundered against the dirt road, the night air cutting like knives. My hands trembled where they clutched the reins, Markos' arms braced tightly around me. I could feel the urgency in his every breath, every muscle. There was no room for words between us, not with dread clawing at our throats, with danger lurking behind every gust of wind.

We rode for hours beneath a canopy of stars, haunted by silence. Every flicker of movement sent my heart lurching, but we never found her.

Eventually, the Arcane River tribe's camp came into view, nestled in the valley like a forgotten memory. There was no time for greetings, no firelit reunions. We nodded to those we passed, needing sleep enough to continue on.

Supplied with food and drink, we retreated into the same cave we had once rested in. It felt colder now. *Emptier.* I slipped into the spring, the water warm against my aching body, and Markos joined me, washing the dirt from our skin in silence. Even his touch, usually grounding, felt distant tonight, muffled beneath the weight of fear. I felt adrift, as if the tether holding me together had frayed under the pressure of losing her.

When we climbed into bed, our limbs heavy and hearts heavier, there were no words left to say.

As the darkness of sleep claimed me, one thought burned through it all: I prayed she was alive. I prayed she could survive until we found her.

And beneath that prayer, hidden in the undertow of my heart, was the fear I couldn't shake:

What if the sea had taken her back?

Chapter Thirty-Three

Losing Hope in the Storm

The first light of dawn cut through the fog like a blade, gilding the mountaintops in gold, but it could not pierce the heaviness lodged in my chest. Not when Azure was still missing. Not when each moment dragged her further from reach.

Waking after only a few hours of sleep, Markos, Elios, and I went to the stables to retrieve our horses. The tribal camp buzzed quietly behind us, but I barely took notice. We had refilled our water skins and packed enough dried meat to last the journey, but no amount of preparation could settle the unease coiling in my stomach.

A thick band of gray clouds loomed in the distance, but the sky remained clear. Even so, the air was heavy with the promise of a storm. The scent of salt from the Lamalis Sea carried faint traces of Azure's presence, guiding us in the right direction. The familiar scent brought a brief flicker of hope, then pain. I clung to it, trying to believe it meant we were close, but I knew there was a chance we were already too late. The thought clenched around my ribs like a vice, but I shoved it aside. I couldn't accept that possibility.

"We need to move quickly," I murmured, my voice barely audible over the wind.

Elios' jaw was tight, his gaze shifting toward the darkening sky. "It's going to storm soon."

Though my senses were sharper than a human's, I knew he could feel it, too. The tension in the air, the charged stillness before the sky opened up.

Markos tightened his arms around me as we rode, his warmth pressing against my back. He dipped his head, his lips grazing my neck. "Hopefully, we can outrun it. Once we clear this pass, we'll pick up the pace."

I nodded, clutching my cloak tighter as the wind bit through the fabric. Stopping wasn't an option when every moment put more distance between us and Azure.

The hooves clattered like war drums beneath us, each one echoing the frantic rhythm of my heart. I tried to focus on the path ahead, but my mind kept drifting back to Azure. *Was she cold? Afraid? Bleeding?* The brine of the sea grew stronger, but we were still far from Starspell. The wind had picked up, carrying the thick scent of rain, and when I glanced skyward, the clouds had gathered into a heavy, menacing mass. The storm was closing in fast.

I knew Elios wouldn't want to stop. Neither did I. But nature wasn't giving us a choice.

The first droplets hit my skin, cool and sharp. When the first rumbles of thunder reverberated across the sky, the horses grew restless beneath us, their movements jittery, ears flicking back in agitation.

It wasn't long after lighting tore through the sky, illuminating the jagged cliffs, before the storm truly broke.

Rain lashed down in torrents, soaking through my cloak and drenching my hair until it clung to my face. The wind howled through the mountains, whipping against us like an invisible force trying to knock us from our saddles.

The storm roared around me, a reflection of the turmoil inside. Every crash of thunder echoed the dread pounding in my chest.

I barely had time to react before I was nearly thrown from the saddle. Markos' arms locked around me, steadying me before I could slip, but even he knew we couldn't push forward like this.

Elios yanked his reins with a sharp curse, steering his horse toward a lower path. "We need to find shelter *now*."

We veered off into the valley, the horses fighting against us the whole way. I gritted my teeth, frustration curling hot in my gut. Every second we lost meant Azure slipped further away, but we had no choice. If we kept going, we wouldn't survive the storm intact.

By the time we found a cave large enough for the horses, my limbs trembled from cold and exhaustion. Unlike the Arcane River tribe's hot springs, there was no warmth here, only damp stone and an old fire's faint, stale scent. At least there were remnants of charred wood left behind by another traveler. It wasn't much, but it would be enough to dry some of our clothes.

Elios crouched near the firepit, working quickly to reignite the embers, while Markos unrolled blankets in the driest corner of the cave. I lingered at the entrance, staring out into the rain. The storm had not eased. If anything, it had grown fiercer, the wind screaming through the cliffs like a living thing.

Without a word, I stepped outside.

I didn't care that the rain hit me like a thousand tiny daggers. I barely flinched as I waded into a deep puddle, letting the water consume my legs. A shiver rippled through me as my body shifted, skin smoothing into shimmering turquoise scales, my tail unfurling beneath the surface.

I had swum through storms before. I had hunted in them, damning lost souls to the sea. The chaos of the storm should not have unsettled me, but this one did.

The water crashed down harder as if punishing me, and the wind howled its fury, forcing me to tilt my face upward. My eyes closed against the assault, a bitter laugh slipping past my lips.

I deserved this.

The rain, the cold, the storm's wrath was nothing compared to the pain I had inflicted.

I squeezed my eyes shut, my chest heaving. I had to find a way to make amends. To make peace with what I had done. But first, I had to save Azure.

That was the only thing that mattered now.

Just as tears burned the backs of my eyes, I forced my spine to straighten, shoving the emotion down. Taking a steady breath, I shifted back into my human form, the weight of my legs returning as I pulled myself from the puddle and stepped into the cave's shelter.

The rain still pounded outside, relentless, a mirror of the storm churning inside me.

Even though I had never taken a life by choice, only when forced, I could never escape the ghosts of those I had killed. The weight of their deaths pressed into me, inescapable, a constant reminder that no matter what I did, no matter how much I longed for redemption, I would never truly be free.

And I would never be good enough for Markos.

I didn't deserve love. I didn't deserve happiness. That belief had been carved into me by years of servitude, by every life I'd taken under Miris' command. Even now, Markos' tenderness felt like something I could borrow, but never truly keep.

"We'll find her, Little One."

Markos' voice broke through my thoughts, pulling me back before I could slip too far into that dark place. I hadn't even noticed him approaching, but suddenly his arm was around me, guiding me toward the small blanket he had laid out in the back of the cave.

The fire flickered weakly, struggling against the damp air. Elios stood before it, draping our soaked cloaks over a boulder in an attempt to dry them.

With nowhere else to go, no fight left in me, I let Markos lead me down to sit beside him.

He tilted my chin up, his fingers warm against my cold skin. When my gaze met his, the compassion in his eyes nearly broke me. I clenched my jaw, willing myself to hold it together.

"You think I don't see your pain?" Markos whispered. "You carry it like armor, but it's not yours to wear anymore. Let me carry it with you. Let me help."

Then he pressed a soft kiss to my forehead, his lips barely brushing against my skin. "We'll get through this together," he whispered.

I wanted to believe him. *Gods*, I wanted to.

"If Miris gets her, she will—"

Markos kissed me before I could finish, silencing my words with the warmth of his lips.

I melted into him, my body surrendering even as my mind screamed at me to stay guarded. Just for a moment, I let myself forget the storm, the danger, the fear clawing at my ribs. For a fleeting second, it was just us. Just his touch, his warmth, his love wrapping around me like something tangible, something safe.

When he pulled away, his gaze searched mine, his expression etched with certainty. "We will find her," he said, his voice firm. "And we will keep you safe. You will never be a slave again."

His conviction was unwavering, but I knew better. It wasn't a promise he could make.

No matter how badly I wanted to believe him, the fear never truly left me. It coiled in my veins, a constant reminder that my freedom was fragile.

I offered him a small, sad smile, because that was all I had to give. He was trying to reassure me, but after so many years of chains, I had learned not to trust in hope.

Happy endings were rare for people like me.

All I could do now was take it one day at a time, and hope that, for once, fate would be kind.

BENEATH THE CORAL THRONE

We had been at sea for hours, the sun now high above, casting silver light across the endless blue. The journey from the island to the edge of Miris' domain had been brutal. I hadn't slept. None of us had. The only things keeping us moving were dried meat, water, and the sheer, brittle will that desperation fuels when hope feels like a lie.

And fear.

The fear of being too late.

The boat creaked beneath our weight, a patchwork of desperation and battered hope stitched together with fraying seams. Below us, the Sea Goddess's palace waited, hidden in the darkness, waiting to devour the foolish enough to come for it. I could feel it pressing upward from the depths, even before I saw it. The water here was colder. Heavier. Aware.

Markos laid down his paddle with deliberate care, the movement slow and almost reverent, and turned to me. His face was pale beneath the bruised afternoon light, his jaw tight, but his eyes never left mine. He didn't pretend anymore. The fear was there, in the set of his mouth, the tremble just beneath his breath.

I felt it too.

He reached for me, his hand cupping my jaw with a tenderness that undid me more thoroughly than any battle ever could. His thumb stroked over the line of my jaw, a soft, reverent caress, as if he was trying to memorize the shape of me with his hands alone. He drew me forward, and his kiss was slow, aching. It lingered like goodbye, even though no one had said the word aloud.

I didn't want to let go.

My fingers curled into the fabric of his shirt, clinging to him like he was the last warm thing in a world grown cold. I pressed my face against his chest, memorizing the shape of him, the steady drumbeat of his heart, the way his arms closed around me like shelter.

It was the only warmth I had left.

"I'll come back," I whispered, though the words tasted like a lie even as I spoke them.

His hands tightened around me. He didn't say Don't go. He didn't need to. It lived in the way he held me, the way he breathed against my hair, as if he could anchor me to this world through sheer force of will. We both knew there was a chance I wouldn't return. That this could be the last time.

A tear slipped down my cheek before I could stop it. Markos caught it with his thumb, brushing it away with the kind of gentleness that had undone me from the very beginning. His eyes held mine, fierce and shining with something I was terrified to name.

"You'd better return to me, my Sea Maiden," he said quietly, voice rough with emotion, "so I can show you true freedom."

I tried to smile, but it didn't reach my heart. It couldn't. Not when it was already breaking apart inside me.

He leaned in and kissed me again, slower this time, his lips lingering against mine like a promise neither of us dared say aloud. One I wasn't sure I deserved.

"I love you," he said.

The words hit me like a wave, stealing the breath from my lungs. For a moment, I couldn't answer. I could barely think.

Then, in a broken whisper, I gave him the only thing I had left.

"I love you."

It hurt to say it.

Because it meant I had something to lose.

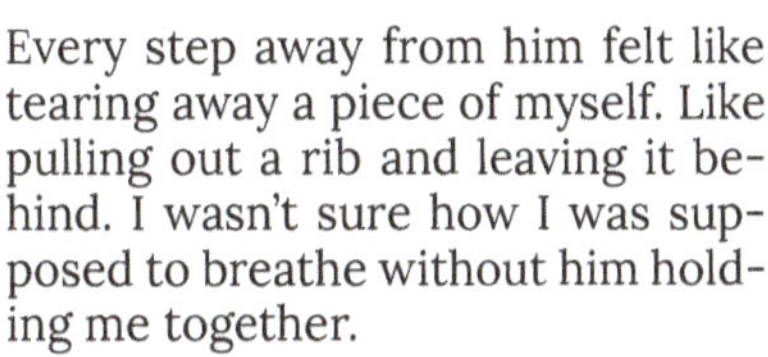

Every step away from him felt like tearing away a piece of myself. Like pulling out a rib and leaving it behind. I wasn't sure how I was supposed to breathe without him holding me together.

I turned and slipped over the edge of the raft, the water rushing up to swallow me. The cold slammed into me like a physical blow, stripping the warmth of him from my skin, stealing the last breath of him from my lungs. The sea didn't cradle. It devoured.

My tail shimmered as it formed, the magic pulsing through my blood like a fading second heartbeat.

For a breathless moment, I hovered just beneath the surface, looking up at him through the fractured lens of water and sunlight. He leaned closer, his hands pressed to the side of the raft, his eyes still locked on mine.

I held that gaze for one precious second longer.

When I couldn't hold on anymore, I let go.

And the sea claimed me.

The ocean embraced me like it remembered who I was.

It clung to my skin, slick and cold, whispering against my body like it knew what I carried inside me, what I had become: a creature shaped by blood and survival, no longer certain where the girl ended and the monster began. My tail shimmered beneath the fractured sunlight, slicing through the water with practiced strength, but even that familiar motion felt heavier now. The sea pressed against me here, denser, older, more watchful. It tested me with every stroke, the currents dragging at my limbs like unseen fingers.

The farther I swam, the dimmer the world became. The brilliant surface softened into ripples, then into shadows, then into nothing at all. Silence closed in, broken only by the dull thrum of blood in my ears and the slow, rhythmic swish of my movement. Every pull of my tail dragged me further from warmth, from Markos, from anything resembling safety.

The water here was different.

Older. Thicker.

It moved around me in deliberate, sentient currents, brushing against my skin with a weight that felt almost alive. I could feel it in the way the shadows shifted a beat too late, the way the pressure curled tighter against my ribs—not to slow me, but to remind me I didn't belong here anymore.

Or worse, that I did.

The Kraken blood stirred faintly behind my ribs, a restless coil whispering promises of strength if I would only surrender. The idea was intoxicating, power without fear, dominance without mercy. But I knew if I gave in, I might not come back. I clenched my jaw, forcing the hunger back down, burying it beneath the crushing fear and focus. There was no room for monsters in a mission like this.

Only a girl with too many regrets and a heart that beat too loud in enemy waters.

Below me, the sea floor stretched into a labyrinth of coral and jagged stone, twisted into cruel shapes by time and hunger. The vibrant blues and greens of the shallows faded into muted grays, the color bleeding from the world until it looked as hollow as I felt.

Ahead, faint lights shimmered, spires of coral rising from the darkness like the ribs of some ancient leviathan. Miris' palace.

I had seen it before. Once. From a distance.

But never like this.

Its towers stretched upward toward the unreachable surface, woven from pink and blue coral that glowed faintly in the dark. From a distance, they looked flawless. But as I drifted closer, I caught glimpses of deep fractures running through the structures. Cracks that pulsed faintly like old wounds hidden beneath a painted mask.

It was beautiful in the way all dangerous things are, mesmerizing until they close around your throat. My chest tightened with awe and dread as I took in the place that had shaped my nightmares. Its splendor was a cruel mask for the horrors within.

I drifted lower, staying just beyond the reach of the glow, and pressed behind a curtain of swaying anemone. Four mermen stood guard at the courtyard's edge, their movements sharp and rehearsed. Their spears flashed when they passed beneath the flickering palace lights, a glint of silver in the gloom.

Their presence prickled against my skin like static, a silent pressure warning that even a single misstep would summon death.

They were trained. They were sharp.

But I had become something else.

I waited, counting the rhythm of their patrol, feeling the subtle shifts in the current when they turned, when they spoke without words.

And then I moved.

Deliberate. Measured. My tail carved through the water with barely a ripple, slipping through the currents like a thought left unspoken. The pressurized entrance loomed ahead, a round chamber carved into the coral's side, hidden behind a veil of waving seaweed. I reached for the switch nestled into a crack in the stone and activated it.

The water drained in a rush, spiraling away with a sound like a dying breath. My tail shimmered and vanished, replaced by weak legs that trembled with the strain of the transformation.

I dropped to the slick stone floor, the cold shock of the shift making me shiver violently. The silence that met me wasn't absence. It was presence—thick, watchful, as if the ocean itself were holding its breath, unwilling to follow me into the darkness beyond.

I stood, heart hammering against my ribs, and crept through the narrow door ahead.

The hunt had begun.

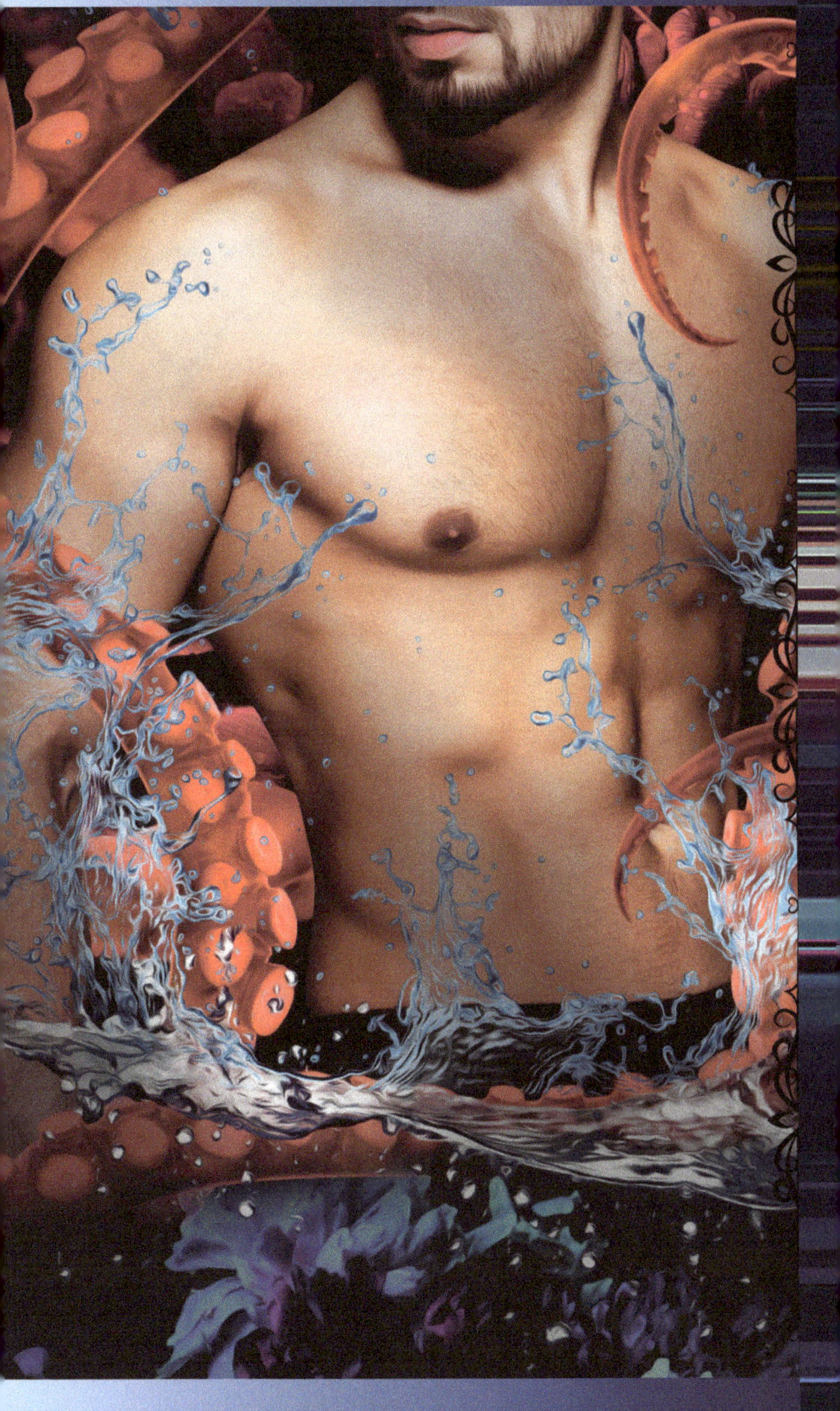

Chapter Thirty-Five

ESCAPING THE LABYRINTH

The key trembled in my grip as I slid it into the metal lock, my fingers slick with sweat despite the freezing air. The moment the lock clicked, a jolt snapped through me, panic and hope colliding in a storm beneath my ribs. I hesitated for a heartbeat, my pulse hammering against my chest, then pushed forward.

No sounds came from the other side of the door. No cries for help. No frantic banging against the metal. No breathing.

If Azure was inside, she wasn't calling for me.

Blowing out a breath, I pushed the heavy door open, each inch groaning with resistance, the screech of metal scraping against stone loud enough to wake ghosts. The air inside the cell felt thin and suffocating, as if the walls were swallowing what little oxygen remained. The smell of blood and salt clung thick to the air, coating the back of my throat.

A dim lantern flickered in the far corner, its glow barely touching the bruised shape curled in the shadows.

My stomach twisted violently.

Azure.

She was a shell of herself—bruised, broken, barely clinging to wakefulness. Dried blood streaked her skin like ink stains, and her turquoise eyes, once vibrant and fierce, were dulled by suffering, dimmed into something barely alive.

I sucked in a sharp breath and stepped inside. "Azure?" I kept my voice low, fear and urgency threading through every syllable. "I'm going to get you out of here."

Her eyelids fluttered. Slowly, painfully, she forced herself upright, wobbling like her bones had forgotten how to hold her. When her gaze finally lifted to mine, something inside her, something precious, cracked open with a soundless scream. Whatever strength she'd clung to had finally given way.

Then, without warning, she was in front of me, cupping my face in trembling hands, her strength flickering and fragile. She clung to me as if I were the last solid thing left in her world.

I crushed her closer, my hands desperate and unsteady. I should have been faster. I should have saved her sooner. That guilt dug into my ribs like barbed hooks even as I whispered reassurances I didn't have words for.

"You're really here. I don't understand." Her voice cracked, scraped raw from screaming. "How did you get past the guards? Where's Elios? What about everyone else? How did you end up with Corileia?"

I glanced over my shoulder, a wry smirk tugging at the corner of my mouth, even as fear gnawed at my heart.

"I hit that guard over the head with a metal lantern and knocked him out. I snuck past everyone else I encountered, but there weren't many guards on the way here." I kept my voice low, just above a whisper. "They figured you weren't a threat while chained up, but they weren't ready for me."

I tilted my head toward the adjacent cell. "Everyone's fine. Dimitris stayed behind with Aris. Elios and Markos are in boats above the palace, waiting for us. Corileia was in the next cell. I opened hers first by mistake, and she told me where to find you. She's been helping you... so I figured she was worth saving."

Azure stiffened, her hand trembling where it rested on my cheek.

"Ocevia, we have to get Elios out of the sea. If Miris realizes he's here, she'll—"

I didn't let her finish. I already knew. I felt it.

I reached for her hand, squeezing tight. "No one's coming," I said, willing it to be true. "Let's go."

Turning to Corileia, I nodded. "Corileia, do you know the way out?"

The healer nodded immediately, her red curls damp from the cold humidity clinging to the walls. Without a word, she moved ahead, her bare feet silent against the slick stone.

The flickering torchlight danced across the narrow corridor as we followed, shadows writhing along the walls like living things.

We climbed upward through the palace's winding halls, the silence pressing tighter around us with every step. It was a thick, waiting silence, the kind that made the hair on the back of my neck stand on end as if the stone itself were holding its breath for the moment we failed.

There were no guards, no voices, no alarms. It was too quiet.

My heart pounded louder than our footsteps. Azure's arm was looped around my shoulders, her body a brittle weight against mine. Every step with her leaning on me deepened the ache in my chest, an ache made of guilt and fierce protectiveness. She tried to stay upright, tried to stay strong, but I could feel the tremble in her limbs, the sag of her weight when she thought I wouldn't notice.

We were almost there. So close. One wrong turn, one sound too loud, and the palace would swallow us whole.

Candlelight flickered from the foyer ahead. I crept forward, pressing my back to the wall as I scanned the corridor. One last guard stood between us and freedom.

Turning to the others, I kept my voice low. "One guard at the exit. We'll have to take him out."

Azure swayed, exhaustion etched into every line of her body, but she nodded, jaw set with stubborn resolve.

I gritted my teeth. I'd already taken down one. I could do it again.

Corileia reached for a fire poker as I lifted a heavy vase from the alcove beside us, fingers tightening around the cold ceramic. We moved in sync, silent as shadows.

The guard never saw us coming.

I swung hard. The vase shattered against the back of his skull, the crack loud in the stillness. He crumpled instantly, blood blooming dark against the coral-tiled floor.

There was no time for guilt.

We ran.

The airlock chamber loomed ahead. I slammed the activation button, the hiss and roar of rushing water answering a heartbeat later. It flooded the chamber, cold and merciless, swallowing us whole. By the time the room filled, we had already shifted.

The sea devoured us as we fled, the world above still impossibly far. Even wounded, Azure swam faster than I'd ever seen, her tail cutting through the water like an arrow.

The magic came almost at once.

A tremor rippled through the deep—a pulse of power that curled invisible fingers around our limbs and tried to drag us back. The sea thickened, pressing inward like a living wall, relentless and cold, choking the light from around us.

I forced my body to keep moving, muscles screaming as I fought against it. The seashell at my throat throbbed in response, alive with the Kraken's restless hunger. It whispered to me of release. Of violence. *Of victory.*

If I gave in, I could end this. I could tear through every guard. I could clear a path.

But as I lifted my gaze, I imagined Markos waiting somewhere above, and the choice lodged deep in my chest like a blade.

I wasn't sure I'd come back from it this time.

One thing was certain: Azure had to make it out.

Another wave of magic slammed into us, heavier than before. I staggered mid-stroke, my tail straining against the pressure. My lungs ached with the need to breathe.

Azure turned, her eyes meeting mine across the dark. She saw the truth written on my face.

I pointed upward and blew her a kiss.

Hesitating just for a heartbeat, she turned, tail flashing in the gloom, and surged toward the surface.

Once she was gone, Corileia swam past me and toward a group of guards. Six of them, descending fast, spears gleaming like teeth in the dark.

With no other choice, I tore the necklace from my throat.

The sea erupted inside me, power surging outward like a dam breaking beneath centuries of pressure. My bones split and reshaped in an instant, every joint cracking apart before fusing again. Flesh twisted and tore as something older, something monstrous, broke free from beneath my skin.

The Kraken rose.

Pain bloomed in every nerve, sweeping through me in brutal, consuming waves. My vision blurred as blood and rage filled every hollow corner of my being. Thick, writhing tentacles burst from my spine and shoulders, unfurling in the dark like roots searching for violence. For one heartbeat, I thought I saw Corileia's pale face near mine, hovering like a ghost.

But the thought dissolved as quickly as it came, swallowed whole by the creature unraveling me from the inside out.

Everything I was—every memory, every tether to who I had been—unraveled. Ocevia slipped beneath the surface, pulled under by the roar in my blood.

Grief rose, sharp and fleeting, before something darker buried it. The Kraken had no use for sorrow. Only hunger.

The guards hesitated, faltering as the water blackened around me, their formation buckling.

But hesitation wouldn't save them. Not now. *Not from me.*

With a guttural snarl that shattered the sea around me, the Kraken surged forward, tentacles lashing through the water like living storms. I caught three mermen easily, my limbs coiling around their struggling bodies, squeezing until their bones snapped like brittle twigs. Blood burst into the sea, unfurling in slow blooms that the ocean swallowed eagerly, as if the sea itself rejoiced at the offering.

The others turned, scrambling upward, their movements frantic with terror, but there was no escaping the hunger that had been unleashed. I chased them like a rising storm, the Kraken's roar breaking through the surface as I erupted from the waves in a violent spray of blood and foam. I caught four more, dragging them beneath the roiling water, their spears glancing harmlessly off my thick, rust-colored hide.

Their pain fed the beast. Their terror stoked the hunger.

The dark sea churned with wild abandon as their blood stained the currents. I ripped them apart, one after another, their broken bodies tossed into the abyss without hesitation, without thought. The Kraken rejoiced, its victory a thundering pulse through my body.

A force stronger than anything I had ever felt slammed into me, hurling my monstrous form downward with such violence that the water seemed to split apart. The ocean shuddered around me, the currents trembling. I recoiled instinctively, my tentacles curling inward, my body bracing against the sudden, overwhelming pressure.

From the darkness below, a figure rose.

The water vibrated with a power that wasn't merely cold but primal, a weight so vast and terrible it stripped the warmth from the sea and left only silence. Thick dread coiled around my spine, choking me. I knew what I was about to face, and still, I was not ready. The currents bent around her, revered her. The ocean knew better than to resist its goddess.

I didn't need to see her face because I already knew her power.

The Sea Goddess had come.

The Weight of Her Crown

The Sea Goddess threw up her arms, a curse spilling from her lips as she surged toward me. A crackling bolt of energy ripped through the water, striking all around like a thousand stinging blades. Pain seared through me, raw and merciless, as my tentacles convulsed in violent spasms. The Kraken inside me roared, fury and agony entwining into a deafening, soundless scream that shuddered through the ocean's depths.

The agony didn't just seize my body; it bled into my bones, a shuddering pain that echoed inside my skull like the crashing of count waves.

Miris' lips moved again, another incantation spiraling through the water, thick with power. The ocean itself seemed to shudder, the seabed trembling beneath us as the weight of her magic bore down on me. I felt its chill clawing against my very soul, trying to force me into submission.

But I would not yield.

The dark water churned in a chaotic mass, but the moment the spell's force began to settle, I was already moving. I threw my tentacles back, propelling myself forward, ignoring the lingering sting of her magic. As soon as I caught sight of her dark hair swirling in the current, the Kraken inside me didn't think. It reacted.

Surging forward, I grasped Miris, my suction cups latching onto her torso and tail. I squeezed, tightening my grip until she could barely move. Her face twisted in pain, her fingers twitching uselessly against my hold. She screamed, but the ocean swallowed the sound before it could reach me.

Instead of submitting, I squeezed harder.

She thrashed like a dying creature, her silver tail snapping against the water in frantic, furious bursts, but I held firm.

Her arms were pinned at her sides, her magic useless, and no one was coming to save her. Still, I had to get back to the surface. I could sense the guards in the water, their weapons drawn, their presence a looming threat against my friends.

The Kraken's hunger aligned with my one thought. *Protect them.*

Breaking the surface, I dragged Miris above the waves, the sudden shift making her gasp. The sea and sky split around us, storm clouds rolling with fury. Her silver tail gleamed like a blade in the weak daylight, but I didn't let her go.

A scream cut through the air, sharp and jarring, snapping my attention sideways. My gaze locked on two boats floating nearby, the quiet churn of water suddenly too loud.

And then I saw them.

Elios. Azure. Markos.

Standing in the boats, only feet away.

Something inside me stumbled. My mind fractured in an instant, two worlds and two selves colliding in a single breath. I saw my friend. I saw the horror on her face. Azure's hand flew to her mouth, her wide, horrified eyes fixed on me. On what I had become.

The water seemed to chill around me, the Kraken's triumph stalling in my chest. Shame coiled tight in my gut, a cold, sick knot that pulled me down from whatever fury had carried me here.

A part of me shattered.

She knew. Even if she didn't understand the how or why, she saw me.

I had never wanted them to witness this. Not her. Not them. I had never wanted them to fear me, but now they did.

And still, I couldn't move. I felt frozen in this monstrous form, anchored by something heavier than water. Words failed. There was nothing to explain this. Nothing I could say to make them see the girl I still was beneath the beast.

All I could do was stay there—exposed, immense, and silent—while everything I had feared stared back at me across the waves.

The Kraken surged inside me, roaring its ancient hatred at the goddess it had long awaited to destroy. But I—I had become something else. Not a beast, not a broken girl. Something more.

"Call off your beast, Azure!" Miris' voice was sharp, unhinged, as she twisted in my grip, her tone laced with desperation and venom. "Or my guards will destroy every last one of you! Do you think my previous threats were frightening, Little Mermaid? You haven't seen anything yet!"

The Kraken roared in fury.

Without thinking, I thrashed my tentacles, slamming Miris into the waves before yanking her back up. Her silver tail writhed, but I held firm, my grip unrelenting.

My gaze shifted back to the boats, and my monstrous heart stopped.

Lucia stood behind Markos.

Her feral grin twisted around her bared teeth as she pressed a dagger to his throat. A cold, dark terror unlike anything I had ever known seized me, a force so all-consuming that the sea around me seemed to close in, tightening like an iron cage.

He struggled, but she covered his mouth, silencing him.

His eyes found mine, filled with fear for *me*.

A panic unlike anything I had ever known clawed through my chest.

My mate was in danger, and I didn't know how to save him.

Everything fell silent.

Markos' gaze never left mine.

Miris, still dangling in my hold, let out a rasping, cruel laugh, and then with a tilt of her head, she screamed, "Kill him!"

Lucia's grin widened. Before I could blink, she sliced the blade across his throat and tossed him into the sea.

A sound ripped through me, a scream, a wail, a monstrous thing birthed from the deepest part of my soul. It tore through every fiber of my being, leaving nothing untouched. That sound became my grief, my fury, my loss made real. Elios dove in after him, but I was already moving, tentacles tightening around Miris' body as rage burned hotter than the sun, obliterating every shred of restraint.

She had taken everything from me.

She had taken *him*.

With a vicious, blinding surge of fury, I tore her apart.

Flesh and bone snapped under the pressure of my wrath, the sound muffled by the raging sea. The ocean pulled at the pieces greedily, swallowing what remained of her with a final, echoing sigh, as if the tides themselves had awaited her downfall. Just before her body broke, I caught a glimpse of her face—Miris' eyes, once brimming with cruelty and command, were wide with fear. She knew. She had underestimated me. And she had lost everything because of it.

I didn't stay to watch her sink to the depths like all the souls she'd taken. Instead, I dove after the only thing that mattered.

The water churned with red, twisting in thick ribbons around the sinking form of the man I loved. Markos drifted downward, his hands pressed weakly against the gash at his throat, fingers desperate to hold his lifeblood inside. His body fought to live, but I knew. I *knew*. The wound was fatal.

A keening wail tore from my chest, a sound not made for mortal ears, shattering the fragile silence of the deep. My tentacles wrapped around him, pulling him close, shielding him from the abyss that clawed at his fading light.

I surged upward, breaking through the surface with a cry torn from the ruins of my soul. With my soul ripping in two, I lifted him into the boat, my trembling tentacles cradling him as if reverence alone could undo the damage, as if gentleness could knit flesh back together and call the soul back home.

He choked, sputtered, blood pooling beneath him, the crimson stark against his waxen skin. Pain like I had never known split through me, carving into my bones, unmaking everything I was. It was a devastation that transcended flesh, tearing straight through my being.

Markos was dying.

I remembered the way he had whispered my name in the dark, low and reverent, as if it alone was sacred. I would never hear it again.

Nearby, Elios and Azure hovered, their faces blurred by the agony clouding my vision. Their hesitation was palpable, their fear unmistakable, not just fear for Markos, but fear of me. I saw it in their eyes, in the way they flinched from my touch, in the stiff set of their jaws.

They were afraid of what I had become.

The realization landed like a blade drawn too slowly, more ache than shock.

The fragile strength I had been clinging to buckled.

For a breath, I hovered there, trapped in the ruin I had wrought, drowning in it. Then the weight of it—the grief, the rage, the monstrosity of my existence—became unbearable.

I let myself slip beneath the surface, hoping to vanish into the dark, if only for a moment. To drown the thing inside me before it swallowed everything else.

The ocean, once my sanctuary, wrapped around me like a tomb. It pressed against every broken part of me, dragging me downward into the abyss. I could feel the Kraken's hunger whispering at the edges of my mind, urging me to surrender, to vanish into the endless dark.

Everything inside me screamed to let go.

But something else stirred, something fierce, something brighter than the rage clawing at my bones.

Mine.

The ocean recognized it too. The current shifted around me, no longer heavy, no longer resisting, but rising to meet me.

The Kraken receded, folding into the marrow of my bones as my suction cups squeezed the seashell necklace. For the first time, it obeyed me.

My body twisted, the monstrous form peeling away with the slow agony of rebirth. It wasn't magic. It was pain. It was memory. It was hope clawing its way back into broken flesh.

And when it was over, I was myself again.

A mermaid. Not a beast.

Without hesitation, I surged toward the surface, every stroke a battle between despair and defiance. I broke through with a gasp, throwing myself into the boat, crawling to Markos' side as panic and hope warred inside me.

He lay motionless. Still. *Silent.*

Death had already wrapped its fingers around him, but I wasn't ready to let him go.

Not yet, *not ever.*

The sight of him sent a fresh wave of panic tearing through my already splintered heart. I grabbed for him, my hands trembling as I pulled his lifeless body into my arms.

His skin was cold. Limp. A hollow stillness clung to him, screaming a truth I wasn't ready to face.

No breath stirred his chest. No heartbeat thudded beneath his ribs.

For one terrible moment, I thought I had been too late. That nothing could call him back.

A sob tore from my throat, raw and desperate, as I rocked him against me, clutching him tighter, praying to the gods I knew would not listen.

Across the boat, Elios pressed his hands against the gaping wound, blood slicking his fingers, his face grim. It wasn't enough. None of it would ever be enough.

My fingers were numb as they touched Markos' face, but something wild and unfamiliar sparked against my skin. A fierce tingling rushed up my arms, lancing straight into the hollow where my heart had been shattered.

Gasping, struggling to draw breath, I whispered, "How? How was this happening? I don't understand." I pressed my lips to his, praying, pleading, hoping against reason.

Then, impossibly, before my eyes, the wound began to close, knitting itself back together as if by magic. Flesh mended beneath my hands, smooth and whole where ruin had once gaped.

As I watched in awe, he inhaled sharply, a ragged breath tearing free of his lungs. His chest rose and his eyes fluttered open.

A broken cry wrenched from my lungs as I smoothed his damp hair back from his forehead, my hands trembling so violently I barely recognized them. None of it made sense. And yet, he was breathing. His heart was beating.

His lips parted, and a breathless word escaped.

"Ocevia."

The sound of my name unlocked something buried deep, something raw and trembling and still alive.

But before I could respond, Azure's voice broke through the fog.

"Ocevia..." she said, her tone hesitant.

Still frozen, I didn't look at her. I couldn't tear my gaze from the miracle breathing in my arms.

"Ocevia," she said again, voice thick with emotion. "You killed Miris."

The world stood still.

The words hit like a blow. I lifted my head slowly, heart hammering against my ribs. I stared at Markos, the man I had almost lost, and saw the flicker of fear still lingering at the edges of his gaze.

Finally, I exhaled, the breath shaky as it left my body.

"I became a mermaid because it was better than being who I was," I murmured, my voice thick with sorrow, weighted by exhaustion.

Turning toward Azure, I met her gaze and saw the full weight of my truth settle across her.

"My family shunned me. They were afraid of me. I didn't tell you because I didn't want you to fear me too. You were my only friend."

Her expression softened instantly.

"I wouldn't abandon you, Ocevia. And I certainly wouldn't fear you."

Her words wrapped around my heart like a balm, soothing the raw, bleeding edges of everything I had lost, and everything I had fought to save.

Azure swallowed hard, her next question barely above a whisper.

"Ocevia... did you see what happened to Corileia?"

Even though I'd only just met her, the reminder of the mermaid who'd helped me save my friend struck like a dagger. Guilt rippled through my already-broken chest.

"A guard captured her and took her back to the palace. I was going to go after them, but then I saw Miris heading for the surface, and..." My voice cracked, dropping to a whisper. "I couldn't be sure you wouldn't shun me if you knew, Azure. My own family feared me. I needed you to leave so I could transform. It was the only way I could protect all of you."

Markos' hand brushed my cheek, anchoring me with a touch that spoke louder than any words. "Everything is going to be okay, my Sea Maiden.".

A knot loosened in my chest, and slowly, numbly, I nodded.

"All that matters is that you're alive, Markos. That everyone is alive."

But Azure wasn't finished. Her brow furrowed, her voice trembling with something heavier than fear.

"Ocevia... you killed Miris. That means—"

I nodded once, cutting her off.

"I know what it means."

Markos tightened his hold around my fingers, sensing the tension that hung thick between us.

"What does it mean, Ocevia?"

I lifted my gaze to his, the weight of the moment settling into the marrow of my bones. It was heavy. *Inevitable.* A crown I had never sought, but one that would never be lifted again.

For a moment, I hesitated, feeling the ancient pull of the sea around me—the slow, terrible pulse of power that now answered to my blood.

It wasn't a gift. It wasn't a prize. It was the price I paid, the piece of myself that would never heal. My freedom had come shackled in grief. It was a chain of salt and blood, wrapping tighter with every breath I took.

I drew in a slow, shuddering breath, steadying my voice, and when I spoke, it was not with fear. It was with the quiet, terrible certainty of someone who had been forged in blood and loss, and had risen not despite it, but because of it.

"It means I'm the new Sea Goddess."

Chapter Thirty-Seven

A Kingdom Reborn

Two Months Later

The sea held its breath, and so did I.

For the first time in centuries, the waters that had once pulsed with terror now stirred with something else... *hope.* I drifted forward through the broken arches of the palace courtyard, the faint hum of the Kraken's power lingering in my veins like the last breath of a dying storm. My hair floated around me in tangled ribbons of silver and gold, and the seashell necklace—the relic of all I had endured—pressed heavy against my chest.

The palace behind me rose in solemn splendor, its coral spires gleaming in the filtered light like the bones of something ancient and enduring. The mosaics along its walls shimmered with memory rather than ruin, untouched by battle, though not untouched by blood. No siege had scarred its halls, but pain had passed through them, quiet and lingering. Now the silence felt changed. Not reverent. Not grieving. Simply suspended, as if even the stone had not yet decided what future it would be asked to hold.

Before me stretched the gathered merfolk, a living current of shimmering scales and wary eyes. Their bodies shifted with the pulse of the sea, coiling and swaying in quiet disarray. They hovered in the open water, uncertain and unanchored, caught in a world that had changed faster than they could follow.

Word had spread like a tidal wave. Miris was dead, and I remained.

The ache twisting in my stomach was sharp and deep as I paused at the edge of the coral dais. For a long moment, nothing moved but the soft shift of tails, the slow drift of kelp and seaweed stirred by the currents.

Then Corileia broke free from the crowd.

She floated forward with slow, deliberate grace, lowering herself until her tail curled beneath her and her forehead touched the seabed. It was a gesture as old as the tides, the purest sign of surrender among our kind. A ripple passed through the court. One by one, the others followed, easing down to the sands not with knees, but with the slow, intentional sweep of their tails and the graceful bend of their bodies. The sea itself seemed to sigh, the water stirring gently between us under the quiet weight of their reverence.

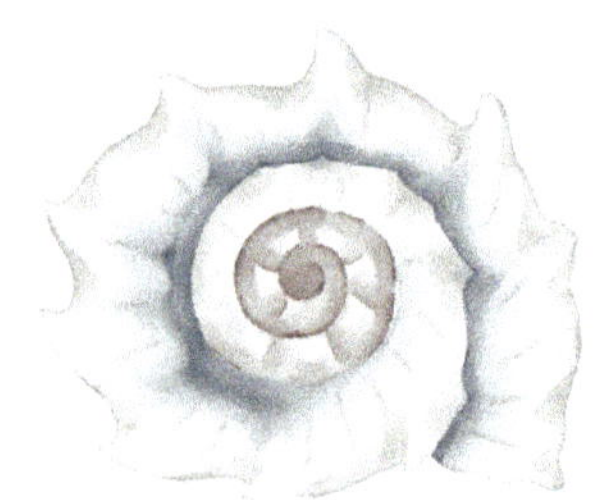

There was no fanfare. No golden crown carved from coral. No parade of sycophants, no choir to carry my name into the currents. Only the palace, quiet and watchful. Only the sea, raw and endless. Only the people, wounded and waiting. And only me, standing at the center of it all, humbled to my core beneath the weight of their silence. I had not asked for this. I had not sought it. Yet in that stillness, I understood that something had ended, and something else had just begun.

For a moment, my body ached with the desire to flee. But I stayed, rooted by something stronger than fear: the knowledge that if I did not carry this burden, it would fall to someone else, someone who might forget the price we had paid.

A voice rose from the gathered court.

"All hail Ocevia, Daughter of Sea and Storm," Corileia cried, her voice echoing through coral and silence alike. "The one who rose not to rule, but to heal."

The words struck a place deep inside me, an ancient hollow I hadn't known was still aching. I did not cry. I did not falter. I simply straightened my spine and lifted my chin, not with arrogance, but with the solemn acceptance of a fate I could no longer deny.

Someone had to lead them, and I would never allow another goddess to rise through cruelty again.

A teenage mermaid swam forward, her long dark hair drifting like ink in the soft tides as she cradled something delicate against her chest. She approached with visible care, her hands trembling despite her effort to appear composed. I lowered myself, folding my tail beneath me as she drew near. When she placed the object into my waiting hands, the crowd exhaled as one, a hush spreading through the court like a ripple of held breath finally released.

A circlet of starlight coral rested in my palms, its delicate branches pulsing with a soft, rhythmic glow. It radiated a quiet warmth, the kind that stirred deep beneath the skin, like memory surfacing from deep water. The magic threaded through it was old and enduring, steeped in tides that had watched lifetimes pass. This was no crown of chains or conquest, but a promise. A vow shaped by storm and salt and grief, carried through the broken hearts of all who had come before.

With careful fingers, I lifted the circlet and placed it against my brow. Its magic touched my skin with a coolness that felt like memory itself—deep as sorrow, steady as tide. It asked nothing of me. It demanded nothing. It only asked that I remember who I was.

The court began to rise around me, tails unfolding, bodies straightening. The energy shifted, uncertain and electric. For a heartbeat, the only sound was the thrum of my own blood filling the silence.

Then the voices began.

Soft at first, like a ripple brushing the surface, then growing louder, swelling through the currents until the entire court sang my name. Not as a goddess to be feared. A ruler to be trusted.

I closed my eyes, the sound breaking over me like a wave—raw, aching, vast. For a moment, the emotion in my chest rose so fiercely I thought it might undo me, might split me open with the sheer, beautiful force of it. But I held steady, breathing through the shudder that moved through me.

This was not adoration. It was not worship. It was *hope*.

When I opened my eyes, I searched the crowd, and I found him.

Markos no longer lingered at the edge of the gathering. He had drawn closer, quiet and composed, pausing just below the dais where the merfolk waited in watchful silence. His dark hair drifted in the current, catching the filtered light in strands that moved like ink through water. His turquoise eyes met mine with a calm that steadied something inside me.

A tail shimmered beneath him, rich with indigo and laced with silver. It moved with restrained power, coiled loosely as the sea brushed gently around him. The ocean recognized its own.

I remembered the moment I thought I'd lost him. His blood in the water. My voice ragged from pleading. I hadn't known what I was offering when I begged the sea to take anything but him, but something had listened.

He wasn't the same man I had cradled in my arms that day. The ocean had remade him. Not through ceremony, not through command, but through the bond between us—through grief, through love, through something older than either of us had understood.

He didn't bow.

There was no need.

He simply lifted his hand, palm open in quiet offering.

I reached for him, and our fingers met. The sea stirred around us, a gentle shift that passed through the watching court. No words were spoken, but something in the current changed.

In that silence, the deep bore witness, and in that space between two heartbeats, a silent promise formed: *Whatever storms still waited beyond the horizon, we would face them together.*

The past lay behind us now, fractured and surrendered to the deep. What had once been carved in fear and silence had been broken open, scattered like shards across the ocean floor.

The sea had changed and so had we.

I was no longer the girl who endured a goddess's cruelty, nor simply the one who inherited her throne. I was becoming something else—something shaped by mercy, and by the quiet power of renewal.

All around us, the water brightened. The court lifted their heads, the shimmer of their scales catching the light like a thousand tiny suns. Eyes once dulled by submission now watched with cautious wonder. I felt the shift echo through them. The ocean no longer pressed against us like a cage. It opened.

This was the beginning of a new covenant. No longer forged in conquest, but in trust. A tide carried not by domination, but by choice.

The future stretched open, vast and unwritten, carried in every current that once pulled us under and in every voice once silenced. Whatever we became next, we would become it together.

And I would rise with them.

Not above.

But among.

EPILOGUE

Beneath the Surface

Moonlight poured through the shifting currents, painting the ocean in bands of pewter and deep sapphire. The palace faded behind me as I slipped into the deep, the weight of the crown and court and endless decisions falling away with every stroke of my tail. Tonight, I wasn't a ruler. I was just a woman in love, swimming to meet the man who made it all worth it.

Markos waited beyond the coral gardens, exactly where I knew he would be. Mischief danced in his smile the moment he spotted me, like he'd been waiting for this—*us*—all day. Gods, he was beautiful like this. Hair loose in the current, shoulders golden beneath the starlight, every line of his body sculpted by salt and sun and freedom. Even now, after everything, he still looked at me like I was a miracle.

He didn't swim to me. He hovered where he was, arms folded, indigo tail flicking with his usual playfulness.

"You're late," he called, voice curling through the water with amusement.

"I'm a goddess," I replied, drifting closer. "Divine beings are allowed to take their time."

"To our secret escape?" he teased. "You're lucky I missed you, my little Sea Maiden."

My heart softened at the nickname. His nickname. One that meant something real.

Gliding into him, our hands met, fingers intertwining like they always did. His thumb brushed over my knuckles, and the sea between us calmed.

Leaning close, his lips nearly brushed mine. "Come on. Bet you still can't beat me there."

"You're so arrogant," I said, narrowing my eyes.

His grin widened. "That's one of the things you love about me."

Without another word, he took off.

Laughter bubbled from my throat as I shot after him, racing through the silent deep. The water shimmered with ribbons of light as we moved through curtains of kelp, past slumbering reef fish, over coral shelves that pulsed faintly with magic. Tiny creatures scattered at our passing, their bodies trailing bioluminescence like stardust in the dark.

As we swam deeper, we veered left at a cluster of obsidian stones that marked the start of a hidden cave system. This path wasn't meant for the court or the curious. It belonged to us. The entrance was barely wide enough for two, its walls etched with the gentle glow of divine magic that warmed the skin without burning. Here, the current quieted and the sea fell away.

Glancing back at me as we approached the final turn, Markos's expression softened.

"Still with me?" he asked.

"Always," I whispered.

The cavern opened slowly, like breath drawn into the lungs of the sea. Around us, the water lit from beneath—soft gold and pale green, the colors of safety, of memory. Moss curled over the stone lip of the spring-fed pool, and far above, veins of crystal caught the moonlight that filtered through the cracks in the ceiling. This wasn't a forgotten place. It was simply private. Sacred. *Ours.*

Drifting forward to where land met sea inside the cave, Markos surfaced first, and I followed, our legs returning as we stepped into the air-warmed stillness.

His gaze lingered as I emerged, eyes raking down my body with something between reverence and want. "I like you better like this," he murmured. "Unburdened."

I wrung the water from my hair, unable to fight my smile. "You always say that."

"Because it's always true."

With more confidence than I'd had when we first met, I moved toward him. "I didn't get a proper kiss hello."

"Then come take it, Little One."

He opened his arms, and I walked into them.

Markos's hands slid around my waist and pulled me closer. There was tension in the way he touched me, like he needed this closeness just as much as I did. At first, his lips brushed lightly over mine in soft, teasing kisses, but it didn't take long for the heat to build, the contact deepening into something more intense, more consuming.

Pressing close, our bodies fit together with the kind of ease that came from knowing one another by heart. The grotto held us in a stillness that made everything outside feel impossibly far away, and as our kisses deepened, the rest of the world ceased to matter.

Pulling back just enough, he murmured, "Tell me what you need tonight."

"You," I breathed. "Only you."

Touching his forehead to mine, he searched my gaze while his hands slid down to my hips. "Then I'm yours."

Moving together, we stepped back onto the moss-covered stone, our breath mingling as his hands slipped beneath the strands of hair clinging to my back. When his mouth found the curve of my shoulder, I melted beneath his touch, a sigh escaping me.

His lips traveled along my collarbone, brushing tender kisses across damp skin, while his fingertips traced slow, reverent patterns at the small of my back. Leaning into him, I slid one hand into the wet strands of his hair and placed the other over his heart, feeling the steady beat beneath my palm.

"I missed this," he whispered against my skin.

Smiling, my eyes fluttered shut. "You saw me an hour ago."

"Too long." Drawing back just enough to meet my eyes, his gaze darkened with something deeper than desire. "Let me show you how much."

Lowering me onto the soft, moss-lined stone, he hovered above me, the heat of his body warming mine before his touch even landed. His fingers trailed up the outside of my thigh, pausing to grip my hips. The way he looked at me sent a shiver down my spine.

I arched into him, craving his skin. "I want to feel you," I whispered.

Markos nodded, the grotto's golden light playing over every sculpted inch of his body.

His hands slid over me, his mouth never far behind as he tasted my flushed skin. He took his time, trailing kisses down my ribs, over my hipbones, between my thighs.

When his mouth found me there, I cried out, hips lifting against his lips. He held me steady, his hands gripping my thighs as he devoured me as though he was a starving man.

"I love the way you fall apart for me," he murmured against my skin.

My fingers tangled in his hair, breath stuttering as my body quivered, a wave building inside me, unbearable and inevitable. When it broke, it left me gasping and boneless.

Kissing his way back up, his mouth found mine as he settled between my thighs.

"I need y—" My words broke off as he slid inside me, every nerve ending sparking as though he were everywhere at once.

Somewhere, barely at the edge of thought, I thought of the old legend whispered about this grotto—that when two lovers came together in its sacred heart, the sea would bless them. That the magic woven into the stone and water could coax life into being, even when hope had faltered elsewhere. It was just a story, told by firelight and half-laughed over by priestesses who claimed not to believe in such things.

But tonight, I wanted to believe, because everything about this man was magic made flesh, and some part of me longed to give him what had always felt just out of reach: something lasting, something ours.

Markos moved slowly at first, like he, too, felt the weight of something larger than the two of us stirring in the stillness. Each thrust felt deliberate, like a vow etched into my bones. His hands cupped my face, his eyes never leaving mine. I clung to him, wrapping my legs around his waist, pulling him deeper, grounding myself in the rhythm of our bodies.

When I came again, it was with a gasp that echoed off the crystal walls. He followed moments later, burying his face against my throat as he let go.

And in that moment, I swore I felt the sea exhale around us, not with power but with promise.

Curled against Markos in the quiet that followed, I let myself imagine what it would mean if the legend were true. Not just a whispered myth passed through generations, but a real blessing waiting beneath the surface.

I had never known what it felt like to belong to a family that would protect its own. But tonight, in this sacred place, with the man I loved wrapped around me like the sea itself, I dreamed of something more.

I wanted to build a family that was not of duty, but of choice. I wanted to raise a child in a world where love wasn't conditional, where support didn't come with sacrifice. A child born not to pay a price, but to be cherished.

And if the sea had truly listened... maybe, *just maybe*, it had heard my heart's quietest prayer.

Enjoyed the journey? Share the magic! If Song of Death swept you away, I'd be so grateful if you left a review.

You can leave a review here:
https://www.amazon.com/gp/product/B0FBD4DCLT

If Goddess of Death swept you away, I'd be so grateful if you left a review. Your words help more readers discover the series and support indie authors like me in continuing to create powerful, otherworldly stories.

You can leave a review here:
https://www.amazon.com/dp/B0FBD48JT8

Thank you from the bottom of my heart for reading. Your support truly means the world. 💛 – C.A. Varian

Also by C.A. Varian

Crown of the Phoenix Series

Crown of the Phoenix

Crown of the Exiled

Crown of the Prophecy

Mate of the Phoenix

Shadowed by Prophecy

Shadowed by the Veil (Coming Soon)

My Alien Mate Series

My Alien Protector

My Alien Rescuer (coming soon!)

Other World Series

The Other World

The Other Key

The Other Fate

Hazel Watson Mystery Series

Kindred Spirits: Prequel

The Sapphire Necklace

Justice for the Slain

Whispers from the Swamp

Crossroads of Death

The Spirit Collector

The Darkness that Follows (Coming 2025)

The Cursed Waters Duet

Song of Death

Goddess of Death

Survivor & Savior Duet

Saving Scarlett
Keeping Caroline

Standalones

Second Chance with Santa

When Everly Saved Emerald Hollow (Coming Soon
with A.A. Weaver)

Spirit of the Dying Flower (Coming Soon)

The Gladiatrix & the Fallen Son (Coming Soon)

Wings of the Forgotten (Coming Soon with J. Paige)

Born and raised in the heart of Louisiana's Cajun Country, I'm a passionate writer of dark, fantasy, paranormal, and even alien romances—if there's a romance involved, chances are I've written it. My stories are filled with mystery, magic, and intense emotional connections that keep readers on the edge of their seats.

When I'm not writing, you'll find me creating special editions of my books packed with all the bells and whistles—character art, exclusive swag, and more for my readers to treasure. I love connecting with fans, whether it's through my TikTok shop, my website, or in person at events where I can share the stories I pour my heart into.

A proud mother and new grandmother, I've faced many challenges in life, including a battle with chronic Lyme disease, but I've never let it define me. Writing is my escape and my passion, and with the support of my amazing assistant Jessica, my husband Trevor, and my daughters, Arianna and Brianna, I'm living my dream of writing full-time. Even my two youngest sisters pitch in, helping me with various tasks for the business—it's truly a family affair!

At home in Alabama, surrounded by love, laughter, and inspiration, I'm never without my two Shih Tzus, Charlie and Luna, along with my three mischievous cats—Ramses, Simba, and Cookie. Whether I'm doting on my furry companions, reading, or soaking up family time, every moment is a precious one.

Join me as I continue to create worlds full of romance, adventure, and unforgettable characters that you won't want to put down!

THE CURSED WATERS DUET ILLUSTRATED OMNIBUS ARTIST & DESIGNER CREDITS

Book Cover Leigh Graphic Designs
Page Edge Design D'Arte Oriel
End Page Design D'Arte Oriel
Hardcase Design G-CAT Designs
Main Jacket Reverse Art Design Just Venture Arts (JV Arts)
Alternate Jacket Front and Back Design Swampy Sloth Studios
Paperback Cover Art Alijah Arts
Paperback Cover Text and Design D'Arte Oriel
Paperback End Page Art Leigh Graphic Designs
Scene Break Purvi Jhavar Sharma
Tip in Artscandare
Omnibus Title Page D'Arte Oriel
Map Paige Annabentleah
After Map Athena Crest Arts

SONG
Before Title Page Graphics by Geka
Song of Death Title Page D'Arte Oriel

P 6 Art Muse Graphic Designs
P 7 D'Arte Oriel
Chapter 1 header Artisan Gallery
P 16-17 D'Arte Oriel
Chapter 2 header JM Designs
Chapter 3 header D'Arte Oriel
p 31 D'Arte Oriel
Chapter 4 header Leigh Graphic Designs
P 41 Alijah Arts
Chapter 5 header Xielle Covers
P 49 Art Muse Graphic Designs
P 50-51 Alijah Arts
Chapter 6 header Doelle Designs
Chapter 7 header SG Désigns
P 69 D'Arte Oriel
Chapter 8 header Xielle Covers
P 77 Alijah Arts
Chapter 9 header D'Arte Oriel
P 85 Rosel Graphic Designs
Chapter 10 header Vylex Art
P 93 ZONE ARTZ
Chapter 11 header D'Arte Oriel
Chapter 12 header SLM Creations
Chapter 13 header Xielle Covers
P 115 D'Arte Oriel
Chapter 14 header D'Arte Oriel
P 123 Artisan Gallery
Chapter 15 header Lune Aesthete Designs
Chapter 16 header Lune Aesthete Designs
P 136-137 Leigh Graphic Designs
Chapter 17 header Leigh Graphic Designs
Chapter 18 header D'Arte Oriel
P155 Achlys
Chapter 19 header Lune Aesthete Designs
P 165 Artisan Gallery
P 166-167 ZONE ARTZ
Chapter 20 header D'Arte Oriel
P 179 Jineus Covers
P 180 Covers by Chan
P 181 Tricia's Art Atelier
Chapter 21 header D'Arte Oriel
P 192-193 D'Arte Oriel
Chapter 22 header D'Arte Oriel
P 203 D'Arte Oriel
Chapter 23 header Obsi Art
P 213 Covers & Berries
Chapter 24 header D'Arte Oriel
Chapter 25 header SLM Creations
P 230 ZONE ARTZ
P 231 D'Arte Oriel

WATER COLOR ILLUSTRATIONS

b.illustrations, young generation team, bad designer, Liudmila Kopecka, Syifa Fauzia Zazuli, Anna Kuzmina, SPRESSO, Anna Szonn, Sontenn, Lordyswiss, Varvara Kurakina, Imgenes de gala ly, Creative Valuation, Anggiena Arifani, Oceanoart, Nichewatercolor, Elena Dorosh Art, johannes.k, deemakdaksina, Okinoma, Christana, Ronnie Morallos, and more via Canva.